SEPTEMBER 23, 2017

FOR MARCY, WITH BEST

WISHES,

D1563781

Cut of the Cross
by Robert L. Gold

Printed in the United States of America.
Published by Marcinson Press, Jacksonville, Florida
© Copyright 2016 by Robert L. Gold

For bulk purchases or to carry this book in your
library, bookstore, or school, please contact the
publisher at marcinsonpress.com.

ISBN 978-0-9967207-3-1

Published by
Marcinson Press
10950-60 San Jose Blvd., Suite 136
Jacksonville, FL 32223 USA
http://www.marcinsonpress.com

CUT OF THE CROSS

ROBERT L. GOLD

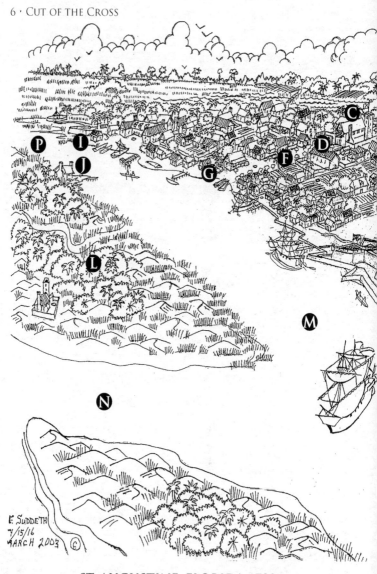

ST. AUGUSTINE, FLORIDA 1788

A Body of Gloria Márquez García   E Mission of Nombre de Dios
B Castillo de San Marcos   F Central Plaza
C Government House   G City Pier
D Catholic Church   H City Gates

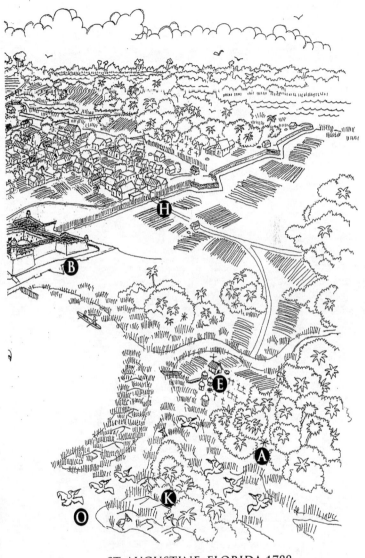

ST. AUGUSTINE, FLORIDA 1788

I	House of Ruiz de León	M	St. Augustine Bay
J	House of Jessie Fish	N	Ocean Inlet
K	Pelican Island	O	North River
L	Anastasia Island	P	Matanzas River

AUTHOR ACKNOWLEDGEMENTS

Once again, I want to acknowledge my brother, Michael, for his unstinting assistance in the completion of *Cut of the Cross*, the second novel in the Colonial City Mystery Series. He was even more helpful in this mystery than *Dead to Rights*. A retired physician, Mike was a consistent source of information in the creation of Carlos Martínez, the iconoclastic doctor who emerges as one of the major characters in the story. He also helped me as a critical reader, researcher and proofreader during the writing process. Accessible on the phone, I could reach him daily to discuss a plot direction, a character description, a theme that needed additional development – actually anything relating to the book. Sadly, Mike died in 2014, before he could see any of the mysteries in print.

Robert J. McConaghie, M.D. was another physician, also deceased, who helped me in the writing of *Cut of the Cross*. Dr. McConaghie was the medical examiner of St. Augustine and St. John's County a number of years ago when I approached him to ask for his help. I went to see him to inquire about what happens to a dead body lying on the ground in the hot Florida summer. Dr. McConaghie not only answered that question in detail, but also suggested murderer types I could use as the villain in my murder mystery. He pointed me to several articles in the *American Journal of Forensic*

Medicine and Pathology and the book, *Modern Legal Medicine, Psychiatry, and Forensic Science* and, in the end, I chose the one we discussed in his office. The autopsy and forensic medicine material mentioned in Chapters 2, 5, 9 and 13 depend on both the above sources and my conversations with Dr. McConaghie.

The eighteenth-century illustrated map of St. Augustine was created by Frank Suddeth, a lifelong aficionado of the city's history. Now deceased, Frank literally lived to draw everything he knew about St. Augustine's colonial history. He must have drawn hundreds of pictures of the garrison town, the great seventeenth-century fortress, the Spanish and British troops, the townspeople – he seemingly missed nothing in the old city's early history.

Once again, I am delighted to see the graphic artistry of Trish Diggins in the interior and exterior appearance of *Cut of the Cross*. I thought her captivating cover for the first book, *Dead to Rights*, in the Colonial City Series could not be surpassed until I saw the second one. The stunning cover alone is evidence of her special talent.

I also want to thank Jim Murphy, Kat LaMons, Gary Nevins, Charles Tingley, Sue Myers and Kristi West for their critical contributions to the completion of the mystery. Kat and Kristi were especially helpful in the editing and proofreading of the book as it passed from a typed manuscript through two page-proof stages to become a completed novel.

In addition to my dedication of *Cut of the Cross* to my wife, LaDonna, I want to thank her for the enumerable hours she spent reading and proofreading the book. She must have read these 400 plus pages at least ten times. Since I am an admitted technology dinosaur, LaDonna also helped me those times when, in a frustrated fury, I would scream at the computer and want to smash it with a baseball bat. At those times, she was there to both calm me down and fix the problem.

CHAPTER ONE

SEPTEMBER 29 – 30, 1788

Fernando Núñez noticed the flies as he reached down to pick up his end of the fishing net. In the beginning dusk of that autumn day, Núñez and his son had dragged the heavy net to shore for the last time when he glimpsed the flies out of the corner of his eye. Núñez ignored them as he pulled his end out of the shallows and dropped it in the sand. The heavy net was full of seaweed and shells and his arms ached from pulling it into shore. He had already freed the numerous tiny fish brought up in the net.

Núñez sighed wearily and straightened up. Hot and hungry, he pictured himself sitting in the shaded patio at the back of his house, a bowl of black beans and rice in his lap. He longed to be home now as the first breeze of the evening blew in from the river. The incessant buzzing of the flies interrupted his thoughts and Núñez turned to look at them.

The flies flew in a cloud around a leafy green palmetto,

only ten steps from where he stood at the edge of the North River. Núñez followed the flies with his eyes and saw a leg and foot sticking out from beneath the palmetto's fronds. He stood stone still. A chill swept over him, cooling the sweat on his back and making him shiver.

"Dios mío!" Núñez crossed himself. "Oh, Mother of God!"

"Qué pasó?" His son, Rafael, heard Núñez cry out and saw him cross himself. The boy kneeled in the shallows, gathering the other end of the net in his hands. He frowned when his father did not answer him.

Núñez continued to stare at the leg. It took him almost a minute before he responded to his son. "There's a body there – beneath the fronds." Núñez pointed to the palmetto, where the bare leg, seemingly detached, lay on the ground.

"A dead body? Let me see it!" His brown eyes bright with excitement, the boy stood, trying to look under the palmetto fronds. But, from where he stood in the shallow water, even on tip-toes, he could not see it. "I want to see it," he announced, coming out of the water.

Núñez said nothing. His eyes were focused on the leg and the buzzing flies circling the palmetto. He waved the boy back without looking at him. The leg held him entranced; he could not take his eyes from it.

"No, you can't see it." Núñez slowly turned to look at his son. He raised his right hand in warning. "Stay where you are! Rafael!" Núñez' tanned face, darkened from the Florida sun, was stern as he stopped the boy with his shouted words. "Don't take another step!" Seeing the boy stop, Núñez lowered his voice. "Rafael, listen to me. Look at me! The presidio must be told what we've found here. You must run to the city gates and tell the sentries. Now!"

"What about our catch?" Rafael cautiously moved two short steps forward and squatted down, trying to see the body beneath the palmetto fronds.

"I'll take care of it. Now, go, Rafael! Hurry!" Núñez, a lean man with muscular arms, motioned the boy away with a sweep of his hand.

As Rafael set out for town, Núñez shouted after him, "Run, hijo, it's getting dark." He watched his son run down the sandy trail through the pine trees, the bottoms of his feet flashing white against the green foliage. Seeing Rafael run without looking down at the ground, Núñez worried the boy would step on one of the many sandspur vines lying along the overgrown path.

Núñez waited only until Rafael disappeared into the woods and then he walked slowly toward the palmetto. He unsheathed his knife and held it ready in his right hand. Núñez was curious, but wary of what he would find under the palmetto fronds. The noise of the buzzing flies increased as he carefully pushed the fronds aside and looked down at the body.

"Dios mío!" Núñez gasped, instantly recognizing the face of Gloria Márquez García y Morera, the governor's seventeen-year-old niece. The young girl was known to every one of the 2,010 residents of St. Augustine. Her beauty alone made her stand out even if she had not been the governor's niece. Men and women alike stared at her as she passed them in the streets. With big black eyes, lustrous hair and a mature woman's figure, young Gloria was the prettiest girl in the colony. Now, the beautiful girl lay dead on the ground, dirt and leaves on her body, her face bloated in death.

Looking down at the dead girl, Núñez smelled the stench of her body and got sick to his stomach. He retched, tasting his midday meal of fish and rice. Fighting the urge to faint, Núñez hurriedly backed away from the corpse. His heel caught on a protruding rock and he stumbled backward, abruptly sitting on his buttocks. He put his head down between his knees, hoping to end the dizziness. It was something he remembered his mother telling him to do, when a boy. Núñez held his head in that position until the dizziness left him and then he stood up again. He returned his eyes to the dead girl, but remained several feet away to avoid the smell.

Núñez stood close enough to see her opened eyes and the tip of her tongue protruding from her mouth. She was nude except for her neck and the upper part of her chest. A wrinkled white bodice was bunched about her shoulders and breasts, but her brown nipples peeked out below the bottom edge of the bodice. Núñez stared at them for a moment and then moved his eyes above the bodice to her face which looked swollen. Her hair fell away in all directions and several strands fluttered in the breeze. Her slender arms extended outward and her hands were cupped as if they had held something round.

Núñez then looked at the beard of black hair below her stomach and he felt his cheeks flush with shame. He inhaled deeply and then let out his breath slowly. Núñez had avoided looking there for as long as he could, but now he intended to stare at her no matter the shame. It was where he had wanted to look as soon as he saw she was naked.

Maintaining his distance, Núñez walked a few steps to his left to look between her legs. He had never seen a naked woman so closely before. He knew his wife, Margarita, only by touch since she hastily undressed at night well away from the bedside candle. Even in that faint light, she always made certain her back was turned to him while undressing. She would then blow out the candle before coming to bed.

Núñez had seen Margarita only once without clothing in daylight, a month before they were married. He recalled hiding in the bushes and watching her bathe in the brook beside her family's home in Santiago, Cuba. He saw her only in profile from the far away woods. It was in 1775, the year when he had entered the king's army before coming to Florida. Núñez never saw Margarita naked again and, although it was something he wished, he was too shy to make such a request of her.

As he stared at the dead girl, a big brown cockroach emerged out of the high grass and scurried along her right leg. The two-inch long insect stood defiantly on her thigh, seemingly twitching its antennae at him. Núñez gagged, the bitter taste of bile in his mouth. He instantly pushed himself farther away from the girl's corpse and collapsed in the weeds.

"Dios, perdóname por favor (Please pardon me, God)," Núñez prayed, certain he had been punished for staring at the girl's naked body.

Núñez got up slowly and lurched unsteadily to the river. He fell upon his knees, leaned forward and thrust his face into the water. The salt stung his eyes, but the nausea left him. He sat back on his haunches with water dripping down his face. Núñez stood a few minutes later and went to see if the fishing net was still secure in the shallows.

When Núñez returned to the palmetto, he sat down several feet away from where the girl lay unmoving in the grass. He could not take his eyes away from the body. There were insects all over her – ants, beetles, centipedes, cockroaches and other hideous things he could not even name. They had been there all along, but his eyes had been focused on her nudity. Now, he saw them with an inescapable clarity – they were everywhere, on her lips and tongue, in her eyes, ears, nose and mouth, crawling and scuttling over every part of her body.

"Oh, my God!" Núñez groaned and he turned his eyes away from the hideous scene. The nausea returned and Núñez held a hand around his throat, hoping he would not vomit. As a boy, he had seen his drunken father choke to death as he vomited.

The flies were everywhere, buzzing incessantly. They hovered above the body, flying on and off her chest and stomach. Most were blowflies, easily recognized by their blue-green bodies and orange-red faces. Núñez had seen them countless times on dead and dying animals in the woods. He knew the blowflies were laying maggot eggs that would hatch within hours. Núñez shuddered, picturing hundreds of hungry maggots feasting on the girl's body. The very thought made him retch, but he still could not take his eyes from the sight.

The blowflies had laid a broad line of white eggs from where the bodice bunched up on her chest to the black hair between her legs. He could see a mass of eggs there within the hair. It looked as if the flies had followed a plan to lay their eggs in a straight line down her chest to end in a cluster below her stomach. Puzzled by the apparent pattern of the egg-laying, Núñez stood to see it more clearly. But, even standing, he could see nothing to explain the pattern. Núñez knew he would see it better if he went closer to the dead girl, but fearful of being sick again, he resisted the temptation to go any nearer.

"No," he thought, "I won't make that mistake again."

Núñez suddenly realized that he did not know why the girl was dead. "What happened to her?" he wondered aloud. "Something must have killed her, but what?" He studied her face as if she could reply to his question, but the only answer he got was the buzzing of the blowflies. He ran his eyes over her looking for a wound, but saw only the disgusting insects on her body. Nothing he could see on her or around her body explained why she was dead.

"Probably bitten by a snake, most likely a rattlesnake," he mumbled to himself. In the previous week, he had seen four of the distinctive diamondback snakes while fishing along the river. "Or maybe one of those big water snakes bit her."

An hour earlier, he had warned Rafael when he saw a water snake slither into the marsh grass close to where they were standing in the shallows. It was said a strike from one of those snakes would kill a man in minutes.

Núnez studied the body again, looking for a snakebite. Seeing nothing, he wondered if a snake had struck her on the back of one of her legs – likely on her ankle where people usually were bitten. If so, someone examining the body would see the marks. Whatever had happened to her, Núñez knew he eventually would hear about it. Nothing ever remained unknown in the presidio for very long. Within hours, there would be tavern talk about it and the gossips would spread the news around town.

Núñez held his nose as a gust of wind brought the sickening smell of death to him again. It was then that he heard a horse and cart clattering along the oyster shell road. The voices of men reached him as a horse drawn cart turned off the main road and followed the narrow path through the woods. Núñez stared through the trees, looking for his son.

Rafael and three soldiers in blue uniforms emerged out of the darkening woods. The boy and an officer rode in the wagon, while the other two soldiers walked single file alongside the horse. Núñez recognized the officer as Lieutenant Roberto Dorado Delgado y Estrada, a young nobleman from Spain. Núñez hurried to meet them and saluted the officer as he stepped down from the wagon.

"Where's the body?" The lieutenant fixed his blue eyes on Núñez. He patted Rafael's back as the boy jumped off the wagon and ran to his father.

"Under that palmetto, sir." Núñez pointed to the tree, where the flies still buzzed about the body. He nodded a greeting to the soldiers as they followed the lieutenant to the palmetto.

"No, not you! I don't want you to see it." Núñez

stopped the boy, who had fallen into step behind the soldiers. He held his son's arm. "Let's pull in the net and take our catch home." He put a hand on Rafael's shoulder and gently urged him to the river where the fishing net still lay in shallow water. Núñez had left half of the net in the water to keep their catch alive.

Rafael said nothing, but his glum face showed his disappointment. He looked toward the palmetto, reluctantly following his father. The boy glanced over his shoulder as he walked to the river. A shout from one of the soldiers made them both turn to look.

"Oh, my God! It's the governor's niece!" The first man to reach the corpse stood still in shock. The officer pushed the stunned soldier aside and looked down at the corpse. Waving the flies away, he squatted down beside the body and covered it with a stained piece of canvas he had carried in a roll under his arm. He quickly wrapped the body in the canvas. One of the soldiers handed him a length of rope, which he ran around the body and knotted it at the neck, waist, knees and ankles. The lieutenant made sure that no portion of the corpse was exposed.

According to the official regulation regarding the disposition of the dead, soldiers were ordered not to touch the clothing, face or any other bodily surface. It was said the dead could carry sickness, even the plagues. The officer willingly followed the regulations, having heard all his life how the Black Plague had killed almost half the population of Europe.

When the lieutenant finished tying the last knot, the two soldiers picked up the wrapped corpse and carried it over to the cart. They carefully loaded the girl's body aboard as if it were fragile and could be broken. By the time the body lay in the wagon, only the last light of the day was left to show the men the way out of the woods.

The lieutenant talked to Núñez, while Rafael was sent

to pack up the fishing gear. He led him to a spot near the shore, where they could not be overheard by the soldiers waiting near the wagon. "How did you find her ... the body?" The lieutenant's voice wavered as he spoke.

"I saw it from over there, sir." Núñez pointed to where his son was hastily thrusting their catch into a woven-twine bag. "We were pulling the net in when I saw the flies."

The lieutenant nodded. "Tell me, Fernando, of all the fishing spots close to town, why do you come here to fish?" The officer gestured to the few crabs and fish in the bag.

"We usually do much better here, sir." Núñez scowled. "This time of year, the fish are spawning and we usually get a bag full. In September, I come out here every day after duty."

"I see." The lieutenant sighed. "I'll need to talk to you some more, but it's getting dark now and we better leave. See me in the morning at the fort after the change of guard."

"Sí, señor." Núñez waved to Rafael, who ran to his father's side.

While the lieutenant rode in the wagon with the wrapped body beside him, the men and small boy walked ahead, one soldier leading the horse. Núñez, carrying the heavy fish net over one shoulder, guided them out of the dark woods. Rafael walked beside him clutching the bag that held their catch. No one spoke until they reached the shell road to town and then the men talked about the dangers of walking in the darkness. With almost no light left of the day, they feared stepping in a hole or on a venomous snake.

Dorado, as the lieutenant was called by the other officers at the Castillo, sat silently in the wagon thinking about the girl. With a soldier leading the horse along the road, Dorado was free to think about her without distraction. He had met her aboard the schooner *La Esperanza* that brought them both to St. Augustine. Dorado saw her on deck as they sailed out of Havana harbor and entered the Caribbean Sea.

"It was only six months ago in April." He sighed, recalling his first sight of her.

He clearly remembered the day. It was a sunny spring afternoon with few clouds in the sky. The forested island of Cuba stood out in striking green against the blue sea. It shrank in size as the ship caught the current and heeled in the wind. And, when there was only a speck of land to see, Dorado turned and, for the first time, saw Gloria Márquez García.

The girl stood looking astern, her face profiled against the sea, her black hair blowing in the wind. Like Dorado, she had been watching the island slowly disappear from view. He watched her for several minutes until she abruptly turned from the sea and caught him staring. Their eyes met and she smiled at him. He returned her smile and they continued staring at each other until she was called below. Although they never exchanged more than a passing greeting thereafter, their eyes met a number of times on the seven-day voyage to St. Augustine. Nothing else was possible. Despite Dorado's hopes for a few minutes alone with Gloria, every attempt he made to approach her was blocked by her chaperone, an ever-watchful elderly woman. The woman, named Elsa, maintained a careful distance between them.

In St. Augustine, Dorado saw Gloria occasionally at Government House, but always in the company of other people. He found it all but impossible to be with her alone. Whenever he saw Gloria, she was accompanied by her chaperone or surrounded by other officers. The closest he ever got to Gloria was sitting beside her during a flamenco guitar performance in the plaza. Even then, her chaperone sat on the other side of her and other officers sat in front and behind them.

Dorado finally found a time alone with Gloria on a sultry night near the end of August. At an officer's fiesta held in Government House, they signaled each other with their eyes and met in the garden under the limb of a live oak. There, in the humid mist, they squeezed each other tightly and kissed with wet lips. A servant calling the girl's name ended their embrace. She blew him a kiss as she went inside and, after a minute, Dorado, making sure his wig was on straight, followed her into the building.

A week later, they had another unexpected encounter in Government House. Dorado met Gloria as he was delivering the monthly rations report to the governor's office. Abruptly turning a corner, he nearly collided with her coming the other way. They smiled at each other, said hello, and hastily held hands. As she stood so close to him, the scent of rose perfume in his nostrils, Dorado yearned to stroke the soft skin of her face and kiss her lips.

Staring into her eyes, Dorado was surprised when she took him by the hand and led him into a hall closet. And there in the musty darkness, they hugged and kissed with open mouths. Dorado kissed her eyes and ears, licked her neck and when she boldly pushed her bodice down, he sucked her nipples. Kissing her unceasingly, he reached up under her dress and into the wet and warmth between her legs. Gloria gasped and wrapped her arms around his back. Clinging tightly to him, she rubbed her body rhythmically against him. They were panting and moaning when footsteps sounded outside in the hallway. They instantly stopped every movement, even their breathing, and waited silently until the sounds receded down the stone corridor. When it was quiet again, they sighed with relief and stepped apart. Fearing to be found together in the closet, they knew they had to leave. Gloria pulled up her bodice and hastily patted her hair into place. With flushed faces, they cautiously peeked out and then tiptoed from the closet. Gloria went first after squeezing his hand. She turned to whisper "Hasta pronto" in the hallway.

In his hurried departure from Government House, Dorado saluted two senior officers as he went by. He felt their eyes on his back and worried his appearance might have given away his tryst with the governor's niece. That night, Dorado lay awake in bed for hours. He could not stop thinking about his passionate few minutes with Gloria and the possibility of the governor or commandant learning about it. He worried the remainder of the week, expecting at any time to be ordered to explain his lengthy presence in Government House. But no one ever asked for explanations and he went about his duties as if nothing had happened.

As for Gloria, she was never in his arms again. Despite her cross-her-heart promise to meet him again, she seemed unable to escape her chaperone's scrutiny. Their only encounters thereafter were with their eyes in the company of other people. He saw her on other occasions at Government House, but never by herself. He never caressed or kissed her again. He never even sat near her again. "Until now – lying dead in this wagon." Tears formed in his eyes and he cleared his throat loudly to disguise the sobs that followed. When Dorado finally composed himself, he felt a lump in his throat. He swallowed several times, but the lump remained stuck in his throat.

Earlier, Dorado had barely managed to hide the shock of seeing her naked and dead on the ground. In the last light, his loss of color and widened-eyes had not been seen by his men. Nor did they see him almost collapse as he dropped to his knees to cover her corpse. Dorado looked at Gloria only once before he threw the canvas sheet over her. He closed his eyes for the rest of the time it took to lift her body onto the sheet and wrap it around her. Struck by the stench of death, Dorado clenched his teeth and barely breathed as he tied the wrapped corpse with a rope. He stumbled clumsily rising from the ground, but neither of the soldiers saw it happen. They were busy carrying the dead girl to the cart.

On the dark road to St. Augustine, it suddenly occurred to Dorado that he did not know how or why Gloria had died in the woods. But the memory of her lifeless body on the ground concerned him more than the cause of her death. The terrible sight seemed stuck in his mind, no matter how hard he tried to push it away. Over and over again, Dorado saw Gloria lying dead on her back, her beautiful face bloated, her body insulted by a horde of insects.

Distraught by Gloria's death, Dorado was unaware they had reached the city gates until Núñez shouted a greeting to the sentries. He looked up and saw the flickering lanterns of the Castillo de San Marcos. The great stone fortress was a welcome sight for the men coming in from the darkness on a moonless night. Núñez and his son left them at the city gates.

Dorado, his two men and the horse and cart bearing the corpse continued on toward the Castillo. While the soldiers took the dead girl to the doctor's office, Dorado went to the guard station to write a death report. Aware his superiors and, perhaps, even the governor himself, would read his report, he wrote it with care and in the best Castilian Spanish he knew.

Dorado used the sharpest quill he could find and carefully lettered each word to assure clarity and easy reading. A number of pieces of paper were balled up and thrown on the floor when the ink clotted or he made mistakes. He finally finished his report two hours later and left the fort shortly after eleven o'clock.

Dorado's last act before leaving for home was to submit his report to the Night Officer of the Guard, Lieutenant Elías Ramírez Villanueva. It would be Ramírez' unenviable duty to go to Government House and inform the governor of the death of his niece. Dorado trudged wearily away from the Castillo, forgetting to sign out for the night. His mind was on the lovely Gloria, knowing he would never hold her in his arms again. He shook his head still struggling to believe she was dead and gone forever.

Dorado arrived early at the Castillo the next day. Unable to sleep for more than an hour during the night, he got up before dawn, dressed quickly and walked to the fort. As he crossed the drawbridge over the moat, the lone sentry standing guard that morning saluted him.

"Buenos días, Teniente. El Capitán Martínez left orders for you to report to him – after reveille." The sentry nodded to emphasize the message.

"Gracias, Salazar. He's already in his office?"

"Yes, sir. El Capitán was the first officer to sign in this morning."

As Dorado entered the fortress, he saw Núñez ahead, waiting for him in the entry room. He paused at the guard's table to sign his name in the officer's duty register.

"You're here early, Fernando." Dorado walked over to Núñez and returned his salute.

"Yes, sir. I try to be early every day. But today I'm here early because I couldn't sleep after yesterday."

"I understand, Fernando." Dorado gestured for Núñez to follow him. "Let's talk on the upper deck. It still should be cool up there and we won't hear as much of the morning drill."

Núñez followed Dorado as he strode across the parade grounds, located at the center of the Castillo. They climbed up the broad stone stairway at the eastern and seaside of the fort and reached the upper deck as the first light appeared on the horizon. The lieutenant led Núñez past the northern watchtower to a pair of cannons facing the Bay of St. Augustine.

"Another hot day." Dorado was already wet under the arms after climbing the stairs. He leaned his back against the barrel of one of the cannons and motioned Núñez to the other.

"Yes, sir. Not a wisp of wind off the sea this morning."

"Fernando, we need to talk about what happened ... yesterday. Do you know the time you got out to the river?" Dorado pointed his finger north to where the sunlight was spreading over the forested land.

"I don't own a timepiece, sir, but I'd say it was three o'clock or so."

"So early? The duty roster shows you on the morning shift."

"Yes, sir. I was working under Sergeant Santana mending those old cracks in the moat. When we ran out of mortar, he sent us home. After lunch, I took Rafael fishing. With him, it takes me a while to get out to the river. He stops to look at every animal in the woods; knows them all, too. Rafael's small for his age, but smart." His smile showed the pleasure he found in his son. "So, I'd say it was about three o'clock más o menos when we got there."

"I see." Dorado nodded. "Did you see the governor's niece anywhere along the way? In the woods or on the river?"

"I never saw her until ..." Núñez made a face. "I'll never forget how she looked."

"I understand." Dorado paused to look out to sea. His eyes had misted, but Núñez, busy wiping sweat from his brow, was unaware of it. "Did you see anyone else on the way?"

"Only a couple of fishermen at the city gates. They'd been fishing on the San Sebastian River. They had a small catch, too. They're from the old barrio and I've seen them before."

"What about out where you found the governor's niece?"

"No, sir. Not many men fish there. Too many mosquitoes and snakes and too far from town. I can't guess what the governor's niece was doing out there." Núñez scratched his ear.

"I can't either. Tell me, Fernando, when you and your boy reached the river, did you go directly to that fishing spot?" Dorado stared at Núñez.

"No, sir. We started farther south and walked north along the shore. It was a bad day for fishing, but we still went on. We couldn't fish most other days because of the rains."

"Do you know about when you reached the spot where you saw the body?"

"I can't say for sure, sir, but the sun was going down by that time. We fished one place after another without any luck and that was the last spot to try. We cast out twenty-some times with only a few small crabs and a couple keepers for our effort." He made a face.

"Did you see her clothes anywhere?"

"No, sir. I never saw her clothing or shoes. I can't guess what she was doing out there without clothes." Núñez shook his head from side to side. "Surely, she wasn't bathing there."

"I wouldn't think so. Did you see any wounds on her? Or blood?" Dorado squinted as a beam of sunlight crossed the seawall and struck him in the eyes.

"No, sir. I didn't see nothing and I looked at her for a time." Núñez blushed, but with sunlight in his eyes, Dorado did not see his reddened face. "I stayed away and never touched her – you know what they say about the dead carrying the plagues."

Dorado nodded. "Tell me, Fernando, what do you think happened to her?"

"I don't know, sir. Yesterday, I thought she was struck by some snake. Today, I don't know. I didn't see a bite on her and her face was bloated from something." Núñez shrugged. "Maybe, the señorita ate some tainted berries."

"We'll see. Captain Martínez is looking at her now." Dorado paused and waited as a roll of drums announced reveille. "One more question, Fernando. When you sent Rafael into town, did you know the dead girl was the governor's niece?"

"No, sir. It was only when I walked to the palmetto and looked at her face." Núñez blushed. "The governor's niece is *well-known* in town."

"What do you mean *well-known* in town?" Dorado noticed Núñez' flushed face.

"She's the governor's niece, so everyone knows her." Núñez' face remained red.

"Speak up, Fernando. What do you mean by *well-known*?" Dorado's knuckles whitened as he gripped the handle of his sword.

"Well, sir." Núñez rubbed his chin. "Can I speak frankly?"

"Yes, of course." Dorado frowned. "Speak up! That's an order, soldier!"

"Sí, señor." Núñez saw the anger in the lieutenant's face, but he hesitated to tell him the truth. "Well, sir ... the governor's niece was ... the talk of the town. They said she flirted with all the young officers."

"Is that so?" Dorado grimaced. "What else did they say?"

"It was said la Señorita Gloria had much more experience in the ways of the world than other girls her age. The women said she was sure to get herself in trouble – sooner or later."

"Oh and what did the men say about her?"

"Sir, what the men said was tavern talk."

"Let me hear it anyway." Dorado clenched his teeth.

"Yes, s-sir." Núñez inhaled audibly. "When la Señorita Gloria was first seen in town the men called her *El cuerpito glorioso de Gloria* (Glorious Body Gloria). Later, they called her *el cuerpito* (the body). Not to her face, of course."

"No, of course not. What else was said?"

"Nothing else, sir."

"Are you sure?" Dorado looked into his eyes to see if he was lying.

Before Núñez could reply, a soldier appeared and saluted Dorado. He stood at attention before him. "Sir, Captain Martínez wants you to come to his office immediately."

Dorado dismissed the soldier and then turned to Núñez. "We'll talk later, Fernando." He returned Núñez' salute and walked toward the stairs.

Watching the officer step down the stairs to the parade grounds, Núñez knew he would never tell him what was said about the girl. He had heard countless comments in town as well as in the barracks about how she needed a good hard ride. Only yesterday, the two young men working with him on the moat talked endlessly about lying between her legs. They took turns boasting how they would give her a ride she would never forget.

Dorado headed toward the northeast bastion of the fortress. It was called the Bastion of San Carlos and stood on the bay front facing the inlet channel, where ships sailed in and out of St. Augustine. Heavy cannons pointed toward the inlet on the upper deck of the bastion, while below the interior space was divided into two chambers. The much larger of the two chambers held the Castillo's munitions; the other contained a small medical office with an adjoining and equally small surgery. The little office was occupied by the biggest man in St. Augustine, the six and a half-foot physician, Captain Carlos Martínez Medina.

Dorado recalled visiting the doctor six months earlier for a routine medical examination, required of all new officers in the presidio. "You're healthy, Lieutenant," Captain Martínez told Dorado, after briefly listening to his heart. "I see from your service records you're twenty-six. At your age, you should be. See that you stay that way, so avoid the putas (prostitutes)."

Dorado looked healthy. Slender and almost six feet tall, the young man stood straight and walked with long strides. The son of a noble family from Asturias in northern Spain, he had the blue eyes and light colored hair and skin commonly seen in the Cantabrian mountain country. His face was free of pox marks, but was made conspicuous by a long, hooked nose that suggested a Semitic ancestor. Aware of anyone staring at his nose, Dorado was quick to say there must have been a Moorish princess in his family history. He had a thick mustache which he also hoped might minimize the prominence of his nose.

As Dorado entered the open door of the medical office, he saw the physician was not alone. Captain Ricardo Ruiz de León, the senior staff officer at Government House and close advisor to the governor, sat in the office talking to Martínez. Swiping futilely at a buzzing fly, the doctor looked up when Dorado stepped into the room.

"Well, Lieutenant, I'm glad to see you finally found the time to meet with me." Martínez frowned during the exchange of salutes. "Sit down over there on the stool. I assume you are acquainted with Don Ricardo? He's here to listen to your report."

"Yes, sir, we've met at Government House. It's good to see you again, sir."

Ruiz de León nodded, but made no reply

Dorado arranged his sword at his side and sat on the wooden stool assigned to him. It had been put in front of the closed door to the surgery, facing both the other men. The young officer felt uncomfortable under their gaze, but he tried not to show it.

"Well, Lieutenant, what do you think about the unfortunate death of the governor's niece?" Martínez closed the outside door.

"I was shocked to discover it, sir." Dorado looked back and forth between the two older men. He noticed that neither man wore a wig.

"Where's your report, Lieutenant?" Martínez stood with hands on his hips. "You did write a death report, didn't you?"

"Yes, sir. I left it with the Officer of the Guard late last night. Hasn't he given it to you, sir?" Dorado worried the report somehow had been lost.

"No, Ramírez hasn't arrived yet. Damn it! And no one else has a key to his office or the munitions room. Can you imagine it? God help this poor presidio, if we are ever attacked early in the morning. We wouldn't be able to open the munitions room and arm ourselves for battle." He sat down heavily in his chair.

"I'll write up another report immediately ..."

"No, Lieutenant. Tell us what you know, now." Martínez spoke sharply. "We'll read the report later."

"Sí, mi Capitán."

Martínez tilted his desk chair backward so he could lean his head against the stone wall behind him. The chair squeaked in stress under his weight. The physician was a big man, big in bone and bulk. Martínez was not only the tallest man in the presidio, he also was one of the heaviest, probably weighing more than two hundred and fifty pounds. Dorado was staring at his large shoes when Martínez snapped at him impatiently.

"Let's hear what you know – now!" He spoke rapidly, swallowing word endings in the style of city people from Spain. "How about beginning, Lieutenant, before the girl is buried."

"Yes, sir. I'll tell you what I know, but it's not much."

"I'll be the judge of that." Martínez frowned. "Tell us what you know."

"Sí, mi Capítan. La Señorita Gloria Márquez García was found dead during my night shift of guard duty in the presidio. A few minutes after seven o'clock, a young boy reported the discovery of a dead body on the shore of the North River. The boy's name is Rafael Núñez; he's the son of Fernando Núñez, a soldier from the Havana Regiment. Rafael informed one of the sentries at the city gates, Luis Velasco, that his father had found a body. Núñez sent his son to tell the sentries, while he waited with the corpse in the woods. The boy ran all the way to the presidio. He did not know if the body was a man or woman; his father wouldn't let him see it." Dorado saw Ruiz de León nod approvingly.

"Isn't Núñez stationed here at the Castillo?" asked Martínez. "I'm sure I've seen him."

"Yes, sir. Núñez is one of the men in the maintenance crew at the Castillo."

"So, he's one of the chief engineer's men."

"Yes, sir." Dorado shifted his feet to relax the tension in his back.

"I see. Continue, Lieutenant."

"Yes, sir. I was walking along la Calle Real (Royal Street) toward the plaza when the boy found me a few minutes later. The guards at the gates, as instructed, didn't leave their post. They sent Rafael to tell me what he knew." Dorado paused to clear his throat.

"I then went over to the Castillo to requisition a horse and wagon to collect the body. I also took two men from the barracks, José Calles Cruz and Esteban Solana, to accompany me to the North River. Rafael rode with me in the wagon and the boy led us into the woods where his father was waiting. Núñez showed us the corpse lying under a palmetto and we saw it was the governor's niece. Of course, we were all shocked." Dorado inhaled deeply, thinking of the lovely girl lying dead behind him in the surgery.

"I covered her corpse and followed the instructions in the officer's manual, avoiding all contact with the body. The dead girl was carried to the wagon and we then left for town. By then, it was almost dark. At the city gates, Núñez and his son went home and I took her – the corpse to the Castillo. It was carted here and, when a key was found to open the outside door, the body was carried into the surgery. I then wrote my official report and gave it to Lieutenant Ramírez Villanueva, who was the Command Officer at the Castillo last night. He told me to go home and sent someone else to make my final rounds of the presidio."

"Who notified the governor?" Martínez crossed his arms over his chest.

"Lieutenant Ramírez. I think he notified the governor after reading my report. On my way home, I saw him walking behind me as I passed the sentries at the end of the drawbridge."

"When was that?"

"It was a few minutes after eleven o'clock, sir."

During Dorado's account, the two senior officers held their eyes on him the entire time. Concerned about their impression of him, he wondered what they were thinking as he looked from one to the other. Martínez was the one who asked questions, but both of them scrutinized him as he responded.

From their lined faces and gray hair, he guessed both

of them to be in their fifties. Ruiz de León, a short, slender man, appeared some years older than Martínez. He had a bald spot at the back of his head, which he covered with carefully combed hair. His long, narrow face was accentuated by a thin mustache, trimmed to the exact length of his mouth. Ruiz de León rarely smiled and then only slightly with his lips. He spoke softly and infrequently.

Carlos Martínez appeared to be the opposite. He smiled often and laughed easily. He spoke loudly and bluntly and was regarded as a man with a ready wit, all too often spiced with sarcasm. At the Castillo, his sarcasm had insulted a number of the other officers including the commandant of the Castillo. They considered him arrogant and tended to avoid all unnecessary contact with him. Even in town, where he spent little time drinking in taverns, Carlos Martínez was said to be a man with *too much mouth*."

"Well, Lieutenant, so that's your report, is it?"

"Yes, sir." Dorado fingered the yellow band on his hat which he had placed in his lap. "I have nothing else to report."

"Nothing else? You noticed nothing else, Lieutenant? Surely, you noticed the nudity of the dead girl? Didn't you find that odd?" Martínez glared at Dorado.

"Yes, sir." Dorado did not know what Martínez wanted him to say. He looked at Ruiz de León in bewilderment.

"Since you saw she was naked, didn't it occur to you to look for her clothes? Do you think girls like the governor's niece go wandering about the woods without clothing?"

"No, sir." Dorado's face flushed in anger.

"Were you too engrossed staring at her naked body to think of looking for her clothes? She was a pretty little piece, wasn't she? And there the girl was with her legs spread and her chocha in sight for anyone to see it."

"No, sir." Dorado's face remained red. He was searching for something to say, when Ruiz de León spoke up for the first time. Unlike Carlos Martínez, the small man spoke slowly and softly. In order to understand everything the captain said, Dorado found it necessary, not only to listen carefully, but to watch the words form in his mouth.

"Pardon me for interrupting, Lieutenant." Ruiz de León looked at Dorado and then he turned to Martínez. "Carlos, you shouldn't be using such vulgarities with the lieutenant. Those are the words of a common man, not a man of culture and knowledge."

"I've heard it said that common words often carry the most meaning."

"Is that so? Well, not to me!" Ruiz de León pointed his finger at Martínez. "You need to show more respect. It's the governor's niece you're talking about." He looked at Dorado. "I'm sure the lieutenant is still quite shocked by at what he saw in the woods last night. After all, it's not even twelve hours since he returned to the Castillo."

"That may be, but he doesn't need you to speak for him. So, Lieutenant, tell us what you saw when you looked at the dead girl – the governor's niece."

"Yes, sir, I was shocked. I still am – seeing her dead. I knew la Señorita Gloria and I liked her very much." He looked at the doctor. "Yes, I saw her nudity, but only dimly in the darkness. I covered her body up as quickly as possible. Still, what I saw will stay forever in my mind's eye." His face paled.

"What did you see?" Martínez pushed himself from the wall and sat forward in his chair. With his elbows resting on the desk, he held his head on crossed hands under his chin.

"Her face was all bloated, her tongue was sticking out of her mouth. Her body was stained with dirt and leaves were stuck to her. Insects of all kinds were running all over her and the flies were everywhere. It was revolting!" Dorado grimaced and shook his head.

Martínez nodded. "Was there anything else about the

body that you noticed?"

Dorado paused before answering. He tried to recall his first sight of Gloria's body as one of his men pushed aside the palmetto fronds. "Yes, sir. Now that I think about it, I recall she lay on the ground in a manner reminding me of the crucifixion of our Lord, Jesus Christ."

"What do you mean?" Martínez stared at Dorado.

"She lay on her back with her arms extended out to the sides and her head leaning down to the right." Dorado felt his stomach tighten as he pictured Gloria's face and opened eyes.

"What about her legs? They were spread open – wide open! Unlike the concept of the crucifixion the painters, sculptors and writers have given us to believe." Martínez gave him a look of disdain. "It's amazing what Spaniards still believe in this so-called Age of Reason."

Dorado was silent. He wondered how Martínez knew the position of her legs.

"You need not reply to that blasphemy, Lieutenant." Ruiz de León spoke up again.

"What about the girl's clothes?" Martínez sighed in exasperation.

"I didn't see any clothing – there was only her white bodice, bunched up on her chest." Dorado furrowed his brow, trying to remember what he had seen in the few seconds before he covered her body. He remembered little after his first sight of her lying dead at his feet. Once he had seen her open eyes, Dorado had closed his own as he draped the cover over her body.

"I don't suppose you saw her shoes either." Martínez exhaled his breath loudly.

"No, sir." Dorado shook his head. "I wondered what had happened to her clothes, but by that time it was too dark to look for them. I know they were not anywhere near her – body. I can't believe she went out there nude."

"I can't believe it either. Did you see anything else on or around the girl?"

"No, only the insects." Dorado shuddered, remembering the ants running over her face as he wrapped up her corpse.

"Were there any wounds on the body?" Martínez lowered his voice.

"None that I saw."

"Blood?" Martínez stared at the lieutenant.

"No, sir." Dorado shifted his buttocks on the stool.

"What about scratches on her body?"

"No, sir." I didn't see any scratches on her." Dorado shook his head, knowing he had not looked carefully at her body or the place where she lay.

"Were there signs of a struggle there – where her body was found?" Martínez watched Dorado intently as he answered his questions.

"No, sir. Not that I could see." Dorado worried that he had missed seeing something that Martínez knew had been found. "It was at day's end and the light was fading fast."

"What about Núñez? Did you talk to him?"

"Yes, sir. I talked to him last night and then again this morning. I met with him before reveille and we talked until you sent for me."

"What did he say?" Martínez cocked his head to the side.

"Nothing important. Núñez found her while fishing along the shore. He saw her body from the shallows where he and his son were pulling in the net. Núñez only went close enough to identify her; he was afraid of getting the plague. He thought she might have been killed by a venomous snake or poisoned by eating some tainted berries."

"She was not bitten by a venomous snake nor poisoned by tainted berries. Do you have any suspicions of Núñez?"

"No, sir, I would never suspect Núñez. He's one of our best men. He was fishing after serving his shift at the Castillo. His only concern was to keep his boy from seeing the corpse. Rafael is only nine years old. He was ..." Dorado abruptly stopped speaking. When he spoke again, his voice was barely audible. "You're saying Gloria was murdered!" Dorado shook his head in disbelief. "Murdered! No, I don't believe it."

"The girl was murdered." Martínez spoke with certainty. "Murdered and mutilated."

"Mutilated." Dorado repeated the word as if it was unknown to him.

"Yes. Severely mutilated as you'll soon see if you have the stomach for it."

"I don't believe it." Dorado shook his head, stunned at what he had heard.

"Can you think of anyone here who could have killed her?" Martínez sat back again, his arms crossed over his chest. He looked at Ruiz de León, who was quietly studying Dorado.

"No. Who could even think of hurting her? She was so alive, such a sunny girl. Always smiling." Dorado visualized Gloria as he had first seen her aboard ship. "I liked her the second I saw her. What man wouldn't want her on his arm or in his house? She was beautiful."

"She was beautiful." Martínez nodded. "Maybe, too beautiful for her own good. Well, Lieutenant, I can't think of anything else to ask you for now ... but, I may have more questions later. Ricardo, do you have any questions for him?"

"Yes. Lieutenant, you said you knew la Señorita Gloria. How well did you know her? I don't recall ever seeing you with her at Government House." Ruiz de León sat straight in the chair, his hands clasped in his lap.

"I met her in April, sir. We sailed to St. Augustine on

the same ship. We also talked at the governor's fiesta in August." Dorado did not mention his clandestine meeting with her in the garden that night or their time together in the hall closet, two days later.

"Ah, that explains it. One more question. Were you on duty before your late shift as Officer of the Guard in town?"

"Yes, sir. I had morning duty here at the Castillo. I was in charge of musket training for the militia. Afterwards, I carried out an inspection of the sentry posts around the presidio."

"Where were you in the afternoon?"

"I played chess with Lieutenant López Contreras in the plaza."

Ruiz de León nodded and waved another fly from his face. He looked at Martínez. "I have nothing else to ask."

"Well, Lieutenant, is there anything else that needs to be said?" Martínez stared at him.

"No, sir." Dorado did not repeat the town gossip he had heard from Núñez. "I assume you will talk to Fernando Núñez?"

Martínez scowled. Abruptly standing, he gave Dorado a hard look. "There are many people to be interviewed, Lieutenant. And that's my responsibility – not yours!"

"Sí, señor." Dorado stood at attention. "Captain Martínez, please permit me to assist in the search for the murderer. I want to do something."

"Who knows, perhaps you can be helpful. We'll see." Martínez exchanged looks with Ruiz de León, who was rising from his chair. "For now, I need someone to assist me with the autopsy. Don Ricardo must return to Government House and I need an assistant to record my findings. Do you think you have the stomach for it?"

Dorado nodded slowly. "I think so."

"I want you to take notes while I examine the girl's

corpse. I trust you write clearly?"

"Sí, señor." Dorado took a deep breath.

"Good." Martínez nodded to Ruiz de León. "I'll see you at dinner, Ricardo. Thanks to one of my patients, I've got a good size piece of wild boar for us to eat."

"I'll bring the chess set. Adiós, Teniente."

"Adiós, mi Capitán." Dorado saluted.

As Ruiz de León walked from the office, Dorado noticed he limped. It surprised him and his eyes followed the officer as he went through the door. He had seen the governor's aide many times before, but always seated in his office.

Martínez saw Dorado's look of surprise. "Don Ricardo was badly wounded in the war with England. A cannon ball almost cost him his leg as well as his life. He's very lucky to be alive." He motioned Dorado to follow him.

The doctor opened the door to the surgery and led the way into the dark room. Dorado followed him, feeling the cool of the interior once the door was opened. In the room, the smell of death made him cover his nose with the palm of his hand. Dorado stood behind Martínez and was unable to see much of the room.

"The cool feels good, doesn't it? It's like that most of the time in here, though at times too damned damp. The thick walls of the Castillo keep it that way." Martínez turned to face the lieutenant. "You'll have to get used to the smell; there's nothing I can do about it. When it gets really foul in here I smoke a cigar. Do you want one?"

"No, sir. I'll be fine in a minute or so." By that time, Dorado's eyes had adjusted to the darkness and he now could see the outline of the furniture in the room.

"Good." Martínez nodded. "May I call you Dorado? I'm told that's what everyone calls you here in the Castillo."

"Yes, sir." Dorado responded softly, not looking at the doctor. His eyes were on the small covered figure lying on the table in the middle of the room. He saw Gloria's body in the light that fell across the table from the outer office. It was covered by the same stained canvas sheet he had used to cover her corpse in the woods.

"The body is covered, as you can see." Martínez, aware of where Dorado's attention was focused, spoke reassuringly. "You know, after all these years in the king's service, I still don't like looking at the death of youth – especially, as in this instance, such a lovely girl." He patted Dorado on the shoulder to distract him from staring at the corpse on the table.

But the young man's eyes never left the small shrouded body. Dorado worried about what he would see when the sheet was removed. He could feel his heart pounding in his chest.

CHAPTER TWO

SEPTEMBER 30, 1788

Martínez moved around the dark chamber, carrying the fish-oil lamp from his office to light the candles around the table, where the body lay covered. The candles stood on wooden stands that could be easily moved to provide needed light for examinations, medical treatment and surgical procedures. The room was ten feet square and sparsely furnished. In addition to the blood-stained table, where the corpse rested, the room contained a stool, a smaller table and a tall cabinet in the corner near the entrance to the outer office. During medical examinations or surgical procedures, Martínez sat on the stool and employed the smaller table as a stand for his various instruments.

When not in use, the instruments lay on a towel on the top shelf of the cabinet. The next two shelves held an assortment of corked bottles of chemicals, ointments and medicines. Rolls of bandages of all shapes and sizes filled the fourth shelf and other apparatus and equipment, including seldom used surgical instruments, were piled below on the fifth shelf. The remaining shelves of the usually open cabinet were cluttered with a variety of empty bottles, flasks, charts of the human body and piles of dusty papers. A row of medical books, most with torn or worn covers, extended along the bottom shelf.

None of the furniture was new and every piece showed the signs of years of use. Made of split pine, the examining table had been splintered, scraped and stained over time. The seven foot long table was made sixty years earlier when the first Castillo physician had been assigned the two small rooms for an office and surgery. Martínez requested a new table when he arrived at the presidio in 1786, but the carpenters, busy replacing the fort's cannon carriages, were told to ignore his requests. The cabinet and small instrument table had been made a year before his arrival, but appeared similarly abused. One of the doors of the cabinet hung loose on a broken hinge and the other had a split panel in it. The oak stool, purchased in town by the previous physician, was the one sturdy piece of furniture in the surgery. Martínez' only contribution to the room was a human skull with a toothy smile, which he set atop the cabinet.

Upon his arrival, Martínez had been given a newly made desk and chair in his office, but nothing had been added or replaced in the surgery. The battered examining table remained in use despite his monthly written requests to the commandant for a replacement. In August, at the monthly officers' meeting in the Castillo, the commandant angrily reprimanded the doctor for "his damned requests." The commandant spoke vehemently, telling him the fort's defenses were his principal priority, not the medical facility.

In addition to the stench, Dorado was struck by the dirt and litter he saw on the floor of the surgery. Dust deposits seemed to be everywhere he looked and, even in the dim light from the outer office he could see black mold on the farthest wall. The stone floor was littered with leaves, sand and other debris brought in on the doctor's shoes and large dust balls lay beneath the cabinet and examining table. And, when Martínez lit the candles in the surgery, Dorado saw mold on every wall, especially in the lower corners and along the base of the walls.

Spider webs, one of them almost two feet in diameter, hung down from the ceiling in three corners of the room. Long-legged, black and yellow striped spiders stood motionless on their webs waiting for prey. As Martínez lit the last of the candles, the spiders moved suddenly as if awakened by the light and darted among the insect mummies they had wrapped in silk.

"They're pets." Martínez smiled, seeing Dorado's expression of distaste. "I keep them here to catch some of the flies that get in through the open door. The spiders do as well as can be expected, considering the number of flies and other insects that come for the bits of flesh lying about. There are other spiders somewhere else in the room. I don't know where their webs are, but I see them now and then when I light the candles."

Dorado strode to the center of the room, away from the webs. Spiders frightened him. As a small boy, only seven years old, he had been bitten by a viuda negra (black widow) in his bed and he was sick for more than month from the bite. He still had a red spot on his shoulder where the spider had bitten him.

Martínez turned to Dorado after closing the office door. "As you can see, I covered the body. I will keep it covered and only expose the portions I am examining. That should spare you from seeing too much. But inevitably during the autopsy, most of the corpse will be exposed; it can't be helped. If that bothers you, look away; if you feel faint, leave the surgery. The strongest of men can faint at the sight of a corpse. Is that understood? Lieutenant!"

"Yes, sir." Dorado paused before answering Martínez. He had been watching the black and yellow spider in the corner web nearest to him. The large spider held a struggling fly in its grasp and Dorado knew the doomed fly soon would be immobile and wrapped up in a cocoon. "My God," he said to himself, "that spider is bigger than a silver peseta."

The doctor, unaware of where Dorado's eyes were focused, continued talking to him as he walked around the table positioning the six candle stands for the autopsy. Two were placed close to the table just above the top of the head, two others at the sides of the waist and the last two at the soles of the feet. Martínez then lit a thick candle that stood on the table. The candle was set in a six-inch metal stand that could either be slid along the table's surface or held in his hand when a particular portion of a body needed more scrutiny. Martínez called the candle his examining light and held it in his huge hand as if it were as light as a feather.

In the flickering light from the six candles, the covered cadaver looked sickly yellow to Dorado. Occupying less than two-thirds the length of the table, the shapeless form looked too little to be the body of Gloria Márquez García. His stomach turned as he looked closely at the canvas cover and saw the brown stains of blood and bodily fluids that soiled it. Swallowing several times to suppress his nausea, Dorado stepped back from the table.

"Get a chair from the office and sit over there." Martínez motioned Dorado to a place on the opposite side of the table where the upper portion of the corpse lay concealed under the cover. "Before you sit, get a quill and the pot of ink from the top of my desk. There's paper in the top drawer. Use that flat slab of wood lying on the desk to write on." Impatient to begin, the doctor peered under the cover while Dorado was in the outer office.

Martínez carefully pushed the cover aside when Dorado was seated. He made sure the girl's head remained hidden as he exposed her breasts and abdomen. He glanced at the young lieutenant, then looked down at the corpse.

Dorado avoided the sight of Gloria's naked body. Instead, he studied Martínez. "What a massive man," he thought, observing his broad shoulders, chest and long muscular arms. In the small room, looming over the body, Martínez looked as big as a bear. The shadow he cast on the wall was in fact a black bear. Dorado watched the doctor adjust the candles for the last time and then look over at him. He nodded, signaling Dorado the autopsy would now begin.

"Write down only the facts. The physical findings are what I need to determine how, when and, maybe, why she was killed. Don't record everything I say. If you're unsure what's significant, ask me. I'll use your notes to write up my report later. Is that understood?"

"Yes, sir." Dorado crossed his legs and placed the slab on his upper knee.

"I didn't do much to the corpse when I arrived this morning. Of course, I removed the bodice and thoroughly bathed the body with alcohol. I use alcohol to remove the insects and dirt; it also somewhat lessens the stench of death. I applied a lot of alcohol since the body was crawling with ants and cockroaches." Martínez glanced at Dorado. "Are you feeling well?"

"Yes, sir." Dorado now looked at her exposed chest and abdomen. With Gloria's head covered, the sight of her body did not sicken him as he had expected. It looked unreal, like the marble and stone figures so commonly seen in Spanish churches and city plazas. He sighed in relief. His worst fear had been that Gloria's dead body would make him vomit.

"Good. The body lay outside for about a day. I know that because of its strong smell. That's the sign of bodily decomposition; the stronger the odor, the longer the corpse has been decomposing. In this humid climate, heat hurries the process of decay and bodies soon stink." Martínez saw the young officer twitch his nose.

"You shouldn't smell much of anything where you're sitting – not after all the alcohol I applied to the body."

"No, sir," lied Dorado, smelling the fetid odors that filled the room. He wanted to clap his hand over his nose to shut out the stench. Even when inhaling through his mouth, he could not avoid the smell of defecation, urine and the other sickening odors he could not identify. He swallowed again to stifle the nausea that welled up from his stomach.

"Insects hasten the bodily decomposition. Before you know it, they can strip a corpse of all its flesh." Martínez waited while Dorado finished writing his first notes. "Although they do what we consider disgusting things to the dead, insects and all the other scavengers serve us well. They remove all dead things along with their diseases. Some say it's God's service they perform and that's as suitable an explanation as any others I've heard."

Martínez moved one of the candles closer to the girl's chest. He leaned across the body to move a second candle and his shirt sleeve brushed the girl's breasts. As he placed the candle close to her side, Martínez casually rested his forearm on her covered face.

Dorado frowned. "Respétala! (Show her some respect!)" he said to himself.

"What's the matter?" Martínez noticed Dorado's grimace.

"Nothing," he lied. "Though I can't imagine praising insects for doing God's work."

"Is that so? Well, Lieutenant, let me tell you something. Without the insects and the other carrion eaters, there would be animal corpses rotting everywhere in the world. So, I say praise be it to the ants, cockroaches and even the filthy flies. Oh, yes, and let's not forget our ever hungry friends – the vultures." The doctor studied the girl's neck and chest as he talked.

Dorado watched him without speaking. His stomach

churned, but the nausea was gone.

"Are you ready?" Bent over the body, Martínez briefly looked up at Dorado.

Dorado looked quickly at the wounds and then returned his eyes to his notes. "Listo (ready), mi Capitán," holding the quill in his right hand.

"There are four deep wounds in the torso," Martínez reported, as he leveled the candle over the girl's chest. He moved the candle horizontally from side to side down the entire length of her body and then repeated the process from her feet to her head.

"Four wounds?" Dorado did not follow the candle with his eyes.

"Yes. One wound is located in the lower neck, at the throat, two others are in the chest, one in each breast, and another is situated in the lower abdomen. The latter cited wound begins in the pubic hair above the female opening and extends downward deep into the body. It looks to be the deepest and widest wound. The two wounds in the chest are separated, each situated in the upper portion of a breast. Those wounds are almost a foot apart."

"I didn't see any wounds on her ... when I wrapped the body."

Martínez nodded. "You wouldn't have seen the upper wounds; they were out of sight beneath her bodice. But the lower one between her legs should have been obvious to you."

"Yes, sir. I must have missed seeing it in the dark." Dorado knew he had closed his eyes after seeing Gloria's bloated face.

"It was that dark, was it?" Martínez smiled. "Let's continue. The size and shape of the wounds indicate they were made by a knife's blade. The flesh around the wounds seems to be torn suggesting ..." Martínez paused to look at Dorado. "Suggesting the knife was thrust into her body and, then, turned or twisted."

"What! He twisted the knife!" Dorado's face reddened. "Hijo de puta! (whore's son!)" he said to himself. Out loud, he exclaimed, "The fiend!"

"A fiend indeed." Martínez nodded. "He wasn't satisfied stabbing her. No! He twisted the knife as if to torment her as he did it."

"Why in God's name would he do that to her?" Dorado sighed. "I can't believe it."

"It is hard to believe someone would do such a thing."

"So, she was tortured to death." Dorado leaned forward.

"I'm not sure she died that way."

"What do you mean?" Dorado frowned.

"I'm not sure she was stabbed to death."

Martínez held his hand up to stop Dorado from asking additional questions. He leaned over her chest and abdomen, his nose almost touching her skin. Martínez held that position for almost a minute, moving the candle slowly over the body.

"Here's something strange. I didn't see it this morning when I bathed the body."

"What is it?" Dorado raised his voice and leaned forward to look. "What do you see?"

Martínez held up a huge hand. "Tranquilo! I'll tell you, but you need to be patient."

"Sorry, sir." Dorado sat back in his chair.

"All of the wounds are connected by lines – lines cut into the corpse." Martínez moved the candle slowly up and down her chest and abdomen and then repeated it. "It looks like a line was cut vertically from the throat wound to the one between her legs. Another intersecting line was cut across her chest from one breast to the other. I wonder why?" He looked up at Dorado, the candle still in his hand.

Returning his eyes to the body, Martínez again used the candle to follow the lines cut on her chest and stomach. He repeated his examination a third time and then set the candle down on the table. Martínez frowned and stood back from the girl's body, his arms crossed over his chest. He shook his head.

"Dios mío! He cut a cross on her."

"A cross?" Dorado's mouth dropped open.

"Yes. The cut-lines connecting the wounds make a cross – a Christian cross."

"Santa María! What man would do such a thing? He must be a madman." Dorado shook his head in disbelief.

Martínez shrugged his shoulders. "I don't know what to think. The murderer might be a madman, but we know too little to say that. Let's get on with the examination."

Martínez picked up the candle and steadied it over the girl's chest and stomach again. He looked along the lines connecting the wounds and saw some maggot eggs still stuck to the body. "Ah! Now I know why the maggot eggs were laid in a linear pattern on the corpse."

"Why? What do you mean?" Dorado stared at the doctor.

"When the girl's body was found, fly eggs were located in a vertical line running down between her breasts to below her belly. A mass of them were laid in her pubic hair. Blowflies typically lay their eggs in moist areas and the cut line and pubic wound, wet with blood, were perfect places for them to lay their eggs. The flies lay their eggs in such places so the maggots will have nourishment as soon as they are hatched."

Dorado swallowed tasting bile in his mouth.

"That's why there were no maggots found above the breasts. The bodice covered those wounds on her breasts, chest and throat. The flies couldn't lay eggs in the wounds beneath the bodice. Do you understand?"

"Yes, I see." Dorado shifted the slab of wood from one knee to the other. His stomach felt queasy again, but he no longer tasted the bile.

Martínez returned to the table still frowning. "That's strange. Where's all the blood?" He asked himself the question, but spoke it aloud. He looked at Dorado. "Was there blood on the girl's body when you saw it yesterday? A lot of blood?"

"No, only a little, señor. I got a spot or two on my fingers."

"Under or around the corpse? Any areas wet with blood?"

"No, sir. I don't recall seeing blood or feeling anything wet when I covered her body. Maybe the blood drained into the ground. There wasn't enough light to see anything clearly." Dorado worried he would be reprimanded for missing the blood.

"But there was enough light to see a lot of blood, if it had been there – on the body or the ground. Is that right?"

"Yes, sir." Dorado tried to remember what he had seen the night before. "There wasn't much blood – only a little on her bodice that I could see."

Martínez muttered something to himself and moved the candle slowly along the length of the body. Walking around the table, he repeated the same process on the other side. He then shifted the lifeless girl on her side to look at her back and buttocks.

"Ah, there's the lividity."

"The what?" Dorado brushed a fly off the writing slab.

"Lividity. When a man's heart stops beating, blood flows down to those parts of his body closest to the ground. It happens because of the Law of Gravitation. Surely, you have heard of the Englishman, Isaac Newton?" He saw Dorado nod. "Those surfaces of the body lying on the ground therefore show the livid signs of blood or what we call lividity. I assume you saw a dark coloration on her back, buttocks and legs? It should have been distinct."

"I saw it." Dorado made a face. The doctor's condescending attitude annoyed him.

Unaware of Dorado's irritation, Martínez lifted up an edge of the cover and looked at the dead girl's face. He held the cover so Dorado could not see her face. After a few seconds, the doctor dropped the edge of the cover and adjusted it over the entire body.

"Now, I know exactly how she died," he said, nodding to Dorado.

"How?" In his excitement, Dorado did not say "sir," but Martínez did not rebuke him.

"She didn't die from the stabbing. He cut the cross on her corpse after he killed her. That's why there was so little blood in the wounds. I'm certain that's what happened."

"Then, how did he kill her?"

"She was first strangled, then stabbed. The bloated face, lack of blood flow on the body and significant lividity are the signs showing me what happened to her. They indicate the girl did not die from his stabbing." He smiled, pleased with himself. "I'll tell you how I think she was murdered, then mutilated." Martínez saw Dorado grit his teeth. "Are you feeling sick?"

"No, sir. Please say what has to be said." Dorado sighed loudly. "I'll be fine."

"Here's how I see it happening." He glanced at Dorado, who held the quill poised over the paper, ready to write. "These are only speculations, so don't take notes for now."

"Yes, sir." Dorado laid the quill on the wooden slab.

"They met – the murderer and the girl – sometime in the morning; I don't know when as yet. He strangled her with his bare hands." Martínez held his hands around an imaginary neck, showing how the girl was killed. "I assume she then fell at his feet. He then stripped off all her clothing except the bodice. Who knows why?" Martínez shrugged. "It makes no sense to me, but he must have had a reason."

Dorado watched the doctor's every movement.

"The murderer placed the girl on her back for the stabbings. I suspect he stabbed her corpse sequentially; first, in the throat, then between her legs and, finally, in her breasts – the left first and then the right breast. He stabbed her following our Catholic practice of crossing ourselves – in this manner." Martínez raised his hand, made into a fist, as if it held a knife and thrust it down to the body. He stopped the knife at the throat and then repeated the pantomime stabbing the girl's body between the legs and into her breasts. He twisted his wrist each time.

"Dios mío! What blasphemy!"

Martínez nodded absently, but his mind was on the stabbing sequence the murderer had followed. He stepped back from the body and studied it from a distance. He then looked at the lieutenant, who was waiting for him to speak.

"The murderer followed our practice only partially." Martínez pointed to the wound in the girl's throat. "He started the top of the cross at her throat instead of her forehead and ended it between her legs instead of the middle of her chest as we do it. The two wounds marking the horizontal length of the cross are also out of place – in the breasts instead of the shoulders."

"Perhaps, he realized the bones in the head, chest and shoulders would have prevented his knife's penetration." Dorado instantly regretted speaking up without permission.

"That may well be the explanation." Martínez nodded in agreement. "If so, it shows us the mutilation was planned and, perhaps, was practiced on other victims before."

Dorado shook his head in disbelief. "He must be a madman."

"I wonder. Madmen who mutilate their victims usually slash them in a frenzy – leaving wounds all over the bodies. There's no plan or pattern to their stabbing. But this murderer had a plan in mind and he executed it step by step: first, the strangulation, then, undressing her and finally, the designed mutilation – a cross cut on the corpse. Keep in mind, the cross was cut in steps as well – first, the four points of the cross were made with a knife, and then the lines were cut to connect the four points and make the cross. I should also mention the lines were cut as straight as possible. The murderer knew exactly what he was doing." Martínez shook his head from side to side. "No, I don't think this murderer is a madman."

Dorado frowned. "If not, how would you explain what he did to her?"

"Religious fanaticism! It has long been a Church problem."

Dorado did not argue with Martínez, a superior officer, but he was sure the murderer was a madman. "Who else would do such a thing?" he thought. "What happened next, sir?"

"It appears after the mutilation he took the time to spread out her naked body beneath the palmetto." Martínez shrugged. "Why, I can only guess. Whatever his purpose since that place is so remote, he probably was in no hurry to make his escape."

Dorado nodded. "Yes, sir. I wonder where he went – St. Augustine, I suppose." He frowned, thinking the madman could be anywhere in the presidio.

"Yes, he's here in the presidio. Unless he lives on one of the plantations outside town or in an Indian village – though I doubt he's an Indian. This isn't the kind of killing one of them would commit. I can't imagine an Indian, even if Christian, cutting a cross on someone."

"He must be found wherever he is. I want to see him hung in the main plaza." Dorado still pictured the doctor's description of Gloria's mutilation.

"Yes, this fiend must be found and arrested as soon as possible. Who knows what he might do next." Martínez leaned forward with his hands on the examining table. "It's time to take notes. I need a record of what I've observed on the autopsy report."

"Yes, sir." Dorado dipped his quill into the pot of ink he had put at his feet.

"I know the girl was strangled because of her swollen face,

protruding tongue and the bruises on her neck. When some-one is strangled, as you surely know, breathing stops and the victim simply starves for air. Without air, the face becomes swollen and the tongue sticks out of the mouth. The bruises on the neck, which I found a few minutes ago, confirm that the girl was strangled to death. There are two bruises on her throat, which I'm sure were made by the murderer's thumbs – as well as marks – finger marks – on both sides of her neck."

Dorado waited while Martínez held his examining light over the girl's corpse.

"The evident lividity and lack of blood on the body in-dicate the strangulation preceded the stabbings." Martínez looked up from the body at Dorado. "If the girl had been stabbed to death her heart would have continued to beat for a while before she died, pumping blood out of the four wounds. As a result, her body would have been bathed in blood and there would have been little, if any, lividity. So, it's obvious she wasn't stabbed to death."

"I see." Dorado added a sentence to his notes.

"One more related observation. Since this body shows li-vidity on the back side, I know she was on her back when the murderer stabbed her. Surely, you understand."

"Yes, of course." Dorado was annoyed by Martínez' con-tinued condescension. It was no wonder the other officers at the Castillo detested him. He had heard one man after anoth-er complain about his arrogance. "The big bastard thinks he knows everything and he treats you like you're slow witted" had been one remark he remembered hearing. It seemed any-one who encountered Martínez sooner or later complained about his overbearing manner or sarcasm.

Martínez sat back with his hands behind his head. "So, now, Lieutenant, we know the man murders with his hands and mutilates with a knife."

"Is that unusual? Have you ..."

The doctor stood and silenced Dorado with a raised hand.

"Lieutenant, I want you to ride out to where the body was found and look over the site. Look for any signs of someone being there. See if you can find the girl's clothing and shoes – search in the woods and along the shore. Tell today's duty officer I've sent you on a special assignment. If he wants more information, tell him to talk to me."

"Yes, sir. I'll go immediately, but what about the autopsy notes?" Dorado wanted to ask Martínez other questions about the murder, but dared not delay his departure. So far, the man had not intentionally insulted him and Dorado wanted to keep it that way.

"I'll finish the notes myself. I want you to search the site thoroughly. You probably have time for a quick lunch, but make sure you get there well before the afternoon rains. I'll be here all day, so see me upon your return."

"Sí, mi Capitán."

Martínez waved off his salute. "¡Ándale! (Go!)"

Dorado set out for the North River after a hasty lunch of beans and rice. It was almost one-thirty by the time he requisitioned a horse from the stables and walked across the wooden bridge over the moat. As Dorado mounted the horse outside the Castillo, he sensed someone's eyes on his back. He turned in the saddle and saw a man standing high above him on the top deck of the fort. Squinting in the sun, Dorado shielded his eyes with a hand, but by the time he focused on the spot again the man was gone.

Dorado guided his horse through the city gates and then urged him to a gallop on the road north of town. He rode fast, feeling the wind against his face. As he left St. Augustine, he saw a line of dark clouds on the western horizon and knew a storm was coming. Dorado thought he could smell it in the air. September was the wettest month in Florida and it rained almost every day in the late afternoon. Thunderstorms had struck the town seven consecutive days with the exception of the day of the murder and Dorado knew it would be no different that day. He spurred his horse to a faster gallop, hoping to finish his search before the rains arrived. He had been drenched twice during the weekend and hoped to avoid another soaking.

Ten minutes later, Dorado turned off the main road and took the narrow path leading to the river. He followed the path cautiously to avoid sinking sands and any undergrowth where snakes might be lurking. His horse led him to the spot where the cart stopped the night before. Dorado dismounted and tethered the horse to a pine tree and looked around. The wheel tracks of the wagon were still visible in the sand, but nothing else suggested human presence at the site. Even the tall grass flattened by the soldiers' shoes had risen in the morning dew. Nothing moved except a pair of green lizards running over the stump of a rotted tree. The only sounds he heard were the squawks of a flock of seagulls flying over the bay. Even the river seemed to be flowing soundlessly toward to the sea. It was a quiet time before the coming thunderstorm.

Dorado studied the darkening sky he could see through the trees. Clouds now covered the sun, but not the black ones he knew brought the rain. It looked as if he still had an hour or more to search the area. Dorado exhaled his breath loudly, knowing what had to be done, but not wanting to do it. He had to look at the place where the girl of his dreams had been killed.

Dorado walked to the palmetto, where her dead body had been found, and stooped to look at the ground. Below the fronds, he saw a few traces of dried blood in the weeds, but no other sign of the murder anywhere around the tree. Avoiding a busy ant hill near the base of the palmetto, he got down on his hands and knees and crawled around the trunk.

Dorado swore when his left knee struck a string of sand spurs and he immediately stood to pull out the painful spines. He swore again when he saw a tiny tear in his red stocking. He resumed his search, this time squatting rather than kneeling as he circled the palmetto's trunk. Once away from the tree, he stood as he moved slowly around the tree scrutinizing the ground. On his fifth trip around the palmetto, Dorado thought he saw a scrap of white paper, but when he leaned over to pick it up he realized it was the underside of a leaf. He looked everywhere, eventually working his way in concentric circles that took him ten feet out from the palmetto. Though he saw the flattened grass where the girl's body had been, there was nothing else there that indicated the presence of anyone other than the soldiers who accompanied him from the Castillo. Dorado noticed the shoe marks he and his men had made in the sand, but nothing the murderer might have left near the body.

After more than an hour of futile searching, Dorado had found nothing. He had gone over the area six times without any luck. Dorado knew it would be useless to search anymore, but he still looked in all directions, hoping something might eventually turn up. But nothing appeared except a gray rabbit that raced across the ground to a patch of brambles.

Disillusioned, Dorado sat on the ground under a pine tree, thankful the day was cloudy and not too hot. In his woolen uniform, he appreciated any cloudy day without sunlight. Even in the shade, his face and hair were wet and drops of sweat trickled down the back of his neck. He took off his hat and mopped his head with a handkerchief, glad he had not worn his wig. A sudden wind from the west signaled the approaching showers and he quickly rose to finish his search. Dorado did not want the storm to catch him as he rode on the open road to town.

As he stood up and turned toward the river, Dorado noticed something he had not seen before. What he saw was observable in a seated or low position near the tree, but he had been looking the other direction and missed it. Dorado squatted down to see better and exclaimed, "There's a trail there!" He saw a path through the underbrush that had been made by someone pressing the weeds down as he walked on them. The weeds were late summer grasses that had died, become brittle in the sun and, under foot, lay flattened on the ground. Dorado followed the path with his eyes and saw that it stretched away from where he crouched to somewhere closer to the shore. Obstructed by the fronds of three other palmettos, he could not see where the trail went beyond the underbrush. He stood on his toes, but still could see no better.

Dorado immediately followed the trail of flattened grass through an overgrown area full of vine-covered bushes and stunted pine trees. The trail led him to the edge of the river, where the water lapped against the bank. He stopped beside a dead pine tree lying on the ground and looked out into the river. It occurred to him that Núñez and his son might have made the path through the weeds on one of their fishing trips to the river. Dorado frowned and turned to look along the bank and then into the thick underbrush where the pine woods began. He propped a foot on the termite-infested trunk and scanned the shore.

He saw nothing unusual at first and was about to leave when he spied something white in the weeds. Dorado might have missed it even then, if he had not turned hearing the splash of a fish surfacing in the water. As he looked toward the river, he saw it and quickly ran to the spot. Staring down at the folded pile of white clothes, Dorado instantly knew they had been worn by Gloria; they were, in fact, her underclothes. He sighed, exhaling his breath slowly.

Dorado stood there a moment longer, thinking of Gloria. He recalled her last intimate touch. She had briefly squeezed his hand as he passed her in the church on Sunday morning.

Tears filled his eyes as he thought about her and what might have happened between them in the days and weeks to come.

The faint rumble of thunder ended his thoughts of Gloria. Dorado knew he had to hurry to finish his search of the site. The storm was still some distance away, but it would not be long before the lightning and rain reached the woods. He felt the air cooling as the thunderstorm's winds began to blow through the trees.

As Dorado bent to pick up the clothing, something else in the river caught his attention. Out of the corner of his eye, he spotted something red in the water. Dorado suspected it was a piece of cloth from the way it moved with the current. The cloth seemed to be held in a thicket of the thorny weeds found in so many places along the shore. From where he stood, it seemed to be within reach in the shallows.

Dorado went as close he could to the cloth without stepping into the water and stretched his arm out to grasp it. But no matter how hard he strained his arm, the floating cloth remained out of his reach. Reluctant to use his sword or step into the water, Dorado finally snared it with a broken tree branch he found on the bank. He then tried to pull the fabric free, but found the work much harder than expected. The water plants seemed unwilling to relinquish their catch to him. Finally, leaning far forward over the water, he turned and twisted it out of the thorns. He needed another few seconds to pull it through the weeds.

Hot and soaked with sweat, Dorado was panting when, at last, he dragged the length of fabric from the river. He knew immediately it was Gloria's red skirt. He had seen her wear it any number of times about town. Breathing hard, Dorado dashed into the woods and hung the dripping skirt on a tree limb. He started to squeeze the water out of the skirt, but stopped when a loud clap of thunder sounded overhead. He quickly pulled the soaked garment from the limb, rolled it up and tied it on the horse's back. Dorado felt the first drops of

rain as he ran back to the river to retrieve the pile of clothing left on the ground. Running to his horse, he hugged the
clothes tightly against his chest. He would not allow the rain
to touch them.

It was only sprinkling as Dorado stood beside the horse
wiping out his saddle bag. He used his handkerchief to remove the remaining dirt his fingers had missed. Dorado felt
a lump in his throat as he withdrew Gloria's clothes from
beneath his jacket. He had put them there to keep them dry.
Now, he gently stroked the little pile, thinking the few pieces
of clothing in his hands were the last things of Gloria he
would ever hold. Tears trickled down his cheeks as he pictured the mischievous smile she showed him when no one
was looking. Dorado buried his face in her underclothes, hoping to find one last scent of the lovely girl he had so longed
to be near. But all he smelled was the familiar smell of the salt
river and sea so close to the presidio.

Seeing a bright burst of lightning above him, Dorado
knew he had to hurry to finish his search. He circled the palmetto tree one last time and, finding nothing there, he ran to
the spot where Gloria's clothing her had been left. Dorado
hoped to find her shoes somewhere nearby, but he never saw
them in his hurried search of the high grasses and underbrush. The rain had fallen intermittently and lightly earlier,
but now heavy drops struck his hat and shoulders as he started away from the shore. He took long strides at first and then
ran. By that time, the woods were dark beneath black clouds
and lightning struck every second or so.

As Dorado turned and took the path of matted grass, he
saw the glint of something shiny out of the corner of his left
eye. He stopped, squatted down and looked around. Dorado
parted the grass to look at the ground, but, other than a few
broken sea shells, he did not see anything shiny in the area.
A brilliant flash of lightning overhead made him run again
and he hurried away, assuming a shaft of light had made a

seashell shine.

He mounted his horse and rode cautiously through the dark woods to the road to town. Ever increasing explosions of thunder and bright lightning flashes accompanied him as he made his way along the narrow path. Once out of the woods and on the hard shell road, Dorado spurred his stallion to a gallop. Trying to ignore the shafts of lightning in the sky about him, he thought about his meeting with Martínez, worrying the unpredictable captain would not be satisfied with what he had found and would criticize him for not finding Gloria's shoes.

Dorado reached the Castillo before the heavy rains reached St. Augustine. He rode in and out of light drizzle as he spurred his horse from the woods to the city gates. The day had appeared to have darkened to night by the time Dorado entered town. He took a lantern from a sentry to see his way in the gloom. No sooner had he dismounted at the drawbridge when a downpour fell on the fort. The thunderstorms continued throughout the afternoon and into the early evening, temporarily cooling St. Augustine until the heat and humidity returned with the morning sun.

Ruiz de León and Martínez were discussing the murder when Dorado returned from the North River. He found them in the office seated in the same places as that morning. Martínez stood and smiled when he saw the clothing Dorado held in his hands.

"Buen trabajo (good work), Lieutenant!" Martínez smiled. "I knew they must be there somewhere. Take off your hat and jacket and sit down." Martínez motioned him to the stool.

Dorado handed him the clothing and sat on the stool. Martínez hung the red skirt on a window shutter and put the white clothing on his desk. He nodded to Dorado.

"Now tell us what you found; we can look at the clothes later."

Dorado told them about his search and how he had found the girl's clothing. They did not interrupt him and Martínez made no mention of the missing shoes. The rumbling thunder forced him to raise his voice as he finished his report.

"With your permission, sir, I would like to offer a few observations about my report."

"Bueno." Martínez nodded. "Let's hear them, Lieutenant." He exchanged looks with Ruiz de León as Dorado began to speak.

"First, I think Gloria – the girl was killed near the river rather than where she was found. She was then dragged about forty feet to the palmetto. The path through the weeds indicates where the murderer dragged her. I believe he used her bodice to drag her away from the river. That's why her bodice was bunched up on her chest. That also explains the dirt on her body. Perhaps, that's also why he left the bodice on her."

"Muy bien, Teniente!" Martínez smiled. "I looked at the bodice again and saw that it was stretched well beyond its size and shape. So, we know it was used as a handle. Her body told me the rest of what happened. There are several bruises, five in all, on her left arm below the elbow, so I assume he pulled her by the arm as well as the bodice. He used both hands to drag her away from the shore."

Dorado frowned.

Martínez saw the frown. "You don't agree, Lieutenant?"

"I agree, sir. What puzzles me is why he didn't carry her? She was slight and certainly didn't weigh very much."

"No more than ninety or so pounds." Martínez shrugged. "What do you think, Ricardo?"

Ruiz de León thought a few seconds before answering. "Perhaps, he's a small man and she was too heavy for him to carry that far or it was simply easier to drag her by the bodice. What do you think, Lieutenant?"

"Yes, sir. I think the body was dragged away from the shore so it wouldn't be seen by someone paddling on the river. Many of the men fish from canoes this time of year."

"That makes sense." Martínez nodded. "A body on the river bank also could have been seen by the Franciscans. The monks are always on their way to and from the Indian villages north of town. They even paddle canoes at night."

"Let's not forget the Indians." Ruiz de León looked at Martínez. "They're on the river more than anyone else. They are also easily angered and quick to resort to violence."

"True, but I doubt an Indian killed the girl." Martínez shook his head from side to side. "I can't imagine an Indian, even a Christian Indian, cutting a cross on a body, can you?"

"I suppose it would be unlikely. Continue, Lieutenant."

"I think the murderer stripped and stabbed her on the shore where I found her clothing. The thick underbrush there would hide what he was doing once she lay on the ground. After the mutilation, I assume he dragged her to the palmetto, where she would be out of sight from the river. Maybe he didn't carry her there for fear of being seen with a body in his arms."

Martínez nodded. "That's a possibility."

"Or perhaps he was worried about getting blood on his clothing." Ruiz de León made a face as he crossed his legs, carefully folding his bad leg on top. "What makes you suggest that sequence of events, Lieutenant?"

"Well, sir, her underclothing was left at the river, rather than near the palmetto. There isn't blood on those things, but there are traces of blood in the weeds along the path from the shore to the palmetto. That's why I think he murdered and mutilated her at the river's edge."

"Anything else, Lieutenant?" Martínez saw that Dorado had something else to say.

"Yes, sir. I wonder why the murderer left the bodice on her body after he dragged it to the palmetto. He removed her other clothing. Why then leave the bodice on her – especially since he planned to stab her in the throat? I don't think he stabbed her through the bodice; at least, I don't recall seeing any knife slits last night."

Martínez nodded. "There were no knife slits in the bodice. Except for the stretching and dirt, the bodice was as she had worn it that day. The murderer pulled it up to expose her breasts when he stabbed her and put it back over her when finished. The wounds in her throat and breasts were covered and the wound between her legs left exposed. I don't know why he left her that way, but it must have some meaning to him."

"One more thing, sir. I think he threw her skirt in the river expecting the tide to take it out to sea." Dorado pointed to the red garment. "Instead, of course, it got caught in the weeds."

"Good thinking, Lieutenant. That makes sense to me." Martínez tapped his fingers on the desk. "What do you think, Ricardo?"

"I think he has figured out what happened. Well done, Lieutenant."

"Now, we need to know what Gloria was doing there in the woods." Martínez looked at Ruiz de León. "What or who brought her there? Surely, she didn't go all the way out there to meet some stranger. I doubt that, don't you? The girl must have known the man and met him there according to a pre-arranged plan. It appears she agreed to a secret rendezvous with the murderer. Why else would she go out there to that remote place?"

Ruiz de León nodded. "From what I have learned at Government House, we know the governor's niece left her room early yesterday morning and was not seen again that day – until Núñez found her. That's all we know. She was missed at seven-thirty, when the maid went to awaken her for breakfast. She simply disappeared and no one inside or outside saw her leave Government House. Not one single sentry! No one in the building, the plaza or in town saw the governor's niece that morning. Can you imagine it?" He sighed in frustration.

"It's hard to believe no one saw her. Surely someone eventually will recall seeing her that morning. How could she possibly get out to the woods without being seen? "

"It doesn't seem possible, does it?" Ruiz de León stroked his cheeks, searching for the stubble he had missed after shaving.

Martínez shook his head. "I can't believe a lovely girl like Gloria could ever escape the notice of the men in this town. You know they called her *el cuerpito* (the body), don't you?"

"Yes, I do." Ruiz de León made a face, suddenly smelling the corpse's odor. He looked at the door to the surgery and saw that it was closed.

Martínez saw his expression and smiled. "I can't do anything about the stench of death. It seeps in here even with the door closed. By this time, you should be accustomed to it. Keep in mind that's what you will smell like someday – hopefully not too soon."

Ruiz de León glared at Martínez, but said nothing. He got up from his chair and pushed it closer to the partially-open outer door where drops of rain blew in from the parade grounds. He moved his chair again when several drops struck his shoes.

Martínez smiled as he watched Ruiz de León. "Let's look at her clothing," he said when the governor's aide was seated once again. He spread out the red skirt on his desk. A distinct brown stain stood out at the hem of the garment. "Obviously blood. See that little tear in the cloth?" He put his forefinger on it. "I would guess it was made by the murderer's knife as he wiped off the blade."

The two men watched Martínez shift the skirt about on the desk. He studied both sides, but only found a thorn caught in the material. He then hung the skirt on the shutter and used a rag to wipe up the wet spot left on his desk. Next, he examined the small pile of underclothes that had been placed aside. Martínez unfolded each piece slowly, scrutinizing it intently. He frowned, seeing nothing unusual.

Martínez looked up after dropping the last piece of clothing on the pile. Exasperated, he exhaled his breath loudly. "I wonder why everything was folded so carefully and placed in such a neat pile. Why would the murderer waste the time and then leave the pile there?"

"Surely, she didn't undress herself out there in the woods." Dorado pointed his finger at the clothing. "That pile looks like the work of a woman. It's neatly folded like the pile of clean clothes Señora Sánchez leaves for me every Monday evening. She washes that day and, when dry, she folds my clothes and leaves everything in a pile on the bed exactly like that. You don't think the murderer could be a woman, do you?"

"No." Martínez shook his head. "Women don't murder in that manner. It's too vicious. They prefer poison. Although I know cases where women have stabbed their victims to death, it's quite uncommon. I've seen only one such murder myself, but I've never seen or heard of a mutilation carried out by a woman. Not once in thirty years of service for the crown!"

"It's only a thought that came to mind. The neatness of the clothing pile made me think of a woman." Dorado worried that the doctor would ridicule his suggestion.

"Some men are neat, too – like myself." Ruiz de León looked at Dorado.

"That's true." Martínez chuckled. "But, you're one of a kind, Ricardo. Muy distinto!"

"One other possibility occurs to me." Dorado risked another suggestion. "The murderer might have forced her to undress in front of him before strangling her?"

Martínez thought for several seconds and then shook his

head from side to side. "It's a possibility, Lieutenant, but I doubt that he would risk it even in that remote place. Wouldn't he worry about someone unexpectedly coming upon them even in that isolated place?"

"I would think so." Ruiz de León nodded. "Even if he paused briefly to fold her clothes, I can't imagine him wasting time watching her undress. The former would take only seconds, the latter minutes." He leaned forward in his chair and massaged the knee of his wounded leg.

"I doubt it, too." Martínez nodded. "I think the man killed the girl and then undressed her himself. Why he folded her clothes so neatly in a pile, I don't know. But that's something to keep in mind about him. Everything he did seems so well planned, especially the mutilation of the body. It was so cruel and yet carefully executed – a cross carved on a human body! I've never seen anything like it in all the years I've been a doctor. It obviously has something to do with the crucifixion, but we know nothing else. It certainly doesn't explain why the murderer would mutilate her that way. What do you think, Ricardo?"

Ruiz de León shook his head. "I don't know what to think. I can only guess. Perhaps he was punishing her."

"Yes." Martínez raised his voice. "That makes sense. The mutilation suggests he was punishing her for something she did – perhaps for some religious transgression. Quién sabe? (Who knows?) Even if we don't know the reason for the mutilation, I think we can assume he was punishing her." He held up his finger. "And twisting the knife as he stabbed her is one example of his punishment of her."

Ruiz de León nodded.

Dorado raised his hand. May I ask a question, sir?" He saw Martínez nod his head. "Wasn't the deed of dragging her body through the dirt also a punishment?"

"It was indeed. But, whatever cruelty he inflicted on the girl's body as punishment, it did not affect his other plans for her. Afterwards, he cut the lines connecting the four wounds to make the cross and then displayed her nearly naked for all to see. Without any concern for her body, he dragged it through the dirt to the palmetto, but then he carefully arranged it on the ground. The girl was placed on her back with her arms and legs spread wide. The placement of her body was purposeful, not accidental. It was as if an Inquisitor from the sixteenth century had found her guilty of whoring and exposed her mutilated body to show the consequences of such sin. You know, 'The wages of sin is death.' It's from Corinthians, isn't it, Ricardo?"

Ruiz de León grimaced. "No, it's from Romans, 6:23, 'For the wages of sin is death, but the gift of God is eternal life in Christ Jesus our Lord.' And you, Carlos, should keep the entire passage in mind." He saw Martínez scowl and was about to scold him for his ignorance of the Bible, when he heard Dorado's raised voice.

"You're saying the murderer regarded Gloria as a whore." Dorado spoke up without asking permission. His face was flushed and he had to keep himself from shouting.

"It appears that way." Martínez saw the anger in Dorado's face. "I know it's not what you want to hear, Lieutenant, but keep in mind, it's only the murderer's view of the girl. Isn't that so, Ricardo?"

"Yes, it's his view of the girl."

Martínez looked at Dorado and saw that the color in his face had faded. "Let's continue then. There's more to be said about the murderer. Though we don't know his identity for now, we do know he is man of mind. A clever and orderly mind! The murder and the mutilation, in particular, are not only acts of cruelty, they are also acts involving shrewd thinking and careful planning. Think of it – he was able to entice the governor's niece from Government House to the remote woods to kill her. He then mutilated her in a precise step-by-step manner not unlike the weapons-use instructions in an officer's training manual. This man is a brutal killer with a cunning mind." Martínez patted the small pile of clothes on his desk. "We don't yet know who has such a mind, but let's hope we do so soon. I fear for the presidio with him at large. "

"Surely, we know he's mad." Dorado could think of no other explanation for the man's mutilation of Gloria.

"Maybe, but mad or not there's much thinking in his mind. Don't you agree, Ricardo?"

"Yes, it seems he's a clever one."

"You didn't find her shoes, did you?" Martínez looked at Dorado.

"No, sir. I didn't see her shoes anywhere. I searched the site where I found her clothes twice to see if I missed anything."

"It's all incomprehensible." Martínez shook his head. "The bodice left on the body, the skirt thrown into the river, the rest of her clothes placed neatly in a pile and her shoes missing – perhaps, thrown into the river as well. It's bewildering to me, but I suppose the murderer had his reasons for what he did."

"It would seem so." Ruiz de León turned abruptly as a bright flash of lightning lit up the parade grounds outside the office.

Martínez sighed. "Well, there's nothing else to be done for now. Let's meet tomorrow after lunch. I want to work on the corpse in the morning. By the way, when is the funeral?"

"Friday morning. I know you expected more time for the autopsy, but the governor wants the funeral over quickly. He thinks it would be best for the community."

Martínez frowned. "Is that so? Does the governor also think it would be best for those investigating the murder?"

Ruiz de León looked at Martínez, but made no reply.

"Now, there's only one more day to get the examination done," complained Martínez. He pushed the clothing aside.

"So, we'll meet after the funeral on Friday. Four o'clock?"

"Bueno." Ruiz de León uncrossed his legs, preparing to stand.

"That will leave me only the morning light to look at the body. Let's hope it's sunny. I suppose we're finished here."

Ruiz de León nodded. "It's only drizzling, now. Let's leave before it rains any harder. I don't want to get soaked."

Martínez nodded and withdrew his watch from his jacket pocket. "We still have enough time for dinner and maybe even a game of chess."

"Obviously, the former is far more important to you than the latter."

"Of course, that shouldn't surprise you."

"We eat together twice a week," Ruiz de León told Dorado, "and then play chess unless he falls asleep after eating too much – something that's becoming customary these days."

Martínez smiled. "It's because of the fine wine we drink." "Ricardo serves excellent Castillian Rioja. Only the governor has Rioja of such character. And if I fall asleep after eating a good meal and drinking a little wine, what better way is there to end a good evening?"

"A little wine!" Ruiz de León frowned. "I wouldn't call two bottles a little wine."

"You know what they say? 'Without wine and women, what worth is there to life?'"

"Who said that?" Ruiz de León sneered, "Some sensualist from ancient Rome?"

Martínez stood up and stretched. "A man of wisdom."

"Wisdom of the damned."

Martínez pushed his chair behind the desk and looked outside into the parade grounds. He made a face. "It's dark as death out there, another storm must be on ..." His words were lost in a nearby explosion of thunder. "Wait!" Martínez held his hand up. "We must keep what we know about the mutilation to ourselves. No one else needs to know it, except of course the governor. And surely he should be spared the grisly details."

Ruiz de León nodded. "There's no need to upset him any more than he is already. As you suggest, let's keep what we know to ourselves. We don't want to do or say anything that might alarm the townspeople. There are enough problems here as it is."

"We must avoid panic at all costs." Martínez leaned over the desk and lowered the wick of the oil lamp until the flame disappeared. "News of the murder alone will frighten everyone, especially our women. Many now will walk the streets looking over their shoulders."

"Exactly, the less the presidio knows the better." Ruiz de León turned to Dorado, who stood at door. "We'll see you here tomorrow, Lieutenant. In the meantime, you are ordered to say nothing to anyone about what we discussed today. Is that understood?"

"Yes, sir, completely understood." Dorado was pleased to be included among the few men who knew the details of the murder. He left first, striding out into the moonless night.

Dorado found his way by following the flickering lights of the town lanterns. Situated on every street in St. Augustine, the lighted sentry posts guided him all the way to the two tiny rooms he rented in town. Since the rain had slackened, he arrived relatively dry except for his shoes and stockings which were soaked when he ran through a puddle outside his house.

Ruiz de León waited while Martínez stuffed the autopsy notes into the lower drawer of his desk and locked the office door. It started to rain harder as they hurried across the parade grounds to the entrance of the fort. Crossing the Castillo's drawbridge, they were buffeted by gusts of wind, but the rain lightened as they left the fortress. On the way to the doctor's house, they discussed the death of the governor's niece.

After midnight in another part of the presidio, an exhausted man rose wearily from his bed unable to sleep. He had tried every trick his mother taught him and even counted sheep, but he could not fall asleep. It had been the same the night before. He had tossed and turned until the dawn's light entered his bedroom window. Now, he yawned, thinking of the long day ahead of him and the probability of another night with little or no sleep.

He could not sleep because of his incessant thoughts of the dead girl. Uninvited, she entered his mind every time he closed his eyes. Hoping to free himself of her, he left his bed and went out into the empty streets in the rain. But even on the bay front in the middle of the night, the thoughts of her accompanied him. He could not escape the thoughts and the vivid pictures they showed him.

They showed him gruesome scenes from the woods and made him listen to her words over and over again. The words reminded him of what had happened to the flirtatious little girl with the smiling face. They made his head ache. Finally, finding no escape from her ceaseless chatter, even outside in the wet streets, he went home knowing her foolish words would follow him there as well.

Somewhere close to home, he spoke back in his own words. His head throbbing with pain, he hissed at her through his clenched teeth. "Puta! Ustedes son todas putas (Whore! You're all whores)! Always teasing and tempting. Well, you won't be doing that again, will you? No, puta, nunca más! – nunca más (never more)!"

CHAPTER THREE

OCTOBER 2, 1788

Everyone of significance in St. Augustine attended the solemn service held for Gloria Márquez García y Morera. By dawn the central plaza was almost full of the townspeople awaiting the governor's arrival. At eight o'clock, the governor, Vicente Manuel de Zéspedes y Velasco, accompanied by his wife and children, walked across the plaza and entered the parish church. An entourage of the presidio's senior officers followed Governor Zéspedes and his family. At the church, a line of the town's principal civilian officials and distinguished townspeople formed silently and stood with heads bowed as the governor of Florida walked by them. They waited respectfully until the grieving family was seated in the front row benches, with the Castillo's officers behind them, followed by the town's prominent civilians. The remaining benches were taken by merchants, tradesmen and other townspeople, who entered quickly one by one until the church was full. When everyone had been seated, Auxiliary Bishop Cirilo de Barcelona began the funeral mass.

Following the service, six soldiers carried the girl's casket out of the church and all the way to the cemetery, a half mile northwest of the central plaza. A long procession of army officers and townspeople walked behind the priests, pallbearers and the bereaved family. The Commandant of the Castillo followed the governor and his family with Captain Ricardo Ruiz de León next in line. According to rank and seniority, the other army officers of the garrison, including Captain Carlos Martínez, strode in order behind their superiors. Lieutenant Roberto Dorado Delgado, who held the lowest rank and had the least seniority in St. Augustine, was the last officer in the procession. The civilian officials and townspeople trudged after the men in uniform. It was a humid autumn morning and everyone sweated in the sun.

The long funeral cortege passed slowly through the cemetery gates and then between the headstones to the grave site. As the church bells tolled ten o'clock, the last of the people in the procession entered the cemetery and gathered around the other mourners. The governor's wife, Concepción, wept quietly while Bishop Barcelona performed the Rite of Committal and the oak casket was carefully lowered into the ground. An eagle screeched overhead as the first shovelful of dirt was dropped into the grave. Everyone stood silently watching the grave being filled and the governor's family prayed on bended knees. Beneath a moss-encrusted limb of a large live oak, Gloria Márquez García y Morera was laid to rest.

Governor Zéspedes returned to Government House after the funeral. Head in his hands, he sat upstairs in the family quarters thinking of his niece. Minutes passed before he looked up at his wife, Concepción.

"She was so young," he said. "Who would ever think she would die so young?"

"No one. Gloria was still a child. Why would anyone want to take the life of a child?" Tears rolling down her cheeks, Concepción held a handkerchief balled up in her hand.

"I don't know." The governor shook his head. "Maybe he's a madman. But whoever the fiend is, we'll find him sooner or later and put him to the sword. You can be certain of it! The man will wish he never was born."

"It was a lovely funeral. Everyone in town was there." Concepción dabbed her swollen eyes with a handkerchief already wet from her tears. "Everyone was so kind."

"Thank God it was brief. For once, the bishop's sermon was short. It was sweltering in the sun even that early in the day. I'll be relieved when they finish the roof on the church."

"The bishop was wonderful; I'll never forget his words." Concepción blew her nose. "It was as if he could see Gloria's soul rising up to heaven. What he said filled my heart."

"Yes, yes, he was quite eloquent." Zéspedes grimaced. "Let's hope the bishop is as brief and eloquent when he consecrates the reconstruction of the church – that is, whenever it's finally finished. Que Dios nos ayuda (God help us), let's hope it's soon."

"I'm glad some of the children were here for the funeral." Concepción crossed herself. "Gracias a Dios. They're still full of youth."

"At our age, it's our funerals the children should attend, not the funeral of their cousin."

Zéspedes was sixty-eight years old at the time of his niece's death. He had arrived in St. Augustine four years earlier after his appointment as Governor of East Florida. His assignment followed the transfer of East and West Florida from British to Spanish rule after the American Revolutionary War. A treaty signed in Paris in 1783 ended the international war, recognized the American colonies as a new nation and, among other territorial changes in the New World, awarded the two Floridas to Spain. Soon afterward, the king, Carlos

III, selected Zéspedes to be Governor of East Florida.

With the appointment, Zéspedes reached the pinnacle of his career in the king's service. He was promoted to the rank of brigadier in the army and given authority over a critical colony in the Spanish empire. It was what he had always wanted to accomplish. East Florida included the presidio of St. Augustine, the entire peninsula and all the territory along the Gulf coast west to the Apalachicola River. The colony was large in land, but extremely small in population as the new governor learned when he arrived in the hot summer of 1784. With the exception of the Indians who still occupied most of the province, East Florida was sparsely populated with fewer than 3,000 people living in St. Augustine. Unfortunately, the new governor learned that most of the residents of the capitol city were Englishmen who spoke little or no Spanish.

Still, Zéspedes was pleased with what he knew would be his last position in the king's service. He had been appointed governor at an older age than most Spaniards sent to America and he appreciated the opportunity to do something meaningful in the final years of his career. Zéspedes knew he owed his assignment to the powerful Gálvez family who recommended him to the king. General Bernardo de Gálvez, hero of the war against England, and his influential uncle, José de Gálvez, Minister of the Indies, had sponsored his appointment. Without their help, Zéspedes would have ended his military career in some dreary office in Havana signing papers that no one would ever read.

Zéspedes sighed wearily and stood, a hand pressed on his back. He looked at his wife, who was still weeping. "I can't sit here all day, Concepción I'm going down to my office."

She nodded, her head bowed as she wept.

Zéspedes walked to the door and went out on the landing. He shouted down to the lone sentry standing in the hallway. "Landa, go find Capitán Ruiz de León and tell him to meet me in my office." Zéspedes waved him away with a flip of his wrist.

Ruiz de León was busy talking to Bishop Barcelona in front of the church when the sentry finally found him. The governor's aide acknowledged the soldier's salute and gestured for him to wait while he finished his conversation with the bishop. He turned to him a few seconds later when the bishop paused to nod a greeting to a parishioner and his wife walking in the street.

Landa saluted again. "Sir, Governor Zéspedes wants you to meet him in his office."

"Thank you, Landa." Ruiz de León returned his salute. "Tell the governor I'll be there in a few moments."

"I agree with you, Ricardo." The bishop spoke when the sentry was gone. "Gloria was a terrible problem for the governor, a constant embarrassment. As I'm sure you know, she was the talk of the town. The girl was so willful and sensual! It was said she was possessed and I wondered about her myself. In fact, I had begun to think it necessary to request an experienced exorcist from Havana. Of course, that's of no matter now. What does matter is the governor's standing in the presidio and I've heard it said he will be much the better regarded without her here. In time, her shameless behavior would have surely dishonored him." The bishop blinked several times, a mannerism that made his parishioners think he had trouble seeing them.

Ruiz de León nodded. He suspected the bishop himself had made those comments.

"You know, the girl never said a word to me all the time she was here. Not one word! She went to Father Hassett for confession. At Communion, instead of showing me some piety, never mind respect, she brazenly looked into my face without the slightest shame." Barcelona, a small slender man with a bulbous nose, sniffed and blinked his eyes again. "Yes, that willful girl may well have been possessed." He nodded and then crossed himself.

"I wouldn't be at all surprised from what I saw of her." Ruiz de León shook his head up and down. "I must go now. We should resume this conversation another time."

"Sí. Vaya con Dios, Don Ricardo."

Ruiz de León served Zéspedes as the officer in charge of internal affairs in the colony. He also served on the governor's council along with Colonel Miguel Montesinos y Cárdenas, Commandant of the Presidio, Tomas Hernández Torres, Treasurer, and Captain Mariano de la Rocque, Chief Engineer. The four officials formed an administrative staff used by Zéspedes to govern the king's colony of East Florida. With the exception of the commandant, appointed by the king, the other officials were selected by Governor Zéspedes.

Ruiz de León met Zéspedes in Santiago, Cuba, in 1782, two years before the governor received his appointment to Florida. At the time, Zéspedes was interim governor of the eastern seaport. The two men met when Ruiz de León was sent to Santiago to recover from the wounds he suffered in the war with England. Ruiz de León was told to take as much time as he needed to recuperate, which he knew meant his service as a field officer would not be required again.

During his so-called recovery in Santiago, Ruiz de León spent much of his time in the governor's office. The wounded man had been bored sitting idly by the sea and, after a month of rest, he went to meet Zéspedes and offered to work as his assistant. Ruiz de León quickly became a valued aide and later when Zéspedes was named to his position in St. Augustine, he requested the assignment of Ruiz de León to serve with him in Florida. The king's officials in Havana approved the captain's transfer and he sailed with Zéspedes to St. Augustine. During their eight days aboard ship, the two men talked for much of the trip and became close friends.

In St. Augustine, Zéspedes assigned Ruiz de León to be an aide on his administrative staff. He had no specific responsibilities, but served the governor as his representative on the town council and intermediary between the military and civilian officials in the colony. Ruiz de León served the new governor well, earning appreciation for his intelligence, hard work and reliability. Six months later, when the supervisor of colonial operations died of a winter plague, the governor appointed Ruiz de León to the vacant position. Now, three years later, the captain held the same administrative office on the governor's staff, but with an expected promotion to the rank of major. The governor sent his promotion papers to Cuba in August and the captain general's written approval was anticipated to arrive by the end of November.

Only a short walk to Government House from the church, Ruiz de León reached the building a few minutes later. He walked along the hall on the first floor and knocked on the door to the governor's office. Sargento Raúl Suárez, who managed the office, admitted Ruiz de León and told him to wait while Zéspedes finished his lunch upstairs in the family quarters.

"Don Vicente will be down in a few minutes, Don Ricardo. He's almost done. He said you should sit and enjoy one of the wines on the sideboard, while waiting." Suárez pointed to two decanters on the sideboard. "The governor also said you should take off your wig and coat and make yourself comfortable."

Both men smiled, knowing the governor's demands for comfort in his home and office. Outside of Government House and in all official ceremonies, Zéspedes always appeared in full uniform. But, in meetings, he insisted on comfort over propriety, especially in the hot Florida summers. In his office, shunning a wig, he wore only a white shirt and the blue linen breeches of his uniform. He dressed formally in Government House only when he entertained Spanish officials or foreign diplomats visiting St. Augustine. He also wore his brigadier's uniform on the rare occasions when he held audiences in his office. Zéspedes had managed the governor's office the same way in Santiago Cuba.

Ruiz de León poured a glass of wine and sat down to wait. He did not remove his wig or coat. Such informality was unacceptable to the captain, who was perfectly attired except in the hot months when he sometimes removed his wig. At home, he ate, read or worked at his desk in full uniform and, after a long day in his office, he habitually bathed and dressed before dinner, even if eating alone.

His friend Carlos Martínez teased him unendingly about his rigid formality. "Ricardo," he would say, "If you died in bed at night, I'd wager they would find you fully dressed the next morning." At other times, Martínez would suddenly inquire with a smirk, "Tell me, Ricardo, is it true you haven't a body beneath your clothing – only layers of uniforms?"

As Ruiz de León sat savoring one of the governor's fine red wines from Spain, his eyes roamed about the room where he had spent so many hours working with Zéspedes. It had been repainted recently and the smell of whitewash freshened the room. He could now take a deep breath without inhaling the stale odor of pipe tobacco.

The captain liked the governor's office and approved of its furnishings. He especially liked Zéspedes' desk, crafted from live oak and now gleaming from rubbed oil. The massive desk stood in front of the fireplace, filling one end of the room. Zéspedes' chair was made of the same wood. It was head high, with wide flat arms and a black leather back and seat. His family's coat of arms, featuring stone castles, red, white and yellow striped shields and broad swords, was engraved in the leather back. Five similar chairs, a foot shorter in height, faced the desk in a semicircle.

A long oak sideboard stood near the door to the office. It held several cases of Castilian Rioja and a dozen crystal glasses. Above the sideboard, four one-foot square Roman mosaics were mounted on the wall. The mosaics showed helmeted men in combat. When Ruiz de León first saw them in Santiago, Zéspedes proudly informed him the mosaics were more than fifteen hundred years old. A wooden chair was situated beside the sideboard for an attending servant. The captain sat in that chair while waiting.

Ruiz de León sighed as he looked around the room. Under different circumstances, he could have occupied the finely furnished office and held the title of Gobernador de la Florida. He possessed all the essential qualifications to be a colonial governor. He had a famous family name, a long and exemplary military record and years of administrative experience in Cuba as well as St. Augustine. Ruiz de León also knew with certainty he had the ability to governor a colony and command a presidio. In fact, he had more colonial experience and knowledge than Zéspedes, who had spent most of his military career as an infantry officer. Though devoted to the governor, Ruiz de León knew his many limitations and witnessed every day how dependent he was on his staff to administer the colony. Zéspedes had turned over colonial administration to him because he had no notion of how to carry out the required duties of the office.

"Yes," Ruiz de León thought, "I already do all the necessary work of the office even if Zéspedes holds the governor's rank and title." But whatever he did in St. Augustine, Ruiz de León knew was of little matter to the king or Council of the Indies. He would never be appointed governor of Florida or any other province in the Spanish empire. What he lacked and Zéspedes had in abundance was influence in Madrid at the court of King Charles III.

Ruiz de León sighed and closed his eyes. "Tranquilo (Be calm)," he said to himself. It was foolish to wish to be the Governor of Florida. Wishing was a waste of time. It would not change his status in St. Augustine. His current position in the presidio was as good as it could possibly be in the twilight of his life and he should thank God for the opportunity the governor had given him. "And soon I'll be a major in the army," he thought with a smile.

Ruiz de León looked across the room and saw himself reflected in the tarnished mirror that hung across from him on the white-washed wall. The wide mirror covered most of the wall and revealed everything on the other side of the room. For a few seconds, Ruiz de León stared at himself sitting in the chair. Then, draining the last of the wine from his glass, he rose slowly and limped across the room for a closer look in the mirror.

"How old I look," Ruiz de León thought, studying his fleshy neck and jaw, which once had been so firm. Now, he had the beginning of jowls and his cheeks were discolored by tiny red veins. Scrutinizing his face, he noted the sagging skin around his eyes and the deep lines running down his cheeks along his nose and mouth. So close to the mirror, he also saw the fine lines covering his forehead and the many surfaces of his scalp that could be seen no matter how his thinning hair was combed. Ruiz de León exhaled a long breath, knowing there was nothing to be done about it. Looking into the mirror, his eyes then moved to his ears, which seemingly overnight had sprouted long gray hairs. Ruiz de León shook his head in disgust.

"What is it they say? Ah, yes. 'As a man ages, he loses the hair on his head and gains it on his ears.' How true! I'm already a viejo (an old man) at fifty-six." He sighed. "Yet, I'm still strong, Gracias a Dios, almost as strong as the young officers." Ruiz de León realized he was exaggerating his strength and smiled at himself.

Governor Zéspedes entered the office and saw his aide staring into the mirror. "Never look in mirrors, Ricardo. They tell much too much truth. My mind's eye tells me what I prefer to look like – a man twenty years younger. Mirrors show me that my mind's eye lies. I surely prefer the lies." He chuckled in self-amusement.

Ruiz de León nodded as they moved together and briefly hugged. Zéspedes stood close to his aide, looking into his face. "I'm very glad you're here, Ricardo." He placed his hand on the shorter man's shoulder.

"How are you, Don Vicente?" Ruiz de León looked closely at Zéspedes. "I know this has been a very difficult day for you."

He saw sadness in the pallid face of Zéspedes. A tall, almost gaunt man, the governor had lost a lot of weight in the last six months. At one time he had been plump, if not corpulent. Now he seemed shrunken, his white shirt hanging like a bulky bag on his shoulders. Zéspedes' recent appearance worried his aide, who felt a special affection for the superior he had served for so many years in Cuba and Florida. Ruiz de León feared the governor was suffering from an unseen illness that was slowly stealing his weight away.

"Oh, I'm fine. Let's sit down. We have much to talk about."

The governor went over to one of the chairs in front of his massive desk and motioned his aide to another beside him. It was not an unusual place for him to sit. In monthly meetings with his staff, Zéspedes always sat among them rather than behind his huge desk. Sitting so far away, he said, made him feel removed from the discussions.

Zéspedes liked being close to those who talked with him. Whether sitting or standing, he would try to place himself a foot or so away from them. He wanted to be near enough to have eye-to-eye contact or make a point with a pat of his hand. The governor was considered good humored with only occasional fits of anger and a tendency to disparage those of his staff who disappointed him.

Zéspedes held the back of his chair and waited while Ruiz de León eased himself into a chair beside him. The governor sat down wearily, exhaling his breath loudly. The strong smell of garlic struck Ruiz de León as the governor sighed and breathed in his direction.

The incident reminded him of Martínez and his comments about Zéspedes. The doctor was one of a number of officers who complained about the governor's garlic breath. They also objected to him standing so close to them. Martínez spoke of it as a Zéspedes assault. After a meeting with Zéspedes, Martínez would hold his nose, saying he had been wounded in battle.

With a smirk, he would add, "You know, Ricardo, after only one assault it takes me a week to recover my sense of smell. Do you think Concepcíon worries some wench will lead him astray? The food she cooks will surely keep one away as well as everyone else in town."

Ruiz de León turned his full attention on the governor when he saw the exhaustion in his face. He nodded in sympathy as Zéspedes told him of his wife's grief.

"This is an especially sad time for Concepción. As you know, Gloria was her sister's only child. We took the girl in when her mother died last winter. Her father was lost at sea a year earlier – you of course already know that. So, Gloria came to us only a few months ago. In the spring, wasn't it? I can't keep up with the passing of time anymore. I'm too damned old! A wine that ages is supposed to be best – isn't that what they say? Well, if the wine ages too long it loses its body and in my case, its mind, too." He smiled sadly.

"That's not true, Don Vicente. You know your mind still works well, very well! We all have trouble remembering names of people and places from the past. It happens to me, too. I sometimes even forget them in the present."

"So do I. That's another of my memory losses. Well, let's put aside the self pity of this old man – a sixty-eight-year-old man at that. Oh well, at least, I still can remember my age." Zéspedes, who had been studying his wrinkled hands, looked up at Ruiz de León.

"Poor Concepción has suffered two terrible years. First, her father died suddenly. Then, only four months later, her sister, Constancia, died of the plague. Now, her niece is murdered here in St. Augustine." The governor shook his head from side to side in disbelief. "Can you believe it? My own niece murdered here in this little frontier town which I govern."

Ruiz de León nodded his head, but made no reply.

"We both feel guilty about the girl. Although, as you know, she was quite a problem for us. We tried to give her a good home, a home away from the worldly hazards of Havana. Yet, now, she's murdered by some madman in St. Augustine! Here in the community I command. I am dishonored!" Zéspedes' sad face reddened and his eyes filled with tears. Embarrassed, he covered his face with his hands.

Ruiz de León felt sorry for his superior. He was glad Zéspedes did not know the details of his niece's murder; he knew only that Gloria had been stabbed to death. Giving him enough time to recover, Ruiz de León looked away and pretended he had not seen the tears. He busied himself by brushing lint off the sleeves of his army jacket. It was a mannerism that earned him the inevitable mocking of Carlos Martínez. Whenever he caught his friend in the act, Martínez delighted in mocking him. "Be careful, Ricardo, you'll brush away the nap of that jacket. You surely know how much a new one would cost."

The governor rose to get himself a glass of wine and regain his composure. He stood by the sideboard, behind

Ruiz de León, and wiped away his tears with a handkerchief. Zéspedes noisily opened another bottle and filled a glass with wine. He calmed himself with the help of two glasses of wine and then poured one for Ruiz de León. Zéspedes filled a third glass before returning to his chair. Steadying the glass in his hand, he sat slowly to avoid spilling the wine.

"Well, what's to be done, Ricardo? Tell me, how do we find this diablo? It seems he got away without anyone seeing him."

"So it seems. No one was seen anywhere near the woods where Gloria was found. A few fishermen were out at the river that day, but they fished farther south – close to town. We will talk to them, of course, but it's unlikely they were involved in what happened. We should know more in a day or two."

"How in God's name did Gloria ever get out to that remote place without being seen?" Zéspedes frowned. "That's what amazes me."

Ruiz de León nodded. "It is hard to believe. But so far we haven't found anyone who saw her that morning. Not here at Government House nor in the central plaza – not anywhere in this town! It seems she simply disappeared."

"You mean to tell me that not one sentry in this presidio saw her? How did she get out of Government House without being seen? Dios mío, there are sentries everywhere."

"No, Don Vicente, not one sentry saw her leave Government House or the presidio. It is hard to believe in this walled city."

"I should say so. Well, Ricardo, what do you suggest we do?"

"I suggest you order an investigation immediately. A small squad of three or perhaps four officers should direct the investigation. I suggest one man be selected from the Castillo, obviously with the consent of the commandant, and another man from Government House. A third man might be the doctor. With your permission, I will represent Government House."

"I want you to lead the investigation." Zéspedes pointed a trembling finger at his aide. "It appears you already have a plan in mind. Let me hear it." The governor slurred his words as he spoke. He had drunk too much wine that morning.

Zéspedes seldom consumed more than two glasses a day, except for his customary dinner wine and what he called a medicinal libation before going to bed. On the day of the funeral, he had gone well beyond his limit. Before coming down to his office, he had downed three glasses of wine upstairs. All the wine he had consumed made him dizzy and he blinked his eyes trying to see clearly. Unsure of what had been said, he repeated himself. "Let me hear your plan."

"I recommend that you assign Lieutenant Roberto Dorado Delgado y Estrada from the Castillo to help me in the investigation. He was on guard duty when Gloria was found. I suggest him because he is young and can do the necessary walking about. I'm getting old, too, Don Vicente, and I can use his youth. As my dear mother, God rest her soul, often would say to her older sister, María Teresa, 'What do you think, you're the only one getting old?'"

"Bueno." Zéspedes smiled. "I like that expression. I must remember to use it the next time Concepción complains about one of her female ailments." He slurred his wife's name.

Ruiz de León nodded as he reached for his glass of wine.

"Fine. I'll speak to the commandant about releasing the lieutenant. What's his name? Oh yes, Dorado Delgado. He'll be freed from duty – his normal duty during the investigation and assigned to work with you. By the way, what do you know about him?"

"Not much. From his accent, I would assume he's from the mountain country, perhaps Asturias. I doubt his family is prominent."

"I've never heard the family name. Have you?" Zéspedes shook his head slowly. He felt dizzy when he moved it quickly.

"No. The family obviously has an hidalgo (noble) background, but probably a petty one. I assume the name Dorado comes from an ancestor who fought with Francisco Pizarro during the conquest of Peru. As you know, the Pizarro expedition searched in vain for the legendary El Dorado. They found silver, but never the golden man or his city of gold."

"I see." Zéspedes rubbed his eyes. "So the lieutenant is a provinciano (rural noble)."

"Yes, but apparently better tutored and more knowledgeable than most provincianos."

"Can he read and write?"

"Yes, he wrote a careful and thorough death report, which the commandant forwarded to me this morning. He seems quite alert, but I don't know much else about him."

"Well, hopefully, he'll be useful in the investigation. Now, let's talk about your friend, the *esteemed* Doctor Carlos Martínez. You know only too well what I think of him."

"Sí, Don Vicente." Ruiz de León knew Zéspedes was speaking slowly, word by word, to avoid making mistakes. He watched as the governor took a handkerchief from his pocket and paused to wipe his eyes and the corners of his mouth.

"As you know, Martínez has given me a number of problems. The damned man can't keep his hands off women. It was the same in Havana. I heard all about his reputation there, too. After a bottle or two, he's got his hand up some woman's dress. Married or unmarried, it doesn't matter to him. Verdad?" Zéspedes gestured clumsily with a shaking hand.

"Sí, Don Vicente."

"As I'm sure you will recall, some years ago – I don't remember the year. An artillery officer wanted to duel him to the death for some dishonorable deed he did to the man's wife. What a situation! I don't recall the man's name, but I think he was a captain. I didn't dare ask him what happened.

He was angry as a hornet and wanted satisfaction with swords. I suppose Carlos Martínez happily helped the man's wife cuckold him." Zéspedes studied his aide. "I can see from the color in your face that you know exactly what happened. Tell me, Ricardo. What did that rogue do with the woman?"

"It was told to me in confidence, Don Vicente."

"Don't worry. I won't punish him. It's over now."

"All right. The artillery captain – I can't remember his name either, discovered his wife and Carlos Martínez in an intimate embrace that couldn't be explained away. The woman was ruined. It happened here in Government House on the second anniversary of the restoration of La Florida to His Catholic Majesty. You ordered a community celebration and invited all the presidio's officers to a fiesta in the courtyard."

"I remember it well. How could I forget that first year?" He sighed and again Ruiz de León smelled garlic on his breath. "What work we had to do to make this colony livable after the foreign occupation. Dios mío! What a filthy people the English seem to be. Never mind such memories. Continue with your account."

"As I was saying, all the presidio's officers were here at the fiesta. The officers' wives, of course, were invited as well. In a short time, everyone was enjoying themselves thoroughly. Bottles of your Castilian Rioja were consumed and Concepción's food was delicious. No one makes tastier arroz a la marinera (seafood and rice) or flan (custard with caramel sauce). Then there were those two soldiers from Granada who played Flamenco guitar so well. Everyone, of course, drank too much and Government House was a mess when the fiesta was finally over." Ruiz de León scowled, recalling the empty bottles, broken glasses and vomit on the floor.

Zéspedes smiled. "That's to be expected, Ricardo. It was a fine fiesta."

"I suppose so. The Castillo's officers ate and drank everything in sight – they were like locusts in a field of corn.

When they finished gorging themselves, they went into the garden to drink. They left the table immediately after you made your anniversary speech. In the garden, they sang dirty songs, told disgusting stories and drank endlessly. Meanwhile, Carlos and the artillery officer's wife talked at the dinner table. They conversed while her fool of a husband got drunk with the other artillery officers. And, later, as we were giving toasts to the king, Don Carlos III, our own Carlos was busy giving carnal pleasure to the artillery officer's wife. They went into the hall closet for their rendezvous. At the time, her husband was busy, too, drinking who knows how many bottles of your wine. I saw him finishing a full bottle myself."

"Those artillery officers always drink too damned much. What else happened?"

"When the drunken fool finally missed his wife, he looked everywhere without finding her. Eventually, in exasperation, he threw open all the doors on this floor and, when he opened the closet door ..." Ruiz de León paused to sip his wine. "The drunken fool found Carlos and his wife engaged in an adulterous intimacy. I don't know what else to call it." Embarrassed, Ruiz de León's face was flushed. "According to Carlos, the cuckolded officer saw his wife's body exposed; her bodice was pulled down, her dress up above her waist. He also saw Carlos kissing her breasts and rubbing his hand between her legs. She was moaning with pleasure – so he told me later. Worst of all, the shocked man saw his wife holding Carlos' huge member in her hand."

"Dios mío!" Zéspedes put his hands over his face.

"What could she say to her husband? What excuses could she offer?" Ruiz de León held out his hands, palms up. "There was nothing she could say – she was caught in the act."

"Oh yes, so she was." Zéspedes nodded, a smile on his face. "What happened then? What did the cuckolded husband do?"

"Furious, the man slapped his wife and then punched

Carlos in the stomach. According to Carlos, he intended to hit him in the groin. But, in his drunken state, he missed his mark."

Zéspedes snickered. "Dios mío! What a situation."

"Well, Carlos responded to the punch as you would expect. He knocked the officer to the floor and threatened to beat him to death with his bare hands. The man had a bloody nose from the brawl. He met with you the next morning and not surprisingly demanded satisfaction for his dishonor. Despite the wronged officer's insistence and Carlos' willingness to accept his challenge, you refused his official request for a duel to the death. As I remember his request, the humiliated man wanted a duel with swords, at noon, in the plaza."

"I recall it all too well, now." Zéspedes scowled. "I paid off the husband with twenty-five gold pieces and a case of wine. I suppose it was a small price to pay for his dishonor."

"That's exactly what you said at the time. Fortunately for everyone concerned, a day later, a frigate arrived from Havana and you transferred the artillery officer to Cuba. His wife, badly beaten, accompanied him abroad." Ruiz de León wiped his mouth. "I remember you said, 'The Castillo needs a doctor much more than an artillery officer.' Now that I think of it, man's name was Contreras Guevera."

"Did I say that, Ricardo?" Zéspedes chuckled. "The artillery officer would have easily dispatched Martínez to his maker. How could any decent swordsman miss such a target? The duel would have been over in seconds."

"I'm sure you saved his life, though Carlos would never admit it."

"I know Martínez is very clever and works hard, so, of course, I'll assign him to you. But for my sake, please keep him far away from women in the investigation. Make certain he works with men or the dead, who won't complain about his behavior to me." Zéspedes shook a finger of warning at his aide.

Ruiz de León shook his head. "I don't think you will have any more trouble with him, Don Vicente. He seems to have settled down with the widow Valdez. He visits her several times each week. Carlos has slowed down, too, like all of us older men. He admits that lust even abandons him, now and then. You, of course, know what aging does to desire."

"Unfortunately, I do know – all too well. It amazes me these days to realize I would rather read history or philosophy than lie down with a woman. I now know why most great thinkers were older men. We seem to gain our minds as we lose our desire. I wonder if God gives us more mind as a compensation for getting older and weaker?" The governor, who no longer felt dizzy, looked directly at his aide. "What do you think, Ricardo?"

"Possibly." Ruiz de León stroked his chin. "Perhaps the loss of our lust is God's gift – the gift of a new life for us. It is sad to lose desire, but there are benefits from it. It's easier now for me to spend time playing chess, walking or simply looking out to sea. We older men also can find new ways to know God. That's what has happened for me here in Florida."

"It's true." Zéspedes nodded. "At this time in our lives, it should be easier to look into our souls and find God. Quién sabe? Are these simply the thoughts of two older men trying to explain the loss of machismo? It's such a convenient explanation. I wonder."

"I wonder, too." Ruiz de León looked down at his wrinkled hands. "Perhaps, old age permits us such thoughts that youth can never know. I don't know. I do know my desire for women comes and goes. I can live a long time without feeling it. Then, at times, lust seems to be an irresistible force in my life. Sometimes it's intolerable."

"Lust comes and goes for me, too. Now, unfortunately, it comes much less often than it goes." The governor chuckled. "I suppose lust is still strongly present for Carlos Martínez. Of course, he's so much younger, isn't he?"

"No, Don Vicente, he is not much younger. He's fifty-three, though he doesn't look it. As you know, I'm fifty-six and I know I look much older than Carlos. From what he tells me, he still functions three times a week. He claims to wear out the widow on those occasions and spends three other evenings with me, playing chess. On Sunday, he rests."

Both men laughed and the governor clapped his hands. "Martínez and God!" Zéspedes said, still laughing.

Ruiz de León was pleased to see Zéspedes laughing. He had looked haggard after the funeral. Now, at least, he had a smile on his face.

"Tell me, Ricardo, when does Martínez rest his stomach? From the look of his bulk, it would seem there's no day of rest from food. Even a rabbit rests."

"Never to my knowledge. The man eats enormous quantities of food. When we eat at my house, I buy enough for four men. Three of those portions are for him. His expression for eating so much is, 'I'm scraping the bowl.' Apparently, it relates to his youth, when his family suffered poverty in the south of Spain."

"Is that so? He certainly doesn't look like he has lacked for anything in the past."

"No. His bulk gives the opposite impression."

"So it does. It suggests a man of unrestrained appetites."

"Carlos is indeed a man of unrestrained appetites."

"Obviously, too often unrestrained for the good of this presidio." Zéspedes nodded.

"Don Vicente, I want to say one thing in his defense."

"It's not necessary; I know his worth. He's a very good physician and a useful member of my staff. Martínez speaks up and says things no one else will dare to say. His comments at meetings are often the most helpful I hear from anyone and he refuses to flatter me. That's why he remained here in St. Augustine and I sent the cuckolded artillery officer to Cuba. I respect him, though I can't say I like him.

But you know that."

"I still would like to say something about his involvements with women."

"Then do so." The governor drank down the last of his wine and gave his glass to Ruiz de León, who got up to refill it. "Only a sip or two, I've had more than enough."

"Carlos has not always been the one who initiated the intrigues that have concerned you." Ruiz de León handed Zéspedes his wine and returned to his chair. "Women often have made advances to him and I'm not speaking of whores."

"Is that so?"

"Yes, strange as it seems. Both married and unmarried women have made advances to him over the years. It happened in Havana as well. So, they too must bear some of the blame for the scandals involving him. He is one of those men who attract women. Who knows why? They seem to go to him like moths fly to candlelight. At one time, I surely envied him."

"I understand such envy." Zéspedes glanced at the door and spoke softly as if afraid his wife might hear what he was saying. He leaned forward toward his aide and whispered, "That damned Martínez has bedded some comely women. I must admit I would have welcomed any one of them to my bed – of course, when I was young and unmarried."

"Yes, of course, Don Vicente."

"It astonishes me that women are so drawn to him. I don't see him as handsome. Do you, Ricardo?" The governor sat with his arms folded across his chest.

"No, nor does he. In fact, he sees himself as too large, if not fat, and ungainly."

"Then, what is it that attracts women to him? Surely, it can't be the rogue's reputation. It's well known Martínez seduces them and then walks away without the slightest worry. I've heard it said he discards women like so many worn-out shoes."

"Yes, that certainly was his practice in the past, but he seems changed in recent months. Carlos no longer looks longingly at every woman he sees on the street. Instead, he appears to have settled down with a Mestiza (a woman of Spanish and Indian ancestry). She's a soldier's widow and her name is María Valdez." Ruiz de León made a face. "Not only does the woman lack sangre pura (pure Spanish blood), she is also quite common. She speaks Spanish poorly and comports herself in a coarse manner, at times even bickering with Carlos in public. Yet, I have seen Carlos treat her with tenderness. It's as if he's courting her for the first time and that may be what women see in him."

"It must be the tenderness that attracts them to him; I've heard women talk much about it. Concepción says Spanish men only show it to charm women."

"Perhaps." Ruiz de León toyed with a loose button on his sleeve. "Of course, Carlos is moody and his tenderness comes and goes. It depends on a woman's willingness to meet his needs. He expects women to satisfy his carnal desires as well as to cook and clean his house."

"That's what we all expect, but most of us have to marry for it." Zéspedes made a face.

"Yes, but Carlos wants it all without marriage, without any willingness to pay the piper. And, when asked why he hasn't ever married, Carlos will say with that loud laugh of his, 'Why marry? When the cream is free, why keep the cow just for her milk?'"

Zéspedes smiled. "Now, that sounds like the Carlos Martínez we know so well." He leaned back and put his hands behind his head.

"On the other side of the coin, Carlos is quite kind to older women. He treats Amalia Camacho, the widow who cleans his house, like his mother. There's much affection between them and Carlos allows her to order him about as if he were a small boy."

"That doesn't surprise me. His concern for older women costs him nothing." Zéspedes sneered. "Tell me, where's his concern for the women he has seduced? Does he worry about the married women he has ruined? Probably, no more than his last fart."

"Yes, Don Vicente, he does show concern for them. I've heard him express it myself."

"Is that so? It's hard to believe." Zéspedes tapped his fingers on the arms of the chair.

"It's true, Don Vicente. There are times when he regrets his past and worries about the penalties he must pay for what he knows are his sins of the flesh." Ruiz de León did not tell Zéspedes that Martínez' regrets were usually expressed when sick from drink and moaning in self-pity. Knowing he had not told the whole truth, Ruiz de León prayed for forgiveness.

"So he should. He has a lifetime of sin to worry about." Zéspedes nodded. "God only knows what will become of him."

"I'm certain Carlos has a deep commitment to God, though he's not one to speak of it."

"No one would ever know it. I never see him in church."

"It's true. He rarely goes to Mass now because of the crowded conditions of the church; he says there's always a smell of body odor inside. Carlos also complains endlessly about what he calls the 'incredible ignorance of our priests.'"

"Is that so? What church doesn't have that smell? And what are his complaints about our priests? Tell me." Zéspedes glared at his aide.

"Carlos regards Father Hassett as an ignorant, unenlightened man with what he calls a Middle Ages mentality. He refers to him as 'that foolish Irish priest.' He says Hassett would have better served the Church five or six centuries ago, when most people believed that priests knew something about the world of men – as well as God."

"Oh." Zéspedes smiled in spite of his annoyance. "And what does Martínez say about our visiting bishop, Cirilo de Barcelona?"

"Carlos finds the bishop unbearably boring and pompous. I can repeat the exact words he uses to describe him; I've certainly heard them enough. He says, 'The bishop's mind seems to be empty of anything except religious platitudes and senseless Latin phrases.' Barcelona's lifeless sermons, he says, are boring and endless. He says the bishop could put a storm to sleep, if given a chance to speak to it. Carlos calls him, 'Bishop Boring.'"

Zéspedes snickered. "Martínez never misses anything, does he?"

"No, never." Ruiz de León smiled. "You should see him mimic the bishop giving one of his long sermons. It's very funny."

"I can well imagine. No one ever can say Martínez lacks good eyesight or a keen sense of humor." The governor yawned and the smell of garlic again made Ruiz de León turn away.

"He can be clever. But his criticism of our clergy does not deny his devotion to God."

"I'll believe that when he forswears his philandering and marries that widow." What is her name? Oh yes, Valdez."

"It's true. Carlos must change his ways and make the best of the life he has left to live. He is already deeply in debt to God for the life he has led." Ruiz de León sighed, wondering when his friend had last made his confession and taken communion.

"We all owe debts to God." Zéspedes spoke softly and stared off into space.

"Yes, we all do." Ruiz de León clucked his tongue. "I'm no exception. I certainly have a lifetime of debts to pay, too."

A knock at the door ended their conversation. It was a signal from Sergeant Suárez advising the governor that his wife wanted him upstairs. Final preparations were in progress for the community visitation following the funeral.

Zéspedes tilted his glass up and finished the wine. "I must go upstairs and get ready for the visitation. It's for the foreigners who have asked to come to pay their respects. You need not come. I assume you already have spoken to Concepción?"

"Yes, I saw her for a few moments after the funeral. I will certainly come up, if I can be of any help." Ruiz de León flexed his bad leg, which had stiffened as usual after sitting.

"No, no. You will need to make the necessary arrangements to begin the investigation. I'll see you later today."

The men shared an abrazo (hug) as they parted company. Ruiz de León walked behind the governor to the stairway in the hallway and waited while he mounted the stairs. He saluted the governor when he reached the landing to his living quarters. Ruiz de León then arranged the sword on his left side and set out for his meeting at the Castillo de San Marcos.

CHAPTER FOUR

OCTOBER 2, 1788

Dorado saw Martínez in the central plaza after the funeral. A head taller than anyone near him, he stood out in the milling crowd of soldiers and townspeople. Dorado approached the big man indirectly through the throngs of people, pretending to be unaware of his presence. As he hoped, Martínez spotted him as he passed nearby and called out.

"Dorado! Over here! Come join us." Martínez gestured with his hands as if sweeping the young man closer.

Dorado moved his eyes over the mass of people before settling on him at the south end of the plaza. Smiling at the discovery of Martínez, he moved past a mother and a crying child to reach him. The big man stood with three dark-haired women beneath the limb of a huge live oak. They all turned to look at him as he approached.

"This is Lieutenant Roberto Dorado Delgado y Estrada."

Martínez motioned to the officer. "Dorado, meet Señora María Valdez Chávez, her sister, Señorita Esperanza Chávez Camacho and their cousin, Señorita Serena Rodríguez y Orellano. They're all from Havana."

The women smiled politely as the lieutenant bowed and kissed each of the hands held out to him. Dorado used the formal custom to charm them as well as to scrutinize the women from beneath his lowered eyelids. It was one of the many tips his Uncle Ernesto had told him when he first became interested in girls.

"What a gentleman," muttered Martínez.

"Yes, he is a gentleman." María Valdez smiled at Dorado. "Courteous, too. Something seen so rarely here in St. Augustine – especially among the older officers of the presidio." She tightened her lips and stared directly at Carlos Martínez.

"True." Martínez nodded. "There are all too few gentlemen in Florida. It's a critical shortage I'm sure that concerns the king. He probably doesn't sleep at night thinking about it."

"Very funny." María Valdez glared at Martínez. "Of course, you, Carlos, of all people should know about such shortages. Anyone who has eyesight can see the lack of quality in the older officers sent to Florida in the past. Now, at last, it seems some young Spanish gentlemen are coming here." She smiled again at the lieutenant.

"Oh, yes. There're certain to be many more Spanish gentlemen on their way here soon. I understand the king has commanded the Council of the Indies to search all throughout Spain for titled officers to serve in St. Augustine. Surely, this remote presidio is the perfect place for them to meet their future wives." Martínez grinned, seeing the angry look on María's face.

During the exchange of sarcastic remarks, Dorado studied the three women in front of him. María Valdez was a buxom woman, whose calloused hands revealed the hard work she had done in her life. He guessed her to be about thirty.

She had thick black hair, dark skin and large black eyes. Her broad face and coloring made him suspect an Indian ancestry, common among colonists in the Caribbean. She wore a white blouse, red bodice and a brown skirt.

Despite her sullen expression, Dorado thought there was something distinctly sensual about María Valdez. Maybe, it was her full lips and fleshy figure that appealed to Martínez. He knew Uncle Ernesto would have warned him away from such a woman. His uncle would have predicted she would be stout someday soon and no longer voluptuous.

Esperanza Chávez, her obviously older sister, was already a stout woman. A heavier version of her sister, she also looked sullen. Her mouth seemed fixed in a sneer as if she were waiting for the chance to complain or criticize someone. Dorado quickly moved his eyes away from Esperanza Chávez and to her cousin, Serena Rodríguez.

While Martínez and María continued to quarrel, Dorado studied Serena Rodríguez. A slender young girl, she appeared shy, looking down rather than meeting his eyes. Dorado had instantly liked her when he kissed her hand. Now, he looked her over, noting her long brown hair, large oval eyes and what he saw of her figure in the green dress she wore that day. Serena blushed, aware of his scrutiny, and turned her eyes to María who still glared at Martínez.

Tired of the bickering, Martínez turned to Dorado. "I'm glad we met here, Lieutenant. We can go to the Castillo together. I intended to suggest it when I saw you walking behind me in the funeral procession." Martínez smiled at the women. "We must leave you now."

"So, you're involved in it, too." María shifted her scowl from Martínez to Dorado. She squinted in the sun. "Don't look so surprised. Everyone in town knows about the murder."

Dorado said nothing. He looked at Martínez for guidance. Martínez frowned. "What everyone knows is street gossip – nothing more."

"What a terrible, terrible thing! The governor's niece murdered! Can you believe it?" Esperanza Chávez spoke up for the first time.

"What makes you think she was murdered?" Martínez stared at her.

"Of course, she was murdered! Everyone knows it. We're not stupid!" She glared at him. "It's obvious! Surely, you don't expect us to think the girl died of a sudden heart attack? In the woods, without a stitch of clothes on her body!"

"We don't yet know with certainty what befell the girl." Martínez shook his head.

"Mentiroso (Liar)! You know she was murdered." Esperanza narrowed her eyes and looked at her sister. "I tell you, this wretched place is perilous for us all. What with its pests, plagues, low-class people everywhere you look and now murder, this frontier town frightens me and should frighten you, too. We should go home to Havana."

"Let's not go over that again." María Valdez scowled at her older sister and turned her eyes to Martínez. Her face softened as she spoke to him. "It's true – the murder frightens us all. It frightens me simply to know some madman dared to strike down the governor's niece in St. Augustine, of all places. If the governor's family isn't safe here, who is? Everyone in town is afraid – especially the women. I know I am."

"And with good reason," added Esperanza who lived alone in a tiny one room house, south of the plaza. "We could all be murdered in our beds at night and no one would know it."

"Stop!" Martínez held up his big hands. "Let's not exaggerate what happened. The girl was found dead in the daytime, well outside of town, in the woods. There's no reason to think other women are in danger even if she was murdered. So, let's not panic."

"Well! That's certainly easy for you to say, Doctor. Men

aren't being murdered here."

Esperanza stood with her hands on her hips glaring at him. "And, as you know, the governor's niece isn't the only girl killed here either."

Martínez grimaced. "I assume you are referring to the missing girl in 1784." He saw Esperanza nod. "That girl drowned! She was last seen paddling a canoe in the river and, after her disappearance, the canoe was found overturned on Anastasia Island. What was her name? I can't think of it at the moment." He looked at María.

"You see, the good doctor doesn't even know the girl's name." Esperanza sneered. "So like a man. Her name was Patricia Hernández Parral. The girl was only seventeen. I've heard it said there were many in town who thought she had been murdered."

"Well, whatever her name, she was never found dead or alive."

"Which means she might well have been murdered." Esperanza Chávez thrust out her chin, defying the doctor to disagree with her.

Martínez sighed in exasperation. "Perhaps, but it's much more likely she drowned and her body was devoured by alligators. Anyway, there's absolutely nothing known to connect the disappearance of the Parral girl with the death of the governor's niece. Besides, there are some unusual, ah, elements involved in her death that can't be compared to any other ..." Martínez stopped himself from saying, "any other murder."

"What unusual elements?" María Valdez spoke softly.

"You don't want to know." Martínez reached over and gently patted her arm.

"Do those unusual things have anything to do with the little hussy's many escapades in town?" Esperanza Chávez glared at Martínez, the sneer evident on her lips. "Everyone knows what she was doing."

"What do you mean?" Dorado frowned. He intended to

defend the dead girl's honor.

"Tsk. Tsk. You don't want to know." Esperanza nodded her head knowingly.

"Tsk. Tsk." Martínez mimicked her in a falsetto voice. "I guess beauty has its price – the envy and gossip of other women."

Esperanza put her hands on her hips. "Well! Let me tell you, Doctor, with that one, beauty was only skin deep."

"It's well known she was a saucy wench." María turned to Dorado. "Like it or not, it's true and everyone knows it."

"What does everyone know?" Dorado's face was flushed.

The doctor motioned to Dorado. "It's time for us to go, Lieutenant. We can talk about the girl later." He reached over to María Valdez and gently squeezed her shoulder.

Dorado bowed before the women. He said "Adiós" to them all, but fixed his blue eyes on Serena Rodríguez. She smiled shyly and softly responded, "Adiós, Teniente."

When he was far enough away not to be overheard, Martínez muttered "Mierda (shit)!" out of the corner of his mouth. "Damned women! They think they know everything. The old Castilian saying is so true, 'The sweetest of women have sour mouths.'"

Dorado nodded as they walked side by side across the plaza. He looked back and saw the women still standing in the same place talking among themselves. Esperanza Chávez stood with one hand on a hip and the other pointing toward where the men were walking. Even at a distance, Dorado could see the scowl on her face.

"They're still talking about us," he told Martínez as they reached the bay front.

"It's that nasty bitch, Esperanza." Martínez briefly looked back. "Someone should do us all a favor and strangle her. Believe me, she wouldn't be missed."

"She certainly can be trying." Turning north toward the Castillo, Dorado increased his stride to keep up with Martínez.

"Trying, you say! She makes me furious. Many are the times I'd like to slap her sullen face, but what can I do – she's María's sister. Anyway, they have that sullenness in common. I call them the *sullen sisters* to myself, of course." He chuckled at his own cowardice. "Happily, I seldom see Esperanza. María keeps her well away from me most of the time."

"Do you see her cousin, Serena Rodríguez, seldom, too?"

Martínez laughed. He stopped walking and took Dorado's arm. "I wondered when you would ask about her." He continued to snicker. "Serena's quite comely, isn't she? Yes, indeed, a pretty little piece!" He whistled *Los Ojos Mios* (Those Eyes of Mine) as they began to walk again. "No, Lieutenant, but I can arrange for you to meet her. That's what you want, isn't it?"

"Yes, sir." Dorado's face reddened.

"Next time, say what you want to me. Don't try to be clever. It was quite obvious to everyone that you were interested in Serena. Of course, women always seem to see and hear everything. They miss nothing, especially if it involves men. Serena will be here in town for a while since she's visiting from Havana. There will be plenty of time to meet her."

"Gracias, señor." Dorado looked sideways at Martínez.

"If I may ask, Dorado, what are your thoughts, now, about la Señorita Gloria? Is she out of your mind now? It's certainly understandable, of course."

"I still think about her." Dorado inhaled deeply. "It's hard to accept that she's dead and gone; Gloria was such a lively girl. She will be on my mind for a long time to come. But I know I wasn't the only man interested in her and the more I hear about her reputation in town, the more I wonder about her propriety. Even the common soldiers talk about her flirting. I know I should look elsewhere. As they say, 'life goes on and love is never far away.'"

"Spoken like a man of reason, Dorado. You'll be fine sooner than you think. A good bottle of wine and a warm woman in your bed and you'll feel much better, believe me. I'll see to it you meet Serena soon. María will be happy to arrange it."

"Muchas gracias, mi Capitán. What was María going to say about Gloria?"

"Quién sabe? There's much gossip about the girl. Among other accusations of her so-called wanton ways, I've heard she brazenly flirted with men, even the married men in town. Then, there's the story about her purposely exposing her breasts on Merchant Street in August. The sullen sisters say she showed them off while stooping over to soothe a crying child. The little boy had apparently stubbed his toe. According to María, the girl bent over slowly 'with her breasts all but falling out of her bodice.' She said that Gloria smiled, well aware the men nearby were staring at her."

"What do you think about such stories?"

"I don't know what to think. I'm generally suspicious of gossip, but where there's so much smoke, it seems to me there must be some fire."

"I suppose so." Dorado frowned.

They proceeded along the bay front toward the Castillo de San Marcos. It was balmy for early October and they enjoyed the breeze blowing off the bay. Gusts of wind sent rolling waves crashing against the seawall and water sprayed over the path where they walked. In the bay, they saw a schooner struggling in the heaving seas. It was on its way to the city dock.

They stopped walking when the schooner disappeared in the steep trough of a wave and even its masts were gone from sight. Seconds later, the vessel reappeared, righting itself in the rolling sea. They turned to leave when the ship smoothly rode out the next wave and looked to be on course to the docks of St. Augustine.

Hearing a shriek, the men looked toward the seawall, but saw nothing. Another scream came from the same spot and they rushed over to the wall, Dorado leading the way. He quickly pulled himself up on top of the five-foot high wall. Martínez followed him to the wall a second later. Panting from the effort, he looked over the wall.

Below them on the bayside of the wall, they saw a man on top of a woman, his hands around her throat. The man was fat and his body almost completely covered hers. Only her head and face, contorted in pain, appeared free of his weight. Her upper arms pinned beneath his heavy body, she weakly slapped her hands against his fleshy sides. She screamed again when he tightened his grip on her throat.

Dorado jumped down, drew his sword and struck the man's back with the flat side of the blade. "Get off her or I'll take off your head." He leveled the sword over the man's neck.

Groaning, the man rolled off the woman and lay on the ground looking up at the sharp edge of Dorado's sword. He shuddered and held his arms up over his face. "Please don't kill me. She stole my money." He spoke in barely discernible Spanish.

"Mentiroso." Free of the fat man's weight, the woman gasped for air. She pulled her skirt down from her waist where it had been and fitted her breasts into her bodice. Helped up by Dorado, she brushed the dirt from her clothing and straightened her hair. "Cerdo gordo (fat pig)," she spat at the man on the ground.

"Puta!" The fat man crawled over to the seawall and sat back against the stones. He pointed a dirty finger at the woman. "She stole my money."

"Pendejo! (Prick!). I don't have your filthy money," she snarled and kicked sand at him.

The man held up his hand to protect his face, but the sand

never reached him.

"Go on home, Graciela." Martínez exhaled his breath loudly. "Not another word or I'll tell your husband what you've been doing."

The woman hiked her skirts up and climbed nimbly over the seawall. She turned her head and shouted "Pendejo" as she walked away.

"How much did you pay her?" Martínez made a face and looked down at the man.

"Three pesetas, but she stole four more out my pocket while we ..." He stood slowly.

"I know what happened; it's an old trick of hers." Martínez dug his hand into his jacket pocket. "Here are the four pesetas she took from you. Now, get out of here." He handed the man the coins and booted him in the buttocks as he hauled himself over the wall. "And stay away from her," Martínez shouted as the fat man waddled away.

"A Minorcan?" asked Dorado as they watched him walk toward the northern section of town. "I've seen him in the streets before."

"Yes. He lives near the cemetery in one of those hovels with straw roofs. Like the other Minorcans, he spends most of his time drinking in the taverns. God only knows where they find the money for wine or whores."

"It looks like the schooner made it in." Dorado pointed to the pier, where passengers were walking over the gangplank to the shore. "For a time, I thought the sea swallowed it up."

"So did I." Martínez stood with a hand shielding his eyes from the sun. He turned back to the path and grunted. "Well, look who's coming our way."

Dorado saw two townsmen approaching them along the path. "Who are they?"

"The old man is Jesse Fish. The other one is Enoch Barton. They're English and own property in and around town. In my opinion, they own too damned much property."

"What's wrong with Fish? He looks crooked."

"Nothing. He's simply bent from age. The old bastard has to be close to seventy. But look at him, he still gets around. What is it they say, 'Death comes all too soon to the good and too late to the evil.'"

Dorado studied the Englishmen as they approached. Stooped and apparently stiff in the joints, Jesse Fish moved slowly. He was wrinkled, worn and looked very old. As they walked closer, he could see that Fish's clothing was soiled and patched in places. With his wispy white hair blowing in the wind and a few yellow teeth remaining in his mouth, the old man reminded Dorado of a childhood goblin who had haunted his dreams.

Moments later, when the Englishmen stopped to exchange greetings, Dorado saw that in addition to his shabby clothing, Jesse Fish looked dirty as well. He could see dirt embedded in the wrinkles of his face as well as blemishes and blackheads all over his forehead. The bald back of his head looked the same, Dorado discovered, when Fish turned to speak to Martínez. The few strands of oily hair that remained on his head stuck out like the quills of a porcupine. Dorado turned away in disgust. Instead, he studied the serious-looking man beside him.

Enoch Barton appeared to have nothing in common with Jesse Fish. He stood straight and was properly dressed in blue breeches and a gray frock coat. A fringe of neatly-barbered hair encircled his bald head. Barton listened to the conversation, but made no comment.

"The governor's niece! What an awful calamity!" exclaimed Jesse Fish. "I can't believe something so horrible could happen here in the presidio. Does anyone have any idea what happened to the girl? It's said in town she was murdered. If so, I surely hope the man is arrested soon." Fish raised his eyes to Martínez, who, because of the old man's bent posture, appeared twice his height.

Dorado was surprised to hear Fish speak excellent Spanish. He spoke fluently without the slightest accent. Also surprising was the old man's deep voice, which seemed to surge out of some hidden place in his puny chest.

"Thank you, for your concern, Señor Fish. We are not yet certain what happened to the governor's niece." Martínez, his head raised, stood back from the Englishman. "Of course, our investigation has already begun and we will announce our findings in good time. If murder is involved, we will find the guilty man and arrest him."

"I surely hope so. What a shame! Such a lovely girl. I'm so sorry for our governor." Fish looked briefly at Dorado and then returned his eyes to Martínez, who moved away to prop a foot on the seawall.

"It is indeed a terrible tragedy for the governor. A terrible tragedy." Enoch Barton stood still beside his stooped companion, his long arms hanging loosely down by his sides.

"It is a tragedy indeed." Fish stepped closer to Martínez. "I'm here to pay my respects to the family and express my sympathy to Don Vicente. He has suffered such a terrible loss."

Martínez nodded. "It must be several months since I've seen you in town, Señor Fish." He again moved again away from the old man. Martínez took off his hat and stood with the wind in his face. He inhaled the air and then looked down at Jesse Fish.

"It may be even longer. I seldom come to town anymore. It's too hard on me. My old bones take a beating in a boat these days."

"You seem to be getting around well enough, even at your age. You are a fortunate man." Martínez smiled. "It must be the salubrious climate of Spanish Florida."

"I'm not feeling all that well, you know. I come here only to conduct a little commerce. These are bad financial times what with the freeze that ruined the orange crop last winter."

"That must be the reason why you haven't yet paid for your last visit to my office. It was in early March, seven months ago, as I recall." Martínez crossed his arms over his chest and glared at the old man.

"I thought I already paid you – five pesetas wasn't it?"

"No, you never paid me and it was ten pesetas for the treatment. As you know, it is the crown's policy that Spaniards pay five pesetas and foreigners pay ten for medical treatment." Martínez raised his voice to emphasize the word foreigners.

Fish made a face. "Ah yes, we pay more for everything in this presidio, even those of us who have served the king for over fifty years."

Martínez smiled, but said nothing.

"I'll pay you the next time I come into the presidio. But that may well be awhile. The constant pain I suffer and the poor state of my bones forces me to remain at home much of the time these days. I can hardly get out of bed some mornings." Fish sighed sadly, holding his back with an age-spotted hand.

"If you wait long enough, your debts will undoubtedly outlive you." Martínez again smiled at Jesse Fish.

"That's not at all amusing as you will see if you should live into your sixties. Old age has so many hardships. Gracias a Dios for good friends like Enoch Barton, who paddle across the bay to visit me. Without him, I wouldn't be able to get into town at all." Jesse Fish turned his entire body to smile at the slender man beside him.

It was a hideous smile to Dorado and his stomach turned when he looked into the man's open mouth. He saw a few dirty yellowed teeth rooted in red gums. "Dios mío. I hope I never look like that," Dorado said to himself, "He looks like a living gargoyle."

"Well, we must be on our way now." Fish tapped Barton's arm. "We don't want to be late for the visitation." As he started to leave, Jesse Fish turned and faced Martínez. I walk so slowly and with such excruciating pain these days. Que Dios me ayude! (God help me!) Tell me, Doctor, do you think there will ever come a time when old age will be less painful?"

"Who knows, Señor Fish?" Martínez looked at the old Englishman, a trace of a smile on his lips. "But if you think about it, your pain may not be all that bad."

"What do you mean?" Fish raised his eyebrows.

"You might think of it as old age's way of telling you that you're still alive. So, enjoy the pain while you still can." Martínez chuckled as he saw the Englishman's mouth fall open. Dorado laughed with him. Even the ever serious Enoch Barton smiled briefly.

"I'll try to keep that advice in mind, Doctor. You do have a way with those who suffer. Yes, indeed. What a prescription for my aging – pain!" Jesse Fish showed the two Spaniards another one of his gargoyle smiles and turned to leave.

"What a weasel!" Martínez shook his head as they continued walking. "These are bad financial times," he mumbled mimicking Jesse Fish. "Qué mierda! (What shit!) That bastard is the wealthiest man in all of Florida. At one time, he owned more property here than the king."

"That dirty old man?" Dorado stopped walking and stared at Martínez. "He looks and smells like a street beggar." Fish's odor reminded Dorado of a sweat drenched, sour towel.

"Fish always comes to town in grubby garments like some poor campesino. He's afraid if he looks prosperous, his vast land holdings might be taxed some more. So the man's forever poor-mouthing and going about looking as shabby as the poorest man in the presidio. I doubt the man ever bathes; he stinks. I prefer the odor of death to that disgusting smell."

"He does stink. I stood upwind, well away from him."

"So did I, but Fish's stench doesn't keep Enoch Barton away. Oh, no! Barton rows over to Santa Anastasia Island to visit Fish or fetch him to town because he's in debt to the old bastard. That's why. 'Good friends' row over to that rundown plantation he calls El Vergel (the garden) only to pay debts or borrow money. They like his smell no more than we do."

"I believe it." Dorado glanced over his shoulder at the two Englishmen walking away into the distance. He saw them enter the crowd still gathered in the central plaza.

"Greedy men like Enoch Barton do whatever Fish wants. But that's the merchant class for you. They row across the bay whenever Fish beckons them – that is if they want to hear the sound of his silver coins dropping into their pockets."

"Even with all his money, how does he dare call the governor, 'Don Vicente?' Surely, Fish doesn't address him in that manner."

"He does. It astonishes everyone – even Ricardo. There must be something between them, considering what he gets away with here."

"What does he get away with here?" Dorado stopped and stood facing Martínez.

"Too much. Among other regulations for foreigners, Fish has never accepted Catholic instruction, even though the governor ordered it for all Protestants."

"Fish has defied the governor?" Dorado gasped.

"It would seem so despite Zéspedes' well-known intolerance for the English. Yet, Jesse Fish, an English Protestant, has been allowed to own vast tracts of land in Spanish Florida. At one time, that old bastard owned an enormous territory in the center of the peninsula as well as most of the property in town. Fish also claims to own all of Anastasia Island where his orange plantation is situated."

"That's the plantation he calls El Vergel?"

"Yes, the Fruit Garden. It's now a garden of dead and dying orange trees, wild animals and weeds. At one time, El

Vergel was a productive citrus plantation, but Fish has let the place fall into ruin. Now, it's dilapidated – like its owner."

The two officers stood by the city pier where Enoch Barton's boat had been tied up. An old black freedman sat on the gunwale smoking a pipe. Martínez motioned Dorado toward the Castillo. As they walked away, he touched his ear and then pointed to the Freedman.

Dorado realized Martínez did not want their conversation heard by Barton's freedman. A few minutes later, when the pier was well behind them, he asked. "Fish said he had served the king for fifty years. Here in St. Augustine?"

"Yes. Fish came to Florida sometime in the early thirties. Though only a lad of twelve or so, he worked as an agent for the William Walton Company of New York. The foreigners sold foodstuff here. As you know, we've never grown much in this desolate place."

"So that's why he speaks such excellent Spanish."

"Yes. While working for the Walton Company, Fish learned all about us. He learned our language and customs so well that people said he seemed more Spanish than English."

"Surely, that's not why Fish gets special privileges?"

"Quién sabe? All we know is that Jesse Fish has the governor's ear. The Englishman is allowed in his office almost anytime he comes to town."

"That's hard to understand, seeing how dirty he is." Dorado frowned.

"What's even harder for me to understand is the vast land empire he possesses in this Spanish province. Fish is an English Protestant, por el amor de Dios (for God's sake)! I don't know why the king's officials allow it."

"It is bewildering. How did Fish acquire so much land?"

"He got it twenty-four years ago. It was when we turned Florida over to the English following the Seven Years' War. At that time, our people put all their property in his hands."

"Why, for God's sake?" Dorado looked sideways at the doctor.

"Because our people left before their property could be sold. At the urging of the king, everyone abandoned Florida and went to Cuba." He swatted at a fly buzzing around his brow.

"Everyone, sir?"

"Yes, except for a few who didn't sell their land. According to the treaty, our people were allowed eighteen months to sell their property. A reasonable period, right?"

"It would seem so." Dorado brushed the hair out of his eyes.

"Yes – except it didn't work out as expected. Little of the land was sold in time. Too few English settled in Florida to purchase the property. Only simple soldiers came here at first and they had too little money to buy anything. As usual, royal policy made in Madrid couldn't be put into practice in the colonies." Martínez sighed, exhaling his breath loudly.

Dorado nodded. He had heard the same complaints in Havana.

"Can you imagine what happened – how our people suffered? They expected money in their pockets when they moved to Havana. Instead, they sailed away with only what could be carried on their backs. Except, of course, for the wealthy. They always manage to escape all calamities with their riches intact."

"Surely the choice houses and lots were sold in time."

"Not many. La Florida was emptied faster than anyone expected. To the astonishment of everyone, the royal officials evacuated this province of all its people and portable goods in ten months. Can you imagine that?"

"That is astonishing." Dorado stood with his back to the wind.

"The entire colony of 3,700 soldiers and civilians, including the Christianized Indians, sailed to Cuba and Mexico.

Most went to Havana. Even the recent dead were taken. I saw most of the evacuation myself since I was here during the last months of the colony. They sent me to St. Augustine to help the ill and older people move to Havana."

"They evacuated Apalache and Pensacola as well, sir?"

"Yes, those outposts were also closed. We left the English a province empty of people. But, sadly, our people left before their homes and lands could be sold. It's so typical! Spain succeeds in a colonial operation and our people pay the price. It happens again and again."

Dorado nodded, not knowing what to say.

"When the English came here they found a deserted city. According to Ricardo, it was as if a plague had swept through the colony killing everyone. He sailed aboard one of the last evacuation ships to leave St. Augustine in 1764. I left a month or so earlier with the remaining ill and older people."

"So that's why so little land was sold."

"Exactly. Our officials were forced to transfer the unsold houses and lands to someone – someone who promised to represent our people in the new English province."

"And that someone was Jesse Fish." Dorado nodded.

"Yes. Fish said he would sell the unsold lands beyond the time limits of the treaty. He pledged to sell the property at the highest possible prices and then pay our people the proceeds, of course, after expenses and profitable fees. Greedy to get those profits, Jesse Fish lied to the English – his own people. He told them the property was his, purchased from the owners."

"So, Fish became a secret agent for all the unsold lands. That was risky and might be why he has the governor's ear."

"Maybe. What Jesse Fish did was risky and he would have been hanged if the English had learned of his lies. But what he possessed was worth the risks. Fish made a fortune from the agreement and became the largest landowner in Florida."

"Was that when he got his plantation over on the island?"

"Yes! The damned Englishman got that plantation and so much more. After our people left Florida, Fish owned most of the property in this province. He held houses, lots and tracts of lands in such quantity that the English accountant sent here by their king never had the time to appraise them all. In twenty years!"

"Dios mío! Does he still own it all?"

"No, he sold most of it. At first, he rented the houses and later sold them to immigrants who came here in the seventies. The so-called English Loyalists from the north purchased most of the properties; they're the people who fled the revolution in what they now call the United States. Even the miserable Minorcans bought some houses in and around town."

"They're the peasants from the islands in the Mediterranean?"

"Yes. The Minorcans were lured to Florida to settle Mosquito Inlet, thirty leagues south of here. The English brought the Minorcans here to grow indigo in that godforsaken place they called New Smyrna. Of course, the settlement failed. What would you expect in a place called the Mosquito Coast?"

"What a site for a settlement. Those poor people!" Dorado knew the Mosquito Coast from a reconnaissance mission he had led south of St. Augustine. He remembered draping a blanket over his head and body as he rode his horse through clouds of mosquitoes.

"It was madness to settle them in the swamps. I'm told a number died from snakebites and a couple of their children were taken by alligators. But it was mainly starvation and fevers that killed most of them. Only a third survived of the 1,400 who went to New Smyrna. When the colony failed, those who still lived came here looking for help. They still do."

"When did Fish pay our people? He did pay them, didn't he, sir?"

"No one is certain. Fish sailed to Havana in the seventies, but what happened there no one knows. Most of the people who left La Florida remained in Cuba and are now dead. Those who returned to St. Augustine after the English occupation, including the heirs of the deceased, were paid for their property. It's said Fish paid them little after subtracting his fees and upkeep expenses." He scowled. "Even then, the old bastard had the audacity to show his irritation as he handed them the pesetas they were due. So, all we know with certainty is that Fish became filthy rich from handling our people's property."

"It's astonishing what he's allowed to own here and English at that."

"Isn't it? Now, I'll tell you something else that will astonish you even more. Jesse Fish was with the governor's niece the day before she was killed. He was also with the Parral girl the day before she disappeared." Martínez smiled, seeing the startled look on Dorado's face. "What do you think of that, Lieutenant?"

"I don't know what to think." Dorado shook his head. "What were those girls doing with that disgusting old man?"

"Nothing to worry you. Fish sometimes invites young girls, always well chaperoned, to visit El Vergel. They are rowed over there to pick oranges and stroll in what remains of his flower garden. He invites them simply to watch the pretty young things prance about his place. That's all the old fart can do anyway. He gives each girl a silver coin, which is quite unusual considering how stingy he is. He does no more than say a few words to them. Except for a freedman, Jesse Fish lives alone and, now and then, enjoys such company. Still, it's an odd coincidence that both girls visited El Vergel before they disappeared."

"It is. How do you know about their visits, sir?"

"I always know what's happening here if it involves disease, death or the dalliance of pretty girls." Martínez snickered. "So, Lieutenant, are you suspicious of me?"

"I'm not suspicious of you, only surprised you knew of their visits to El Vergel. That's all. I'm more suspicious of Jesse Fish. It seems too coincidental that both of girls were with him before they were murdered."

"Wait! We don't know the missing girl was murdered. We only know she disappeared and was never found. Though now as we talk about the coincidence, I wonder." He looked at Dorado. "I recall her canoe was found overturned on the bay side of Fish's plantation. "At the time, we thought the girl's canoe was washed up there by the current. Now, I don't know what to think. Maybe, that girl was murdered too. Quién sabe? I wonder if we'll ever know."

"Did anyone talk to Fish about the lost girl – at that time?"

"Yes, I had that duty. I went over to talk to him after the canoe was seen lying on its side in the sand. It was a waste of time. Fish knew nothing that was of any help. And since the man seemed so feeble, it was hard to imagine him killing anyone. The old bastard looked then much as he does now. Of course, Fish has strong hands – like mine." Martínez held up his huge hands and flexed his fingers.

"What about Jesse Fish and his way with women? You said he invites young girls to El Vergel and only watches them prance around. Is he too old to function?"

Martínez nodded. "Fish can't get it up; it's known all over town. They say he had such an affliction even when he was younger. I wonder if that's the price we must pay for becoming wealthy in this life? If so, I prefer to remain poor." He guffawed loudly.

Dorado grinned.

"People say that's why his pretty little wife, Sarah Warner, left him some years ago. As you can imagine, she's the subject of much gossip and shaking of heads."

"What's said about her?"

"I'll tell you, Dorado, but, keep in mind, what I've heard comes from the sullen sisters." He smiled. "So, who knows how reliable their gossip is? What a pair, they are! It's certainly no surprise Esperanza has never married – who would be foolish enough to marry such a mean woman? Not only is Esperanza unsightly, she finds fault with everyone and everything. It's no wonder she hasn't been courted, even in this presidio where women always seem to be in short supply. Though she would never admit it, Esperanza came here hoping to find a husband."

"That might explain her unpleasant manner. Who would want to be with her with such a face and manner?" Dorado stepped over a puddle in his path.

"María isn't as mean as Esperanza, but she too finds fault with most people. It must be a family manner. Anyway, Sarah Warner married Jesse Fish in the late sixties when she was just sixteen. Her father, James Warner, was the harbor pilot at the time. It was a good marriage for Sarah, even though Fish was well over forty at the time. Of course, there's nothing remarkable about that. Fish was hale and hardy and making much money."

"Was he in possession of his plantation at that time?"

"Yes. After a few years, they had a son and, somewhat later, a daughter. Not too long after the second child was born, they parted company. Sarah took the children and moved into town, while Fish stayed on alone at El Vergel, living the life of a hermit."

"What happened to his marriage with Sarah Warner?"

"There are a number of explanations told in town. According to the sullen sisters, Sarah Warner deserted Fish because he rarely bedded her. They speak of the woman as a shameless hussy, whose bodily needs cannot be met by any one man. Their gossip has Sarah going from man to man and bed to bed. They say her shameless behavior so distressed her husband that he retired alone to his island refuge. And, there, 'the lonely old man has lived ever since to escape the embarrassment of the lustful slut's numerous trysts in town.'

Those are María's words. The two sisters see Sarah Warner as a wicked sinner sure to be punished by God."

"How much of what they say do you believe, sir?" Dorado smiled.

"It's hard to believe the stories of hypocrites. Neither of them ever mentions María's sin for the lustful life she lives with me. Everyone knows she shares her bed with me. Isn't that sinful, too, since we aren't married? Of course not. For women, it's only sinful when another woman does it."

"What do you know about Sarah Warner? What's the truth?"

"I've heard she left him because he neglected her and the children." Martínez scratched a mosquito bite on the back of his hand. "It's said he was more concerned with his commercial dealings. His life has been consumed by the need to acquire more and more land and money."

"So it's true what they say about the English. They're much more interested in money than family. What a people they are."

"Indeed. No matter his enviable wealth, Jesse Fish wanted more. The fool! He never ceased seeking it. Apparently, Sarah accepted the situation without the slightest complaint for years. She also accepted his affliction. Women are often like that. In time, he could not get it up, except by his own hand. What then took place between them were – strange practices which shocked his innocent young wife."

"What kind of strange practices?" Dorado stopped walking and waited for the doctor to turn back to him.

"I don't know." Martínez shook his head. "What little I know was told to me by the English physician, Doctor Dennis West. He was the only physician who stayed here after we regained Florida from England. He stayed only a year and then sailed to Savannah. Anyway, it seems some years ago, he treated Sarah for a female ailment. At the time, Doctor West said she complained of her husband's strange practices, but would say no more than that."

"Did Doctor West have any suspicions of what the practices might be?" Dorado could not imagine the strange practices Fish had required of his wife.

"None that he mentioned to me, but his case notes for Sarah Warner suggested several possibilities. I read them later when she became my patient upon his departure for Savannah. I don't recall the words he used in his notes, but they implied her female ailments were probably caused by Fish's strange practices." Martínez smiled, assuming the young man had few, if any intimate experiences with women and would not have any notion of what the notes suggested.

"I see." Despite his curiosity, Dorado did not ask Martínez anything further. He did not want appear to be an ignorant provinciano (rural noble). Dorado saw the doctor's smile and suspected the older man thought him to be inexperienced with women.

"No, but your question makes me wonder if anything happened between them the day before she was murdered. It's unlikely, of course, in the presence of a chaperone. Yet, it's possible a rendezvous in the woods could have been arranged."

"There is also the visit of the other girl, who disappeared."

"Yes, someone will have to speak to Fish. The problem will be getting the governor's permission. The last time I interviewed the old bastard I had to go see Zéspedes and beg him to let me do it." Martínez looked up into the sky as if seeking understanding in the heavens.

"But, now after his own niece was murdered, do you think the governor would hesitate to have Fish interviewed?"

"No, I don't. Nor do I think he would ignore the coincidence of both girls visiting El Vergel the day before one was killed and the other disappeared. Even if Fish has his ear."

"No, sir, it doesn't seem likely."

Martínez looked at his pocket watch. "Well, it's time to be on our way. We'll be meeting Ricardo in a few minutes."

CHAPTER FIVE

October 23, 1788

Ruiz de León saw them approaching from the upper deck of the Castillo. He arrived earlier and was enjoying the cool wind and the panoramic view from the eastern watchtower. From where he stood, forty feet above the waves that struck the seawall, the captain could see the entire area around St. Augustine. No other place offered such a clear view of the city and the bay and he often would walk over to the Castillo to look out to sea.

From his favorite lookout spot beside the tower, Ruiz de León could see the blue ocean beyond Santa Anastasia Island, the narrow inlet flowing into the bay and the entire seaside of St. Augustine. The town, only a mile in length, lay out before him with all the buildings on the bay front in sight. Behind them, he could also see the rooftops and upper stories of the bigger houses that stood on the streets to the west of the bay. The two sentry towers at the city gates and the shell road running north along the river were also in view from where he stood. Ruiz de León watched a lone horseman on the road riding out of the city.

From his position, he could even see a portion of the plaza with its citrus trees, now in full bloom. The spacious plaza, set in the center of St. Augustine, served as a parade ground for the presidio's troops, a popular meeting place for the townspeople and the site of most of the vendor stalls in the city. It extended from the bay front to Calle Real (Royal Street), which ran north and south the entire length of the colonial city. Government House stood on the west side of Royal Street diagonally across from the city's church. The church, still damaged and under repair after the English at-tacks of the 1740s, was prominently positioned as the only building on the north side of the plaza. Squinting, Ruiz de León saw some of the mourners still lingering in front of the church.

St. Augustine was a walled city. Since the presidio had been built beside the bay, the walls stood on three sides of the rectangular shaped community. The bay lay to the east while the walls, constructed of shell-stone blocks and layered logs, were erected on the north, south and west sides of the city. Spanish engineers built the walls earlier in the century fol-lowing the first English attack on the colony in 1702. Troops from Carolina invaded Florida and destroyed the entire town with the exception of the Castillo. The Spaniards rebuilt the city and encircled it with barricades, but forty years later, in 1742, the colony was besieged again and sacked by the Eng-lish army. Spain strengthened the presidio's defenses after the second attack, but no other assaults were made against the presidio in the forty-five years that followed.

As Ruiz de León looked over St. Augustine, it struck him how stark the presidio seemed. With so few trees, it reminded him of one of the bleak desert towns he had seen while sta-tioned in North Africa. A series of severe winters in the last two decades had forced the townspeople to cut down most of the shade trees for firewood. Only five of the enormous live oaks survived in town, one sixty-foot tree growing in the garden behind Government House and the others in the plaza. There were also two rows of citrus trees planted on the north and south sides of the plaza, but no other vegetation except a flower bed planted in front of the church. It occurred to Ruiz de León that the plaza looked like an oasis surrounded by sun-bleached buildings and yellow sand streets. He knew colorful flowers and citrus trees grew elsewhere in the city, but they were not in view from where he stood.

St. Augustine still showed signs of the battles fought earlier in the century. Buildings with broken down walls and exposed foundations were a common sight and stone rubble lay in piles on most streets. Most of the town's houses had been rebuilt after the last English assault and included flame-blackened blocks removed from earlier dwellings destroyed in the war. The wooden planks of many structures were pock marked from musket shot or scorched from fires set by soldiers of the invading army. Razed during the siege of the city, the church had been partially reconstructed, but still needed renovation. Along with war damage, during the twenty years of English occupation, many houses in St. Augustine had been stripped of wooden beams and planks to provide winter firewood for the English army.

St. Augustine looked much better since the beginning of the Zéspedes governorship in 1784. The majority of buildings had been both repaired and renovated. Within five years of the governor's arrival, most families had houses, some for the first time in a decade. There was still overcrowding in town, but at least everyone had a roof over their heads. The townspeople also had planted vegetable gardens that now flourished almost everywhere, as well as red, white and yellow flowers which filled patios, hung from balconies and decorated entrances of houses and stores throughout the presidio.

Looking about the town, Ruiz de León considered the small settlement a pleasant place to live. At times, he missed his homeland in the scenic mountain country of northern Spain, but the captain was content in St. Augustine. The little town had everything he needed and his bad leg seemed to ache much less in the warm climate. At his age, he had no hope of promotion or preferred assignments elsewhere in the king's service. Ruiz de León expected Florida to be his last military appointment and he suspected his life would come to an end in St. Augustine.

Beyond the presidio, thick forests spread out endlessly as far as the eye could see. The dense woodlands were impenetrable in many places, in or under foul water in others and full of unexpected perils. Home to scores of venomous snakes as well as alligators, bears, wildcats and blood-sucking insects, the wilderness would test any man's claim to courage. All too many men had gone recklessly into the uncharted lands, never to return. Ruiz de León sympathized with the presidio's soldiers, who were routinely sent on reconnaissance patrols into what they called the tierras perdidas (lost lands).

He thought of the clouds of insatiable mosquitoes and gnats that engulfed the forests at dusk and into the night. During the day, the biting flies attacked men and horses alike, leaving welts where they had taken their meal of blood. Day or night, there were prickly plants, sharp spurs and thorns to infect the flesh of those who foolishly went into the woods.

"God knows what else waits in that wilderness." Ruiz de León shuddered remembering a chance encounter with a ten foot alligator and a close escape from the strike of a rattlesnake.

Seeing Martínez and Dorado walking across the drawbridge, the captain paused for one last look at the bay before descending the stairs to meet them. Santa Anastasia Island, fourteen miles long, stretched out like a man's bent leg to the south. Against the dark blue sea and sky, the island appeared like a green paradise where God had placed the earth's precious jewels. He pictured himself gathering up the sparkling stones to bestow upon the beautiful woman who so often frequented his daydreams. The sight of her smiling face remained with Ruiz de León as he limped down the stairway.

"Well, Carlos, what have you learned?" Ruiz de León waited until Martínez had closed the office door before speaking.

"Much. But before I tell you about it, I want to know what the governor has decided to do about the murder of his niece. Who has been assigned to the investigation?" Martínez sat down in his desk chair and immediately tipped it back against the wall.

"The governor has assigned us all to the investigation." He looked at Dorado. "You will be relieved of all your duties at the Castillo during the time it takes to conclude our work. You will still serve weekend guard duty – once a month, isn't it? I spoke to the commandant today and he temporarily assigned you to serve under ..." He glanced at Martínez, "our direction."

"Thank you, sir." Dorado smiled.

Ruiz de León nodded and turned to Martínez. "Carlos, the governor wants us, you and me, to lead the investigation together." He lied to avoid an angry outburst from his friend.

"I'm surprised." Martínez sat with his arms crossed over his chest. "I expected him to choose an official like you to be in charge." He chuckled. "No offense intended, Ricardo. You know me, I never expect our superiors to make any sensible decisions. Why would I, after what I've seen all these years in the king's service?"

"I'm not offended. It's true that I'm a royal official and not an investigator of crimes. I make no such claim. But, my friend, neither are you. Let me finish." He held up his hand.

"I know this investigation will certainly require your doctor's mind. It will also need knowledge of the presidio and its people, which I possess. So, we should be able to work well together, of course, with the help of the lieutenant here, who will do the needed leg work."

"You're right, Ricardo." Martínez smiled. "We should make an excellent investigation team. It makes sense that the three of us will be involved."

"There is, ah, one concern the governor has voiced about you, Carlos." Ruiz de León spoke slowly, selecting his words with care. He wished the subject could be avoided.

"Oh, here it comes. What's his concern?" Martínez stuck his huge hands out, palms up as if to receive something from Ruiz de León.

"Do you want me to speak about it in private?" Ruiz de León glanced at Dorado.

"No. Let me hear it now." Martínez exhaled his breath loudly. "The lieutenant needs to learn what concerns our superiors."

Ruiz de León paused, thinking what to say. "The governor is worried about, ah, your past affairs with women. He wants me or the lieutenant to interview any women who might somehow be involved in the investigation."

"So, that's his concern, is it? I'll be damned!" Martínez shook his head. "I can't believe it! Here in this tiny town on the frontier, a fiend has murdered and mutilated an innocent girl, the governor's niece, and could very well kill another unsuspecting girl. And the governor is concerned about me and my past affairs with women. Now, isn't that something?"

Martínez' face reddened as he pushed himself from the wall and stood. The chair fell on the floor and he kicked it out of the way. He pointed a trembling finger at Ruiz de León.

"What is Zéspedes thinking? What in God's name do my past affairs with women have to do with this present murder? My women weren't murdered, they were pleasured! They left my bed, perhaps a little sore, but alive! Do you hear me, Ricardo? They were not murdered by a man who never even entered them. What stupidity!" Martínez shouted, his eyes blazing. "I suppose it's what we should expect from the king's officials. Stupidity!"

"Calm down, Carlos." Ruiz de León held his hand up. "I want to say ..."

"God damn it! What stupidity!"

"Please listen. Keep in mind what the governor has suffered. He has lost his own niece in the presidio he commands. It's a terrible shock for him and he sees himself as dishonored by her death. He needs our concern now. You know I fear for his life. A year ago he was almost fat and now he looks frail. Surely, you see his health is failing." Ruiz de León put out a hand to touch his friend's knee as Martínez stood with his hands on his hips.

The big man sighed, knowing there was nothing he could say to counter Ruiz de León's argument. "Yes, of course, I see something is afflicting him. It's obviously internal, but I have no notion of what's wrong with him. He refuses to speak to me about it. Whenever I tell him it's time for an annual examination, he only smiles at me. You know the damned smile he uses to say his mind won't be changed. So, tell me, what can I do with him? He's one of those stoic Castilians. I suppose he questions my medical skill because of my past affairs with women."

Ruiz de León shook his head. "You know that's untrue, Carlos. He highly respects your intelligence and knowledge of medicine. I've heard him say that many times and he repeated it again today. But you are right about his stoic streak. He never admits anything could be wrong with him and refuses to talk about his loss of weight. Only a few days ago, I was ordered not to mention it again. He's much too stubborn for his own good."

"I'm surprised to hear you criticize Zéspedes. You usually

make excuses for him. The man is too damned stubborn. If he won't let me examine him, I can't possibly help him."

"I intend to keep urging him to see you."

"He needs to be examined and soon! The loss of weight is certainly significant, though not necessarily a threat to his life. I've seen people lose much more weight and live for years. Still, it isn't a good sign, no, not a good sign at all! Zéspedes has been a better governor than I expected. The presidio functions about as well as possible under his command. The governor even made a few decent selections in the choice of his staff."

"Is that a compliment? I can't believe it."

"Oh, don't take it personally." Martínez grinned.

"Let's continue. Tell us what you learned from the autopsy."

Martínez picked up his chair and sat in it again. "I spent two hours yesterday morning examining the girl's cadaver. But before I could finish the autopsy, the body was taken away. They said the body had to be prepared for the funeral." He scowled. "By that time, however, I knew she had been dead for three days. That means she was murdered Tuesday morning. I've got medical proof for that opinion and some of it won't be pleasant to hear."

"We'll put up with it, but please don't give us unnecessary medical information." Ruiz de León cleared his throat.

Martínez made a face. "There are a number of methods to determine the time of death. One is related to bodily change caused by the climate, another involves the activity of insects on a dead body."

"One method will be enough, Carlos. Give us only the pertinent facts."

"All right." He showed them a devilish smile. "The body was beginning to look black, when I first saw it the morning after the murder. That was Wednesday. Dead bodies become black after a day or so in this hot climate. At death, corpses look gray, hours later, green, then purple and finally black.

Eventually, a dead body has a marbled look, much like the marbling of fat in a good piece of beef." He snickered seeing their looks of disgust. "The dead are not attractive, no matter what they looked like in life. They also smell like rotting meat."

"Must we hear all these grisly details?" Ruiz de León frowned.

"I'm only giving you the pertinent facts."

"Are you, indeed? Well, then, let's finish it. It's getting late."

"Fine. When I saw the body becoming black Wednesday morning, I knew the girl was murdered sometime Tuesday morning. The beginning of body bloating also indicated that time of death. I assume this account interests you, Ricardo."

"Oh, yes, it's certainly as fascinating as one of the bishop's sermons on the wages of sin and the eternal suffering of the damned."

Martínez laughed loudly. "You do have a sense of humor at times."

"What about lividity?" Dorado wanted Martínez to know he recalled his explanation.

"By Wednesday morning, the livid areas on her back looked black as well. Her face also changed color because of the blood in her head; that happens when someone is strangled. There's also some bleeding around the eyes."

Exasperated, Ruiz de León exhaled loudly. "Tell me, Carlos, do we really need to know these details? I can't believe they're useful for us."

"I'm giving you only the facts that will go into my report." Martínez grinned again. "You do want the pertinent facts, don't you?"

"Yes, yes. Do continue." Ruiz de León grimaced and shook his head.

"There's other bodily information for the murder on Tuesday morning. When I saw the corpse on Wednesday, bloody fluid flowed from the mouth. That's fluid from the lungs and it typically appears in a day's time."

"What about rigor mortis?" Dorado recalled his father telling him what happened to dead men after a battle. "Does that also suggest the girl was murdered in the morning?"

"No. Rigor mortis appears three to four hours after death. But, in this hot climate, all stiffness will disappear in eight hours. So, if the girl died in the morning and developed rigor mortis by the early afternoon, all the stiffness should have been gone by that night. When you moved the body, it wasn't stiff, was it?"

"No, sir. She seemed limp when I wrapped up her body."

Martínez nodded. "There is one more indication of her death in the morning. There were no significant signs of bodily excretions in her underclothing or on the cadaver. In the struggle for life, the body usually loses control of both the bowels and bladder. It would be expected in murder by strangulation. Yet, there were only a few tiny stains on her clothing. Why? Because she used the chamber pot before leaving her room. I think the girl left soon after awakening that morning. She ate no breakfast according to what the maid told you."

"That's right." Ruiz de León nodded.

"Knowing she would be outside for a while, the girl didn't drink or eat anything. She didn't want to stop anywhere to relieve herself for fear of being seen. I assume she was going to a secret rendezvous. What do you think, Ricardo?"

"So it seems."

"I think it suggests something else, sir." Dorado saw Martínez nod his head for him to continue. "I wonder if she would chance walking all the way to the woods. The time it took to walk there – at least an hour, would increase the risk of being seen. It would be faster and less risky for her to paddle a canoe to the spot."

"Good thinking, Lieutenant." Martínez nodded. "It certainly would be easier if the girl went by water. If she paddled along the shore, where the marsh grass is high, she would also be less likely to be seen. What do you think, Ricardo?"

Ruiz de León nodded. "A canoe can easily be paddled in the shallow water along the shore. It would offer speed as well, but how could the girl get a canoe without being seen?"

"I don't know. That's another good question." Martínez shook his head.

"It is and there are many more." Ruiz de León grimaced. "How could the governor's niece leave Government House, walk through the plaza, get a canoe at the pier and then paddle away without being seen by someone, especially a sentry." He raised his voice. "Why wasn't she seen by someone? A sentry at Government House, a vendor in the plaza, a pedestrian in the street? If the governor's niece can leave town unseen in full daylight, it suggests that the presidio itself is not protected. That worries me as much as the girl's disappearance."

Martínez nodded. "What you say is true, Ricardo. The common soldiers they send us here are from the bottom of the barrel."

"The commandant says the same thing." Ruiz de León sighed loudly.

"Let's return to Gloria's unseen trip out of town." Martínez looked at Dorado. "The use of a canoe is a good possibility. Perhaps it was hidden somewhere along the shore, not far from the pier. We also need to know how the murderer got out to the North River as well and how he returned to town. I assume the girl knew him in St. Augustine."

"I would say so," said Ruiz de León quickly. "It's unlikely the governor's niece would be acquainted with anyone outside town or outside of Government House for that matter."

"With one exception – Jesse Fish. I told the lieutenant about the strange disappearance of Patricia Hernández Parral and the discovery of her overturned canoe on Fish ... ah, Anastasia Island. There's a man who surely must be interviewed."

"That foul old Englishman! What wouldn't Fish do that's

dishonest or depraved? The governor lets him get away with murder in this town." Ruiz de León scowled, realizing what he had said.

"That's an interesting choice of words, Ricardo."

"They are appropriate words. You know what I think of him."

"It would be easy to suspect him. His illegal schemes suggest he's capable of anything, especially if money is involved. But murder of a young girl? I doubt it. His insatiable quest for land and money has marked his life in the past – not women. He's never been interested in them to my knowledge. Nor does he seem to be an ill-tempered man who might kill someone in a fit of rage. I've never heard about even one act of temper. Have you?"

"No." Ruiz de León shook his head.

"Still, the man must be interviewed. The coincidence of both girls visiting him before their deaths is too much to ignore. I think we can assume the missing girl is dead." Martínez looked at the lieutenant. "We'll let Dorado do that interview."

"Fine. I know how to do it." Dorado held his nose.

"That's the only way," said Ruiz de León, with a brief smile.

Dorado raised his hand. "Sir, I want to ask about something you said before. You said the murderer didn't enter her even though he took off all of her clothing?"

"That's right. Gloria was a virgin at the time of her death; her maidenhead was intact. What do you think of that? Whatever the girl did with men, she did not let them enter her."

Dorado was relieved, but only said, "I'm surprised, after all that's been said about her."

"So am I," said Ruiz de León. "I would have thought she had been bedded before."

"Well, now we know better. What we do not know is how she left town without anyone seeing her. She had to go through the plaza whatever way she went. So, someone should have seen her, perhaps one of the vendors or craftsmen?"

Ruiz de León nodded. "They're there at all hours. We'll need to talk to them."

Martínez looked at Dorado. "That's another task for you, Lieutenant."

"Yes, sir. I'll start as soon as I leave the Castillo."

"Good." Martínez frowned. "What puzzles me is how she could get out of the presidio without being observed in the plaza or on one of the streets. None of the sentries on the walls saw her nor was she seen by the guards at the city gates. Lieutenant López de Gómara, Officer of the City Guard that day, told me he talked to all thirty men and not one of them saw her – at any time that morning."

"It's unbelievable." Ruiz de León shook his head.

"It is, but, sooner or later, I think we'll hear of someone who saw her," said Martínez. "There're too many busybodies in this town for Gloria to escape notice that or any other day. She was too pretty to be missed by the townspeople, especially the men."

Dorado raised his hand. "Sir, I think she took a canoe to go to the woods. I therefore suggest we make a search of the shore from the pier to the site of the murder. We might find some signs of her trip along the way. With your permission, I'll take a canoe out there in the morning and see what I can find." Dorado saw both officers nod in approval.

"I'll join you, Lieutenant," said Ruiz de León. "It'll do me good to get away from the office for a while. Let's leave at first light before the heat of the day. We can meet at the pier."

"Sí, mi Capitán."

"Look out for snakes, Ricardo." Martínez smiled. "Keep in mind, they have no respect for royal officials, even those on the governor's staff."

Ruiz de León looked at Martínez, but said nothing.

At that moment, the outside door opened and the commandant of the Castillo, Coronel Miguel Montesinos y Cárdenas, stepped into the room. Despite his raised hand, the officers all stood and saluted him. He motioned them back to their seats.

"Sit. Sit. I only stopped by to wish you well."

The commandant stood in the doorway, blocking out the bright light of the afternoon. A short muscular man no more than five feet tall, he stood erect to maximize his height. Though born in Barcelona, his dark coloring made him look more like a man from the southern coast of Spain. With an unlined face and thick black hair and beard, he also looked much younger than his late forties. The commandant, standing straight and smartly dressed in his sky blue uniform with red cuffs and gold lace, appeared to be the perfect commander of a Spanish garrison.

The colonel nodded in turn to each of the three officers and then focused his eyes on Ruiz de León. "Is there any progress to report, Don Ricardo?"

"Not as yet. We are discussing the investigation now. Don Miguel, why don't you join us? Lieutenant, get the commandant a chair." He gestured to the door of the surgery.

"No, don't get up, Lieutenant. I came by only to wish you well in the investigation. We need to find this fiend as soon as possible. With so many foreigners living among us, we need to show them the competence and strength of Spanish rule. As you surely know, the murder is the talk of the town and we don't want the talk to lead the townspeople to panic. The murderer must be arrested as soon as possible. We have too many problems here in the presidio already without our people, particularly our women, worrying about a murderer at large among them." He sighed. "Let me know how the investigation proceeds. Buena suerte (Good luck)."

About to leave, the colonel looked once more at the seated officers and moved his eyes to Dorado. "This is a valuable assignment for you, Lieutenant. You're fortunate to be serving under Don Ricardo and Doctor Martínez. Take advantage of this unusual opportunity to learn from their experience and wisdom." The commandant turned and walked out the door.

Dorado blushed as both of the older men smiled at him.

"Well, Lieutenant," said Martínez. "Which one of us will you choose for experience and which for wisdom?"

Ruiz de León held up his hand. "Don't answer that question, Lieutenant. He has one of his sarcastic remarks ready for whatever you say."

"Me? Not me!" Martínez grinned. "I'm only interested in the lieutenant's opinion of us. You always expect the worst of me."

"With good reason."

Ruiz de León stood. He made a face straightening his bad leg. "I must be getting back to Government House. I'll see you at dinner, Carlos."

Martínez nodded absently. His mind was occupied thinking about how Gloria managed to reach the woods without being seen. "I hope you find something tomorrow. It's possible, of course, that both the girl and the killer paddled out to their meeting place – perhaps together."

"It is." Ruiz de León turned to Dorado as he reached for the door handle. "Do you play chess, Lieutenant?"

"Yes, sir."

"One of these nights, then, I hope you will come join us for dinner and a game or two."

"Thank you, sir. I'll be pleased to join you."

Martínez smiled. "Careful, Lieutenant, he's the best player in the presidio." He shook an accusing finger at Ruiz de León. "Is he to be your next victim, Ricardo? I hope you play well, Lieutenant."

"I hope so, too."

"I'll see you in the morning, Lieutenant." Ruiz de León nodded to each of them and limped away into the late afternoon sunset. Dorado followed him out after saluting Martínez.

The next morning was unseasonably cool for early October. A sharp wind dropped out of the northeast in the middle of the night and blew through the city. The unexpected cold sent the townspeople scurrying for blankets as they awakened shivering in the dark. Early morning fishermen later claimed to have seen their breath as they set out for the day. By first light, the bay was besieged by whitecapped waves and the two ships at anchor bobbed up and down like corks on a fishing line.

Dorado arrived early at the city dock to await Ruiz de León. It was still dark when he set out from his rooms in the north of town and walked the half-mile to where the bark canoes lay in the sand by the bay. He sat on a ship's timber lying beside the pier. From his position, Dorado could look out to sea as well as to the west where Government House stood on the other side of the plaza. The church was also visible from where he sat. He saw the first light appear on the horizon and, seconds later, when the sun emerged from the ocean, there was enough light to see the Spanish flag whipping in the wind at Government House.

"It must be a northeaster," he thought. "That means two more windy days." The chill in the air made him think of his homeland in northern Spain. For a moment, he felt homesick for his faraway family and his home in the forested hills of Asturias.

Dorado saw Ruiz de León approaching across the plaza. In spite of his injured leg, the captain walked with an erect posture. He held his head high and his shoulders back. Dorado watched him draw nearer, thinking how impressive Ruiz de León looked in his blue uniform and tricorne hat with its red cockade. He stood and saluted the captain as he reached the pier.

"Buenos días, Don Ricardo."

"Buenos días, Lieutenant. What a beautiful brisk morning, but gracias a Dios, we're not at sea in such weather."

"Yes, sir. The crisp air reminds me of my home in Asturias."

"Me, too. As you know from my name, I'm from León. My family lives in the high country. Where is your home in Asturias?"

"Our land is located south of Oviedo, near the lower Cantabrian mountains." Dorado pushed the hair out of his eyes.

"So, we're neighbors separated only by the mountains. I haven't been home in years." He squinted his eyes and looked out to sea. "Dios mío! It's fifteen years ago. How time flies like an eagle after a field mouse. I still miss León very much."

"Yes, sir, especially this time of year. I think of the autumn leaves changing color and the cool breezes blowing down the mountains. I went home after the war and arrived in time to see everything in color. The hills looked to be full of every color in the rainbow."

"I can recall those days when I was a boy hunting in the woods with my father. It seems like only yesterday." Ruiz de León sighed. "Well, let's be on our way; we can talk as we go. By the time we get there the sun will be up and the light should be good." He patted Dorado's shoulder as they walked to the dugout canoe the lieutenant had requisitioned for their trip.

Several minutes later, gliding rapidly north on the current, the canoe passed the Castillo de San Marcos. Ruiz de León steered from the stern, while Dorado, kneeling on the bottom of the canoe, paddled from the bow. In the fast flowing current he worked leisurely, occasionally dipping his paddle into the water to guide the canoe.

"Tell me about your family, Lieutenant. Who now resides on your lands in Asturias?" Ruiz de León sat back on the stern seat and stretched his bad leg out in front of him.

Dorado, holding the paddle out of the water, looked over

his shoulder. "My mother, my oldest brother and his family and three younger sisters. There are six of us and I am the third son. My father served as an artillery captain in the last war and was severely wounded; he was shot in the chest, during the defense of Havana. They sent him home afterwards and he spent the rest of his life trying to manage our lands. He was only thirty-five when he died. My father was bedridden during his last three years and we played chess almost every day. He was a very good player." Dorado's eyes filled with tears and he turned his head forward. "Please pardon me, Don Ricardo, for speaking so long about such personal matters."

"No apologies are needed. I am honored you would speak to me of such matters."

Dorado turned forward to push a cluster of floating branches out of their way. He held the paddle against them as Ruiz de León steered the canoe away into deeper water. One of the branches, almost striking the captain, scraped bark off the stern as they passed.

"Sorry, sir," said Dorado as he looked back at his companion.

"It wasn't your fault. Please continue your account."

"My oldest brother, David, my father's namesake, holds the family lands. He cares for my mother, who is now quite sick, and raises my sisters as well as his own children. I do not envy him with so many responsibilities and property of limited worth. In spite of little salary, I prefer service in the king's army. My other brother, Miguel, is a captain of artillery in Cuba."

Ruiz de León nodded. "We've had similar experiences. My father also died of musket fire; it happened in the forties' war with England. He too was a captain, though in the infantry. I was ten years old when he died. My brother, Rafael, manages our lands; he's sixty-four and in good health. My mother has been dead twelve years. Dios mío! Where did the years go?"

"I was ten years old, too, when my father died."

"We do have much in common. Look out for that branch!"

Dorado quickly turned to see a thick tree limb in front of him. Extending over the river, the moss-covered limb was head-high and almost hit him. He barely had time to bend over as the swiftly moving canoe passed beneath the branch. It scraped his left shoulder as he ducked. He turned his head to see Ruiz de León lean out of the way.

Dorado was exhaling in relief when he saw the water snake in the canoe. Thick as a man's upper arm and at least four feet long, the big snake slithered toward Ruiz de León, who sat wide eyed in fear. Dorado stood up, almost capsizing the canoe.

He prodded the snake with his paddle even as the canoe shook perilously from side to side and water splashed inside. The snake twisted away from the paddle thrusts and turned to extend its huge brown head toward him. Dorado saw the snake's mouth open wide and fangs come into view. Repeatedly thrusting the paddle at the writhing snake, he tried desperately to keep it at bay while holding the canoe steady under his feet. He knew if it capsized, the deadly snake would be able to strike them both in the water.

Parrying his futile lunges like a skilled swordsman, the big snake suddenly curled itself around the shaft of the paddle and thrust its triangular head toward Dorado's hand. He gasped as the snake struck and missed his thumb by an inch. He instantly slid his hand upward to grip the paddle handle at its end. The snake's open mouth, cotton white inside, loomed before him as it coiled most of its length around the paddle and drew its head back for a second strike. He saw its forked tongue flick out and then its fangs flash toward his fingers as he cast the paddle out into the river. The snake disappeared as soon as it splashed into the water.

Dorado kneeled down in the canoe and took the paddle from Ruiz de León's hand. He used it to retrieve the other one floating in the river. Dorado reached for the paddle only when he was sure the venomous snake was no longer near it. He sat in the bow, drenched in sweat.

"Dios mío!" exclaimed Ruiz de León. "How did that thing get into the canoe?"

"It must have fallen from the tree when the limb hit my arm. I've seen them curled up on overhanging tree limbs before." Dorado inhaled deeply and expelled his breath loudly.

"Well done, Lieutenant. That snake could have killed us both."

Several minutes later, still carried on the current, the canoe reached the marshy shores north of the Castillo. They scanned the banks and shallows, but saw only a few turtles and a multitude of tiny fish in the water. At times, they paused to glance into the underbrush, where cypress trees stood in the water and Spanish moss and leafy vines obstructed their view of the interior. They saw no sign suggesting anyone had come that way by canoe. The overgrown shoreline and dense woods beyond looked impenetrable.

By mid-morning, they had worked their way well beyond the presidio's limits and were paddling close to the place where the girl's corpse had been discovered. Dorado knew the area from previous reconnaissance trips on the river. When they reached the dead tree lying on the bank, he pointed toward the shore. Ruiz de León turned the canoe about and paddling together they brought it into the shallows. Dorado pushed aside floating tree debris and water plants as the canoe glided into the thicket of thorns that had held the dead girl's skirt.

When the canoe came to a stop in the sand, Dorado climbed out of the canoe and tied it to a cypress root. "This is the place where I found her clothes. They were piled up over there." He pointed to the grass, five or six feet from the canoe. "I suggest we go ashore here, sir, and look around. I may have missed something when I searched here yesterday."

"Good idea. It'll also give us a chance to stretch our legs."

Dorado steadied the canoe as the captain struggled to climb over the stern. His bad leg had stiffened during their time in the canoe. Dorado did not offer him a hand. He knew Ruiz de León would be insulted by such a gesture.

After flexing his leg a few times, Ruiz de León followed Dorado through the weeds to the grassy patch of ground. "This is where her clothes were left," said Dorado. "Her body was dragged that way." He pointed through the underbrush.

Ruiz de León looked down at the ground. "Why don't you search in the woods? I'll look around here, where you found the clothing. We can then look at the other spot."

While Dorado walked into the woods, Ruiz de León got down on his knees and carefully searched the place. He raked his fingers through the grass, twigs, and pine needles and even looked beneath the dead leaves on the ground. Although painful for him to crawl on all fours, Ruiz de León looked everywhere, grimacing when his knees struck something hard or sharp. He heard Dorado thrashing through the woods as he searched the ground.

Ruiz de León finished before Dorado returned from his search in the surrounding area. The captain struggled painfully to his feet when he heard the sounds of snapping twigs coming closer. He did not want Dorado to see him in pain as he got up from the hard ground. He was flexing his leg as the young lieutenant walked out of the woods.

"I found nothing," said Dorado, frowning. "I only succeeded in startling a small rabbit in the bushes. What about you, Don Ricardo?"

"I didn't find anything either and I searched the entire place on my hands and knees," Ruiz de León sighed wearily. "Let's sit here awhile and then we can proceed to the other spot. There are no mosquitoes for the moment, thanks to the wind. These northeasters do have their good sides, I suppose. Gracias a Dios."

They sat on a cedar log lying alongside the river. The dead tree had been dragged there by Núñez, who stood on it when casting his fishing net into the river. From the log, they could watch the water rushing rapidly past them as well as flocks of pelicans in flight.

The birds were flying on and off an island in the river, about a hundred feet from where they were sitting. Thousands of pelicans nested on the mile-long stretch of sand and shells and the place was appropriately known as Pelican Island. The local townspeople typically ignored the ever present birds, not known to be tasty, and the pelicans avoided the presidio, only flying near it when fishing in the nearby bay.

On that windy day, the bird community was in chaos. Because of shifting crosswinds the pelicans could not smoothly take off and land on the island. The birds were graceful over the sea and adept aloft on the air currents, but too weighty to fly well over land. Hapless in the capricious wind that morning, they fell from above like so many brown stones in an avalanche. The pelicans collided with each other, sprayed sand and shells in all directions and awkwardly collapsed on their neighbors' nests. In the raucous commotion, their squawking stifled all other sound. Pecking and posturing with flapping wings, they were fighting all over the island.

"What a sight!" Dorado laughed. "It's like a comic puppet show with pelicans."

"It is indeed." Ruiz de León rubbed his sore knees which he had bruised while crawling on the ground. "They remind me of ourselves, fighting senseless wars without end. I wonder if we look like the foolish pelicans to God. We aren't that different from animals, you know."

"Do you mean in war – the way we fight?"

"No, the way we live. We spend our lives stuffing our

stomachs, satiating our lusts and blundering about without any meaningful purpose like those pelicans. We even fight endlessly over land and females as they do. There aren't nearly as many differences between the animals and us as we would like to believe."

"Of course, they lack souls and they don't know what's right and wrong. Nor do they know of God." Dorado pushed his hair out of his eyes.

"Verdad. We have such knowledge, but unfortunately not often the will to do what we know God wants of us." He glanced again at the pandemonium on Pelican Island. "I suppose we should finish our search and start back to town."

Dorado stood and stretched. "I wish we had found something here," he said making a face. "I doubt we will find anything near the palmetto. I looked everywhere there."

They spent another half hour searching around the palmetto, but found nothing new. Dorado walked quickly, while Ruiz de León seemingly scrutinized every inch of the site as well as the path that led from where the clothing had been found to the palmetto. He moved very slowly, his upper body bent over to examine the ground.

"I still think she came by canoe; it's the only sensible way here," said Dorado as they went back to the canoe.

"We could search again along the shore."

"No, I doubt if we missed seeing anything." Dorado frowned. "I guess we won't ever know how she got here."

"Quién sabe? It may yet be known in time."

The chaos on Pelican Island continued unabated as Ruiz de León steered their canoe away from the shore and into deeper water. They paddled slowly watching the frantic birds flying over the island. With the wind now blowing toward town, the canoe quickly reached the end of the sand bar. They stopped paddling and let the prevailing wind push them into the bay. As they passed the last of land, both men turned for a final look at the pelicans.

Staring at the island, Dorado saw something in the surf at the end of the island. He shielded his eyes to see it better. What he saw was partially buried in the sand and beaten by the surf as high tide flooded the shore.

"Look! There's something there at the end of the island. See it there?" Dorado pulled his paddle out of the water and pointed to the spot where it stood out in the sand.

"I see it."

They paddled hard to turn the canoe about. With the wind in their faces, it was difficult to point the bow toward the island. Once the canoe came about, they had to paddle against the water current as well as the wind. When they were finally secure in the shallows and close to the beach, Dorado leaped from the canoe and ran through the surf, holding his scabbard out of the water. Within seconds, he had reached the object in the sand.

"It's a canoe!" he shouted, seeing Ruiz de León limping toward him. Dorado kneeled in the sand and, cupping his hands, began scooping water out of the half-buried boat. He worked hurriedly, but the canoe was still full of water when Ruiz de León arrived at his side. Dorado was panting from his effort.

A thick layer of sand lay on the bottom of the canoe under at least a foot of water. Ruiz de León kneeled beside him and also scooped water out with his hands. When they had bailed out most of the water, Dorado removed as much of the sand as possible. He used a flat piece of broken wood he found nearby to scrape the sand from the bottom. He worked until the canoe was light enough to turn over. Dorado waited briefly as the remaining sand and water fell on the ground and then, when the canoe was righted, he began his search. It did not take long.

Dorado found the brown garment in the bow of the canoe. It had been rolled up tightly and shoved between the bow brace and the front seat. Soaked with salt water and full of sand, it was still easy to identify. A shower of wet sand cascaded from its folds when Dorado held it up to show Ruiz de León.

"Well, we've found what we were seeking," he said, with a broad smile. "Much more, in fact! Now, we know exactly how Gloria got out of town unnoticed." Dorado stood beside the canoe, one foot propped up on the bow.

"You were right, Lieutenant; she came here by canoe." Ruiz de León patted him on the shoulder. "Carlos will be pleased. Why don't we all meet tonight at my house for dinner?"

"Thank you, Don Ricardo. What time should I come?"

"Come at sunset. Carlos should be there by then. Let's tow the canoe back to town. It can be examined there for anything we might have missed. Let's hurry now before the current changes; it'll be moving south soon." Ruiz de León was weary from the long morning on his bad leg and looking forward to drying his wet feet in his office.

"Yes, sir. There's rope in our canoe, I'll get it."

It was midmorning when they paddled away. The wind and currents quickly carried them to the city dock. They said little on the return trip to town and parted company in the plaza. Ruiz de León walked to Government House, while Dorado went home to change his stockings. He stopped briefly to speak to the sentry at the pier on his way. Although wet, he held the brown garment under his arm.

The towed canoe was seen by two boys at the dock and soon became the main topic of conversation in the presidio. The boys also saw the bundle under Dorado's arm. By evening, everyone in town as well in the outlying homesteads had heard about what had been found on Pelican Island. By the end of the week, cattle ranchers as far away as Alachua (central Florida) were talking about the canoe and what it contained. Within a fortnight, all of East Florida knew about it and its meaning in the death of the governor's niece.

The canoe the girl had taken to her death was tied up at the dock. Anyone could see it from the seawall and, at high tide, the empty canoe could even be seen from the central plaza. Before the boat was found, what little was known about her death in the woods came from the two soldiers who brought her body back to town. What was unknown had become the subject of rumor and speculation. Most townspeople suspected she had been murdered, but whatever happened to her, the canoe she paddled to the woods that morning floated in plain sight at the city pier. It bobbed up and down on the current, reminding everyone of her mysterious death.

CHAPTER SIX

OCTOBER 3 – 10, 1788

Ruiz de León lived in a small cedar house at the south end of St. Augustine across from the army barracks. For most of the century, the barracks had been a Franciscan monastery and the nearby house had served as a dormitory for novices. During the twenty years of the British Period, both buildings had housed soldiers but, once contaminated by heretics, they were never used by the Franciscans again.

Ruiz de León bought the old house soon after coming to town. He had intended to pull down the building and put up a new house on the stone foundation. However, on the advice of Emiliano Orozco, a local carpenter, he had the house rebuilt.

"Don't waste your good money building a new house," counseled the toothless old man in a commanding tone. "The structure's sound and I can make it comfortable enough, even for a governor's aide."

The house needed a new roof, windows and a complete interior reconstruction, but even after six months of Orozco's carpentry, the renovation cost much less than a new building. The unexpected savings allowed Ruiz de León to add a few extra conveniences, which he could not otherwise have afforded. His rebuilt house included a bedroom separated from the main room and such luxuries as a cedar bath closet, oak furniture and a coquina fireplace for cooking inside and heating in the winter. The shellstone for the fireplace had come from the rubble left by the masons after a broken section of the seawall was replaced near his house.

The carpenter also constructed a second story balcony facing the bay. Cantilevered at the roof line, the balcony offered Ruiz de León a clear view of the ocean channel into the city, Santa Anastasia Island and the Matanzas River running southward to its inlet. He could even see the ocean farther in the distance beyond the island. A staircase built against the southeast wall reached the balcony door from inside his house. Favoring his bad leg, Ruiz de León was able to mount the eleven steps of the stairway one step at a time. He climbed the stairs holding a wooden railing that was nailed to the wall. Once outside on the balcony, Ruiz de León would often sit in a sun-bleached straw chair, looking for groups of porpoises or the occasional whale that chanced to enter the bay.

Awake early, Ruiz de León began each day on the balcony. He never tired of seeing the sun rise up over the sea and imagined it as a Spanish conquistador casting out his shining cape to seize the morning sky. Looking into the distance, he often thought of his faraway homeland in Spain separated from Florida by the infinite ocean he could see from the balcony. At sunset, he enjoyed an aged brandy on the balcony alone or with Carlos Martínez on the evenings when the big man came to dinner.

Ruiz de León spent most of his money on the house. The cost of construction consumed his savings and the tiny inheritance left him by his mother's spinster sister. Despite a lifetime of frugal living, the captain had little money to show for thirty-five years of poorly-paid service in the king's army. Only seven silver coins remained in his money box when he handed Orozco his last payment. Despite that pittance, Ruiz de León knew the house was well worth the cost since he had decided to live in St. Augustine for whatever number of years were left to him.

It was ten o'clock and the three men were still talking in the main room of the house. They sat at the table after dinner and a lingering look at a colorful sunset from the balcony. Purple and pink clouds had covered the eastern sky as a brisk wind blew in from the ocean. They went inside when the sky darkened and the wind increased in intensity. Ruiz de León gave each of his guests a glass of brandy as they settled in their chairs. He then lit the table lamp and placed his chess board between Dorado and Martínez.

Dorado played one game with Martínez and two games with Ruiz de León. He easily beat the big man because of a careless move which cost him a castle and gave Dorado a clear opening to check his king. Martínez was semi-drunk and swore loudly at the time. A moment later, when Martínez saw the coming checkmate, he struck the chessboard with his huge hand, scattering the pieces across the floor. Disgruntled, he sprawled on the floor and propped his head against the east wall. He set the glass of brandy on his stomach.

Dorado did not do as well playing against Ruiz de León. He barely escaped defeat with a draw in the first game, but lost the next one decisively. The game lasted a long time, but the end result was never in doubt.

As the men played chess, they heard the wind blowing outside and the shutters rattling on a neighbor's house. It rained hard on and off throughout the evening, but let up after eight o'clock. The wind also let up, but they still could hear the waves washing over the seawall.

"Let's hope it doesn't rain any harder or the town will be under water again. It's only raining lightly at the moment." Martínez, who had just returned from the outhouse, spoke as Ruiz de León was putting his chess pieces in a box. The doctor stretched out on the floor in a corner of the room, while Dorado and Ruiz de León sat facing him across a blue and burgundy Persian rug. Faded and worn, the rug had been purchased years earlier in Granada.

"I certainly hope so. The last storm flooded all this side of the city. My house was one of the few off the bay without water in the first floor. Gracias a Dios for old Emiliano Orozco. He raised the foundation because of his fear of flooding."

"Didn't he die recently?" Martínez yawned loudly. "It seems to me a patient told me about his death awhile ago."

"He died in August. The old man was seventy-seven and never sick a day in his life. He died in his sleep." Ruiz de León sat in his favorite chair facing the window on the bay.

"We should all die in our sleep." Martínez belched. "Well, Ricardo, that's one way to taste your delicious food again."

Ruiz de León turned his mouth down in disgust.

"You know, I liked that crabby old carpenter. He had cojones grandes (big balls). The viejo (old man) said whatever he wanted to anyone who annoyed him. It didn't matter who he was. Once, I heard him giving the governor some of his spleen. Zéspedes made a suggestion about the chest Orozco was making for him and the old man snarled, 'If you don't like the way I'm doing it, you do it!'"

Ruiz de León smiled. "What did the governor say?"

"Nothing. Zéspedes showed Orozco one of his little knowing smiles and walked away without saying a word." Martínez chuckled recalling the expression on the governor's face.

"Well, Orozco was a good carpenter, even if grumpy. This

house is as sound as a gold escudo. The walls are so well caulked the wind never gets in – even on the north side."

"It is solid." Martínez sat up and leaned his back against the wall. "Well, Lieutenant, let's hear what you discovered. Knowing the lord of this castle, I'm sure he told you to wait until after dinner to talk about the investigation."

"I did, indeed. As you know, it's a custom of my family in León. We never talk about anything serious during dinner. I hear it's also the king's custom at court. Do begin, Dorado."

"Yes, sir." Dorado described everything that happened that morning from the time they left the pier until they returned to town at midday.

"Well done, Lieutenant." Martínez nodded. "It was as you suspected – she went by canoe. One of our questions has been answered."

"We've answered another question as well, sir." Dorado looked back and forth between the two other men. "We also know how Gloria got out of the city without being seen."

"You are referring to the monk's habit found in the canoe?" Martínez pointed to the brown bundle lying on the floor.

"Yes, sir. No one saw her because she wore the hooded monk's habit that morning. She simply walked to the pier, took a canoe, and paddled away. It was that easy. No one recognized her. She was seen as simply another Franciscan monk going up river."

Martínez nodded.

"The sentry at the pier, Alberto Alvarez, saw her take the canoe and paddle up river. I spoke to him today when we returned from Pelican Island. Of course, in the habit, he thought she was a monk. Alvarez remembered the monk because he thought it strange he had his hood up on such a humid morning. Alvarez said nothing to the monk about it since he assumed the man might be following some form of penance. He had seen the Franciscans do other unusual things in the past since he sees them every day. On his morning shift, they take the canoes and paddle upriver to the Indian villages."

"Didn't she look much smaller than the other monks?" Martínez looked up at Dorado.

"Alvarez said nothing about the monk's size."

"So, I assume she left Government House in the same disguise?" Martínez moved his eyes to Ruiz de León.

"Yes. We now know exactly how she did it." Ruiz de León paused to sip his brandy. "Do either of you want another glass of brandy? The bottle is about empty. No?" He saw his guests shake their heads. "I'll finish it then."

"Cuidado, Ricardo, you could become a wine connoisseur like me." Martínez laughed.

Ruiz de León shook his head. "I doubt it. Anyway, we now know a sentry did see the girl leave Government House in the monk's habit that morning. In fact, he knew a day earlier of her scheme. Gloria told the sentry, Juan Solís, she was playing a prank on her cousin. Solís was quite taken with her, so he did as she asked and said nothing as she went out the building. She probably put the habit over her clothes on the first floor – perhaps, in one of those closets in the hall. She walked away well-disguised, without a worry."

Dorado wondered if she put the monk's habit on in the closet where they had embraced so passionately. He blushed thinking about it, but no one noticed his flushed face.

Martínez smiled. "What a clever girl. No wonder she wasn't seen anywhere in town."

"Of course, Solís said nothing when he heard what happened to her. He lived in dread of being blamed for her death. Solís was terrified he would be court-martialed and then sent to 'a dark dungeon in the Castillo,' those were his words, where he would be tortured for hours." Ruiz de León smiled. "Afterward, he expected to be hung in the plaza – in front of everyone."

They all laughed.

"Dios mío! What ignorance!" Martinez snickered. "Does Solís think some priest from the Inquisition will put him on the rack? Tell me, where do they find these soldiers? Portugal? How did you get the doomed man to admit what happened?"

"It was surprisingly easy. I looked at the sentries' duty roster for the morning shift and Juan Solís was on the roster for duty that day at the main door. So, I called him into my office; he was on duty in the hall today. His face was as white as the walls when he arrived. Seeing his obvious fear, I knew he was involved. I told him I knew everything and expected him to confess. That's all there was to it. He told me what happened and then got down on his knees and begged for mercy. He said he didn't want to die so young."

The three men laughed in unison.

"Where in God's name did Solís get such a notion?" Martínez shook his head. "Has he been reading Las Casas about Spanish cruelty in the conquest of the New World? No, I'm sure Solís can't read a word. What ignorance! Where is that fool from – Minorca?"

"He's from the Canary Islands."

"What happened then, sir?" asked Dorado, still smiling.

"I assured him he would not be tortured or hung, but would be severely punished for his dereliction of duty. He was still on his knees, crying like a baby."

"If you used the words 'dereliction of duty,' I'm sure he still expected to be tortured and hung in the plaza." Martínez rubbed his hand over his head.

"I told him the governor would decide his punishment."

"He's lucky the commandant isn't deciding his fate."

"Indeed. Knowing the governor's leniency, I expect Solís will get away with some hard physical labor – like a road repair detail."

"He should be sent on permanent patrol to the swamps." Martínez finished his brandy. "So much for Solís. We now need to know why Gloria went to the woods. It's time to talk to anyone who knew her – her cousins, friends and even Doña Concepcíon."

Ruiz de León nodded. "I'll talk to Concepcíon. I doubt the girl knew anyone outside Government House. She was carefully chaperoned whenever she went into town."

"We also need to know how the murderer went out to the woods." Martínez stood up and stretched. "Lieutenant, speak to Alvarez again. Ask him if anyone else took a canoe that morning other than the monks. Although I think it unlikely, maybe the murderer also took a canoe out to the woods."

"With your permission, sir, I have a couple of suggestions." Dorado stood and, seeing Martínez nod, he continued speaking. "I think it would be useful to speak to the sentries at the city gates. They might remember who left the presidio that morning on foot or horseback."

"That's a good idea, Lieutenant." Ruiz de León looked at Dorado.

Martínez nodded. "Ask them if anyone unusual left the presidio that morning. What else do you suggest?"

"I think the master of the stables should be questioned about who requisitioned a horse early that morning. Maybe the murderer rode a horse to the woods."

"Good thinking, Lieutenant." Ruiz de León laid a hand on Dorado's shoulder. "Let's meet again in two days' time. We can talk about what we have discovered then. Come at dusk, we'll eat first. Perhaps, there will be time to play a little chess as well."

"Be careful, Lieutenant." Martínez pointed his forefinger at Ruiz de León. "He wants your scalp on his belt. Mine's there already."

"We'll see. I hope to do better next time."

"I'll look forward to another delicious dinner, Ricardo." Martínez smiled. "As you can see, Lieutenant, the governor's aide sets a fine table. Where else in this bleak town would you eat fresh flounder in lemon sauce or any better beans and rice? Who else, except the governor, serves such fine red wine from Castilla? Such luxuries aren't usually available on a captain's table in the colonies, even in Havana."

"That's enough, Carlos. Thank you for your compliments, Lieutenant."

"No, such fine food is not at all common in the colonies. Surely not here in this frontier presidio, where most of us pay little old ladies to cook our simple meals and keep our houses in order. But not in Ricardo's little castle. Oh, no! The widow woman next door, Señora Salgado, comes in nightly with specially prepared foods for him, as you have seen. It's only possible if you have family wealth or large land holdings in Spain." He grinned at Ruiz de León.

"That's quite enough, Carlos! As you well know, I'm not wealthy. I simply like good food and I'm willing to pay the cost." Ruiz de León smiled at Dorado. "I enjoyed our games. Let's play again soon – the two of us. We can devote an evening to chess when Carlos is busy with – what's her name? Oh yes, María Valdez."

"You know her name." Martínez smiled.

"Thank you for your hospitality, Don Ricardo."

"Mi casa es su casa."

"Muchas gracias, señor." Dorado saluted both men before walking to the door.

A biting wind blew through St. Augustine that night following the rain. It came from the north and carried a damp chill off the sea. During the night, the temperature fell steadily into the forties until the morning sun warmed the town. The cold snap killed the last of the vegetable plants and the wind invaded every house in town. In spite of tightly sealed doors and windows, the wind found its way inside through long neglected cracks and gaps in the shutters. It was a night when the townspeople went to bed early simply to escape the cold.

Outside on the street, Martínez led the way in the dark with Dorado following behind him. He took a path between two houses that brought them into the Street of Merchants, one of the three main thoroughfares in town. Lanterns lit the street, helping them avoid potholes in their way. The two men shivered as they hurried toward the plaza. Their turned up collars did little to shield their faces from the wind. It brought tears to their eyes and stung their ears and noses. Buried in pockets, only their hands were spared the biting cold.

"This is unusually cold for October." Martínez pulled his coat collar up trying to keep the wind off his neck. "I hope it's not a sign of a bitter winter to come."

"How cold does it get here in St. Augustine?" Dorado, shivering, looked at the big man beside him. "I thought the weather in Florida would be much like Havana."

"No, here we get some winter. We get a freeze or two, but they don't last long. Three or four days, at most. They say the hard freezes are needed to kill off some of the biting flies and mosquitoes. I'll gladly suffer the cold if it lessens the number of those blood suckers."

"I agree. I surely haven't missed them these last few days."

"No one misses them. As you know, the absence of mosquitoes and the girl's murder are the main topics of conversation in town."

Before the plaza, Martínez stopped at the intersection of a small side street. It ran west for two blocks from the bay front. In the darkness, the narrow street was difficult to see from where they walked in the middle of the road.

"I'll leave you here, Lieutenant. I live down the street. Buenas noches."

"Buenas noches, señor." Dorado saluted and turned to leave.

"Lieutenant!" Martínez' voice stopped him.

Dorado looked over his shoulder. In the dark, he could barely see the outline of the big man only a few feet away. "Yes, sir."

"This Saturday, at sunset, Serena Rodríguez will be in the plaza. Quien sabe? Perhaps, she will be willing to talk to you." Martínez chortled and then disappeared into the darkness.

Saturday morning seemed warmer with the sun bright in an almost cloudless blue sky. The cold weather had ended. A brisk wind still blew in from the northeast, but by afternoon, it had abated and become a light breeze. The bay remained choppy until the tide turned that evening.

In the middle of the afternoon, Lieutenant Arturo Robles Rivera, Officer of the Guard that day, shouted to Martínez as he was leaving his office to see a sick soldier in town.

"Captain Martínez." Robles ran to him from the entrance of the Castillo.

Martínez, who was locking his office door, turned to Robles. "Yes, what is it?"

"Sir, another body has been found. I was just notified." The lieutenant, a new officer from Havana, had heard about the sarcastic captain and was afraid of what he might say.

"Mierda! A girl?" Martínez stared at the young lieutenant.

"Yes, sir." Robles nodded, bobbing his head up and down.

"Where's the body?" Martínez exhaled his breath loudly.

"What was left of her was found on Santa Anastasia Island, sir."

"What was left of her?" Martínez glared at Robles. "Speak up – what do you mean?"

"Alligators g-got her, sir," he stammered.

"Dios mío! Who reported the body?"

He pointed to the two soldiers standing at the entrance

to the fort. "Sergeant Casasola sent Artigas and Santana to report it. They have a boat waiting to take you over to the island."

"I see. Go inform the commandant of the body and tell him I'm on my way to examine it. Don't stand there gawking at me, Lieutenant, go!"

A half hour later, after a rough trip in the rolling rowboat, Martínez stood looking down at the covered corpse. Sergeant Casasola, shivering in the wind, had placed his overcoat on the body. He and four other soldiers huddled around Martínez.

"Here's your coat, Sergeant." Martínez knelt down on the ground and handed the coat up to Casasola. "Move the men back, they're in my light."

"You heard the captain, stand back." Casasola motioned the soldiers to a spot several feet away. They stood nervously watching the doctor examine the body.

Martínez looked at the mutilated body. Both arms were gone as well as her left leg and her right foot. The skin on her torso was scraped raw. Gaping holes dotted her head and chest and a tooth was stuck in one of the holes in her chin. The girl's head had been crushed and her face so flattened it lacked discernible features. What pieces of clothing remained on her body were stained from blood. One of the pieces covered her breasts and crotch. A silver crucifix around her neck was the only thing on her corpse that appeared intact.

"Where was she found?" Martínez knew the body had been carried to where it lay on the ground. He looked up at the five pale-faced soldiers, who stood awkwardly shifting their feet from side to side.

"Over there, sir." Casasola pointed a trembling finger at the pond in front of them. "We found the body at the water's edge and carried it here away from the alligators. I put what little clothing was left over her."

"Well done, Sergeant. Now, send one of your men to get that piece of canvas I brought in the boat. Use it to wrap up the girl's body and put it in the boat." Martínez stood and walked to the edge of the pond.

The tidal stream flowed a quarter mile from the bay and widened at that point to create a large pond of brackish water. Looking over the pond, Martínez was surprised to see so many alligators in one place. He stopped counting their floating heads when he reached twenty-five. He also saw several mounds of beach debris on the other side of the pond which he knew were nests where the alligators laid their eggs.

An overturned canoe floated in the shallows. Caught in the weeds, it moved only when the wind rippled the water. Martínez looked over the pond, but did not see the canoe's paddles. "Did you find the paddles," he asked Casasola, who had followed him to the water's edge."

"No, sir. They're not under the canoe either. I looked myself."

"How did you find the body, Sergeant? Do you come this way on patrol?"

"Yes, sir. That's how we found the body. We come this way on patrol; it's the best way to cover our section of the island. Once we reach the creek, we go overland to the sea."

Martínez smiled. "Tell me the truth, Sergeant. You come overland this way looking for wild boar. I've heard they burrow somewhere around here."

"Sí, señor." Casasola looked down at his feet. "But it's still a good way to cover ..."

Annoyed, Martínez scowled at him. "Just tell me what happened, Sergeant."

"Sí, señor. As we walked here from the bay, we heard a lot of hissing and splashing in the pond. Then we saw the girl's body. There must've been at least ten alligators fighting over it. We shot a couple and, when they went for the wounded ones, we carried it here."

Martínez nodded. "I want this entire area searched thoroughly, Sergeant. That means all around the pond.

Now, tell your men to drag the canoe up on shore. Let's see what's in it."

Dorado spent most of Saturday thinking about Serena Rodríguez. She was in his mind from the time he awoke until he set out to meet her at sunset. Over and over, Dorado pictured her face as she initially turned to look at him in the plaza. Her big brown eyes entranced him then and, now, in his thoughts, she stared lovingly at him. Impatient to be with her, time passed much too slowly for him, even though he had been busy from breakfast to lunchtime.

Nagged by the widow Sánchez, who incessantly mothered him, he ate a hearty breakfast of fried bread, bacon, honey cake and tea. Although not hungry after eating everything she put before him, Dorado could not refuse the cake, which she had made specially for him. The old woman sat with him and watched as he ate the large piece she had placed on his plate. He saw her delighted smile when he finished the cake and used his fork to spear every last crumb.

Dorado spent the morning interviewing the presidio's sentries. He spoke to every man who had guard duty the day of the murder. He walked all over town from the central plaza and pier to the southern end of Royal Street and, then, to the city gates and the Castillo. He missed speaking to only one man on his list, the master of the stables, who was sick in bed with a high fever. Despite all his effort, he had learned nothing new.

Tired and thirsty, Dorado left the fort and went to a tavern near the city gates. Nodding to two vegetable vendors he recognized at a table near the door, he went to the rear of the room and sat at an empty table. He ordered a bottle of cheap wine and impatiently tapped his fingers on the table until the scowling bartender brought it to him. Dorado drank three glasses of wine and then leaned back in his chair and stretched his legs out under the table. He closed his eyes for a few moments and fell asleep. A man's loud voice awakened him.

"Lieutenant. Lieutenant Dorado Delgado."

"Sí." Dorado opened his eyes abruptly and sat up straight in his chair. A townsman stood beside his table. Short and muscular, the man had thick gray hair and a beard to match.

"Pardon, Teniente. May I speak to you a moment?"

"Yes, of course." Dorado gestured him to the chair opposite him.

"My name is Francisco Urquiza." The man sat down on the edge of the seat. "I'm the blacksmith at the north end of the street."

Dorado nodded. "Have we met before?"

"No." The blacksmith rested his brawny forearms on the table. "But I have something to tell you about the governor's niece."

Dorado leaned forward. "What is it?"

"I'm not sure it's important, but I heard her talking to someone at Government House, uh, two days before she died."

"Tell me about it." Dorado looked Urquiza in the eyes.

The blacksmith glanced away at his three companions, who sat at a table near the door. "It happened when I went to Government House to get paid for shoeing the governor's stallion. I was told to wait in the garden, uh, until Sergeant Suárez would pay me. I charge the governor and the army seven pesetas. Everyone else charges eight pesetas for shoes."

"I see." Dorado sat with his arms crossed over his chest.

"The governor's niece was picking flowers when I, uh, went into the garden. She went inside as I came to the back door. As I stood there waiting for Sergeant Suarez, uh, I heard her speaking to someone. I could tell she was angry."

"How do you know she was angry?"

"She shouted, 'That's stupid! I won't do it!'"

"Did she say anything else? Dorado saw the blacksmith shake his head. "What about the other – a man I assume?"

"It was a man's voice I heard, uh, but he was farther away so I didn't hear all he said. I did hear him say, 'Don't do it then, but if you want to ...' I didn't hear the rest of what he said. She said something else, but I couldn't hear it. I think she was walking away at the time."

"Did you hear anything else?"

"No, nothing except a door closing."

"I don't suppose you know whose voice you heard?"

"No, he was too far away, uh, to be heard clearly. That's all I know." The blacksmith saw his companions getting up to leave. "I must leave now, Lieutenant. I hope what I heard, uh, will help you with the investigation."

"We'll see. Thank you for speaking to me, Señor Urquiza." Dorado and the blacksmith rose from the table at the same time. "I've one more question, Señor Urquiza. Can you wait a moment longer?" Dorado saw the blacksmith nod his head. "How long after that conversation did Sergeant Suárez come out to the garden to pay you?"

Urquiza paused to remember. "A minute or so later."

"How did he look?"

The blacksmith frowned. "The same as always."

When he saw the sun starting to settle above the western woods, Dorado began to get ready to meet Serena Rodríguez. Using a handheld mirror, he shaved slowly and carefully, but still managed to nick his left earlobe with the razor. "Mierda!" he shouted, stemming the bleeding with his forefinger and thumb.

Dorado trimmed his mustache without incident and then soaped his face and neck. He stood nude facing the dresser where Señora Sánchez had placed a ceramic basin full of heated water. Dunking his head into the basin, Dorado washed his face and hair in the water. He then used a soapy cloth to wash to rest of his body. After rinsing off, he dried himself with a towel and dressed slowly, putting on his best shirt and the uniform he saved for important occasions. He had polished his boots earlier and put them on after he was dressed. Ready to leave, Dorado looked at his watch and saw it was only five o'clock. With an hour left before sunset, he waited in his room rather than walk to the plaza and stand there conspicuously looking for her to arrive.

Instead, Dorado spent the next hour daydreaming about Serena Rodríguez. Lying on his back in bed, his hands cupped behind his head, he closed his eyes and pictured Serena in his room. He saw her prancing toward him, removing pieces of clothing as she came. Naked beside his bed, Serena leaned over and covered his face with wet kisses and then pounced on him, pressing her breasts against his chest. Over and over, he saw her loving him in his bed.

Fifty minutes had passed when Dorado got up to leave. He was in no hurry since the plaza was only a short walk from his rooms, which he termed the small upstairs bedroom and sitting nook rented from Señora Sánchez. Before leaving, Dorado washed his face once again, combed his mustache and then placed his powdered wig on his head. He looked in the mirror for the last time and descended the stairway to the sitting room.

Señora Sánchez was there awaiting him. "La señorita will be unable to resist you," the old woman said as she scrutinized him. She smiled as he bent down to kiss her on the cheek.

The plaza was full of people when Dorado arrived at six o'clock. It was a market day and the townspeople were shopping for food and other goods sold in the vendors' stalls. Some of the families, finished shopping, sat on the seawall watching the porpoises swim by. Others strolled leisurely around, talking to people they knew. Brisk and bright without a cloud in the sky, the mild afternoon brought almost everyone in the presidio to the central plaza. Children ran about wildly, laughing and screaming as they played hide-and-seek among the crowds of conversing people. Groups of off-duty soldiers looked over the unmarried girls, who walked by them, flirting with their eyes. It was a pleasant day after the cold night and the townspeople came out to enjoy the fresh air and the company of their friends and neighbors.

Dorado spent several minutes amid the milling crowd searching for Serena Rodríguez. He looked everywhere, but did not see her. Inhaling the smell of sweating people, he frowned and went to a less crowded spot in the center of the plaza. At last, he saw Serena walking with María Valdez on the east side of the square where the vegetable vendors had their stalls. Both women were wearing white shawls on their heads.

Dorado wend his way to her through the throng of townspeople and soldiers, some who saluted him or said hello. He smiled at two young girls who stared boldly at him and saluted an infantry captain as he passed them. María Valdez was busy bargaining for vegetables when he walked over to where they were standing. Startled, Serena blushed and María gave him a grim look during their greetings. María turned to Dorado when she had completed her purchases and carefully looked him over. She held a woven bag full of greens and groceries and Serena held another heavier one with flour and rice.

"Ah, Lieutenant. How are you today? I hear you men enjoyed yourselves last night. And did you drink too much, too?" She went on speaking without waiting for answers to her questions. "One must wonder how much you men can eat and drink in one night. Of course, it's well known how much Captain Martínez can consume at any time. It shows, too, as anyone can clearly see!" María rolled her eyes. "Nothing to say, Lieutenant? It's true and you know it. I suppose you spent all night playing chess?" She looked at Serena. "At least, that's what they say they do."

"That's exactly what we did." Dorado nodded to Serena.

María waved his words away and went on complaining as if Dorado had not spoken. "They're supposed to play chess twice a week, at most, but, now, it seems Friday is to be set aside as a men's night as well." She glared at Dorado, a lined frown between her eyes.

"We only played a little chess; we spent most of our time discussing the investigation."

"Why is it that such meetings aren't held during the day?" She scowled at Dorado. "I guess the governor's aide is too busy then. Of course, he holds court anytime he wants. His inferiors come whenever he requires. There's no woman in his life so what does he care."

Dorado said nothing, knowing his words would be disregarded. Though he wanted to look at Serena, he politely listened to María. He found it hard to listen to her since she seemed so much like her sister, Esperanza Chávez. "They are the sullen sisters," he thought.

"Well," María continued, "let's hope the murderer is arrested soon! Everyone will be relieved. Don't look at me that way, Lieutenant. Everyone knows the girl was murdered, even if no one in Government House admits it. We know they never tell us the truth."

Dorado kept silent.

She glared at him. "Esperanza is right. Gloria is the second girl killed in St. Augustine. These last years have been awful here – one calamity after another. It's no wonder. What with the surly looking Indians coming and going as they please and the freed slaves everywhere you look – never mind the miserable Minorcans."

Dorado said nothing.

María stepped closer and took his arm. She squinted and looked about for anyone near who might hear what she was saying. She lowered her voice, almost whispering.

"We must watch our backs with the Minorcans. God knows there isn't anything awful they wouldn't do. They're forever squabbling and stabbing each other with knives. This place is full of foreigners and colored people who don't speak Spanish. It's not safe here – not at all! Before the governor's niece was killed, that man Delaney was murdered, too. Then there's the Parral girl. One of them Minorcans or indigentes (low class people) probably killed them all."

"Delaney? Who was he?"

"Serena will tell you what happened to him. She knows all we know." María looked at Serena and gently squeezed her arm. "I'll finish the shopping. Go on now and enjoy this lovely afternoon." She took the bag from Serena and shooed them away with a wave of her hand.

They walked side-by-side toward the bay front. Dorado looked over at Serena. "It is a beautiful day, isn't it?"

"Yes, especially at this time with the sun setting."

As Dorado strolled along beside her, Serena studied his profile out of the corner of her eye. She liked his looks and had found him attractive the day she met him in the plaza. Serena told her cousins how she felt about him on their way home. Then, to her delight, she heard that Dorado wanted to meet her. Serena had waited impatiently for Saturday to come and now here she was walking beside him in the plaza. Dorado fit all her fantasies, but she worried he would never take her seriously because of her common background. She knew about his aristocratic ancestry in Spain and worried his noble family would consider her unacceptable, except as his mistress. But now walking close to him, the hem of her dress brushing against his leg, she put aside her fears and let her happiness fill her mind.

"The cool weather feels refreshing, especially after last week." Serena watched Dorado as he returned the salute of a soldier passing them.

"It does. Without the humidity, it's almost like autumn at home. I'm from the mountain country of Asturias. Where are you from?"

"I was born in Andalucía in a village along the coast of Málaga. Have you ever been to Málaga?" Serena focused her brown eyes on him and smiled.

"No. I've visited Sevilla, but not the southeast."

Their eyes met briefly and then moved to the path ahead. They talked as they strolled about the central plaza, sometimes looking at each other openly and other times surreptitiously out of the corners of their eyes. They talked into the early evening without any notion of the number of times they went around the plaza.

"When did your family move to Havana? I was stationed there for eighteen months before coming to Florida." Dorado stepped aside abruptly to let a little boy run by him. "I've been away from home three years now and, at times, it seems much longer than that."

"My family went to Cuba when I was a small child. Don Antonio María Bucareli was governor then and my father was his accountant. My parents died of the plague in 1779. So did my two-year-old brother, Rafael. Havana was full of the plagues at that time."

"They say the plagues killed hundreds of people. It was Yellow Fever, wasn't it?"

"Yes. It did horrible things to people before they died." She paused to look at Dorado. "I'm glad I wasn't allowed to see my parents, though I sobbed at the time. Now, I thank God I didn't see what the sickness did to them."

"I understand the victims turned yellow and vomited up a black substance before they died." Seeing Serena turn away, Dorado apologized. "I'm sorry, that was stupid of me."

She nodded. "I was only eight years old when they died. Our cousins, the Chávez family, took me and my sister, Isabella, into their home. We were raised by Esperanza and

María's mother, Mama Claudia. I'll never forget what she did for us. She treated us like her own children in every way. Gracias a Dios, Mama Claudia is still alive and well."

While Serena spoke, Dorado looked sideways at her. Although certainly not beautiful, he found her to be a comely-looking woman with clean white teeth and fair skin. Her luxurious brown hair was beautiful. A pock mark below her right ear, the size of a small button, was the one blemish on her face. Dorado felt proud to walk with her in view of everyone in the plaza.

"Where is your sister, now?"

"Isabella married Lieutenant Raúl Navarro Ospina three years ago. They haven't any children yet. I haven't seen her in a long time since she lives far from Havana in Trinidad. I miss her." Serena stopped and turned to him with a soft smile. "Tell me about yourself."

When they reached the bay, Dorado led Serena to a spot on the seawall south of the city docks. It was a quiet spot away from the noise in the plaza. Once seated, he told her about his earlier life. He spoke about his family in Asturias, his brother in Cuba and his life in the king's service. Dorado also talked about his homeland in the Cantabrian mountain country.

"I like Florida, although at times I find the heat intolerable. It makes me wish for the cool air that blows down from the mountains. The last few days here remind me of home."

"I'm accustomed to the heat here, it's like Havana."

"Will you be in St. Augustine long?"

"I don't know. María and Esperanza want me to stay on and there's nothing in Havana that makes me want to go back." Serena sighed. "I like it here, too. It's quiet and peaceful. At least, it was until the death of the governor's niece. Do you know if she was murdered?"

Dorado frowned and then looked out into the bay.

"You are not allowed to say anything, are you?" Serena

saw him nod his head. "Well, everyone thinks she was murdered and most women here are fearful. Many now won't leave their houses without a man beside them. And those women without husbands hesitate to leave their homes except in the full light of day."

"I understand. But be assured an investigation is now in progress."

"Are you involved in it?" Serena looked into his eyes.

Dorado nodded. "What made you want to come to St. Augustine?" he asked, anxious to change the subject. He also remembered Uncle Ernesto's words of advice. His uncle had said, "Women will warm to you if you ask them about their lives."

"I came to visit my cousins. I'm staying with Esperanza." Serena sighed, deciding to tell him what María had urged her to keep from him. "He doesn't need know it," she had said. "You never know what a man will think of what you tell them."

Dorado wondered why she had sighed and looked away from him.

Serena met his eyes and then shyly lowered her eyelids. "I came to Florida to avoid the attention of someone – someone who persists in courting me against my wishes. Although I have told him I'll not marry him, he continues to pursue me. Nothing I say seems to discourage him. So, I came to St. Augustine on the advice of Mama Claudia."

"Who is the man?" Dorado looked intently at her.

"It doesn't matter who he is. What matters is that I am not interested in him." Serena looked directly at Dorado without lowering her eyelids.

"Who is he? Tell me ... please." Dorado wanted to reach over and touch her hand, but he hesitated to be too forward.

"He's a man of prominence in Havana. That's all I will say."

"I see." Dorado was annoyed that she would not tell him the man's name. He glanced at a passing family and then back at Serena. Their eyes met and Dorado decided to wait before asking her about the man again. It was time to change the subject.

"Tell me about the murder of that man, Delaney." He shifted his backside on the wall and crossed his legs.

"I don't know much except what María told me. It happened in 1785. The man's name was Lieutenant William Delaney. He was struck down one night by two men in hooded cloaks. It happened outside the house of a disreputable woman named Catalina Morain."

"Was she a Minorcan?"

"No. The woman was a foreign seamstress from the north. She supposedly lived here sewing for our soldiers. It's said Delaney was killed over her." She raised an eyebrow. "I don't think they ever found the murderer. The woman herself was suspected. She's no longer here."

"How was Delaney killed?"

"He was stabbed to death in the dark."

"Stabbed! Is that so?" Dorado looked at Serena. He was tempted to ask if Delaney was mutilated in any way, but knew the townspeople would not have been told such things.

"That's what I heard. The governor sent the case to Havana for settlement. There were many accusations and witnesses. No one seems to know how it ended." She shrugged.

"So, no one was arrested for the murder?" Dorado found Serena looking over his face. He smiled, but she had already looked away. Dorado recalled his uncle saying if a woman ran her eyes over a man's face, she would surrender everything to him. He wondered if it were true.

"That's what María told me."

"This presidio has had more than its share of trouble since we returned here – only five years ago. What with the murders, the disappearance of the girl in 1784 and all the foreigners here – this must be a frightening place for our people. Dios mío, you cannot walk anywhere in town without hearing foreign languages. At times, St. Augustine doesn't seem Spanish at all."

Serena nodded. "It's true, there're too many foreigners in this town. It doesn't feel like Havana. The king seems so far away from us here."

"True! There are especially too many Protestants." Dorado believed the murderer was Protestant. He could not imagine a Catholic cutting a cross on the naked corpse of a woman. "No," he thought, "none of our people would do such a thing. Whoever had murdered Gloria had mimicked the crucifixion. It was too blasphemous an act for a Catholic to commit. It was an act insulting God as well as murder.

"Lástima (sadly) there are more of them than us in St. Augustine," Serena sighed. "Gracias a Dios we have the king's soldiers here to protect us."

"It's true. Poor St. Augustine; so far from Spain and so close to the English colonies."

"You know what's said about this town, don't you? I've heard it ever since I arrived."

"What do they say?" Dorado studied Serena's face as she spoke.

"They say St. Augustine is cursed."

Dorado frowned. "Cursed! What curse?"

"God's curse. They say the city has been cursed because of evil deeds done in the past. That's why it has suffered from fire, floods, war and even starvation. Everyone says it."

"I don't know about the past, but I do know the presidio has suffered much throughout this century. You only have to look around to see what's happened here." Dorado waved his hand at the bared foundations, broken-down houses and rubble piles standing all along the bay front. Of course, much of the destruction in town was here when our troops returned after the war. The English left the presidio in ruins."

Serena nodded. "Most of our people complain about living here. Esperanza isn't the only one. There's been so much misery – it's easy to believe St. Augustine is cursed."

"I suppose so. Our soldiers complain about living here, too. No one likes this remote place and many officers have requested transfers. They complain about the shortage of pretty young women in town. Until very recently, I complained, too."

Serena blushed and lowered her eyes. "It's time to leave, now. It's getting late and I want to help with dinner." She accepted Dorado's hand as she stepped down from the wall.

"Look, Serena." Dorado touched her shoulder as she was brushing sand from her skirt.

He pointed to two porpoises swimming alongside the seawall. They were almost close enough to touch with an outstretched hand. The porpoises appeared to be taking turns leaping high out of the water and diving down in front of each other.

Serena laughed. "They look like they're playing the game of catch-me-if-you-can."

"Yes, they do." Dorado was entranced by the warmth of Serena's smile. "I'll escort you to Esperanza's house."

As they started to walk away from the wall, Dorado saw Martínez coming up from the pier. A group of soldiers followed him and one man carried a bulky bundle over his shoulder. He leaned forward from the weight of it. As the soldiers came closer, Dorado saw the object was wrapped in canvas and tied in three places with a rope. He knew the man carried a dead body and he shivered, feeling a cold sensation run through him.

"Please wait here a moment, Serena, I'll be back in a moment."

Dorado saw her nod and he hurried to meet Martínez, who had reached the plaza ahead of the soldiers. He spoke softly so no one near them could hear what was said.

"Not another one?" He inclined his head toward the man with the wrapped bundle.

"I'm afraid so. We'll talk about it later." Martínez turned

to leave. "For now, I need to get her body to the surgery."

Dorado nodded and returned to Serena's side as the soldiers walked by them. Everyone still in the plaza watched the soldiers. Their eyes followed the transfer of the bundle from one man to another as the squad proceeded along the bay front toward the Castillo. No one spoke until the soldiers were well away in the distance.

Dorado and Serena left the plaza with the last townspeople. Serena waited until they were alone before she asked about the bundle. Even then she whispered. "Is it a girl's body?"

"Yes." His teeth clenched, he replied without looking at her.

"What happened to her?" Serena touched his arm.

Dorado turned his eyes toward her. "I don't know. The doctor said nothing else. He was in a hurry to get to the surgery."

They walked without speaking into the southern section of town. A light breeze blew in off the sea as the sun set. Without clouds in the sky, the sunset was swift and subtle in soft orange. In the last light, they walked down narrow sand streets darkened by oyster-shell walls and wooden balconies. Sentries were setting up their night stations as they passed.

Dorado did not try to hold Serena's hand. Such attention, he suspected, would be too forward for their first time together. He only held her elbow to guide her around piles of stones and over the potholes in the road. They exchanged occasional looks, but said little during their walk to the house of Esperanza Chávez. It took only five minutes to reach the small structure, on a side street off the Street of Merchants. They said goodbye in the darkening street.

"I would like to be with you again," announced Dorado as he bowed briefly and kissed her hand. "Would it be possible for you to meet me in the plaza – next Saturday afternoon?"

"Yes. I would like that very much."

"At the same time?"

"Yes." She smiled at him. "Hasta luego."

He returned her smile. "Hasta pronto."

At the same time Dorado and Serena were leaving the plaza, a lone man entered it from the north side of town. He also had been sitting on the seawall watching the sunset, but farther away, below the Castillo's southeastern watchtower. By the time he reached the square, it was empty of townspeople except for a few clothes vendors. Busy packing away their unsold goods for the night, they paid no attention to the solitary man strolling through the plaza.

His mind full of painful memories, he trudged along without interest in anyone around him. He was preoccupied with a series of pictures that passed one by one through his thoughts. They were repulsive pictures, which he could not dismiss no matter what he tried. The mental struggle gave him a headache. It always happened that way. He made a face as the pain in his head intensified. It was one of those severe headaches that struck suddenly and would then last all night. He dreaded the intolerable pain and vomiting that was sure to follow. The headache would settle behind his eyes and eventually make one of them bulge out grotesquely. It would be his left eye, which was already sore to the touch. His temple throbbed with pain. Each step he took on the ground, no matter how softly, resounded like a banging drum in his head.

He knew the headache was coming when the memories crowded into his mind. They arrived as always, with a picture of his handsome father smiling down at him. He could still see his smile and recall his hairy body beside him in bed. It had happened long ago when he was a boy, but he saw everything as if it were only yesterday.

Now nauseous, the man walked faster worried he would

not reach his house before the vomiting began. His increased pace intensified the pain in his head. The drumbeats sounded louder now and lasted much longer. He suffered a few minutes more in the street before finally stumbling into his house.

He barely managed to unlock the door and throw it open. He vomited in the doorway on the foot mat and entry floor. The man dropped to his knees and continued to retch and vomit until his stomach was empty. Finally finished, he staggered to his bedroom utterly exhausted. Too sick and tired to undress, he fell on his bed fully clothed and hot with sweat.

He closed his eyes to sleep, but the pain and the pictures in his mind would not permit him any escape. They made him see the lovely little girl as she stood before him in the woods. They insisted he see her again and again, a broad smile on her face.

He saw her standing there in front of him, hands on her hips, laughing with glee. "What a wonderful joke! It was so easy coming out here without being recognized. Everyone thought I was a monk on my way to one of the Indian villages." Her eyes sparkled as she laughed.

She stopped laughing when he unbuttoned his breeches and pulled out his member. All the glee was gone from her face. "No, please, no!" She stepped back from him.

He seized her thin arm and gripped it tightly. "It'll be alright," he assured her. Then, he looked down and saw his small member barely poking out of his breeches. With his free hand, he pulled at it to show her it had much more size than she saw. But, despite his frantic efforts, his member seemed to shrink rather than enlarge. It always happened that way. All the while, she struggled to pull her arm from his grip.

"It'll be bigger when we're ready," he said, hoping she believed him. Still, she tried to free herself. Her eyes were wet with tears. Then, he stared at her and she stopped struggling.

Seeking relief from the excruciating pain, he turned his head from side to side on the soft pillow. But nothing helped.

The agony remained no matter what he did.

"Why would she do that to him? Arrange to meet him and then refuse what she knew he expected. Why are they all like that? Flirting, teasing and then resisting. Whores! They're all whores! Well, that little slut will tease no more. No. Not that one."

He saw her face strangely contorted. Hands were around her throat. Her eyes protruded. Her mouth opened and she stuck her tongue out at him. "Such a childish gesture," he thought. Her red face seemed to puff up in front of him. It was his turn to laugh. With her mouth, open and enlarged, she looked like a fish about to seize its prey. "Like a common fish," he chortled.

Then, he saw the rest of it. The hands squeezed her throat harder. She flailed away at the hands, but they would not let loose. They squeezed with all their strength. She could not pry the hands away and, even when it was all over, they still held her tightly.

Many hours passed before his memories finally left him and he fell asleep. It was early Sunday morning when his mind let them go. His headache lingered on through the afternoon and it was not until evening that he felt better. Exhausted from the long ordeal, he stayed home and rested half the next day.

CHAPTER SEVEN

OCTOBER 19, 1788

Olga Gallego Torres knew something important. She was certain of it. She recalled what had happened while walking to early morning Mass. When the memory came into her mind, the shortsighted woman almost stumbled over a large stone in the street.

It remained in her thoughts even in church and intruded upon all her attempts to pray. The old woman was so preoccupied she heard little of what Father Hassett said in his sermon. That had never happened before. She usually listened attentively to the Irish priest. Señora Gallego never ceased to enjoy his lilting speech and accented Spanish as well as what he said about the sundry ways God worked his wonders in the world. He was her favorite priest and Olga Gallego looked forward to his sermons and the time she spent talking to him after Mass. Father Hassett listened patiently to her complaints and always inquired about her family.

But on that early Monday morning, Olga Gallego hurried off after his sermon without speaking to him. The bent little figure in black limped away before the priest stepped down from the pulpit. She was gone even before the last prayers were said.

When Dorado stopped by Government House to talk to Ruiz de León, he found Señora Gallego in the waiting room. The white-haired woman sat in a hard chair, hands folded in her lap, staring at the closed door to the governor's office. She was waiting to speak to Governor Zéspedes and would talk to no one else. All efforts by Sergeant Suárez to persuade the woman to speak to someone else in the governor's office were rejected with contempt.

"Who's he? Who wants to talk to him?" Olga Gallego replied with a sneer, when asked if she would talk to Ruiz de León. "He's not the governor. I'll only talk to Governor Zéspedes. I'll wait here until he sees me or I die – one or the other. You can tell him that." She dismissed Suárez with a sweep of her wrinkled hand. "And don't come over to me again unless it's to tell me the governor will see me."

The sentry, standing at the doorway, told Dorado the old woman had been sitting there for more than two hours. "She arrived here at seven-thirty this morning, sir" he whispered to the lieutenant. "The governor is in a staff meeting. Who knows for how long?"

"He'll be in the meeting most of the morning." Sergeant Suárez saw Dorado come in and joined him at the doorway. "What do you think we should do, Lieutenant?"

"I'll try to talk to her. What's her name?"

"La Señora Olga Gallego."

Dorado combed his fingers through his hair and went over to the old woman. "Señora Gallego." He spoke softly so he would not startle her. "I'm Lieutenant Dorado Delgado. May I sit with you?" Dorado saw her nod and he sat down in the chair beside her.

Olga Gallego gave him only a cursory glance and then returned her eyes to the door of the governor's office. She reached into a side pocket and Dorado could hear her fingering the rosary beads in her hand. Her lips moved and she prayed silently.

Dorado spoke to her when she removed her hand from her pocket. "I'm waiting to see the governor, too," he lied. "We have a long wait, I fear. He's busy in a meeting this morning – so I've been told." He gestured toward the sergeant.

"That's what they told me, too." She stared intently at Dorado. "You can wait with me, young man. I'll be here until I see him. I won't see anyone, but the governor. They tried to get me to speak to some minor official." She sneered. "But, I'll talk only to the governor."

"I understand." Dorado smiled reassuringly. "He'll see you, I'm certain." He reached over and patted her spotted hands now folded again in her lap.

"You know, young man, you're the only one here polite enough to show an old woman some consideration – unlike those two over there." She motioned with a crooked finger to the two soldiers standing in the doorway. "I must see the governor. I have important information for him." Without teeth, she mumbled as she spoke.

Señora Gallego stared at Dorado with a steady unswerving look. Her eyes were small black beans, nearly obscured in the wrinkles around her nose. The old woman had a dark thin mustache, which stood out when she moved her lips to speak. She appeared to be chewing on something, but Dorado realized it was only the movement of her gums. Olga Gallego sat there resolutely in a black dress with a knitted black shawl about her neck, an elderly Spanish widow seen on almost every street in St. Augustine.

She looked at Dorado. "You know, I'm now eighty-one years old. What do you think of that?" Olga Gallego showed him a toothless smile. "A glass of wine every night and God's love. That's what does it for you." She cackled loudly, opening her mouth to reveal red gums and one yellowed tooth in the back of her mouth. "I've already buried three husbands and eight children," she announced with a sad shake of her head. "Everyone I knew is gone. All dead, now. You know, sometimes I think they'll have to shoot me before I'll die."

Dorado burst out laughing before he could stop himself. Señora Gallego laughed with him for a few seconds. But then she seized his forearm as her laughing led to a convulsion of coughing. She recovered following a few soft pats on the back.

Seeing her swallow repeatedly, Dorado realized the elderly woman needed something to drink. "Soldier, get Señora Gallego a glass of wine," he ordered the sentry. A minute later, the sergeant passed a glass of wine through the open door of the governor's office. The sentry handed it to Dorado, who had one arm around the woman's shoulders comforting her.

"With the governor's compliments, Señora." Dorado handed her the wine, careful to place the full glass in her hands.

Olga Gallego emptied the glass in two swallows. "Ah, now I feel better – much, much better." Olga Gallego gave Dorado another toothless smile and took one of his hands. She held it firmly in her wizened hand.

"Would you like another glass of wine, Señora Gallego? The streets are so dusty these days and everyone gets thirsty just walking through town." He smiled and patted her arm.

"It's so true." She returned his smile. "Yes, another glass of wine would be good for me while we talk. They say a glass or two of wine a day keeps a body able."

"Another glass of wine, Peralta." Dorado turned to signal the sentry in the doorway.

"Thank you, young man. I can see you were brought up properly."

Dorado bowed his head to her. "My mother would be pleased to hear that. Tell me, Señora Gallego, how long have you lived here?"

"All my life. I was born on Calle Tolomato. On November 19 of 1708, not long after the English brutes burned our town. You know, Lieutenant, I think I would just as soon speak to you as the governor." She squeezed his hand. "He's not nearly as young and good looking as you are anyway. Are you single?"

"Yes." He smiled broadly and nodded.

"Can I count on you to tell the governor everything I say to you? Will you promise?"

"I promise." Dorado made a cross with his forefinger and thumb and kissed it.

"What I want to tell him," she mumbled, "concerns the murder of a young girl about the age of his niece. It happened in Havana, when we Floridians were in Cuba. It happened in 1770. Let me tell you about it. It was horrible!"

Dorado walked from Government House to the dock, where he selected the best canoe he could find for his trip to Santa Anastasia Island. Minutes later, he was paddling to the place where the second girl's body was found. He had been sent to the island by Ruiz de León, who spoke to him after Olga Gallego left the governor's office. With the tide flowing out to sea and the wind blowing behind him, the canoe glided quickly across the bay. He reached the island pier in fifteen minutes and, in another five minutes, he stood at the edge of the tidal pond.

Dorado looked all around the area, but saw nothing except a number of alligators in and out of the water. He walked halfway around the pond without seeing anything else. About to go the other way, he saw at a huge alligator on the bank below him. The alligator, some fifteen feet long, lay basking in the sun and beside his head, almost completely covered with mud, was a broken paddle. The alligator's eyes were closed, but Dorado knew it would be foolish to try to retrieve the paddle. He waited awhile, hoping the reptile would slide into the water, but it never moved a muscle, even when he clapped his hands.

Dorado waited almost an hour in vain and then decided to search the nearby woods. In a matter of minutes, he found a clearing with a bed of pine needles and the blackened remains of a fire. Someone had built a fire in a dug out circle surrounded by seashells and stones. He picked up one of the charred bits of wood and smelled it. Before leaving, he got down on his knees and carefully raked his fingers through the pine needles.

Dorado returned to the pond only to see the alligator lying in the same place as before. He grimaced in annoyance and then walked around the pond until he reached a wooded knoll that rose about fifteen feet from the ground. He climbed the mound, which was high enough to give him a good view of the pinelands immediately around him. Looking westward through the trees, he could see the bay and the river running south from St. Augustine. But, obstructed by the upper branches of the pines, Dorado could not see the city without using the spyglass he carried in his coat pocket. Even with the spyglass, only the Castillo's watchtowers were visible through the trees.

Turning the spyglass to the east, where there were fewer pine trees, Dorado saw the sea sparkling in the sunlight. A schooner in full sail was sailing in wide circles, awaiting the high tide, when it could safely enter the shallow inlet into St. Augustine. He pitied the ship's crew, knowing they would wait at least eight hours before docking in town.

As Dorado turned the spyglass again to the west, something caught his eye. He brought the glass back slowly and saw two men moving in the woods south of the hill. They were some distance from him, but, with the spyglass, he could see one of the men was white and the other black. The black man carried a shovel on his shoulder. After scrutinizing the second man, who looked bent over at the waist, Dorado realized he was Jesse Fish.

As he watched, the black man began to dig a hole in the ground. After a few moments, the hole was enlarged and then deepened and Dorado knew it would be a grave. His stomach knotted as he continued to watch the man dig into the ground. Dorado kept his glass focused on the digging, fearing he might miss something. The black man dug steadily, pausing now and then to drink from a flagon which Jessie Fish handed to him. An hour passed, as the digging was delayed by the collapse of one of the side walls. When only his chest was visible above ground, the black man hoisted himself up and shook the sand from his breeches.

The two men then went out of Dorado's sight behind a group of palmettos. When they were once again in view, the black man was carrying a wrapped object in his arms. Although much smaller than what Dorado assumed to be a body, he carefully laid the bundle at the edge of the hole. Unconcerned about the bundle, Fish casually used his foot to push it into the hole. And, while the black man shoveled dirt into the hole, he sat against a tree watching him work. He remained seated until the loose dirt was packed down with the shovel. The two men then scattered leaves and pine needles over the site and walked away into the woods.

Dorado saw Martínez in the plaza after tying up his canoe at the city pier. The doctor was on his way to the Castillo.

"Captain Martínez!" Dorado shouted and ran to meet him.

"Buenas tardes, Lieutenant." Martínez returned Dorado's salute.

"What did you find on the island?"

"No other signs of the girl, sir, but ..."

"We know her name now, it's María Rosa Morones. Ricardo used her crucifix to find her parents. She's a Minorcan and her father thought she had eloped."

"Dios mío! I knew that girl – she helped the Señora clean the house on Mondays. She was only a child, no more than eleven years old. Why would he think that?"

"An Englishman named Matthew Harmon had been courting her." Martínez cleared his throat. "Actually, the girl was sixteen, though she looked much younger."

"And the Englishman?" Dorado stood with his arms crossed.

"Eighteen or so. We haven't spoken to him yet. He's gone and no one seems to know where he went. It's said Harmon came off some ship in August and has been here ever since."

"Let's hope he's found soon – we'll need to interview him. What I found on the island suggests the Morones girl was there with someone before she died."

"A man's clothing?" Martínez raised his eyebrows.

"No, sir. I found a small clearing in the woods where a fire had been built. From the smell of the burnt wood, I'd say it was recent. And, now, that I know about the Englishman, it's possible the clearing was a place where they bedded. There was a thick mat of pine needles set up beside the fire hole."

"I wouldn't be surprised." Martínez nodded knowingly. "The Morones girl was not a virgin. The only thing intact on the poor girl was her crucifix."

"Was a cross cut on her?"

"I'm not sure. The alligators did too much damage to her

body for me to know with any certainty. She had puncture wounds all over her chest, but I can't say if the wounds were made by a knife or alligator teeth. There were more than a hundred tooth marks on her torso alone!"

"Madre de Dios!" Dorado winced. "What an awful thing for her poor parents to see."

"Her mother swooned when she saw the body. I warned her what she would see, but I couldn't keep her from looking at her child's corpse. Did you see anything else on the island?"

Dorado told him about the grave he suspected was dug in the woods. He saw Martínez frown as he described the burial in as much detail as he could remember.

"So, Jesse Fish is involved again. First, the missing girl's canoe is found grounded near his place, then, the governor's niece visits him the day before she's murdered and now another girl is found dead on his property. If that's not enough, the old bastard is seen burying a body in the woods. He's like a deadly plague that won't go away."

"It's all too coincidental, isn't it?" Dorado shook his head.

"It is," Martínez made a face. "Maybe now we can get the governor's permission to interview him. I must be on my way, Lieutenant; some of the men are sick with the fevers."

A sultry mist settled over St. Augustine that evening and the humidity made everything wet and sticky. It was one of those hot nights when every window in the city would be thrown open to catch a wisp of wind. Yet, nothing stirred and not one wind chime sounded. Even the sea breeze on the beaches seemed strangely silent.

With dinner over an hour earlier, Dorado and Martínez

were sitting with Ruiz de León on his balcony drinking brandy. A thin streak of orange in the sky was all that remained of the day. The men could barely see each other and, then, only in silhouette.

Ruiz de León sat behind his guests since the tiny balcony could only accommodate two of the wide chairs up front overlooking the bay. Dorado and Martínez were in shirtsleeves, but Ruiz de León wore his uniform jacket and even his wig. Martínez had removed his shoes and stockings and propped his big bare feet up on the wooden railing.

"God, it's hot tonight," he grumbled, turning to Ruiz de León. "I feel like I've been put to the fire by the Inquisition. How do you tolerate this heat sitting here in full uniform?"

"It's mind over matter, my friend. Anyway, as you well know there will be a breeze off the bay soon. So be patient! Should I light the candles? We'll need them if we play chess."

"I don't feel like playing chess tonight. It's too damned hot. I would rather talk about the investigation. How about you, Lieutenant?"

"I'd like to discuss what we discovered today." In the last of the light, he saw Ruiz de León nod his head. Dorado sat sideways along the railing so he could see both senior officers.

"Bueno! You begin." Martínez wiped his face and neck with a rumpled handkerchief. Dorado began by repeating his conversation with Olga Gallego. They all laughed when he told them about her asking if he were single. There was more laughter when he repeated her comments about the governor's aide.

"That's funny!" Martínez clapped his hands together. "That old lady put you in your place, Ricardo. 'Who's he? Who wants to talk to him?'" He snickered.

"What can I say?" Ruiz de León smiled as he stood to refill the glasses.

Dorado then told them what Olga Gallego remembered. The mood of merriment ended. They listened attentively and scrutinized his face in the flickering candlelight.

"She spoke of a young girl in Havana, about the age of Gloria. Señora Gallego did not recall the girl's name, but she said, 'the girl was stabbed in a sacrilegious manner.' She said it happened in 1770."

"Dios mío, que cosa (My God, what a thing)!" Martínez grasped Dorado's arm.

"Those were her exact words. I tried to get more information from her, but she couldn't remember anything else. She said the memory came to her on her way to morning Mass."

"Well, we definitely need to verify what she told you." Martínez shifted his feet on the railing and the balcony shook. "That is startling information."

"It is indeed, if true." Ruiz de León spoke from behind him.

Martínez nodded. "Of course, it could be simply coincidental – the stabbing of a young girl in Havana. There're always stabbings in Havana. But it's her words 'the girl was stabbed in a sacrilegious manner' that interests me."

"How can we verify it?" Dorado looked at Martínez.

"I know the presidio physician in Havana; we are old friends. I'll write and ask him to verify it. All the death records for Havana, including those of this century, are in his office. When is the next ship to Cuba?"

"There's a packet boat sailing early Saturday morning." Ruiz de León tapped Martínez on the shoulder. "That will give you plenty of time to write a letter."

"It will. More than one murder and mutilation – can you imagine it?" Martínez sighed. "Well, let's not make any assumptions yet. Let's see what we learn from Havana."

"Why can't we verify her account here in town?" Dorado looked at Martínez. "What about someone who lived in Havana during the foreign occupation? Isn't there a man here in St. Augustine who went to Cuba or was born there, who might know about the murder?"

"That's a possibility. There should be someone. What do you think, Ricardo?"

"One of the old Floridians would remember it, but I wonder if the old woman's memory is reliable. I fear we'll find what Señora Gallego remembered came from her imagination and not her memory. Old age often does that to people."

"It does. Still, it's certainly worth trying." Martínez made a face. "God, what humidity! I can barely breathe. Where's that sea breeze tonight, Ricardo?"

"Soon, be patient." Ruiz de León sipped his brandy. "The problem in St. Augustine is how to verify it without causing panic among the people. We don't want to frighten them any more than they are already. They now know the girl was murdered and their fear is apparent. I'm told many people walk the streets looking suspiciously at anyone they don't know."

Martínez nodded. "Most people suspected she was murdered before it was announced, but, now that they know it with certainty, they seem to be more frightened. We must go about our inquiry quietly. If we're lucky, we'll find someone who lived in Havana at that time and will tell us about the murder without anyone else knowing about it."

"Yes, a man who lived there during the foreign occupation of Florida." Ruiz de León tapped Martínez on the shoulder as a light breeze began to blow in from the sea. "There's the wind, now. It'll be cooler in no time."

"At last!" Martínez brushed a moth off his hand.

"Well, Lieutenant, do you have any more surprises for us?" asked Ruiz de León.

"No, sir, but I do have more information."

"Let's hear it." Martínez looked over at Dorado.

"The guards at the city gates saw nothing unusual the day of the murder. A couple of Minorcan fishermen were the only men who left town in the morning. I spoke to them today. They fish along the banks of the San Sebastian River and never go to the North River. They said it's too far from town. Anyway, they didn't recall seeing anyone while fishing."

"They're too lazy to walk out there." Martínez snorted. "Even if the fishing is better. Minorcans are afraid of snakes, which God knows are plentiful in the pinewoods."

"Sergeant Cardozo and a squad of soldiers also left the Castillo that morning on a patrol north of town. They saw nothing either, except two Indians hunting in the woods. They went past the path to the murder site and never even knew it. Most of the new men have come from the Canary Islands and know little about the surrounding area."

"That's not unusual even for local residents." Ruiz de León cleared his throat. "Most people are afraid to go anywhere outside the city gates. It's been that way since the war."

"What about the sentry at the city pier?" asked Martínez.

"Alvarez saw the usual monks on the river early that morning. He also recalled seeing Barton's man rowing the Englishman out to the island. Alvarez said he saw them early – not long after the sun was up. But he never saw Barton return to town that day."

"I wonder if Barton was with Jesse Fish when the girl was killed? If not, both of them must be interviewed. We need to talk to Fish anyway about the body he buried. If it's someone he killed, we will finally have him no matter his influence with the governor. Let's hope so."

"What Spaniard would disagree with you?" said Ruiz de León. "Do continue, Dorado."

"Four vendors now say they saw a small monk walking across the plaza that morning. But I don't believe them. By now, everyone in town knows Gloria was wearing a monk's habit when she left Government House. Besides, they are too busy in their stalls to notice anything or anybody. They're only concerned with making money."

"True! I don't believe them either." Martínez nodded. "Merchants are an unsavory lot. They'll do or say anything for a few pieces of silver. They'll tell you, a Castillo officer, what they think you want to hear – anything to protect their stalls in the plaza. The greedy dogs!"

"That's exactly what they would do." Ruiz de León spoke with certainty.

"I've only a couple other items of information, probably of little meaning. According to the master of the stables, José Pérez Farías, a horse and cart were signed out to Government House on the day of the murder. He said the commandant also left early on his horse that day. The guards at the city gates saw him ride out, too, but didn't know the time he left or returned. Pérez was unsure as well, but he knew the commandant's horse was back before noon because he remembered feeding him before he had lunch himself."

"The commandant?" Martínez turned his head to smile at Ruiz de León. "So, I suppose one of us will have to ask him where he went that morning. It should be you, Ricardo."

"I'll talk to him."

"You're the one to do it, Ricardo." Martínez snickered. "I can't imagine the lieutenant telling our commandant he has questions to ask him about the murder of the governor's niece."

"Carlos, you know that's not true. The commandant would certainly assist if asked."

"Do I? I know only that the commandant is very impressed with himself and is much too powerful in this presidio. Sometimes the man acts as if he is the governor of this presidio."

"Carlos! Let's continue. I too have information to report."

"Bueno," grumbled the big man. He crossed his ankles

on the railing and once again the whole balcony shook.

"First, let me tell you why the horse and wagon were assigned to Government House on that day. They were there to dispose of rubbish and pick up fresh vegetables – it's done twice a week. A man carts away the refuse on Monday and Thursday this time of year. He then rides out to the planters west of town and purchases what's in season; I think they're picking turnips and corn now. The horse and cart are brought over the night before. They leave the cart behind the building overnight and stable the horse with the governor's horses."

"I've seen the wagon there. I noticed it while on guard duty." Dorado stood. "Before you continue, Don Ricardo, please permit me a trip to the outhouse."

"Good idea, Lieutenant, I'll be close behind you." Martínez got up as Dorado descended the stairs. "Of course, you know, Ricardo, when the lieutenant was assigned to guard duty, he should have reported the cart for improper standing on a city street." Martínez grinned. "I must point that out to the governor the next time I see him." He then went down the stairs.

"Carlos, I really wish you wouldn't criticize the commandant or the governor in front of the lieutenant." Ruiz de León looked down at Martínez from the top of the stairs. "He's young and impressionable and needs to respect his superiors. We must be good examples for him."

"I don't need a sermon on what to say or do. Dorado's a good young man. He seems more mature than his years would suggest. He is also intelligent, more intelligent than I first thought. He's surely clever enough not to repeat what we say in our meetings."

"That may be true, but ..."

"I must go to the outhouse. I can't wait any longer unless you want me to pee here over the railing." He grinned. "I know you wouldn't want that."

"Carlos!" Ruiz de León spoke as Martínez reached the bottom of the stairs. "Keep my request in mind. Please be more circumspect."

"That will be hard to do." Martínez looked up from the bottom of the stairway. "I like him and want to speak my mind to him, much like I do to you. Do you know what I mean?"

Ruiz de León heard the door close as Martínez left the house. "Yes," he thought, "I know what you mean. I like him, too."

A few minutes later, the men were again seated on the balcony facing the bay. Ruiz de León spoke as he filled the brandy glasses and pressed the stopper back into the bottle.

"Since we were last together, I've learned much about Gloria and her past life, mostly from Doña Concepción. What I tell you is quite confidential and I want it to remain that way."

"You can be sure of that, Ricardo. Nothing about the investigation should be repeated to anyone." He looked at Dorado and saw him nod in agreement.

"Good. Well, unfortunately little is known of her activities the day she disappeared. No one in Government House saw her that morning. She was up and away before anyone knew it. Not much more is known about what she did the day before. In the morning, she spoke briefly to Concepción about a dress she was making. After lunch, she went over to *Fish Island*."

"Let's keep in mind it's *Santa Anastasia Island* not *Fish Island*!" said Martínez. "The English scoundrel only owns a portion of it."

"Yes, yes, it's *Santa Anastasia Island*. Anyway, according to Concepción who went to the island with her, Gloria seemed in a good mood, smiling much of the time. Incidentally, I saw her in the hall, later that day, and she was humming *Malagueña*. We spoke only briefly."

"So, it was a secret rendezvous she planned." Martínez turned to look at Ruiz de León.

"Yes, the sentry, Solís was the only one who knew her scheme to slip away in disguise. And he knew nothing else. From what I've learned talking to the governor's family and servants, Gloria kept to herself much of the time. She said little other than the usual pleasantries. Doña Concepción thought she spent her time daydreaming. The girl had no friends; keep in mind she was only here six months."

"She had no friends? What about her cousins, the governor's daughters — Josafina and María Dominga?" Martínez again looked back at Ruiz de León.

"They both were gone from Government House before Gloria could get to know them. María Dominga left Florida earlier this year when her husband's regiment was sent to Havana. And Josefina, who married Captain Manuel de los Reyes last summer, spends her time, as she should, making a home for her husband. I'm certain you must remember their wedding, when you accidentally spilt a glass of wine on Bishop Barcelona. Gracias a Dios, it happened after the marriage ceremony."

"What a waste of good Rioja. I remember the wedding, but I don't bother to keep up with the gossip about the governor's household. That's for women. Besides, the looks of those girls don't deserve much comment. Zéspedes is fortunate to have them married off."

"Carlos, you're now gossiping yourself."

"I suppose so. Still, it doesn't change the fact that those girls are distinctly plain — and that's a very generous appraisal. Have you met either of them, Lieutenant?"

"No — yes, sir, I do remember meeting Doña Josefina. I saw her once at the governor's fiesta last summer. She was in the receiving line."

"She obviously made a memorable impression on you."

"To be honest, I have few memories of the fiesta. I spent

my time looking at Gloria."

"Let's continue. I'll now tell you what I learned about the girl." Ruiz de León poured brandy for Dorado and gave his friend a severe look while filling his glass. Martínez returned a wide-eyed look of innocence.

"As I said, Gloria had no friends here. She seemed interested only in men. Even as a child she always went to them. Doña Concepción said it started when Gloria was quite young and continued as she got older. Her mother had to keep an eye on her almost every moment by the time she was ten years old. At that time, they found her nude in bed with a twelve-year-old boy – he was a neighbor's son. Little Gloria boldly invited him into her bedroom one afternoon through an open window. She was fondling him when caught in the act by her mother. It was her idea, the girl admitted without the slightest hesitation."

"That was brazen of her." Martínez snickered.

"It happened again a year or so later. A younger boy – her own cousin! – was involved on that occasion. He was only eight! During a loud thunderstorm, Gloria soothed his fears by bringing the boy to bed. She fondled him, too, and this time with her mouth. The frightened little fellow told his mother what happened the next day. Once again, Gloria readily admitted her actions and was severely punished."

"A very precocious child," said Martínez. He moved his feet off the railing. "What do you think, Dorado?"

"I would say so." Dorado felt his stomach tighten. "What a fool I was," he thought.

"Not only was she precocious, the girl had a woman's body by the time she was twelve. According to Doña Concepción, she was already having her monthlies by that age. A young girl with a woman's body. And she flaunted that body around for everyone to see. Her mother found her, one evening, casually undressing in front of an open window – in candlelight! Can you imagine it? Keep in mind, her family lived on a busy street in Havana."

"She certainly was a wanton little thing, wasn't she?" Martínez tried to see Dorado in the darkness. "Did you know any of this, Lieutenant?"

"No, none of it, sir. I've only heard town gossip about her flirting."

"There's much of that as well." Ruiz de León coughed. "Let me continue. Concepción heard about Gloria's exploits only in the letters once she arrived in Florida. Her sister wrote her of the need to maintain almost constant scrutiny because of Gloria's 'bodily attention to men.' I saw those words myself in a letter written in 1785."

"She would have been fourteen then?"

"Yes, Gloria was seventeen when she arrived here. Aware of her past, Concepción had her chaperoned wherever she went. But the girl was quite clever and despite all precautions, she still managed to escape her chaperones now and then and rendezvous with men even under surveillance in Government House. The chaperones couldn't watch her day and night after all. So, no matter what safeguards Doña Concepción put into place, several known encounters took place in the time she was here."

"Several?" Dorado frowned. It angered him to learn Gloria had been involved with so many men. He now expected Ruiz de León to mention him as one of those men.

"Yes, several men. She flirted with three other men here besides you, Lieutenant. Doña Concepción didn't even know about you. She also wrote to two other officers in Havana."

"She was a busy little wench, wasn't she? It's no wonder Gloria had no girlfriends, she didn't have time for them. She was much too busy manipulating all the men in her life. Well, Lieutenant, what do you think of lovely Gloria now?" Martínez patted Dorado on the knee.

"It seems I was a fool – one of her fools. I lacked only

the foolscap and bells." He hit the railing with his fist. "Maybe she got what she deserved."

"Maybe so," muttered Martínez. "No one likes to be fooled."

"No one," said Ruiz de León. "It's a matter of pride and it would infuriate any man."

"You're right, Ricardo, it would surely infuriate me." Martínez raised his voice. "If she had made a fool of me, I would have wanted to wring her neck. I hate being humiliated."

"Humiliation is hard to take." Ruiz de León sighed. "I know it all too well."

"I do, too. I've been a fool with women all too often and every time it happens, I vow that I won't go near them again." Martínez chuckled. "Of course, in a short time, my desires make me change my mind."

"That's happened to us all." Ruiz de León sighed

"Women beguile us – especially Spanish women. We're like wet clay in their hands."

"How different are Spanish women from other women?" asked Dorado.

"Well, Ricardo, what do you say to that question?" Martínez looked back at his friend.

"I think it's a question better suited to you and your many amorous experiences."

"Well, for one thing, Spanish women enjoy playing the game of love with men. It suits their romantic nature. Outside of Spain and our colonies women seem coldhearted. Quién sabe por qué (Who knows why)? It might be because of their Protestant beliefs. Our women look for love and show it; that's why they flirt so much."

"You're right, Carlos," agreed Ruiz de León, "Spanish women are flirtatious. Some are much too flirtatious as it appears little Gloria was here in St. Augustine."

"So it seems. There's another difference about Spanish women – they're so much more passionate in bed." Martínez laughed loudly. "Gracias a Dios. There's more fire in them than the other women I have known."

"My Uncle Ernesto often said – he's dead now, 'Spanish women possess a fire that even the Church can't put out.'"

"Your uncle was a wise man, Lieutenant." Martínez slapped a mosquito on his arm.

"Yes, sir, he taught me much. Since my father was sick, I spent time with him when he came home from the wars. Uncle Ernesto was a naval officer on one of the king's warships."

"You were fortunate to have an uncle with such wisdom," said Ruiz de León. "When my father died, my older sister was the only one who spent time with me."

"Let's return to our discussion. It's late and I'm getting a headache." Martínez rubbed his forehead. "Who are the men Gloria encountered? One of them may have murdered her out of jealousy – in a rage."

"One of them is Lieutenant Luis López Sierra."

"López Sierra!" Martínez turned around to look at Ruiz de León. "I know him well. He was stationed in Havana when I was sent there in 1780. I didn't know he was here in St. Augustine. What's he doing here?"

"He's on an assignment for the Governor of Cuba. How do you know him?"

"I know him as a randy fool, always following his member after some puta. So López Sierra knew Gloria. Why, he's old enough to be her father – no, her grandfather. He must be in his late fifties at least!"

"Actually, he's fifty-four. He's in our generation, Carlos."

Martínez shook his head. "Why in God's name would Gloria have any interest in that decrepit dandy? I can understand her attraction to Dorado, but not to that old fart?"

"You know what they say in Castilla, Carlos. 'The ways of women will never be known to men no matter how long they live.'"

"That's true, but if Gloria wanted to be with an older man ..." Martínez paused.

"She should have selected you?"

Martínez turned to Ruiz de León. "Actually, I was about to say she could have chosen a man with cojones – his are gone. But, yes, I would be a much better choice than López Sierra."

"Anyway, he's married." Ruiz de León clucked his tongue.

"That's right, I had forgotten. He fell for a Flamenco dancer and married her after only knowing her for a few weeks. The damned fool! She soon became as big as a wine barrel."

"Are you still friends with him?"

"No. We had a falling out over a woman." Martínez chuckled. "I won that one and he wouldn't talk to me afterwards. Luis always was a bad loser. I'll bet that's why he has tried to avoid me here. What was his involvement with the girl?"

"I don't know. He was seen whispering in her ear and their faces were flushed when Concepción saw them together. It could have been their sole encounter or one of many."

"He must be interviewed. And obviously I shouldn't be the one to do it."

"I'll interview him, sir." Dorado looked at Ruiz de León.

"Are you certain you want to do interview him?"

"Yes, sir. I don't have anything against him. He's only another one of her fools."

"Who were the others?" asked Martínez.

"The second man is Sergeant Suárez."

"Suárez? Zéspedes' man in Government House? That's hard to believe."

"I know, but it's true. He was seen with her on several occasions, once with his hand on her shoulder. When

Concepción heard of it, she told him to stay away from Gloria. Suárez didn't touch her again, but, whenever possible, he followed her around like a devoted dog. He couldn't keep his eyes off of her. The servants, of course, gossiped about his infatuation."

"Does the governor know about Suárez and Gloria?"

"No. I'll not say anything about him for the time being. He serves the governor well and manages his office efficiently. I suppose he still should be interviewed."

"Yes, sir." Dorado looked at Ruiz de León. "I've recently heard something suspicious about him. I thought it unimportant until I heard of his infatuation with Gloria." Dorado told them of his talk with the blacksmith.

"Isn't that interesting?" Martínez waved his hand at a buzzing mosquito flying around his neck. "Yes, he will have to be interviewed. Who should do it?"

"What about you, Carlos?"

"I think the lieutenant would be a far better choice. We both have known Suarez a long time and such knowledge might hinder our interview. Besides, after his informative talk with the old woman, he should be the one to do it. Unless, of course, his budding romance with her keeps him too busy."

"I'll try to fit Suárez into my busy schedule, though most of my time is taken up with Olga, these days."

Martínez laughed loudly. "Who's the third man?"

"The third man is – I'm certain you will like this information, Carlos. The third man is the commandant of the Castillo."

"So, the commandant also knew Gloria. Why didn't you tell us that earlier?"

"There was no reason to tell you – until now. But let's not make any assumptions yet. I'll talk to him myself and see what he says."

"Good. How do you know he was involved with her?"

"They were together whenever he came to Government House." Ruiz de León spoke softly. "Lieutenant, I am sorry to say, for your sake, what must be said."

"Thank you for your concern, Don Ricardo, but I'll be fine."

"Bueno. Well, to be blunt, Gloria was all over him. Her interest in the commandant was obvious to everyone in Government House – except the governor. Only days before the girl's disappearance, Doña Concepción had decided to talk to him about her obsession with the commandant. She admitted to me that she hoped a marriage could be arranged."

"Concepción said that to you?" Martínez shook his head and laughed. "That woman is a consummate schemer."

"Concepción has always liked the commandant and considered him a good match for her niece. More important, she wanted her safely married before she dishonored the governor. Concepción lived in fear that Gloria would be with child before a marriage could be arranged."

"Given Gloria's wanton ways, I can understand her fears. With what we know now, I'm astonished the girl still was a virgin when she died." In the candlelight Martínez saw Dorado make a face and nod in agreement.

"So am I. Concepción thought the colonel would be a good choice for the girl, one that would be considered acceptable here as well as in Havana. She was certain her sister would have approved of such a marriage and she expected the governor's approval as well."

"Isn't it interesting that the commandant showed no sadness when he talked to us? One day after the murder! I trust you noticed, Ricardo. It's as if Gloria was someone he had seen in the street only once before. The man showed nothing to suggest it bothered him at all."

"He did seem oddly unmoved, but let's not assume anything yet. It may be that Gloria's infatuation was not shared by the commandant. We'll know more after our talk."

"When will you talk to him?" Martínez yawned loudly.

"As soon as he returns from Pensacola."

"I think he is our best suspect so far, considering his many meetings with the girl and his unknown movements the morning of her murder. Let's not forget, he left the Castillo on his horse early that morning."

Ruiz de León nodded. "What do you think, Lieutenant?"

"I don't think the commandant murdered her, sir."

"Oh! And why is that?"

"There's something I want to say about the murderer. It's been on my mind for a while. I don't think the murderer could be Catholic."

"Why not?" Ruiz de León stared at Dorado. His face stood out as if encircled in a halo of yellow candlelight. It reminded him of a medieval painting by Giotto.

"The mutilation insults God. It's blasphemous! I can't imagine one of our people doing something so sacrilegious. It's more likely the act of a heretic or a Protestant."

"What you say makes good sense, Lieutenant." Ruiz de León nodded.

Dorado looked at Martínez. "At first, when you told me what the murderer did to her, I was certain the man must be mad. But now I doubt it. The method of mutilation, the cross cut on the girl's body, the folded clothing, all seem so well planned. As you said at the time, sir, those are the acts of a man of reason, not a madman. If so, the murderer must be Protestant to have killed her in such a blasphemous manner."

"Not necessarily," said Martínez. "He could be a Catholic fanatic as well. There are a number of them in the presidio, for example there's Lieutenant Portes Gil. I'm sure you know him. He recently told me it's our sacred duty to burn all the Protestants here at the stake."

"Yes, sir, Portes Gil is a fanatic, who talks endlessly

about the Protestant heresy and the need to execute all the heretics. But can you imagine him cutting a cross on a Catholic girl?"

Martínez shrugged. "There are other fanatics here as well; it seems they're everywhere. What concerns me more is why the murderer killed her. I wonder if he went to the rendezvous intending to kill the girl. Was her murder planned or did something happen in the woods that provoked him to do it? Gloria was flirtatious and it may be she flirted with the wrong man."

"There are so many questions without answers," complained Dorado. "I wonder what we will ever know about the murderer and why he killed Gloria."

"I think all will be known in time," said Ruiz de León. "There must be an explanation for what happened."

"I wonder if jealousy could be the reason for their rendezvous in the woods." Martínez again turned to Ruiz de León. "It's easy to imagine a secret meeting, his accusations over her flirtations, her denials and defiance, angry words between them and, then, the murder."

"The mutilation might have followed as an act of fury, maybe, to punish her for playing the puta with other men." Dorado shook his finger as he spoke.

Martínez held up his hand. "Let's not forget that Gloria was flirtatious, a brazen wench, but not a whore. Remember she had not been bedded."

Dorado nodded. "Yes, sir, but I doubt anyone in town knew that. From what I've heard, the men in the barracks as well as in town all believed she had been bedded. We didn't know the girl was a virgin ourselves until you did the autopsy."

"Keep in mind, Carlos, we're not certain jealousy is involved at all. Not at all! It's only one possible explanation for her death at this point."

"You're right, Ricardo. We don't know why Gloria was

murdered and mutilated. What we do know is that she fooled a number of men. And, maybe, the murderer was the one man who couldn't bear being fooled by her. No one likes playing the fool."

Dorado nodded. "No, sir, no one!"

Martínez nodded. "You know the old expression, 'There's no fool like a fool in love.'"

"At our age, there is another appropriate expression." Ruiz de León spoke softly from the darkness behind Martínez.

"Oh, and what's that?" The big man stood and rolled down the sleeves of his shirt.

"Few old men find wisdom, most find folly, especially those with younger women."

"You made up that last part."

"Yes, but isn't it true?"

"I suppose you are referring to me and María Valdez." Carlos Martínez scowled and spoke sharply to Ruiz de León.

"No. I was speaking about all older men of our age, but if the shoe fits – wear it."

"Well, aren't you the sassy one tonight? Do you have any other old adages for us?"

"No."

"Then, I've a question for you, Ricardo. Wait a moment." Martínez bent over to put on his stockings.

"What is it?" Ruiz de León stepped into the light. He frowned, waiting for a reply.

"Tell me, Ricardo." Still bent over, Martínez looked up from buckling his shoes. "How did you get Doña Concepción to tell you about young Gloria getting caught with her mouth on the boy's member?" He grinned as he stood and laid a hand on his friend's shoulder.

Ruiz de León clucked his tongue. "She didn't say that in so many words. Concepción never would have spoken of such a thing. I figured it out from her careful use of language and, of course, her blushing."

"You don't think Concepción has ever done that for the governor, do you?" Martínez smirked and looked at Dorado, who tried not to smile.

"Carlos, that's quite enough." The shorter man glared at Martínez and angrily shook his hand off his shoulder. "Let's meet later – maybe next week sometime."

"Bueno." Martínez turned for a final look at the bay, now lit by a thin crescent moon.

"Let's wait until the lieutenant conducts his interviews." Ruiz de León saw Dorado nod in agreement. "I also want to speak to the commandant when he returns from Pensacola."

"That makes sense. Ah, the sea breeze feels so good." Martínez paused before opening the balcony door and entering the house.

The men went down the narrow stairway with Dorado following behind Martínez. The stairs creaked under the stress of their weight. Ruiz de León descended last, limping down step by step to the living room.

CHAPTER EIGHT

October 20, 1788

Dorado held his interviews in the guardhouse at the south side of Government House. He scheduled his talks with Sergeant Raúl Suárez, Lieutenant Luis López Sierra, and Fernando Núñez. At the last moment, the lieutenant decided to add Núñez to his short list with the hope the soldier might remember something he had forgotten to mention earlier.

Despite its musty smell, Dorado decided to use the guardhouse because of its privacy and lack of distractions. With the guards ordered to stand outside during the morning, the one-room structure seemed well suited for the interviews. His only complaint about the building was its poor lighting, which entered through the cracks between the wall boards and the door when open. After reveille, Dorado walked from the Castillo to the guardhouse and arrived at seven o'clock. He sent the sentry away and opened the door to let fresh air into the room.

There were only two wooden chairs in the building. One stood at an angle because of a short leg at the back. Dorado sat in the sturdy chair and, while awaiting Sergeant Suárez, he amused himself counting the carved initials on the walls. He had reached sixty seven when the shadow of a man darkened the doorway.

Suárez saluted Dorado and sat down in the unsteady chair. Raúl Suárez was a slim man with fair hair and a florid complexion. His face was flushed that day and Dorado suspected he had been drinking, perhaps to fortify himself for the interview. The sergeant sneezed and tried too late to place his freckled hand in front of his face. When Suárez opened his mouth, Dorado saw the man had lost his upper eye teeth.

"Sorry, sir. Every year this time, I get these sneezing fits and itchy eyes." Suárez made a face and leaned away from the shortened leg of the chair. "I'll have to write up a requisition to repair the chair," he said, settling his weight awkwardly on the right side of his buttocks. It was uncomfortable, but he could not think of anything else to do with the chair.

Dorado nodded. He had said "salud" after each sneeze. "Sergeant Suárez, do you know why you have been sent here to talk to me?"

"No, sir." Suárez had known since sunrise when Ruiz de León told him the lieutenant would be questioning him about the murder.

"As I'm sure you are aware, I'm working on the murder investigation with Captain Ruiz de León and Captain Martínez. We know you had several encounters with la Señorita Gloria and I expect you to tell me about them."

"What encounters, sir?" Suárez finally spoke after what seemed to be an endless wait to Dorado. "I'm not sure what you mean, sir."

"You know exactly what I mean, Sergeant Suaréz. Now, tell me everything before it's too late." Dorado recalled how Ruiz de León had questioned the sentry at Government House and used the same method on Suárez. Dorado had spoken firmly, but, to his dismay, the man said nothing. He felt his stomach tighten as Suárez remained silent.

"Do you hear me, Sergeant?"

"Yes, sir." Still Suárez said nothing. He stared down at his scuffed shoes.

Dorado did not know what to do. He saw himself standing at attention in front of Ruiz de León, trying to explain why he had failed to get any information from Suárez. With such a failure, he was certain the governor's aide would dismiss him from the investigation.

Suárez finally spoke in a flood of words. His face wet with sweat, the frightened man blurted everything out about his feelings for the governor's niece. Suaréz spoke so fast and said so much, he did not hear Dorado's sigh of relief.

"I never did anything to her. We only talked – I swear it on my mother's soul. She told me about living in Havana; I told her about my home in Toledo. We spoke about St. Augustine – how desolate it is. That's all that happened. I never put a hand on her. I swear it!"

"I see." Dorado did not know what else to ask him. "Ah, what did you do on the day of her murder, Sergeant?"

Suárez stared at the door trying to recall that day and what he was doing when she went into the woods to die. He rubbed his rough hands together.

"It was a Monday, wasn't it, sir?"

"Yes, three weeks ago, today." Dorado shifted his sword as he crossed his legs.

"That's the day we take out the rubbish. It's one of the two days we do it – on Mondays and Thursdays. One of the sentries goes out in a wagon. On the way back, he buys vegetables and sometimes a pig from the planters west of town. I go with the sentry if the Señora tells me she wants something special."

"Did you go out that day?" Dorado looked him in the eyes.

"No, sir. There was nothing special she wanted that day. I made sure all the rubbish was carried out to the wagon and sent the soldier on his way. He's given more than enough pesetas to pay for everything and usually returns with as many as half the coins he carried."

"Who assigns the men to that detail?"

"I do. The men are assigned to the rubbish detail according to a roster I make out every month. They all want to go because they get something out of it. The planters always give them a bag of fruit or vegetables. It's usually damaged or stunted things they can't sell. It was Rojas who went that day and he brought back melons for us all."

"When is it done? The rubbish detail?"

"Before lunch. In the summer, it goes out earlier because of the smell and the flies."

"When did the wagon leave Government House that day?"

"About midmorning, sir. I don't recall exactly, but I know it wasn't any earlier. No wagon has left earlier since the end of August."

"Where were you that Monday, the morning of the murder?" Dorado studied Suárez to see if he paused or shifted his eyes. Uncle Ernesto had told him those were the signs of lying.

"I was here all day." Suárez responded instantly and never moved his eyes. "Captain Ruiz de León will tell you! We talked in the office that morning."

"I see." Dorado nodded, showing Suárez he believed him. "Now, Sergeant, before you go back to duty, isn't there something else you should tell me ... about you and the governor's niece? Something you haven't mentioned?"

"No, sir." Suárez shook his head.

Again, there was silence. Dorado stared at the sergeant, who turned his eyes downward to watch an ant walk across his shoe. Almost a minute went by before Suárez looked up.

"Nothing happened. Nothing was going on between me and Gloria." Suárez paused to wipe his face with the sleeve of his jacket. "But, I loved her," he said, so softly it was almost inaudible. "I knew I could never have her in any way, but still I loved her." Suárez looked at Dorado through wet eyes. "I wouldn't have hurt her for anything in this world. I loved her so much." Tears ran down his cheeks and he turned away to wipe them on his sleeve.

"I believe you." Dorado waited while Suárez blew his nose into a handkerchief. 'The love of a woman will lead a man to a state of ecstasy and misery,' he recalled Uncle Ernesto saying. "It's so true," Dorado thought as he saw the misery of the forlorn man in front of him.

"Damned eyes itch ... sorry, sir." Suarez wiped away his tears.

"Who knew of your love for the governor's niece?"

"No one, sir! I never said nothing to no one – not ever." He choked off a sob trying to make it sound like a cough.

"Did anyone say anything to you about your encounters with her?"

"Do you mean la Señora, Doña Concepción, sir?"

"Yes." Dorado shifted his buttocks on the hard chair.

Suárez sighed. "The Señora told me to stay away from la Señorita Gloria. She didn't want her niece to get a reputation. That's what she told me, sir."

"What do you think she meant by that?"

"The Señora hoped the commandant would be Gloria's future husband. And she didn't want a common soldier like me in the way." Suárez sneered. "Of course, the commandant was welcome anytime in Government House; he came and went whenever it pleased him, prancing about in his fancy uniforms. He appeared every day to see the governor. While here, he made sure he spent time with the Señora and Gloria, trying to impress them with his high and mighty military honors and medals – not earned in battle, I'll bet. Sorry, sir, I shouldn't have said ..."

"Don't worry, Sergeant." Dorado waved away his worries with a sweep of his hand. "What's said here is between us – only."

"Thank you, sir."

"Is there anything else? Anything more you can tell me about la Señorita Gloria?"

"No, sir. She was such a wonderful girl! So beautiful! Why would anyone want to kill her? I still can't believe it." Suárez shook his head from side to side.

Dorado nodded absently. He looked at the unhappy man and thought of how the sly girl had deceived so many men. "Poor lovesick fool," he said to himself.

"One more question, Sergeant. Did you talk to her the day before she disappeared?"

"No, not that I recall, sir."

"The blacksmith told me he heard someone talking to her, the day you paid him for shoeing the governor's horse. He was outside the door when he heard the conversation."

"It wasn't me he heard talking to her. I remember paying Urquiza, but I didn't talk to la Señorita Gloria that day. No, sir. She was gone most of that day with la Señora."

"Are you sure?"

"Yes, sir." Suárez shifted his position on the unsteady chair before meeting Dorado's eyes. "Can I go now, sir? I've got to prepare the monthly rations report."

"Yes, for now." Dorado returned Suárez' salute. He watched him walk out the door, wondering who had been the man Uriguiza heard talking to Gloria.

Dorado sat in the flower garden behind Government House, awaiting his meeting with López Sierra. He chose a coquina-block bench in the far corner, situated under the limb of a live oak. The enormous tree towered above the roof of Government House, its limbs stretching above the garden and even extending over Royal Street. It shaded much of the garden, though there were a number of places where late afternoon shafts of sunlight reached the flowers that grew on the ground.

Secluded behind high coquina-block walls, the garden offered the governor's family a private refuge amidst Canary Island jasmine and pink and scarlet oleander. It was a peaceful spot and Zéspedes often took time from the paperwork on his desk to go outside and tend the beds of calendula, marigold and zinnia. In the winter, when the colorful flowers were gone, he would sit on a bench in the sun and enjoy the garden's serenity. The thick stone walls dulled the daily noise of the town, even during the busiest of times.

Sitting in the shaded garden, leaning against the wall, Dorado felt completely relaxed. He closed his eyes and nodded off to sleep. He awoke with a start when a soft voice spoke his name. It was Ruiz de León, standing before him, hands held behind his back.

"Buenos días, Dorado." The captain smiled at him.

"Buenos días, señor." Dorado stood instantly and saluted his superior. "You startled me. I didn't see you approaching."

"No, you didn't see me." Ruiz de León smiled again. "It's peaceful here, isn't it?" He motioned Dorado back to the bench and sat down beside him. He stretched out his bad leg.

"Yes, sir, it is. I'm waiting for Lieutenant López Sierra."

"How was your talk with the sergeant?" Ruiz de León folded his hands in his lap.

"I doubt he's the murderer." Dorado told him what Suárez said during his interview. "I think he lied to me about talking to Gloria, but I don't think he killed her. Suárez said he spoke to you the morning of the murder."

"Yes, we talked a while. I never thought Suárez was involved in any way." He pursed his lips together. "Suárez wouldn't dream of doing anything to dishonor the governor."

"I hope we will learn more from López Sierra." Dorado sat back with his hands resting on the bench. The coquina was cool to the touch.

Ruiz de León nodded. "What are your thoughts about the poor Morones girl? What a terrible way to die. I didn't see the body, did you?"

"No, sir, hearing about what happened to her was more than enough for me. However, it's possible she's another murder victim. Captain Martínez said a cross might have been cut on her body, but there were too many tooth marks on her to know for certain. So, I don't know what to think. Do you think she was murdered, sir?"

"We should know more when the Englishman is found. So far, he has eluded capture and there's been no sign of him anywhere about town. But, without a horse or boat, he should soon be apprehended. If the fool fled into the lost lands, he will die."

"If that's where Harmon went, sir, he may already be dead."

"True." Ruiz de León looked at Dorado and their eyes met. "Lieutenant, I would like to invite you to dinner one night this week. What about Friday night? We could spend a pleasant evening playing chess since Carlos will be with the Valdez woman." Ruiz de León twitched his nose with obvious distaste.

"Thank you, Don Ricardo. I would be pleased to accept your invitation. Friday will be fine." Dorado leaned forward and rubbed coquina dust from the palms of his hands.

"Let's eat at dusk." Ruiz de León patted Dorado's shoulder. "Well, I must get back to my paperwork. Carlos calls it administrative trivia. At times, I think the term is accurate."

Dorado smiled.

"Oh, before leaving, I found out how Gloria got the monk's habit. She took it from the sewing room. One of the house servants, Teresa Fuentes, makes extra pesetas sewing for the Franciscan monks. At the time, there were two habits hanging in the sewing room. So it was easy for Gloria to take one as she left the building that morning. She was very clever."

"As it turned out, she was much too clever for her own good."

"So it seems. Well, I must be on my way."

"Señor, before you leave, do you have time to answer a question about St. Augustine? It came up during the investigation."

"Yes, of course. My papers will still be there when I return."

"Don Ricardo, I want to ask about what they say is a curse on the presidio. I've heard it's been a belief here for a long time."

Ruiz de León clucked his tongue. "Yes, everything unfortunate that happens in town is blamed on the curse. It's nonsense, of course, but many townspeople, especially the old ones, believe the colony is cursed."

"That's what I've heard."

"The curse is supposed to have come from our execution of the French Protestants, who tried to take Florida from the king. Some 600 people sailed here, in 1564, led by pirates. They entered the St. John's River and set up an armed camp called Fort Caroline, some miles north of here. Have you heard of it?"

"Yes, sir, I've seen the ruins of the fort. I was sent out on patrol along the river and the sergeant showed them to me."

Ruiz de León nodded. "Well, when King Felipe heard about the intruders on his Florida lands, he sent Admiral Pedro Menéndez de Avilés to destroy the colony. His assignment was to remove the Protestant heresy from the crown's lands and establish a Spanish presidio to protect La Florida in the future. I'm sure you will agree that it was a sensible course of action."

"Yes, sir, it was."

"Don Pedro Menéndez did everything the king asked of him. He founded St. Augustine in September of 1565 and quickly defeated the French Protestants on land as well as at sea. It was a great triumph! Don Pedro destroyed their colony, their fort – everything!" He paused to wipe his lips with a handkerchief. "It was an extraordinary victory, especially since the French had more men at arms and ships."

"I heard some of the French escaped from Fort Caroline."

"Yes. Their shameless leader, Laudonnière, was among the few who escaped in a ship. He sailed away without any concern for his unfortunate countrymen. What a heartless people."

"I've heard that about the French."

"It's true. While Don Pedro was fighting at Fort Caroline, three French warships sailed south to assault the new settlement at St. Augustine." Ruiz de León rubbed his hands together. "God was surely on our side that day. The French fleet sailed into a storm and all their ships were wrecked along what we now call the Mosquito Coast."

"On the same coast where that Minorcan colony was

located, sir?"

"Más o menos. There were some 350 survivors from the wrecks and, since their ships ran aground well apart from each other, two groups of their men started north along the coast. It was their hope to reach Fort Caroline, unaware it had already been destroyed by Don Pedro. The wretched men were starving and too weak to wade across the inlet south of St. Augustine, even at low tide. They therefore stayed on the south bank of the inlet and the Indians informed our people of their presence." Ruiz de León bent his wounded leg and grimaced in pain.

Dorado saw his expression of pain, but he made no comment about his leg.

"When Don Pedro and his army arrived at the inlet, he demanded the French surrender. There were no terms. Without food and knowing Fort Caroline had fallen, the French had no choice." Ruiz de León paused for effect. "Then, Don Pedro put all the Protestants to the sword. They were taken, two by two, across the dunes and executed. Only the Catholics were spared."

"I see. So that's why the inlet south of the presidio is called Matanzas (slaughters)."

"Yes, that's how the French Protestants were removed from Florida."

"That was harsh treatment." Dorado raised his eyebrows.

"It was harsh treatment. It happened at a much earlier time, when the Protestant heresy was much less tolerated than it is today." Ruiz de León stared at Dorado. "An earlier, but not so bad a time at that."

Dorado nodded, not knowing what else to say.

"So, Don Pedro Menéndez became the king's champion! He had destroyed the French colony and founded St. Augustine. What he achieved in America became well known and he was heralded throughout Spain. You know, he was from your homeland?"

"Yes, sir. Even now in Asturias, there is still much admiration for Don Pedro. There is no more famous name there than Menéndez."

"I'm not surprised."

"I suppose the curse comes from the execution of the French Protestants at Matanzas?"

"Yes. It is said the Curse of St. Augustine comes from the slaughter of the Protestants. As if the Protestants haven't been guilty of killing Catholics all over the world. So, why would this one Spanish colony be cursed? It makes no sense."

"None at all." Dorado shook his head.

"But, in the minds of our people, a curse has been put on this poor presidio. The curse is credited with Drake's sacking of the presidio, in 1586, as well as the other pirate attacks that followed. The curse also started the destructive fire of 1599 and brought the many hurricanes here that have devastated this colony. In this century, the curse is also responsible for the two British sieges of St. Augustine, the destruction of most of the buildings in town and, finally, the loss of La Florida following the Seven Years' War."

"That's ridiculous!" Dorado snorted. "Florida would not have been lost if the English had not invaded Cuba and taken Havana."

"Exactamente!" Ruiz de León nodded. "The king had to regain Havana at all cost; it's the one port that serves all our colonies in America. That's why Don Carlos III transferred La Florida to the English to get it back. The king had to make that decision."

"And that decision had nothing to do with the curse."

"Of course not. But everything that fails is because of the curse." Ruiz de León shook his head. "It's as if the tidal waters from Matanzas Inlet carried the curse up to

St. Augustine."

"It's amazing how many superstitions the common people still hold," said Dorado. A sudden breeze blew through the garden and both men held their hats in place.

"I suppose it's understandable since people still think dragons threaten us and unicorns are wandering the land."

Dorado smiled. "Is it supposed to be God's curse?"

"That's what some have said because of the execution of the French at Matanzas. But, if so, why then did God deliver the Protestants to Menéndez in the storm? Don Pedro did only what God willed him to do. He removed the Protestant heresy from this province and put the heretics to the sword! So, why would his settlement suffer the curse of God?"

"It doesn't seem sensible."

"No, it doesn't. Not surprisingly, Bishop Barcelona has suggested that Satan might be responsible for what has happened in St. Augustine. He spoke of it in one of his first sermons after arriving here. More recently, he suggested that Gloria was possessed. If true, her sensual life would be more understandable."

Dorado frowned. "The bishop believes Gloria was possessed?"

"Yes, and now I must get back to the office." Ruiz de León grimaced as he stood.

Dorado came to attention and saluted the captain. "I'll look forward to Friday."

"Bueno. Adiós, Dorado."

"Adiós, Don Ricardo."

With a half-hour to wait before his second interview at nine-thirty, Dorado remained in the garden. He leaned back against the wall and again fell asleep for what seemed only several seconds. Dorado awakened when he heard the clatter of a horse and cart in the outside street. As he stood and stretched, he saw someone else in the garden.

Another soldier stood near the back door of Government House. As Dorado watched, the man bent over the jasmines that bloomed in the shade of the live oak. The soldier squatted there in shirtsleeves and blue knee breeches, obviously out of uniform. Dorado went over to rebuke the man for his breach of the uniform code.

"You there! Soldier!" He called out when still several feet away.

"Yes." Startled, the man straightened. He turned and faced Dorado. "How may I assist you?" asked the Governor of Florida.

"Oh, my God! Governor Zéspedes." Dorado halted in mid-stride. He stood as still as a statue until finally remembering to salute the governor. "I ... I thought you might be someone else," he stammered. "I am s-so sorry to disturb you, sir."

"No, Lieutenant, it is I who should apologize for disturbing you, while you were sitting on the bench over there." His eyes twinkled as he looked at Dorado.

Dorado blushed with embarrassment; he could find no words to say to the governor. He only wanted to disappear as if in a dream, but there was no such escape for him.

"Ah, you're Lieutenant Dorado Delgado y Estrada, aren't you?" He smiled at Dorado. "Captain Ruiz de León has told me much about you, young man. What he has said has been very complimentary." He chuckled. "Now, I've something to tell him about you."

Dorado's face stayed flushed. "Sir, I was waiting ..."

"Don't say anything else, Lieutenant." Zéspedes continued to chuckle. "You'll only make it worse than it was. After all, according to my watch, it was only a thirty-minute nap."

"Sir, I ..."

The governor shook his head, denying Dorado the chance to explain his sleeping. "Now, Lieutenant, tell me how the investigation is coming along. It seems to be a very slow process."

"It is slow, sir." Dorado nodded, still red in the face.

Dorado had never been so close to the governor, even when introduced to him his first week in the presidio. Now, outside in the sun, he saw the wrinkles that lined his face as well as the dark circles under his eyes. Governor Zéspedes looked much older than he had expected.

"It's much too slow." The governor frowned. "We need results soon. The murderer must be found and executed for everyone to see. Do you understand?"

"Yes, sir."

"My niece was killed in St. Augustine, the capital of the colony I govern! Never mind the dishonor, the fact that someone would dare strike down the governor's niece – it's a brazen act that suggests weakness, the weakness of Spanish rule. We cannot abide such a perception, especially with so many foreigners living in Florida."

Dorado nodded, but dared not reply.

"So, we must find this diablo who killed my niece and bring him to justice for everyone to see. And soon! Do you understand what I'm saying, Lieutenant?" Zéspedes used his thumb and forefinger to wipe away the wetness collected in the corners of his mouth.

"Yes, sir. We're doing everything possible, sir. We ..."

"Whatever you're doing, it must be done more quickly. Do you understand? I want this nightmare ended. It's essential for the survival of Spanish rule."

"Yes, sir." Dorado saluted Zéspedes as he turned toward Government House.

"Lieutenant!" Once again, the governor faced Dorado.

"Señor?"

"Don Ricardo told me about your interview of the old woman. Well done." He nodded to Dorado and then walked briskly to the back door of the building.

Dorado watched him. The governor walked stiffly, but with his shoulders back and his head held high. When Zéspedes reached the door, Dorado turned to leave the garden. He was halted by the governor's voice. The governor stood in the doorway, one hand holding the door open, the other pointing at him.

"You know I caught you sleeping on duty and don't forget it!" His laughter lingered as he disappeared into the building.

Dorado emerged from the garden gate and found Lieutenant López Sierra and Sergeant Suárez waiting for him outside the guardhouse door. López Sierra stood with his arms crossed, tapping his foot on the ground. His face was flushed with anger.

"You're a half hour late, Lieutenant!" he said after looking at the silver pocket watch. He glared at Dorado. "I do not intend to be treated with disrespect. Do you hear me?"

"Yes, Lieutenant, I hear you – quite clearly."

López Sierra was a man of medium height with a potbelly. He had rounded shoulders and the look of someone who sat at a desk every day. The lines around his eyes and the gray hair in his mustache and sideburns showed him to be over forty. López Sierrra looked at him with apparent disapproval, his upper lip curled and his eyebrows, pinched together in a frown.

"I'm sorry to be late, I was ..."

"So you should be. I haven't got all day to waste on this interview." López Sierra continued to glare at the younger man.

Dorado ignored the man's scolding. "I was delayed talking to the governor."

"Oh, well, that explains it." López Sierra nodded with new understanding. "You need to know I'm on an important mission for the Captain General of Cuba, Don José de Ezpeleta. I can't wait around here all day. I have much to do here in St. Augustine and only a short time to do it." He pulled his shoulders back and stuck out his chin.

"I only ask for a little of your valuable time, Lieutenant. I wouldn't think of keeping you from your important mission. Hopefully, it won't inconvenience you too much to assist us with this investigation – even if it only involves the murder of our governor's niece."

"Don't get sarcastic with me, young man!" López Sierra pointed his finger in Dorado's face. "You know I'm senior to you even if we do hold the same rank – so I expect respect. Do you understand?" His jaw jutting out, he stood there defiantly with hands on his hips.

"Oh, yes, Lieutenant, I do understand." Dorado, his face flushed, wished he could put a fist into the man's face.

"Good. Now let's get this interview over so I can be on my way." López Sierra cleared his throat loudly and spit on the ground.

"We'll talk in there." Dorado gestured to the guardhouse.

"Sir, may I speak to you a moment?" Sergeant Suárez had listened with amusement as the two officers argued.

"What is it, Sergeant?" Dorado spoke sharply to Suárez.

"Señor, Captain Martínez wants you to meet him at the Castillo – when you're finished here. He sent a man with that message only a few minutes ago."

"Thank you, Sergeant." Dorado smiled, regretting his harsh response to Suárez.

"Yes, sir. And, sir, there's something else I need to tell you in private. It's important, sir." He followed Dorado to a spot several feet away from López Sierra.

Suárez spoke softly so he could not be overheard by López Sierra. "Sir, I thought you would want to know when the horse and cart left that day." His back to the fuming officer, he said, with a smile, "I'm sorry to interrupt you, Lieutenant, but I thought you would like to know the time even if it delayed your interviews." He turned his head slightly to the side to indicate the fuming officer behind him.

"I don't mind the interruption." Dorado grinned. "Let him wait, it'll do him good."

"I thought you would see it that way, sir."

"Yes. Thank you. I owe you a bottle of wine, Sergeant. Now, what did you find out?"

"The refuse wagon didn't leave Government House at the usual time because the horse sent from the stables needed a new shoe. The horse was taken to the blacksmith that morning and he wasn't brought back until noon. So, the wagon left later, after the sentries had lunch."

"I see. Thank you, Sergeant."

As Suárez walked away, the officers entered the guardhouse, Dorado leading the way. Before seating himself, he politely asked López Sierra if he preferred the chair near the door. Instead of responding, López Sierra seized the chair Dorado had indicated and carried it even closer to the door. He clucked his tongue in exasperation when he saw the broken leg. Seeing Dorado's smile, he slammed the chair on the floor and sat awkwardly in it.

Dorado sat down in the stable chair. "Lieutenant López Sierra, I want to inform you why you are here for this interview. The governor of La Florida, Don Vizente Manuel de Zéspedes y Velasco has appointed me, along with Captain Carlos Martínez Medina and Captain Ricardo Ruiz de León to investigate the shocking murder of Señorita Gloria Márquez García y Morera, the governor's niece. The murder took place on September twenty-ninth, on the shores ..."

"I know that." López Sierra again clucked his tongue. "I don't need the introduction. What is it you want to know?" He turned the broken chair on its side and sat on the edge of the seat. A cheek muscle twitched on the left side of his lower jaw.

Showing excessive respect, Dorado spoke to López Sierra in a slow and soft monotone. He sounded like a parent trying to calm an unruly child. The patronizing use of politeness was not lost on López Sierra and he closed his eyes as if to shut out the man who questioned him.

"Lieutenant López Sierra, I must ask you about your knowledge of la Señorita Gloria Márquez Garcia y Morera."

"I'll help as best I can." López Sierra crossed and uncrossed his legs in a futile attempt to sit comfortably on the edge of the chair. "But I don't know anything about her murder."

"Please tell me, Lieutenant López Sierra, how well did you know la Senorita Gloria Márquez Garcia y Morera?"

"You don't need to repeat her full name every time you speak of her. I know it!"

"As you please, Lieutenant López Sierra. How well did you know her?"

"I saw her only occasionally when I went over to Government House for something."

"How often was that, Lieutenant López Sierra?"

"I don't know. Whenever it was necessary to talk to Ruiz de León or the governor."

"Do you mean Captain Ruiz de León?"

"Yes. Captain Ruiz de León!" López Sierra exhaled his breath through his mouth.

"Lieutenant López Sierra, do you have any notion of how often you met with Governor Zéspedes or Captain Ruiz de León?"

"No." The older man momentarily closed his eyes. "I've been here two weeks, so I have no notion how many times I've spoken to the governor or Ruiz de – ah, Captain Ruiz de León. Why would it matter? What does it have to do with the girl's murder?"

"It does indeed matter, Lieutenant López Sierra." Dorado spoke slowly, pronouncing each syllable of every word. "You said you saw Gloria Márquez García y Morera when you went to Government House. Is that correct, Lieutenant López Sierra?"

"Yes – no, I said that I saw her only occasionally when I went over there. Not every single time!" He raised his voice.

"How often was that, Lieutenant López Sierra?"

"I don't know – maybe, three or four times. For God's sake, who would remember?" He gritted his teeth.

"What happened when you were with her, Lieutenant López Sierra?" Dorado tried not to smile as he looked at him. He was pleased to see the older man's exasperation.

"Nothing happened! Nothing! We talked, that's all." López Sierra shook his head.

"What did you talk about, Lieutenant López Sierra?"

"None of your – we talked about nothing important." He glared at Dorado. "We talked about the weather, life in St. Augustine." He struck his leg with the flat of his hand. "For God's sake, what does it matter? What we talked about had nothing to do with her murder!"

"That may well be, but we need to know as much as possible about her conversations, her activities – anyone she knew or met. Surely, Lieutenant López Sierra, you can understand our need to be thorough. No stone, not one, must be left unturned in this murder investigation. I know you want to be of assistance for the governor's sake."

"Look, Lieutenant, I was only with her a few times." López Sierra was sweating and he wiped his face with a handkerchief.

"With your agreement, Lieutenant, we can remove our hats and also our wigs." Dorado felt drops of sweat trickling down his neck. "It's already getting hot in here."

López Sierra nodded. He carefully removed his tricorn hat and then his wig. He held his hair down with one hand and took off the wig with the other. Withdrawing a handkerchief from his jacket pocket, López Sierra then dabbed his moist forehead, making sure the thin hair that covered his bald spot was not disturbed.

"Where were you with la señorita, Lieutenant López Sierra?" Dorado, who snatched his hat and wig off in one motion, almost laughed out loud seeing the man's cautious attention to his hair. It reminded him of what a woman would do.

"I don't know, downstairs somewhere." He scowled. "Usually, there was someone with her, either Doña Concepción or a chaperone."

"Were you ever with her alone?"

"Not that I remember. At least, not for any length of time."

"Was there any intimacy between you and la Señorita Gloria?"

"What do you mean?" López Sierra glared at Dorado.

"I'm sure you know exactly what I mean Lieutenant López Sierra. Were you in any way intimately involved with la Señorita Gloria Márquez García y Morera?"

"I suppose my old friend, Carlos – Captain Martínez, told you to ask me that question?" He sneered. "I know his words when I hear them."

"No," Dorado replied calmly. "It was my question, Lieutenant. Mine alone! No one has told me how to conduct this interview."

"Is that so?" López Sierra smiled on one side of his mouth.

"Should I repeat the question, Lieutenant López Sierra?"

"No, Lieutenant, I know what you asked." He closed his eyes and sighed.

López Sierra wanted to walk away without saying another word, but knew he would be reprimanded for his lack of cooperation. Such a reprimand would be reported to the governor of Cuba and end any possibility of promotion. The assignment in Florida was his last chance for a promotion and he would not risk losing it. López Sierra hoped to retire when he reached sixty with the rank and pension of a captain. Although small, the army pension would provide enough money to raise fighting cocks on the acre of land in Valencia his wife had brought as a dowry to their marriage. With those thoughts in mind, López Sierra knew he would now have to satisfy the smug young bastard questioning him.

"Look, Lieutenant, I want to get this damned interview over. I'll be candid with you and I expect you to be circumspect with what I tell you. I don't want the governor to be told – at least, while I'm here. Is that agreed?" He stared at Dorado.

"Bueno. It is agreed. You have my word." Dorado crossed his arms over his chest.

"That girl, Gloria, was something special! Governor's niece or not – she was a hot little piece. She liked men and not one at a time either. You could see it by watching her when some new man entered the room; she would swallow him up with her eyes. You know the kind, I'm sure." López Sierra looked at Dorado expecting his agreement.

"Yes, of course." Dorado had never known such a woman, but would not admit it.

"No one man would ever be enough for that girl. Not even the commandant! And she threw herself at him whenever he came around. Gloria was all over him like a warm blanket on a cold night." He smiled, pleased with the saying he had often used over the years.

"What was she like when the commandant wasn't around?"

"Well, then she had her big eyes on other men. Little Gloria always had her eyes on some man. Surely you know that already."

Dorado nodded. "No, damn it! I didn't know," he thought to himself. "I was just one of her fools."

"One day, I saw her behind a door with someone else. It was some soldier. I couldn't see who he was because of the door."

"Could you see his uniform? An officer's uniform, I assume?"

"Yes, but I didn't see much more than that. I got the impression he was a senior officer. I don't know why. I didn't see enough of his uniform to know that with certainty."

"Are you sure the man wasn't the commandant?"

"Yes, I'm sure. The commandant came into the room not long afterwards and she threw herself into his lap in front of me. No, it wasn't the commandant I saw behind the door."

"I see. Do you know anything else about her?"

"Yes. One day when I was with her – it was after lunch, about a week before she was murdered. It happened when Doña Concepción went upstairs for a few minutes."

"Where were you – in what room?"

"I was in the waiting room when I met them. They were returning from the cathedral. I was there waiting to see Ruiz de León. When the Señora left the room, the girl gave me the big eyes." He moistened his lips. "I walked over and held her hand. That's all I did – so help me, God! The next thing I knew, she was tight against me and we were kissing. She gave me those French kisses – you know the kind with her tongue in your mouth."

"Yes." Dorado gritted his teeth, remembering that

Gloria had given him the same kind of kisses in the hallway closet.

"The wench pushed her tongue in and out of my mouth like it was a man's member. It shocked me to say the least. In less than a minute, she was moaning and panting and rubbing herself all over me. She was as hot as a flaming log. I was on fire myself, but I did nothing. I knew the Señora would be down any minute."

"All this took place in the waiting room?" Dorado recalled her moaning all too well.

"No. We moved into the hallway, while holding each other."

"What happened then? Did you stay there in the hallway?" Dorado expected him to say she led him into the hall closet.

"Yes, believe it or not, it happened there in the hallway. God, I was afraid everyone in Government House would hear her moaning. The girl was panting like a thirsty dog! She put her hand in my breeches and grabbed my member. And I'll tell you, the wench knew exactly what to do with it. You know what I mean." López Sierra smiled.

His smile disturbed Dorado. "Is the old bastard smirking at me?" he wondered. For a second, he worried Gloria had told López Sierra about him. But, then, he reminded himself of how sly she was and he knew she had kept him secret like her other suitors. "Yes, of course," Dorado said at last. "What else happened?"

"Nothing. We stopped everything, when we heard Doña Concepción coming down the stairs. Gracias a Dios, she's heavy footed."

"Doña Concepción didn't find you kissing? Or touching?"

"No, Gracias a Dios. The Señora didn't catch us in the act, but she knew something had happened between us. Women know those things."

"That's everything that happened?"

"Yes, I'm sorry to say. I never got that close to Gloria again. Of course, I still hoped one day to lie between those firm young legs of hers. Yes, indeed! I'm sure you know what I mean." López Sierra smirked. "Is there anything else you want to know?"

"Again, the damned smile!" Dorado felt another urge to put his fist in the man's face. He pictured López Sierra flat on his back, his nose bleeding. "I have a couple more questions. Where were you on the day of her murder? What were you doing that morning?"

"That was a Monday, wasn't it?" López Sierra grimaced and looked up at the ceiling. "Let me see, where was I ...?"

He was interrupted by a knock on the door. It was Suárez, holding two wine glasses and a bottle of Rioja. "Compliments of Don Ricardo," the sergeant announced as he handed the bottle and glasses to Dorado. He left immediately afterwards.

Dorado poured a glass and handed it to López Sierra.

"Ah! I can surely use this now." López Sierra drank half the Rioja in one gulp. He then drank the remainder of the wine and Dorado refilled his glass.

Dorado poured a full glass of wine for himself and drank most of it quickly. The wine helped quench the thirst he felt in the guardhouse, now stifling in the late morning sun. He was already soaked with sweat under his uniform.

López Sierra finished his second glass of wine in two swallows. He sighed contentedly and placed the empty glass on the floor. He then wiped his face with his handkerchief.

"I remember that day clearly." López Sierra leaned forward with one hand on his knee, the other twirling the pointed ends of his mustache. "I talked to the commandant that morning and Ruiz de León later in the afternoon."

"You were with the commandant that morning?" Dorado recalled the sentries had said he left town early that morning.

"Yes, he showed me around the Castillo. Do you know why I'm here?"

"No."

"Governor Ezpeleta sent me to Florida to make an inventory of the military equipment in the colony. After finishing here, I'm going to Apalache and Pensacola and then to Mobile; I'm leaving next week for Apalache. God help me in that remote place." He frowned. "Never mind the damned Indians — I hear it's full of venomous snakes and man-eating animals."

"What time were you with the commandant that morning?"

"It was around eleven or so." López Sierra scowled, annoyed by Dorado's indifference to his assignment in Florida.

"Where did you meet the commandant?" Dorado finished his wine and poured another glass for himself. He handed the bottle to López Sierra, who drank down the remaining wine.

"Gracias. We arranged to meet at ten-thirty, but the commandant arrived forty minutes late. I was standing outside at the drawbridge when he came riding up. I remember his stallion was well-lathered from a hard run. The commandant was breathing hard, too."

"What time did you meet Captain Ruiz de León?"

"Mid-afternoon — about three o'clock. The commandant went with me to Government House. Everyone there was talking about Gloria's disappearance. She had been missing since early morning, as I'm sure you know." He saw Dorado's nod of agreement.

"What did the commandant say about her disappearance?"

López Sierra looked up at the ceiling again. "The commandant was quite calm. I recall thinking he seemed oddly unmoved about her being missing since there was so much affection between them. I think he said, 'Gloria's here somewhere, probably where we least expect her to be. I'm certain she'll turn up soon.'"

"One more question, Lieutenant. I know it's hot in here. Where were you that morning before meeting the commandant?"

"I don't remember – exactly. I eat breakfast early at six thirty; that's when the widow woman where I'm staying serves it. After breakfast, I read for an hour or so and then go over to the plaza. I spend a little time there looking at what the vendors have to offer. Afterward, I usually go to El Toro Negro on Real Street, north of the square. I assume you know the tavern. You can get a strong cup of tea there; nothing else is worth eating or drinking." He shook his head and used his handkerchief again to pat the beads of perspiration on his forehead.

Dorado nodded. "What else did you do that morning?"

"I didn't go out to the woods, if that's what you're thinking." López Sierra made a face. "How the hell would I get out there? Walk?"

"No one suggested you went there, Lieutenant."

López Sierra wiped the sweat from his face. "Is there anything else?"

"Not for now. If I need to talk to you again, I'll let you know."

The two officers stood at the same time. Dorado held up a finger. "One more question, Lieutenant. Were you at Gloria's funeral? I don't recall seeing you there."

"I wasn't there." López Sierra frowned, anxious to escape the hot room and the endless questions. "I was sick in bed. I ate something that soured my stomach the night before."

They bowed stiffly to each other and exchanged unsmiling looks. Neither of them said "adiós" or wished the other well.

Dorado and Núñez talked outside the guardhouse in the shade of a live oak limb. After suffering in the stifling building, Dorado moved the chairs outside. They sat facing each other. Before sitting, Núñez fixed the unsteady chair by placing a flat stone under the short leg. He then gave Dorado a detailed account of his discovery of the girl's body.

During Núñez' report, Dorado sat silently, listening. The soldier in front of him had brown eyes and hair and a face darkened from working many hours in the sun. Although only in his thirties, Núñez had creases in his neck and leathery skin. His teeth were stained yellow from smoking. Out of habit, he held a pipe in his hand throughout their talk.

Fernando Núñez was well known to Dorado. He had served under him during his first assignment in the presidio. Núñez was in a squad of twelve men Dorado supervised to fill the cracks in the Castillo's floors and walls. The detail took six weeks to complete and, when the squad's sergeant fell and broke his leg, Dorado put Núñez in charge of the other men. He had seen how hard Núñez worked and knew he would make sure the soldiers filled all the holes.

"How did you find the girl's body, Fernando?"

"I'm not sure, sir, if it was seeing the flies or hearing the buzzing that made me look at the palmetto. But when I looked, I saw the leg. Anyone would have seen it from the water."

Dorado nodded. "What did you do when Rafael went to town?"

"Nothing, sir, except to walk over there and see who it was. The smell made me sick to my stomach." He wrinkled his nose. "So, I moved away and stayed away."

"When we talked last, you said you went to that place on the river because the fish were spawning there in September. Is that right?"

"Yes, sir." Núñez cleaned out his ear with his small finger and wiped the earwax on the heel of his shoe. "Even though we did bad that day, it's the best fishing spot this time of year. Two days after I found the girl near there, I got a bag full of keepers – big ones!"

"Do you go out there other times of the year?"

"No, sir. It's too far away and the place is full of sand-spurs and snakes."

"Who else have you seen there in September?"

"No one, sir, not at that spot. I've see other fishermen at the river farther south, but not there. Anywhere on the river is good this time of year. The Indians been fishing there for God knows how long." He scratched the side of his head.

"Did you see any Indians that day?"

"No, sir. We didn't see anyone, except a monk in a canoe. He was paddling to town."

"A monk?"

"Yes, sir. We saw him on our way to the dead tree. It was when we was walking north along the river. He was moving fast with the current."

"Was there anything unusual about the monk?"

"No, sir. Not that I remember."

"What did he look like?"

Núñez smiled. "Short and fat like most of the others."

Dorado smiled with him. "Only one monk was in the canoe?"

"Yes, sir. He looked in a hurry and was paddling hard even with the current. Didn't see us as he went by." Núñez tapped the pipe on his knee. "I do recall something unusual – he had his hood up. We could only see his nose even though he was no more than twenty feet from us. I remember Rafael asking me, 'Why is he wearing his hood on such a hot day?'"

An hour later, after discussing the interviews with Ruiz de León, Dorado walked over to the Castillo. A sentry handed him an envelope as he passed his guard station. It contained two letters and a note from Martínez written in a hurried scrawl.

"I can't meet you now. Must tend to an injured man. Read the enclosed letters and mail them. Meet me here tomorrow afternoon."

"Do you know where Captain Martínez went?" Dorado asked the soldier.

"Yes, sir. He went over to the island – to the coquina quarry. Some fool dropped a block on his foot."

Dorado left the fort. He walked across the drawbridge and down the sloping ground to the seawall, overlooking the bay. He sat in the shade of the wall and read the letters addressed to the Presidio Physician of Havana.

Major Esteban Morales Muñoz y Barrientos
Presidio Physician of Havana
Plaza of the Cathedral

My Esteemed Major Morales Muñoz y Barrientos,

I am writing this letter to you to request your assistance in a murder investigation in the Presidio of St. Augustine. The victim, Señorita Gloria Márquez Garcia y Morera, was the niece of the Governor of East Florida, Brigadier Vicente Manuel de Zéspedes y Velasco. The case is one of murder and mutilation. The girl was initially strangled and then mutilated with a knife.

A former resident of Havana has informed us that a similar killing was committed in the city of Havana in the year of 1770. We therefore request a search be made in the murder files in your possession to verify our information. We anticipate a response at your earliest convenience.

Presidio of St. Augustine
October 20, 1788.

Respectfully Submitted by,
Carlos Martínez Medina, Captain
Presidio Physician of St. Augustine

On another piece of paper, Carlos Martínez wrote a personal note to his friend in Cuba. The note was penned with less care than the official letter and included crossed-out words and inkblots. When Dorado compared the writing on the letters, he realized Martínez had ordered someone else to write the official letter.

Esteban,

I assume you still have the murder files that your predecessor, Doctor Alejandro Vilar Caballido, left in the file closet. If so, look for a case of murder-mutilation between 1769 and 1771. Our information for the date of the murder comes from an old woman, whose memory may not be reliable. I know this request is a nuisance, but we do need your help.

I hope these letters find you healthy and content. I trust the boys and Beatriz are all healthy as well. How are you doing there in Havana? You must be beleaguered with paperwork, never mind the king's men, who are everywhere. I'm told there are more officials in Cuba these days than trees in the woods. There must be times when you regret the appointment as Royal Physician of Havana, even with the promotion to Major!

I'm content in St. Augustine. They leave me alone to do my work. I eat well and show it, have enough women to suit me and live as comfortably as one can in this remote town. One day, I'll pack up and go home to Cádiz, but, for now, I'm satisfied here.

The next time I come to Havana, we must drink to old times and, of course, scrape the bowl together. You know, it occurs to me that I haven't been in Havana since 1785, when your second son, Angel, was born. That's much too long a time!

Abrazos,
Carlos

CHAPTER NINE

October 22-24, 1788

"Lieutenant!" The obese monk shouted from the other side of the street. He waved his hand so Dorado would see him.

"Yes." Dorado stopped walking and turned to the monk in the brown habit. While he waited, the Franciscan lumbered across the street and stood before him breathing heavily.

"Aren't you the one investigating the killing?" The monk's face glistened with sweat even though the morning sun was still low in the sky. He looked at Dorado with pale blue eyes. His eyes were small and almost lost in the flesh of his cheeks.

"Yes, I'm Lieutenant Dorado Delgado." He stepped backward, the smell of the man's sweat strong in his nostrils. "Buenos días."

"Buenos días. I'm Fray Fidel. I have information for you – about the murder."

"The murder of the governor's niece?" Dorado stared at the monk.

"Yes, an Indian boy saw them out there – the murderer and the girl. He told me about it today after Mass. The boy forgot about seeing them until he heard the talk about the killing."

"What do you mean he saw them? He saw ..."

"Not the murder, but the governor's niece and the murderer." Fray Fidel nodded.

"He did?" Dorado's eyes widened. "At the North River?"

"Yes, I'll take you to him. He's waiting with Fray Tomás."

They hurried across the plaza toward the pier. Initially, Dorado walked with his usual long strides, but he slowed when the monk could not keep up with him. Fray Fidel smiled his thanks as he caught up with him. A short distance from the dock, Dorado saw an Indian boy sitting on an overturned canoe. The boy stood and waved to them as they approached.

"Mateo, this is Lieutenant Dorado Delgado." The monk smiled and patted the boy's head. "Where's Fray Tomás?"

"Buenos días, Lieutenant." The boy politely bowed his head. "Fray Tomás had to go relieve himself. He said I should wait here by myself."

"Buenos días, Mateo." Dorado guessed the boy to be thirteen or fourteen from his first signs of a beard. He knew his Spanish had been learned at the Franciscan school.

"Mateo, tell the lieutenant what you saw that morning." Fray Fidel put his arm around the boy's shoulders.

"I saw a girl – she must have been the governor's niece. She was standing at the edge of the river across from Pelican Island." Mateo pointed north. "She was talking to someone – a man, but I couldn't see his face. She was standing in the way."

"Why do you say the girl must have been the governor's niece?"

"When Mateo saw her, he didn't know who she was." Fray

Fidel wiped his face on the sleeve of his habit. "He didn't know it until yesterday when his sister told him the governor's niece had been murdered in the north woods."

"I see. Where were you when you saw her, Mateo?"

"In a canoe, sir. I was on my way to meet Fray Fidel."

The monk nodded. "I was at Nombre de Dios, waiting for Mateo to bring the candles, incense and crucifix for Holy Communion. He was on his way from the Indian village three miles north of the mission church. I went on ahead to make arrangements with the chief. It's not easy getting all the Indians together for Mass, you know."

"So, you were paddling south when you saw them. There where that pine tree is down on the ground along the river?"

"Yes, sir. When I see the tree, I know I'm almost at the inlet to Nombre de Dios."

Dorado nodded. "How far were you from them?"

"I'm not sure." The boy looked at Fray Fidel. "Maybe thirty or forty feet. They were close to the river."

"Did you see the girl's face? What did she look like?"

"I didn't see her face. Her back was to me."

"What was she wearing?"

"Something red. That's what I first saw when I looked that way."

"All red?" Dorado looked intently at the boy.

"No, sir. I think she wore something white on top and red on the bottom."

Dorado sighed, recalling the red skirt floating in the water. "What about the man who was facing you? What was he wearing?"

"I don't know." Mateo shrugged his shoulders. "I couldn't see him clearly. She was in the way and there were palmettos all around them. They were not standing in the open."

"Is there anything you can tell me about him? His hair, his height, his weight?"

"No, she was in the way." The boy scratched his head.

"How do you know she was talking to a man?"

"I think it was a man, but I don't know why." Mateo shrugged. "Oh, yes, I remember he wore a blue tricorn hat – that's how I knew. I could see his hat above her head."

"What about his face below the hat?"

Mateo shrugged. "The canoe was moving too fast for me to see it."

"Mateo only glanced at them." Fray Fidel looked at Dorado. "He didn't want to stare. As I'm sure you know, Lieutenant, we try not to involve ourselves in worldly things."

"I understand, Fray Fidel. With your permission, I have only a few more questions to ask Mateo." Dorado smiled at the boy.

"That will be fine. I'm sure Mateo won't mind." He squeezed the boy's arm.

"Mateo, do you know if they saw you?"

"I don't think so." Mateo shook his head. "The canoe was moving on the current and I wasn't paddling, so they wouldn't have heard me go by. They didn't ever turn around."

"I see." Dorado shifted the sword on his hip.

"Besides, they were busy talking."

"How do you know that?"

"I heard one of them laugh."

"One of them laughed? Are you certain?"

"Yes, sir, I heard it clearly. I think it was the girl; she laughed more than once."

"Did you hear or see anything else?"

"Not that I remember. I was hurrying to meet Fray Fidel. We were supposed to meet and set up for morning Mass."

"Do you know what time you saw them?"

"It was mid-morning, más o menos."

"Did you see a canoe there?"

"Yes. It was ashore and there was something brown on the stern seat. It looked like one of the brothers' habits."

"There was only one canoe?" Dorado held up a finger.

"Yes, Lieutenant."

"What about a horse? Did you see a horse tied up there?"

"No." The boy frowned. "I only looked at them once."

Dorado saw the boy fidgeting and held up his hand. "Only one more question, Mateo. Did you take your canoe back up river that day?"

"Yes, after Mass. I went upriver to my own village to see my father."

"Was that canoe still there on the shore – where you had seen it earlier?"

"No, it was gone."

After lunch, Dorado went into the Castillo to speak to Martínez. He found the surgery pleasantly cool after walking in the midday sun. Martínez was hunched over the face of a dead man when he entered the room. A soldier's blue uniform lay folded in a neat pile on the floor.

The doctor looked up and greeted Dorado with a grin. "Sorry I missed you yesterday." He handed him a lit candle to hold over the body. "Tilt it toward his head."

"Hold the candle closer to his head," he ordered Dorado. "Move it closer, Lieutenant. He won't bite, believe me. He's well beyond that."

"Is that close enough, sir?" Dorado held the candle above the man's head. "I don't want the wax to drip on his face." He worried more about the wax dripping on his uniform jacket; it was the best jacket of the two he bought when he entered the army.

"Don't worry, he won't feel it."

"Who is he? I don't recognize him. He must be one of the new men from Puerto Rico." Dorado thought the man looked pitifully small lying on the table. He was light-skinned with a sunburned face and neck. His head looked larger than normal and his eyes seemed to be buried in the swollen flesh of his face.

"Yes, from Puerto Rico." Martínez nodded. "His name was Montoya Lastarria."

"What's wrong with his member?" asked Dorado.

Martínez moved his eyes from the man's face to the middle of his body. "Nothing. What do you mean?"

"It looks like it's been cut or shaved."

Martínez looked puzzled for a moment and then laughed loudly, slapping his thigh with his hand. "He's been circumcised!" he chuckled. "The man's a Jew or Moslem — that's what they do in those barbaric religions." The big man continued to laugh, holding his sides.

Red-faced, Dorado rested the candle on the edge of the table. He frowned, watching Martínez wipe tears of mirth from his eyes.

"I didn't know they let those kind in the king's army."

"They let anyone in these days." Martínez still had a smile on his lips. "Besides, who would know who they are? Unless they get a thorough medical examination, which is rare except for officers, they look just like us in uniform."

"What happened to him, sir? How did he die?" Dorado held the heavy candle with both hands to keep it steady.

"It's a sad story. He arrived here only a month ago and, after two weeks of guard duty at the Castillo, they sent him south to that miserable Fort Matanzas. Poor lad! I can't imagine a worst assignment for a new soldier."

"That's the usual assignment for new men."

Martínez nodded. "This week, he went with a squad of men to hunt for game. Wild boars had been seen on this side of the Río San Juan and everyone looked forward to roasted pork. They camped near the river the first night and hunted the following day from dawn to dusk. They shot a small deer, but never saw the boars."

"They're hard to find in the woods, sir."

"So I hear. After hunting all afternoon, they got back to camp a little before sunset. Since everyone was exhausted they went to sleep immediately after eating their provisions. Every man took his turn at guard except the new man. The sergeant spared him since it was his first day in the field and he looked too tired to do it anyway."

"That would be Sergeant Flores. He's always easy on the men."

"It was Flores who led the squad. Well, when they got up the next morning, Montoya didn't move; he lay dead on the ground. They assumed the man died before nightfall because his blanket was still rolled up. But they couldn't tell how he died. They saw no wounds, no blood, nothing on him except insect bites – mostly from biting flies and mosquitoes. Montoya was covered with them, but so was everyone else in the squad."

"The damned insects are everywhere. They're a plague!"

"They are indeed. Anyway, Flores was baffled by his sudden death and didn't know what had happened to him until I told him. Can you guess how he died?" Martínez smiled mischievously.

"Don't tell me he was strangled." Dorado bent over to examine the dead man's face. "That might explain the swelling."

"No. Montoya died of natural causes – so to speak."

Dorado looked at the body and noticed the numerous bites on the face and neck. The worst bites were on his neck, which was spotted and swollen. Then he saw them. There were two sets, four in all, on his neck. Dorado looked up with a wide smile.

"You found them. Good for you, Dorado!"

"So he was killed by a snake. A rattlesnake, sir?"

"I'd say so. From the width of the bites, I'm sure it was a big snake – maybe, as long as eight feet. Look at the space between the bite marks." Martínez spread out his left fore-finger and thumb. "His head must have been as big as the palm of my hand."

"Dios mío. It must've happened when he went to his blanket."

"That's what I think. The snake must have slithered beneath the bedroll during the heat of the day. Then, when the unlucky lad went to it in the dark, the damned thing was still there. I can see him bending to open his bedroll and the snake striking him twice before he knew it." Martínez clapped his hands twice. "He died on the spot, probably without making a sound."

"Why would he die so quickly?"

"The snake struck him in the neck, where the blood vessels took the venom directly to the heart. He was dead in seconds."

"What a way to die." Dorado swallowed hard.

"It was fast, anyway. Well, tell me about the interviews."

"Yes, sir. But, before I do, I've something else to tell you and it's important."

"What is it?" asked Martínez, his huge hands resting casually on Montoya's chest.

Dorado told him about the Indian boy and what he had seen on the morning of the murder. Martínez listened intently as Dorado related every detail he could remember.

"Dios mío! He saw them there." Martínez stood back from the table.

"He saw her, but not him. The red skirt tells us it was the governor's niece."

"It does indeed. Too bad she was in the way of his view of the man. Couldn't the boy tell you anything about the man? Not even his hair color or height? What he was wearing?"

"He saw the man's hat, but not the face beneath it."

"That's unfortunate. Did he say why he didn't see the face?"

"Mateo claimed the canoe was moving too fast on the current, but I think his eyes were on the girl – not the murderer. The monk said the boy only glanced at them, but I doubt it. I think Mateo looked all the while his canoe passed them considering what he recalled seeing."

"So do I. I assume Mateo is a novice and wouldn't admit he looked at the girl at length in front of the monk." Martínez smiled. "I guess the boy still has some worldly curiosity."

"So it appears. Even though Mateo didn't see the murderer's face, we now know a bit more about him. We know he's not short since his hat appeared above Gloria's head and she was a girl of ordinary height. Maybe five feet tall, más o menos. We also know he's not a fat man or Mateo would have noticed his clothing on either side of the girl."

"Good thinking, Lieutenant. Of course, we can't be certain about the murderer's height or weight because Mateo's view of him was blocked by the girl's body and the palmettos."

"What about the laughter Mateo heard?"

"I don't know what to think about it." Martínez crossed his arms over his chest. "Why in God's name would they be laughing – especially the girl?"

"It's hard to imagine the murder with her laughing."

"It is indeed. Was the boy certain he heard it?"

"Yes, and I believe him, sir. Mateo seems to be an alert lad. And you know how well sound carries over water."

Martínez nodded. "Mateo also saw her canoe there! We can assume it was hers since he saw the brown habit on the stern seat."

"Yes, sir, and he recognized it as a monk's habit."

"You know, mentioning her canoe makes me realize we haven't yet talked about how it ended up grounded on Pelican Island."

"I assume the murderer pushed it into the river after the murder and the current took it over to the island. Mateo didn't see it on Pelican Island later because he was looking toward the mainland where he had seen the man and woman."

"That makes sense. His curiosity would have been aroused when he saw them earlier."

"Even if he wasn't curious, most people paddling up river look toward the shore rather than at Pelican Island anyway. Except for the birds, there's nothing much to see on the island. It's little more than a sand bar that's often under water in flood tides."

"True." Martínez pursed his lips. "Speaking of islands, we need to know who or what is buried on Anastasia Island. We can't speak to Jesse Fish until we know what he buried there. Ricardo won't request the governor's permission to interview him without knowing what it is. So, he wants you to go over there and dig it up – hopefully without alerting the old bastard."

"I'll request a couple of men from the officer of the guard and go over there today."

"Good." Martínez leaned back on the stool.

"Is there anything new known about the Morones girl?"

"Not that I've heard. Harmon still hasn't been found, but he was seen several days ago south of town in the vicinity of Moultrie's plantation. Ricardo has sent patrols over the area to find him. I expect he'll be found soon."

"If you have time, sir, I've a question for you before I go."

"What is it?"

"How did the insects help you learn the time of Gloria's death?"

"Didn't I already tell you and Ricardo about that last week?"

"No. You mentioned it, but never told us all the details. You told us about the changes of body color after death, but not about the insects."

"Ah, Lieutenant, such is the cost of growing old. Loss of memory is a sure sign. What will be next, I wonder?"

He smiled, tilting his head to the side. "One day soon, I suppose my member won't do what I want it to do. When that time comes, I guess the grave will follow." Martínez threw his head back and laughed.

Dorado laughed with him.

"Well, let me see what I can remember."

"Do you want her file from your office, sir?"

"No. I remember. By the time I saw the body, it was covered with insect bites. Much like this one here, but the bites on the girl were the work of ants and cockroaches. They're the insects that come with death and I can't keep them out of the surgery."

"So I've noticed." The doctor motioned Dorado to a stool, while he talked.

"Ants are usually the first to find the dead. They can be there within minutes. So, her corpse was covered with their bites."

"What about vultures?" Dorado was accustomed to seeing them everywhere he went.

"Vultures come later unless they happen to see a body from the sky. They couldn't see the girl's corpse because it was covered by palmetto fronds. Incidentally, no other wild animals or birds found it either or parts of the body would have been taken. Wild animals tear away the hands and feet and birds peck out the eyes of the dead."

Dorado made a face.

"Ant bites are unmistakable; they cut away tiny pieces of flesh. You can see them with a magnifying glass – they look red to the eye. The numerous ant bites on the body indicated it lay out there for quite a while. More than half a day, I would think. The ants were all over her and some were still on her corpse the next day. I removed them with alcohol."

"Does alcohol kill them?"

"No, but they run from it and so do cockroaches. Cockroach bites were on the body as well – they show up as brown spots. The number of them also suggested she had been dead for hours. From the insect bites alone, I knew she died on the morning of the previous day."

"What gave you the time of death?"

"For the best estimate of the time of death, I am indebted to the blowflies. They usually arrive soon after the ants and instantly begin laying eggs in all the moist areas the eyes, nose, mouth, anus, female opening and in all accessible wounds. It's the blowflies' speed in finding a corpse and laying eggs on it that helps us estimate the time of death."

"How, sir? What do you mean?"

"We know blowfly maggots hatch in about a day and a half and, so, once the maggots appear, we know that death occurred about thirty-six hours earlier."

"I see." Dorado sat fingering the gold band on his hat.

"The maggots had already hatched on the Gloria's body when I first saw it. There were maggot holes all over it by that time; they eat into the flesh as soon as they hatch. So, when I saw the holes, I knew she was murdered in the mid-morning of the previous day."

"So insects can teach us something after all."

"Yes. Insects are among nature's creations just as we are. And nature has an order we need to understand. The more we know about nature, the more we'll know about ourselves. In time, perhaps, we might even be able to improve the way we live our lives."

"Uncle Ernesto said, 'Man would have a much better chance of improving his life if he looked to nature rather than revelation. In time, nature may well be known, but not God who never will be understood.'"

"Well spoken!" Martínez struck the edge of the table with the flat of his big hand. "Yes, indeed. I like your uncle's thinking, though it's something our esteemed clergy would consider blasphemy. A century or two ago those words would have sent him to the rack or the stake."

"Uncle Ernesto was contemptuous of the clergy."

"That's easy to understand. Let's continue. We now know when she was killed within an hour or so." Martínez saw Dorado nod in agreement.

"Midmorning seems accurate. That time fits with what we know about her movements that morning. Gloria left Government House before breakfast, didn't she?"

"Yes. Ricardo said that stupid sentry had no notion when she left. He only knew it was sometime before the guards at Government House got their first tea of the morning, an hour or so after sunrise. It's a wonder the tonto (fool) knew that. Solís didn't even know the name of the Indian boy who brought tea to him every morning. God help Spain with such soldiers."

Dorado nodded. "Alvarez recalled the small monk left about a half hour after he arrived for duty at seven-thirty. He said the monk was the last in line waiting for a canoe. So, it seems likely she left the dock after eight o'clock. It would have taken her another hour or so to reach the place where she beached her canoe. It took her longer than usual because she was paddling against the tide. That means she arrived at the site of the rendezvous sometime after nine-thirty. It was therefore almost ten o'clock when Gloria met the murderer. We know the river current changed while she was there because Mateo said he wasn't paddling when he passed the two of them in his canoe. He also said it was about midmorning when he saw them."

"Everything points to her death at midmorning." Martínez looked down at the body on the table. "Tell me about the interviews, Lieutenant. I need to finish up here and see some sick soldiers. There's a chest cough going around. Let's hope it's not some damned new plague."

Holding the wooden post on the pier with both his hands, Núñez steadied the rolling longboat as Dorado and two other soldiers climbed up onto the dock at Anastasia Island. He followed them a moment later after tying the bow and stern lines to the post. Núñez doubled the lines to secure the boat in the wind.

The four soldiers walked along, bent forward in the face of the stinging wind. Dorado and Núñez went ahead, with the other men, Ospina and Vargas, behind them carrying shovels. They turned east when they reached the alligator pond and went through the weeds alongside the tidal creek. The wind subsided as they proceeded slowly inland to the hill, where Dorado had seen Fish and his servant bury the wrapped object.

On top of the hill, Dorado quickly found the spot with his spyglass and pointed his men to the cedar beside it. Striding through the scrubland in only a few minutes, they reached the place Jesse Fish and his freedman had covered with leaves and pine needles. The grave site, much darker in color than the surrounding dirt, was easy to recognize, even with the layer of leaves and recently fallen tree debris.

Under the supervision of Núñez, the two soldiers swept away the leaves and began to dig into the ground. While they dug, Dorado looked around the area for anything Jesse Fish or his servant might have left behind. He found nothing except the tracks of a wheel barrow the freedman had pushed to and from the spot. The tracks, still etched in the sand, went southward through the pine forest toward what Dorado assumed was Jesse Fish's plantation.

Most of the dirt had been dug out of the grave when Dorado walked back from his look about the area. The two soldiers were standing waist deep in the hole when he arrived. Núñez squatted on the edge above them.

"Dig carefully," he instructed them. "We don't want to damage whatever it is."

"Here it is." Vargas pointed to a white piece of fabric near his foot.

"Use your hands, now." Núñez gestured to Vargas, who had his shovel poised to plunge into the ground. "Pass up the shovels."

"Mierda, it stinks." Ospina made a face as he freed one end of the wrapped object. "It must be a dead body."

"A child's body!" Vargas pushed dirt off what he recognized to be a torn white blanket. He used his fingers to brush the dirt out of the creases in the cloth.

"Move out of the way so the lieutenant can see it." Núñez motioned the men away from the white mound in the dirt.

"It's so short – only two feet or so." Dorado knelt on one knee at the edge of the hole. "It may well be a baby's body."

"Bring it up," ordered Núñez, seeing Dorado nod to him. "Carefully!"

"It's light." Vargas bent forward to take one end of the wrapped object. Ospina picked up the other end and they placed it gently on the ground outside the hole.

Núñez kneeled down and carefully unfolded the tattered blanket. Vargas and Ospina remained in the hole, watching Núñez.

"Madre de Dios!" exclaimed Núñez, when he turned the last fold. "It's someone's leg!"

At their last meeting in the plaza, Dorado had asked Serena to meet him every Saturday afternoon, with the exception of the days when he was assigned to guard duty. Serena agreed and, on the third Saturday of October, they met at four-thirty and walked for a half hour. Few other people were in the plaza at that time. It was a dreary day with steady rain in the morning and a persistent drizzle that lingered on through most of the afternoon. The rain slackened and finally stopped by the time they met, but a wet mist hung over them as they walked around the plaza. Eager to be with each other, they ignored the inclement weather.

As the cloudy day darkened, they left the plaza and proceeded down several streets to the house of Esperanza Chávez. The tiny structure was situated on a short dirt lane known as Cádiz Street. It was one of the narrow walkways that crossed the main roads in St. Augustine.

The major roads ran north and south through the city, parallel to the pier. Royal Street (Calle Real) was St. Augustine's main street and it extended from the city gates in the north to the last residential cross-street in the south. At its center, Government House stood facing the plaza and the church. The Street of Merchants (La Calle de los Mercadores) ran a block east of Royal Street and passed the bayside of the plaza on its way from the fort to the southern end of town. At its northern end, the Street of Merchants split into two narrow roads, one proceeding to the Castillo, the other curving to the city gates. There were two shorter streets, a dirt track to the Holy Spirit cemetery and a path that stretched all along the sea wall from the Castillo to the south end of town.

Most of the houses stood on the two main streets, including the best-built buildings in St. Augustine. Those houses had been constructed of quarried coquina or oyster-shell concrete and were roofed with rough split cypress shingles. Standing out among the more common wooden dwellings, they were at least two stories high and had balconies built over the streets. Designed to entice the slightest breeze off the bay in the summer months, the balconies brought morning shade and afternoon shadows to windows and doorways facing the rising and setting sun. On humid evenings, they also provided the home owners refuge from the sweltering heat indoors.

The majority of the houses in town were one-story structures without balconies. They had been built of split logs and stood on every street. The presidio also had a number of mud-plastered huts with palm thatch roofs and earth floors. They housed the poor and stood on side streets, well away from the center of the city.

The little house of Esperanza Chávez was made of yellow pine. Weather-beaten over time, its whitewash was gone and the planking had come loose on the east side of the building. Many boards were warped and the south side leaned away at an odd angle, apparently sliding off the foundation. It reminded Dorado of the bent base card in a house of cards. Though he made no mention of it to Serena, he doubted the house would survive the next violent storm.

To his surprise, the inside of the house seemed more stable than the outside. An uneven floor was the only structural flaw Dorado noticed as he entered the door. Later, when his eyes had adjusted to the candlelight, he saw that the floorboards ended a foot short of the wall on the leaning side of the house. The bare ground in the space between the flooring and the wall had been filled with a variety of boards of different lengths. Dorado guessed the boards were leftover pieces of wood that had been gathered from building sites around town. Since he doubted Esperanza owned the house, it seemed likely the owner added the boards to rent the property.

The little house looked cozy inside. A stone fireplace stood out from the north wall of the room and the pleasant smell of burning cedar filled the air. The fireplace had been installed, like all the others in town, during the English Period. It provided heat in the winter, when wood was available, and a place for food preparation throughout the year. Esperanza Chávez cooked inside, unlike many other women who prepared food in outside sheds.

Her house also had glass windows, another innovation brought to St. Augustine by the English colonists. The windows had been set in the east and south sides of the building to bring in morning light and the sea breeze in the evening. There was a tiny window in the north wall, but none in the west. From long experience, the townspeople of St. Augustine knew the hottest sunlight in the summer and most of the rain and thunderstorms came out of the west.

The house, spotlessly clean, was simply furnished with crude wooden furniture made in town. Esperanza Chávez had one oak chair, but the other chairs and tables were made of cedar. All the wood showed the conscientious application of tung oil and Dorado could smell it while he sat talking to Serena at the table. There were no Spanish furnishings. Imported and highly taxed, they would have been too costly for most townspeople to own.

Serena made supper for Dorado and they ate alone in the house. Esperanza went to visit María, while her young cousin entertained the lieutenant. Anxious to be with Dorado, Serena instantly accepted Esperanza's invitation to spend an evening with him in the house. Esperanza gave her a knowing smile and, the next day, arranged to spend that night with her sister. At the time, María was furious with Carlos Martínez and would not speak to him. Drunk one night in a tavern, he had pulled down her bodice and kissed her breasts in front of three laughing men.

Dorado felt full and pleased as he leaned back in his chair after supper. He had enjoyed the food and the evening's conversation, but, most of all, he simply enjoyed being with Serena. Dorado was delighted to be sitting so close to her at the table. It gave him the chance to look at her at length and revel in her lovely face. Dorado wished the evening would never end, but for the sake of propriety, he knew it would be necessary to leave before long. Two widowed sisters lived in the neighboring house and they would be certain to mark his arrival and departure.

"Dinner was sabrosa (delicious)." Dorado smiled at Serena as she started to clear away the dishes. "Your arroz a la marinera was wonderful. It's been a long time since I've eaten good Cuban food – and yours was delicious."

"Thank you." Serena lowered her eyes when he looked at her. "I'm glad you enjoyed it. The fish was caught this morning."

"It's the tastiest food I've eaten in St. Augustine." Dorado lied, knowing it was inferior to the meals prepared by Señora Salgado, Ruiz de León's neighbor. "Although I have enjoyed eating with Don Ricardo. His woman cooks in the French style with sauces."

"I've heard the governor's cook also prepares food in that style." Serena briefly looked into his blue eyes.

"So I hear, but I know much more about Don Ricardo's food. I've eaten with him many times. In fact, I was there last night."

"It seems strange that a Spanish caballero like Capitán Ruiz de León has never married. It's said he has lived alone for many years. No one knows why, though María says she heard the only woman he ever loved died before they were to be married."

"I don't know anything about a woman in his life. We haven't talked about such things."

"From what you say about him, it seems you have become friends." Serena sat directly across from Dorado. She had cleared the table and served him a glass of Jerez. "Yes. I eat with him now two evenings a week and we play chess and talk late into the night. We have much in common."

"What are some of the things you have in common?" Serena now looked at him openly.

"Well, for one thing, we speak slowly and carefully." Dorado smiled. "I suppose it's the way of the campo (the country way). Not like they speak in Havana or Madrid. They speak so fast there and cut off the word endings."

"Like Captain Martínez?"

"Exactamente. He's from Cádiz and speaks city Spanish."

"He does." Serena nodded. "Sometimes he speaks so fast I don't understand him. Even María has trouble understanding him at times."

"That's happened to me, too." Dorado smiled. "But his sarcasm is easy to understand."

"How very true." Serena made a face.

Serena poured more Jerez into Dorado's glass, but left her own empty. She wanted to save as much as possible. The wine had been an expensive gift brought from Havana for her cousins. Serena had hesitated to serve the Jerez to Dorado, but Esperanza urged her to share it with him. She wanted her cousin to make a good impression on the nobleman from Asturias.

"What about you? No more wine? It's excellent!"

"No, I've had enough, gracias. What else do you and Don Ricardo have in common?"

"Family. Our lives have been surprisingly similar. His father died when he was a boy, too. His older brother, like mine, holds the family lands. Don Ricardo was raised by his sister, Rosa María, who, he says, spoiled him badly. She's still living in Spain."

"His mother was dead at the time his father died?"

"No. She was still living and went to Mass every day of her life. You know the kind – always crossing herself and saying everything is a sin. She became even more religious after the death of his father and spent the rest of her life praying in church. Don Ricardo described his mother as a 'silent, severe woman, dressed every day in black, staring far into the distance at something no one else could see.'"

"How sad! Tell me about your mother."

"My mother raised us with love and humor. I seem to remember her laughing much of the time. She raised us with the help of Uncle Ernesto. He left the king's service soon after my father died. He resigned his commission because he was tired of the sea and wanted to live the rest of his life on land. At least, that's what he told us. He was well along into his fifties when he came home, but remained robust for many years. For me, he was full of life and wisdom."

"He was your mother's brother?"

"My father's older brother. Since he had never married, Uncle Ernesto helped my mother with everything at home, including me." Dorado smiled as fond memories of his playful uncle entered his mind. "He became my champion – a hero to me in my childhood."

"Does Don Ricardo remind you of Uncle Ernesto?"

"In a way." Dorado nodded. "It may be because we have so much in common. We're from the north lands, close to the Cantabrian Mountains. Both of us also became soldiers in the king's army. We are officers and ..."

"And you are both from families with titles." Serena looked directly into Dorado's eyes as she pointed out their class and family differences. She made the blunt observation hoping he would dismiss it as unimportant. But his reply disappointed her.

"Yes, but it's much more than that." Dorado was aware of Serena's concern, but he did not know what to say to her. He saw her smile disappear.

"Don Ricardo is someone special. He's someone I feel I have always known. He's like someone in my family. Does that sound strange?"

Serena stared at him, but did not answer his question. She was not interested in hearing how special the older man was to Dorado. "How is he like your uncle?"

"He's a loyal soldier of the king – like my father and uncle, he would fight to the death for the king. And I am proud that he selected me to serve with him in the murder investigation. He's a commander I would follow anywhere."

"It sounds like he's very important to you."

Dorado nodded. "But now there's someone else who's much more important to me." He looked into her eyes and smiled.

Serena blushed and looked down at her clasped hands on

the table. A moment later, she raised her eyes and said, "I am glad to know Don Ricardo is such a good friend to you. He can assist you in the king's service. It's well known he has the governor's ear. They say those who seek the governor's assistance must first speak to Captain Ruiz de León."

"That may well be true, but my appreciation of him has nothing to do with my hope for such assistance." Dorado spoke forcefully, even though he was well aware that Ruiz de León could help him with a promotion. "Something tells me we will be lifelong friends; it's just one of those things I'm sure about, without knowing why." He saw Serena nod with understanding. "You know, last night, Don Ricardo said something surprising to me. It happened during our second game of chess."

"What did he say?"

"It concerned something I said to him earlier. At dinner, I told him how much I liked his house. It's a solid little house with many conveniences. Didn't I tell you about them?"

"Yes. You especially liked the balcony and its view of the bay. You also mentioned the smell of the cedar walls inside." Serena smiled, pleased to show him how well she had been listening.

"Yes, the smell reminds me of the mountain woods at home. Anyway, I told him how much I liked his house. I said someday in the future I hoped to own one like his. He thanked me for the for the compliments and we continued playing our game. I assumed that ended all conversation on the subject of his house."

"But it didn't?" Serene asked the expected question.

"No. After we finished the game – it finally ended in a draw, he said, 'I'm pleased you like my home, Lieutenant. It is quite comfortable, isn't it? Who knows, perhaps in the future a house like it one day will be yours.'" He then smiled and began packing the chess pieces away.

"Did he say anything else?"

"No. He turned his face away to cough; he's got that awful cough that's going around."

"What did you say?"

"Nothing. I didn't know what to say. Of course, I wondered if he meant I would be promoted after the murder investigation and then have enough money to buy a house."

"That's what it sounds like to me. Was he serious when he said that to you?"

"Yes. Don Ricardo is usually serious and rarely ever laughs. Unlike his close friend, Carlos Martínez, he never laughs out loud. They certainly are unusual friends. One is quiet, soft-spoken and severe, the other is loud, boisterous and sarcastic as you well know. It's hard to imagine them as friends. Yet, they seem to be very close."

"What do they have in common?"

"I'm sure it's their knowledge. They can talk for hours on every imaginable subject – law, literature, history, politics, science, the Church, even God!"

"I'm not surprised to hear that. María says she never knows what the doctor will say next. He speaks his mind, doesn't he?"

"Yes and I admire him for it. I also like his sense of humor, even though it's often too sarcastic. There's much to admire in him. What a mind he has! He's the most intelligent man I've ever met – with the exception of Uncle Ernesto."

"That's what María says. She also says he can be very moody. He has a terrible temper and is quick to anger. His awful anger frightens her, though he never has hit her."

"I have seen such moods come and go. I never know what to expect from him. Yet, I like being with him and I think we'll be good friends, too."

"I hope so, if that's what you want." The frown on her face showed him she hoped it was not what he wanted.

Serena disliked Carlos Martínez. She considered him to be coarse and insulting, a man surely unworthy of her cousin.

From what María said about him as well as what she had seen of him herself, Serena judged him to be a rude brute. His vulgar language and what she viewed as his repulsive personal manners disgusted her. Seeing him swear and pick his nose publicly, she could not imagine what María saw in the big ungainly man. Serena said nothing to María though she did confide her misgivings about him to Esperanza. She recalled speaking candidly to her one night, following a festive family dinner which included Martínez.

At dinner, the doctor, drunk after drinking two bottles of wine himself, slurped his soup and ate the deer meat from the stew with his hands. When he rose from the table, the drunken man belched loudly and farted, mortifying María. He then casually wiped his greasy hands on her grandmother's embroidered tablecloth. Before he finally left, Martínez kissed María with his tongue and cupped his hands around her breasts, squeezing each one in turn. He laughed gleefully, holding her tightly to him, and leered at her as he stumbled to the door.

"What a disgusting man!" exclaimed Serena, walking home with Esperanza. "What in the world can she possibly see in him?"

"Quién sabe?" Esperanza Chávez clucked her tongue. "I don't know why she puts up with that brute, either. It's probably because there're no decent men in this godforsaken place."

As Serena listened to Dorado, she was tempted to tell him what happened that evening. But she decided not to mention it. Serena worried he might resent her criticism of the man.

They talked until ten o'clock and then Dorado stood to leave. Although he wanted to stay longer, the young man knew it would be improper to stay later. Serena escorted him to the door, where they agreed to meet the following Saturday. It was awkward for both of them as they stood facing each other, making polite conversation. Dorado thanked Serena for dinner and took her hand, intending to kiss it politely before leaving. But the first touch of their hands changed the time of his departure.

Instead of allowing him to hold her hand for a quick kiss, Serena squeezed his fingers and stared into his eyes. There was no shyness now. Her brown eyes beckoned to him, but he hesitated to kiss her. Dorado stood so close to her, he could smell the sweet fragrance she had brushed into her hair. Her very presence made him perspire all over.

Serena smiled. She took her hand from his and put her arms around his neck. Serena stood on tiptoes as they kissed. Their lips met tentatively at first and tightened as they brought their bodies together. It was a kiss neither one wanted to end.

Serena dared not move, not wanting to let him loose. Her face felt as if on fire. The fire spread out of control to every part of her body. She felt the sudden desire to turn herself over to him, to surrender everything to him. As they pressed their bodies together and kissed with open mouths and tongues, Serena knew she loved him. She waited for him to touch her body and do whatever he wanted with her.

But Dorado did nothing more with her. He ended the long kiss and gently loosened his arms from around her back. He stepped away, smiled at her and backed away toward the door. With his hand on the knob, he stood looking into her eyes.

"I should be going home." Dorado smiled. "Buenas noches, Serena. Hasta pronto (until we meet again soon)."

"Buenas noches, Dorado, hasta luego." Serena was sadly disappointed by his sudden decision to depart, but showed no sign of her feelings. Instead, she stood with a smile on her face and nodded if to say she understood.

"Until next Saturday." Dorado looked back at her as he opened the door.

Serena leaned her back against the door after he left. She remained there for several minutes thinking of him and what they had shared. Serena wondered why Dorado had left so suddenly, but, after spending so much intimate time with him, she was too happy to let it worry her. Later, she assumed, as a caballero (gentleman), he had treated her like a lady. Serena told her cousins that Dorado's abrupt departure was an act of chivalry. It made her feel respected and temporarily relieved her fears about their class difference.

Dorado walked happily away as well. His mind was awhirl with memories of kissing Serena endlessly and holding her tightly in his arms. He remembered the feeling of her breasts pressed against his chest, her thighs touching his thighs. The thoughts of how close their bodies had been together made his legs tremble and Dorado reminded himself why he had ended their embrace so abruptly. In the excitement of kissing and caressing Serena's body, he had wet his drawers. Fearing Serena might see the wet spot that had spread out to his breeches, Dorado left as quickly as possible. He deftly turned and sidled out through the doorway. Once outside in the darkness, Dorado sighed in relief, knowing she had not seen the spot. But all the way home, he worried what the widow Sánchez would think when she washed his stained clothing.

CHAPTER TEN

OCTOBER 27-31, 1788

"Thank you for coming over to talk to me, Don Miguel." Ruiz de León saluted and, then, extended his hand as Colonel Miguel Montesinos y Cárdenas entered his office.

"Por nada." The commandant shook his hand and then took off his black felt hat. "I want to help in every possible way."

Ruiz de León held out a chair for him. "How was your journey to Pensacola?"

"Long and hard. I must say it's getting harder to ride day after day, even with the best of saddles. A three-week journey on horseback never bothered me before. I must be my age."

"It happens to us all, I'm afraid; one day, you awake and can't do what you did the day before." Ruiz de León nodded. "You know this interview is awkward for me, Don Miguel."

"It shouldn't be, Don Ricardo. You're doing your duty as

you should. I hope in some way I can be helpful. We must do everything possible to find the fiend who killed Gloria."

"Thank you for your understanding. I've ordered tea for you. Would you like anything to eat? The kitchen women can make you some breakfast." Ruiz de León cleared his throat.

"Gracias, no. I usually don't eat breakfast, but I will have a piece of warm bread with Doña Concepción's sugared blackberries. They're too good to refuse." He smiled.

"How true. Did you walk here from the Castillo?" Ruiz de León covered his mouth as he coughed several times.

"Yes, and I almost stepped on a damned snake in the dark – in the plaza of all places. I was in a hurry and walking carelessly."

"Que Dios nos ayude (God help us)! They're in the plaza now in the light of day."

Ruiz de León paused as Sergeant Suárez entered his office and placed a silver tray with two cups of tea and a bowl of brown sugar on the desk. Suárez held napkins and spoons in his other hand and he placed them in front of the officers.

"Thank you, Sergeant. Please bring us a few pieces of this morning's baked bread and a bowl of the sugared black-berries."

"Yes, sir." Suárez saluted Ruiz de León and walked quickly away.

"Well, Don Miguel, I wonder if you remember the morning of ..."

"The morning of the murder." The commandant held the cup to his lips and sipped his hot tea. "Yes, I recall it quite clearly. I left the Castillo at seven-thirty that morning to in-spect the walls, where they connect at the northwest corner. When the San Sebastián overflowed in that last storm, sea water flooded the corner and loosened the stones. Most of the mortar was gone and a number of blocks had fallen out of the wall."

"Did the chief engineer accompany you?"

"No. The esteemed Captain Mariano de la Rocque didn't arrive at the Castillo on time. He's rarely on time these days." The colonel shrugged. "So I rode off without him."

"Did he join you later?" Ruiz de León looked up as Suárez put a plate, with two pieces of wheat bread and an open pot of blackberries, on his desk. A spoon was in the pot. "Thank you, Sergeant, that'll be all." He smiled at Suárez.

The commandant spoke when Suárez was gone. "No, he decided to repair the leaks in the moat instead. Rocque should do as he's told. If he wasn't such a good engineer, he would have been charged with insubordination long ago. If he disobeys me again, I intend to put him on the next ship to Havana."

"Mariano is easily distracted, but as you say he's a very good engineer." The captain's face reddened as he tried to hold back another cough.

"Rocque's much too easily distracted. I see you've got the cough that's going around."

Ruiz de León nodded and coughed into his handkerchief.

The commandant continued his account. "After inspecting the damage, I rode along the walls looking for other breaks in the line. I found another broken section a little farther on and dismounted to see what needed to be done. By the time I finished assessing the damage, it was time to leave. It was ten-fifteen and I had arranged to meet Lieutenant López Sierra at ten-thirty."

"You met him on time?" Ruiz de León sipped his tea.

"Yes. Exactly – en punto." The colonel spooned berries onto a piece of bread and took a bite. "I rode into the woods and took the hard ground to get back in time," he mumbled with his mouth full. "These berries are delicious."

"They are indeed – I had some earlier. Don Miguel, despite my reluctance, I must ask you about Gloria? As you know, it's not a subject that I wish to discuss with you, but I must inquire about your knowledge of her." Ruiz de León exhaled a long breath.

"Don't be concerned, Ricardo, it's what must be done." He took a drink of his tea and put the cup on the desk. "I'll tell you all about the girl. She was a serious problem for me."

As Ruiz de León interviewed the commandant, Dorado and the doctor paddled a bark canoe across the bay to the dock at Jesse Fish's plantation. Martínez sat in the stern steering, while Dorado kneeled, paddling from the bow. It was an easy crossing in calm water. Above them, the sun shone brightly and there was only an occasional gust of wind at their backs.

As they approached the pier, Jesse Fish emerged from the door of his house and walked slowly toward them. He steadied himself with a thick staff and shuffled along, step by step, on the wooden span leading to the dock. By the time he reached it, the Spaniards had docked, tied off the canoe and climbed up the four-rung ladder.

"What a pleasant surprise." Fish smiled at them. It was the same wide smile showing his few yellowed teeth that had disgusted Dorado the first time he met the old man.

Jesse Fish also appeared to be wearing the same patched and soiled clothes Dorado had seen on him the day of Gloria's funeral. He wondered if the old man ever changed his clothing. While Martínez went forward and stood a few feet from the Englishman, Dorado remained by the mooring post to avoid Fish's odor. He leaned against the post and listened to them talk.

"Buenos días, Señor Fish. I trust we aren't disturbing you this morning."

"Not at all. Distinguished visitors are always welcome here at El Vergel." He smiled once again. "I saw you approaching with my spyglass. Gracias a Dios, I can still see through it. It's one of the few pleasures left to me in my declining years."

Martínez nodded, but said nothing in reply.

"I have some oranges for Don Vicente; they're the first of the year." Fish gestured with his staff to a bulging bag standing near the end of the dock. "I've been waiting for someone to come take them to Government House. I sent a note to the governor a few days ago."

"Gracias, Señor Fish, I'm sure the governor will be pleased."

"Why don't you come to the house? We can sit inside and get out of the sun. My man will make us some cassava tea and we can talk in comfort." Fish leaned heavily on his staff.

"Gracias no, señor. We can't stay long."

"How about a glass of wine? It's excellent Rioja! I'll have my man fetch it for you."

"No thank you, Señor Fish. We don't want to take up your time and I must return soon to see patients. It seems there's a new sickness spreading around St. Augustine."

"Well, that means I won't be going into town anytime soon. Ah! So that must be the reason you're here – to warn me away from the new sickness in town. How kind of you!"

"No, Señor Fish, that's not why we are here." Martínez, frowned. "The governor has sent us to talk to you."

"Is that so? Now, that does sound serious." Fish stepped back and sat on a small barrel standing on the dock. "I better sit to hear such serious business." He leaned back and crossed his arms over his chest.

"It has come to our attention that an unreported burial took place on your property some days ago. We're here to inquire about it." Martínez stared at the old man.

"I see." Fish nodded. "So, would that be what was recently dug up and taken from my land? He turned his head to look at Dorado, who still leaned against the mooring post. "It was you I believe who trespassed on my property without permission."

"Yes, Señor Fish, it was indeed Lieutenant Dorado Delgado. He was sent to dig up the man's leg that was buried on the island. The governor is concerned that no notice of the leg or its burial was given to the colonial authorities."

"Ah, yes, the leg." Fish smiled at Martínez. "It seemed senseless to report the burial of a leg. Of course, if it were a corpse, I would have reported it immediately."

"Whose leg was it?"

"How would I know?" Fish shook his head. "I didn't even know it was a man's leg. In fact, I later thought it might be the girl's leg after what the alligators did to her."

Martínez narrowed his eyes as he looked at Fish. "Tell me, señor, how did the leg come into your possession? Surely, it didn't come walking up to the door of your house."

"Oh, no, Captain Martínez, I would then have heard it knock." Fish grinned. "But I did find it behind the house near the woodshed."

"Is that so?" Martínez glared at Fish. "How did you think the leg got there?"

"One of my dogs found it and brought it home. He was gnawing on the leg, when I saw what it was. The leg was little more than a bloody bone. I thought it best to bury it so no other beast molested it further. Of course, I intended to report the burial on my next trip to town."

"I see." Martínez frowned, listening to Fish's explanation. "We also find it curious that two young girls, one of them the governor's niece, lost their lives soon after visiting El Vergel. In fact, they died only a day after their visits. What are your thoughts on those coincidences?"

"What on earth are you talking about?" Fish's face reddened.

"Las Señoritas Patricia Hernández Parral and Gloria Márquez García y Morera visited El Vergel – both of them – the day before they died."

"Is that so? Am I to be blamed for their deaths? What about the Morones girl? Am I also to be blamed for the alligators that killed her? How about the next storm that strikes the presidio, will I be blamed for the damage it does?" Fish's face remained flushed.

"No one is blaming you. We are only inquiring into the odd coincidence I mentioned."

"I can't control coincidences and I object to your insinuations. They're insults! You can be sure I'll mention them to the governor, the next time I'm in town."

"You do that, Señor Fish. I'm sure he'll be concerned about an insulted Englishman in the investigation of his murdered niece." Martínez turned on his heel and walked to the end of the dock. He climbed down the ladder to the canoe, never looking back.

"Don't forget the oranges." Fish spoke to Dorado, who was about to follow Martínez.

Dorado picked up the bag of fruit and thanked Fish before descending the ladder. He untied the lines, kneeled in the bow of the canoe and used his paddle to push off from the pier.

The Englishman sat on the barrel and watched them paddle away. He remained seated, his hands clasped in his lap, as the Spaniards cautiously maneuvered the canoe past the oyster beds and out of the snug harbor that was encircled by his property. Finally, he stood as they steered the canoe around the bend and out of sight.

"What fools these Spaniards are! What pompous fools!" Fish seized the staff in his hands and snapped it in half. He then walked briskly back to his house.

The men pointed the canoe north along the island's shoreline and avoided the sandbar at the mouth of the harbor. It was hard work paddling against the tidal current, now flowing in from the ocean. Both of them were on their knees paddling furiously to stay on course.

"Let's take another look at where the Morones girl was found." Martínez shouted to be heard above the sound of spraying water. "We might see something that was missed earlier. It shouldn't take too long and the incoming tide will make it easy to cross the bay afterwards."

Dorado looked back at Martínez and nodded his head.

"That old man is a sly weasel." Martínez held his paddle in his lap as the canoe entered the calm water of the inlet north of Fish's property. "Did you notice the bastard didn't disagree with me when I said the Parral girl was dead? He never blinked an eye when I mentioned it."

"Yes, sir, I did. He's so smug – so certain he has the governor's ear."

"He is and obviously contemptuous of us. I'm sure he thinks we Spaniards are beneath him. His condescending smile makes me want to strangle him whenever I see him."

"That's easy to understand. Do you believe his dog found the man's leg and brought it to his house?" Dorado touched bottom with his paddle. "We've about two feet of clearance."

"Good. I don't know what to believe. I doubt anything Jesse Fish says. But there were a number of punctures on the bone that appeared too small to be made by alligator teeth. They might well have been made by a dog. I'll take a look at the leg again."

Rather than risk taking the canoe up the shallow creek to the alligator pond, they tied up at the island dock and walked slowly overland. With Dorado working down at the edge of the water and Martínez, farther up the bank, they searched the ground upstream all the way to the alligator pond. After a half hour, they had found nothing, not even a footprint in the sand.

"It looks like no one has been here since the last rain." Dorado watched the alligators swim almost soundless in the pond.

"So it seems. Let's look all around the pond while we can." Martínez started down the bank. "Fortunately, no alligators are on shore today."

Dorado picked up the broken paddle he had seen on his last visit to the site and, seeing nothing on it, he tossed it aside. While Martínez looked over the ground on the near side of the pond, he jumped across the creek at a narrow place upstream and searched the far side. Neither man found anything belonging to the girl. Dorado, carrying his shoes and stockings, re-crossed the creek and walked barefooted back along the water's edge. As he approached Martínez, the young man suddenly stopped and looked down at the dark sand. "What's this?"

Dorado kneeled and dug his fingers into the sand. He stood up holding a small round object in the palm of his hand. "I think it's a piece of carved wood." He washed it off in the pond and handed it to Martínez, who stood beside him.

"It's the bowl of a man's pipe. See the broken stem sticking out of it?" Martínez used his pinky to remove wet sand from the bowl.

"Yes, sir. It's been carved out of a hardwood. Oak?"

"Probably. I wonder how long it's been buried here." He turned the bowl in his fingers.

"It was here at the high tide line." Dorado pointed down to the dark sand.

"The governor is concerned about how long the investigation is taking." Ruiz de León lit the fish-oil lamps on the table. The two lamps flickered from an unseen draft.

They were sitting in the main room after dinner. As was his manner, Martínez reclined on the floor, his back against the wall. He held a brandy glass on a propped up knee. Dorado sat in a chair with his legs stretched out in front of him. Though it was a cool night, neither of them wore their jackets. Ruiz de León remained in full dress, sitting straight up in his chair.

"I'm not surprised." Martínez made a face. "All the king's officials are the same; they want everything done instantly. But, if you should dare to ask them for something you require, they'll tell you to be patient, while they do it at their leisure, if at all."

"The governor has good cause to be concerned. He worries the foreigners will view the slow investigation – that's his term, not mine – as a sign of Spain's weakness. Since there are so many foreigners living in the presidio now, the governor is worried about the possibility of an uprising." Ruiz de León coughed several times, his face flushed.

"That cough sounds much worse." Martínez frowned at his friend.

"It's not that bad." His face remained flushed.

"Don Ricardo, how many foreigners are here in St. Augustine?"

"According to the census of 1786, there were 720 foreigners, including 500 Minorcans and only 713 of our people, not counting our troops. I doubt the numbers have changed much since then and they indicate why the governor is concerned."

Martínez frowned. "I don't know why. I doubt the Minorcans are concerned about the murder of a Spanish girl, even if she's the governor's niece. By the way, who made the census that year? Oh, I remember, now. It was that ignorant Irish priest, wasn't it?"

Ruiz de León glared at Martínez. "Yes, it was Father Hassett."

"Knowing he did it, I wouldn't trust the figures. With his medieval beliefs, he probably included all the saints in the census." Martínez curled his lips in a contemptuous smile.

"Now, Carlos, you know Father Hassett isn't a fanatic."

"Oh, no. Let me tell you what I heard that stupid priest once say in a sermon. He said thunder and lightning are two of the ways God shows us his disapproval of our sins. Hassett said thunder is God's strong voice telling us not to sin and lightning is God's finger pointing to hell where all sinners will go. It was at the baptism of a baby girl I delivered last September."

"No! He didn't say that? You're making that up." Ruiz de León inhaled deeply.

"I'm not making it up. That's what he said. Where does the Church find such priests? They can't all come from Ireland. It's no wonder so few men go to Mass anymore. These days, it's only the women and children, as well as the old, poor and sick who go to the priests. You know it's true, Ricardo."

"Sí. Que Dios nos ayude (God help us)!" Ruiz de León made a face. "Men need to come to God's church to be in His presence, whether or not they like his priests or what they say. It's not enough for them to go to church a couple times a year at Christmas and Easter. Their need for absolution of sin and Communion is the same as for women."

"Like it or not, Ricardo, most enlightened men find the priests too ignorant to inspire belief in what they say about God, never mind the world outside the Church. Most men also find the Church's ceremonies too long to endure at any one time."

"It's the same in Spain, sir." Dorado looked at Ruiz de León. "Few men go into the Church these days and fewer still go for Confession. They're only in church for baptisms, confirmations, weddings or funerals. They take their families there and wait outside for the end of Mass."

"What a foolish people we have become!" Ruiz de León looked at Dorado. "Anyway, most of us in the presidio think the census was accurate. And, as you would expect, the census greatly alarmed the governor when he saw it. I recall him shouting, 'Look at these figures! We live in a foreign colony. Gracias a Dios, we have 500 Spanish soldiers in the presidio.'"

"That's why so many of our people dislike living here, sir." Dorado sat up in his chair. "There are too many foreigners in St. Augustine."

"That's exactly why the governor is so worried." Ruiz de León coughed several times, one hand holding his wig in place.

"Your cough is getting worse." Martínez scowled at his friend. "You should get some rest or it will linger a long time and eventually send you to your bed for even longer."

Ruiz de León waved the advice away with the flick of his wrist. "I told you it's not that bad. Let's discuss the investigation."

"Bueno." Martínez exhaled his breath loudly, knowing it was useless to say any more. "I have some important information. It concerns what Olga Gallego told the lieutenant."

"Ah!" Dorado put his brandy glass on the table.

"I've talked to a man who was in Havana at the same time as the old woman. It's Luis Llera Gómez. Do you know him?"

"Only vaguely." Ruiz de León nodded.

"Well, Llera Gómez was one of the 3,000 Floridians who left the colony in 1763. He was eight years old at the time and lived in Havana during the foreign occupation. He's a boat builder. He makes dinghies for the king's ships and he learned his craft in Cuba. He ..."

"What does the man know?" interrupted Ruiz de León, impatiently.

Martínez made a face. "Llera Gómez remembered more than the old woman. He said, 'There was a murder, a terrible stabbing – it was in 1770. A young girl was killed in a pasture, near where most of the Floridians lived in Havana. They kept it quiet so we never knew if they found who murdered her.'"

"Well, that verifies Olga Gallego's story." Dorado smiled, pleased with himself.

"It certainly does. I must admit I doubted what she recalled." Ruiz de León wiped his nose with a handkerchief. "I hope Llera Gómez doesn't know our suspicions."

"He doesn't." Martínez drank the last of his brandy. "He came to see me about a minor ailment – an infected thumb. He had a wood splinter under his nail and, while I tweezed it out, we talked about his trade. I often talk with my patients to take their minds off what I'm doing."

"Yes, yes." Ruiz de León closed his eyes and sighed. "What else did he tell you?"

"Patience, Ricardo, it's a virtue as you know." Martínez smiled. "Llera Gómez told me everything I've mentioned without one question from me. He also told me he returned to St. Augustine in 1784, on the first ship that sailed here after the war. He returned to reclaim his family's house and property."

"What luck!" exclaimed Dorado.

"Yes, indeed." Ruiz de León shook his head up and down. "As I've told you so many times, Carlos, God moves in ways we do not understand."

Martínez frowned. "Once I knew he had lived in Havana, I asked him what the city was like in those years. At first, he talked about the storms, plagues, the usual and, then, he told me what we wanted to know. He recalled the killing because it was so unusual, 'even in Havana, where stabbings are as common as striped centipedes in the summer.' Those were his words."

"Did you ask him how it was unusual?" Ruiz de León looked down at Martínez.

"Yes, and he said, 'I recall hearing she was found naked and mutilated in some way.'"

"Ah! He used much the same words as Olga Gallego." Dorado smiled again.

"He did. Now, we'll see what Esteban says in his letter." Martínez yawned. "We still can't be certain the two murders show the same mutilation."

"True." Ruiz de León nodded. "Now, let me tell you about the commandant's activities that day. I spoke to him this morning. Incidentally, he was in Havana in 1770, too."

"So were you and I, Ricardo. That's where we first met."

"That's true. We met in March of that year."

"Don't either of you remember the girl's murder?" Dorado frowned. "If you were both in Havana, at the time, why ..."

"Why don't we remember it?" Martínez interrupted him. "I'll tell you why I don't – I was too busy as medical officer at Morro Castle. Most of that year, I was the only physician at the fort. My superior died of the fevers and I was working twelve hours a day. So I knew little of what was going on outside Morro Castle."

"Ruiz de León nodded. I also was assigned to Morro Castle at that time. But, unlike Carlos, I spent much of my time in the city. I served as an aide to the Commandant, Colonel Carlos Flores Gallardo. I was in charge of communications between the commandant and the royal officials in Havana. I went into town several times a week, but only on official business. I was stationed at Morro Castle for seven years, from 1764 to 1771, and so many murders took place then, at least one a week. So who ever would know one from the other?"

He shrugged his shoulders.

"Why, then, would Olga Gallego and Llera Gómez remember the murder so clearly?" Dorado looked back and forth between the two men.

Martínez sighed. "Because they lived inside the city and heard about every event that happened there. Nothing escapes the eyes and ears of the people of a Spanish city. Some say it's much easier to get news in the city streets than from the royal officials. In this presidio, our people seem to know everything as soon as the king's ships come into the harbor."

"How true!" said Ruiz de León. "The common people often know the king's cédulas (commands) before the royal officials. What we announce is seldom news to them."

Martínez nodded. "Rumor rules our cities. It's the source of most news. Everything is the subject of gossip. If the governor belches at lunch, what he has eaten is discussed within an hour. Of course, it's no mystery what spice his wife adds to his food. Anyone who makes the mistake of talking to the governor after he's eaten will tell you it's garlic."

Ruiz de León glared Martínez. "It's true. Nothing seems to escape the people's notice."

"Nothing!" Martínez laughed. "I knew a prominent man of wealth who lived in Cádiz and died in the middle of the night. No physician was called since he died quietly in his sleep. No one else was notified. Yet, early the next morning, there were fifty women at his front door with plates of food and condolences for the widow."

"I don't doubt it." Ruiz de León looked at Dorado. "You know the saying, 'The only secret is one that nobody else knows.'"

"That's so true." Martínez shook his head. "You know there is already talk in town of the girl's mutilation."

"No!" Ruiz de León made a face.

"The specifics aren't known, but there's talk of a 'cruel stabbing.' That's what it's called. We agreed to say nothing to anyone about how the girl was killed. Yet, somehow it's known."

"I haven't spoken a word to anyone about it," Dorado immediately spoke up.

"Nor have I. Of course, I told the governor, but only in general terms." Ruiz de León sighed. "I wish it wasn't known."

"Well, like it or not, it's now known. What about the commandant, Ricardo? What did he say when you questioned him?"

"As I told you, we met yesterday morning at my office. He was most accommodating and answered all my questions without hesitation." Ruiz de León told them the commandant's account of inspecting the walls.

"So, Rocque didn't go with him."

"No. When Rocque was late, the commandant rode off without him. You know how punctual Miguel is and how he hates tardiness."

"Oh, yes! He claims tardiness is a Spanish disease. He calls it the 'Mañana Malady.' Who hasn't heard him preach that sermon?"

"I've never heard him say that." Ruiz de León coughed.

"You haven't attended any of his staff meetings. Did Rocque follow the commandant out on the inspection?"

"No. When Rocque reached the fort, he spent his time looking for leaks in the moat; it was losing a foot of water a day. It took him awhile to find them and there was one deep crack in the seawall. He supervised the repairs, forgetting to follow the commandant until it was too late to ride after him."

"Was the commandant seen by the sentries on the walls?" Martínez now lay on his side with his head propped up on his hand.

"Yes. All five sentries stationed at the north wall saw

him. They recalled saluting him as he rode by that morning." Ruiz de León refilled their brandy glasses.

"You spoke to the sentries yourself?" Martínez sat up to sip his brandy.

"No. Sergeant Suárez asked them for me. I did speak to Mariano de la Rocque myself and he verified everything Miguel told me."

"I don't suppose the sentries knew when the commandant rode by?"

"No."

"They tell time by the church bells." Dorado pointed in the direction of the plaza. "So they wouldn't know the time unless the bells rang when he went by."

"That's true, none of them has a watch. The common soldiers have no pesetas for such costly luxuries. They only knew he rode by sometime after the seven o'clock change of guard."

"That's no help." Martínez frowned. "Wait! Didn't the commandant ride by them on his way back to the city gates?"

"No. He went through the woods beyond the walls and the view of the sentries."

"How convenient." Martínez sighed loudly.

"He rode that way on the hard ground to get to his meeting on time. He left the farthest walls at ten-fifteen and reached the fort at ten-thirty, as scheduled."

"López Sierra said the commandant rode up later." Dorado looked at Ruiz de León. "His exact words were, 'We arranged to meet at ten-thirty, but he arrived a half hour late.'"

"What do you think of that, Ricardo?" Martínez smiled.

"López Sierra had no reason to lie about it," said Dorado.

"Let's not assume anyone is lying." Ruiz de León sighed. "One of them is mistaken – that's all. We can easily find out when the commandant arrived. It'll be in the duty register."

"Of course!" Martínez nodded. "I'll look in the register

tomorrow morning."

"That should settle it." Ruiz de León grimaced, trying to stifle a cough.

"Perhaps. But there's something still to be said about the commandant's movements that morning." Martínez smiled again.

"Oh, and what's that?" Ruiz de León stared at him.

"We don't know where he went after riding into the woods. We only know he was not seen again until he rode through the city gates. By the way, when was that?"

"We don't know exactly."

"Why not?"

"Because the sentries at the gates didn't know the time he returned. They only knew it was sometime between ten and eleven, when the church bells ring the hour."

"Que Dios nos ayude!" Martínez threw his hands up in the air. "The guards at the main gates of the presidio don't know the time people come and go. It's no wonder we're losing the empire. Pobre España (poor Spain), still living in the seventeenth century."

"The governor would agree with you, Carlos. But, for now, there's no extra money for clocks, so the church bells will have to do."

"There's never money for anything useful in this presidio. I still can't get a new work table for the surgery. So, it seems there was time – maybe more than an hour – for him to meet the girl secretly. The commandant had more than enough time to inspect the walls, make the short ride out to the north woods and return to the Castillo by ten-thirty that morning. You know it's entirely possible, Ricardo."

"I suppose so." Ruiz de León exhaled his breath in exasperation. "Don't forget he has a fine horse that runs well. Didn't his stallion win the presidio's horse race this past year? That big beast could get him out and back in half an hour easily!"

"It would be easy, sir" agreed Dorado. "With an ordinary stable horse, I rode from the Castillo to the woods in about twenty-five minutes without spurring him. It was the afternoon I found Gloria's clothes in the woods. And López Sierra said, when the commandant arrived, he was breathing hard and his stallion was 'well lathered from a hard run.'"

"I recall that, too, Lieutenant. But whatever was possible, I'm certain the commandant had nothing to do with it. Now, let me tell you about his involvement with Gloria. I think that might satisfy your suspicions of him."

Martínez held up his hand. "Wait! I want to say one more thing about the commandant. You know, a man of his importance can be easily missed in a small presidio like St. Augustine. His presence is certainly conspicuous at public ceremonies but, at other times, when he comes and goes in town, he can ride or walk anywhere without being noticed. Everybody here is so accustomed to seeing him that he simply isn't seen. It would be the same for all of the royal officials and senior officers. Do you know what I mean?"

Ruiz de León nodded. "It would be true of me as well."

"Exactamente. A man as prominent as the Commandant of the Castillo can do whatever he wishes in this presidio. No one would ever question what he's doing or where he's going. It would be assumed he was doing his duty. Who would know if he were on his way to a secret meeting with the governor's niece or that he would murder and mutilate her?"

"Who could argue with what you say?" Ruiz de León studied his friend's face. "That would be true for any official or important man in town. But now let me tell you what Miguel said about Gloria. He was never enamored of her."

"What!" Martínez struck the floor with his empty glass. "How can you say that after all the affection seen between them? You saw it yourself, Ricardo!"

"I saw her affection, not his! The commandant claimed

he tried to evade her attentions and even her company."

"If so, he was one of a kind here in this presidio." The more Dorado thought of Gloria, the more he detested her. He would never forget how the deceitful girl had made a fool of him.

"So it seems." Ruiz de León nodded. "The commandant regarded Gloria as too spoiled, a consentida (a self-centered girl), who would never be satisfied as a soldier's wife."

"Was he aware of Doña Concepción's marriage plans for him?" asked Martínez.

"Yes, he knew about the scheme. He also knew why Doña Concepción wanted the girl married as soon as possible. It was obvious to him."

"So, the commandant knew about her other flirtations."

"Oh, yes, Miguel's immediate comment was, 'I have eyes, don't I? Only a blind man or a fool would marry her. That girl was on fire and no man could control her. To marry her would be to condemn yourself to lifelong misery.'"

"Yet, he still accepted her attentions, didn't he?" Martínez smirked. "He continued to go to Government House knowing all about her and the schemes of Doña Concepción."

"Yes and it worried him. The commandant didn't want to marry the girl, but he feared his future career could be compromised if he refused her hand in marriage. With his family's fame and long service to the crown, he has a promising career head of him. The commandant could be governor of a colony like Santo Domingo or even Cuba in the not too distant future."

"What's his ancestry?" Martínez frowned, knowing the commandant's nobility would ultimately determine his future career.

"His family is from Aragón and King Ferdinand's lineage." Ruiz de León coughed into his handkerchief. "One of the commandant's ancestors was first cousin to the king, when he married Isabella of Castilla. With such a family, he will go far."

"Ah, yes, our ambitious and aristocratic commandant would not want to risk his future career, would he?" Martínez sneered. "I can see why Doña Concepción's scheme worried him. He didn't want the governor's disapproval if he didn't marry Gloria."

"There was no need to worry, as I told him today. The governor would never interfere in his personal affairs – in any manner."

"No, that's not his way." Martínez shook his head.

"If the governor had heard of Concepción's marriage scheme, he would have ended it immediately. But he knew nothing of it. As he says, 'As governor, I'm like some cuckolded husband in town. I'm the last one to know what's happening in my own colony.'"

"But the commandant didn't know what Zéspedes would do in that situation, did he?" Martínez stared at Ruiz de León. "So, Gloria's death undoubtedly relieved him."

"It did. His words were, 'I hate to admit it, Ricardo, but I breathed a sigh of relief when I heard she was dead.'"

"That's what he said? No remorse? No sadness? Only a sigh of relief!" Martínez sat up and slapped the floor with the palm of his hand. "Dios mío! That man would walk over his mother's body to get a good command. What wouldn't he do to satisfy his ambitions?"

"He is ambitious." Ruiz de León nodded.

"That's all you can say, Ricardo? With such aspirations and his worry about rejecting the marriage to Gloria, murder would be a perfect solution to his problem."

"I suppose so, but think about it, Carlos. Would a man with his ambitions take such a risk? If discovered, he would lose his life, not only his command. No, it doesn't make sense."

"Maybe not, but he had reason to murder the girl and the time and opportunity as well."

Martínez nodded to Dorado, who had raised his hand.

"What about López Sierra? He also had the time to kill Gloria that morning."

"True, but I can't imagine him journeying out to the north woods. He's in no condition to ride or paddle a canoe there, never mind go on foot. He's become a desk clerk and won't go anywhere distant unless by carriage. Besides, he wouldn't think of trekking out there, not even for the lovely Gloria. López Sierra is afraid of snakes – like you, Ricardo – and would never go near the woods. I can hear the would-be Don Juan now, saying, 'no woman's chocha is worth the risk of a venomous snake-bite.'" Martínez chuckled.

Ruiz de León glared at him. "We can do without that language."

Martínez continued to smile. "Anyway, it's now obvious that the murderer must be an active man unlike the sedentary López Sierra. He is either young or strong of constitution to ride a horse or paddle a canoe that distance – like the commandant."

Ruiz de León shook his head. "You won't give up your suspicion of him, will you?"

"No, not with what we know about him. We know of no other man who wanted Gloria out of his life and who was relieved to hear of her death. Nor do we know of anyone else who was out of sight that morning and near the woods where she was murdered. According to the autopsy, the commandant also was away the same time the girl was murdered."

"What about the monk Núñez saw that day?" asked Dorado.

"It's something, but still not much, sad to say." Martínez yawned loudly. "There could be any number of explanations for the monk being on the river. The only peculiar thing about him was the hood he wore that hot day. It was what Gloria wore that morning."

"That does seem odd. But only one habit was taken from the sewing room, so I doubt the man paddling on the river was in disguise. What do you think, Carlos?"

"I guess he was a monk who didn't want to be recognized by anyone; that would explain the hood. I suspect he was hiding his face after leaving some illicit rendezvous with an Indian girl or even a boy. Don't stare at me that way, Ricardo. You know what the monks are about here as well as I do. Everyone does."

"That's only local rumor."

"Is it indeed? Is it only a rumor that four monks were caught in an orgy? With Indian boys, at that, and at Nombre de Dios!"

"No, but it involved only three monks." Ruiz de León sighed.

"Four! And some of our soldiers have been seen with the same boys." Martínez looked at Dorado. "Did you know that?"

"It's well known. At reveille last week, the commandant warned the garrison about the penalties of such behavior. I've heard it's a common practice among the soldiers of all armies."

"Not in the Spanish army, I hope," said Ruiz de León. "It's a mortal sin!"

"Bedding a woman out of wedlock is a mortal sin, too, but that stops no one from doing it. What the lieutenant said is true – like it or not. Wherever there are men living together, such acts will take place, whether it's in the king's army or in monasteries."

"I can't believe such acts are common in the monasteries of Spain."

"I'm certain it's there, too. Even the Inquisition couldn't stop it. Let's not forget the many incidents involving secular priests and women as well. That isn't uncommon either."

"Unfortunately, it's true." Ruiz de León sighed. "It has

been a continuing problem for the Church. What a shame! Priests should provide the best example for the common people."

"As they say, Ricardo, 'The flesh is weak' – What's the rest of that saying?"

"It's not a saying." Ruiz de León frowned in annoyance. "It's from the Gospel of St. Mathew and you, of all people, should keep it firmly in mind. 'Watch and pray, that you enter not into temptation: the spirit indeed is willing but the flesh is weak.'"

"When the flesh is weak, men will surely practice such acts, even if sinful. When I was in Havana in the seventies I saw some things in a Dominican monastery I'll never forget."

"I'm not interested in what you saw in Havana. We need to finish our discussion here so I can report to the governor."

"Your condition is making you crabby, Ricardo. Do you have a fever?"

"No, I feel fine except for the cough and it's letting up."

"Be sure to stay in bed if you get a fever. Rest is the best treatment for this sickness."

"I'll keep that in mind." Ruiz de León rose to refill the brandy glasses. He spoke when he returned to his chair. "Now, let's talk about other possibilities. We haven't mentioned any of the people who live in or about town. The foreign Protestants, for example, or the Indians and Negroes? What about the Mestizos and other mixed blood peoples? And let's not forget the Minorcans. They always seem to be killing one another."

"The Protestants possibly, but not the others. I can't imagine an Indian, Negro or one of the mixed blood people strangling the girl first and then cutting a cross on her corpse. Nor can I see a Catholic Minorcan murdering her in that manner. It's not the kind of killing one of them would commit – it was too well planned. A Minorcan would have either strangled her or killed her with a knife thrust or two. He would not have done both. It would have happened in a fury, probably because the woman was seen flirting with another man. God knows how many Minorcans I've had to sew up after jealous fights. They even brawl over whores."

Dorado again raised his hand. "I think it had to be someone Gloria knew, not a stranger – someone who persuaded her to paddle a canoe out to the woods to meet him."

"That makes sense." Martínez sipped his brandy.

"What about Jesse Fish?" Ruiz de León felt himself sweating and knew he had a fever.

Martínez sighed. "Unfortunately, we can't consider Fish seriously either. He was with Barton that morning at El Vergel. Of course, we don't know when they were together; we only know Barton was seen early that morning rowing out to the island. It would be helpful to know how long they spent together and what they did afterward."

"I'll see what I can find out," said Ruiz de León.

"Ricardo has paid spies in St. Augustine," Martínez told Dorado. "That's how he gets his information and he refuses to tell me who they are. Isn't that so, Ricardo?"

"Never mind how I do it; I'll find out what we need to know."

"Anyway, it's hard to imagine the old bastard, with his many infirmities, rowing a boat all that distance across the bay to meet the girl, never mind murdering her. He would then have to row back across the bay. He looks too feeble to do all that and, frankly, I don't think he has much time left to live, Si Dios quiere (God willing)." Martínez smiled.

Ruiz de León nodded. "Jesse Fish does look feeble. Yet, he still talks about a voyage to Spain to see the king to settle his land claims. As if the king would see him."

"I doubt he'll go anywhere now, except to his grave."

Ruiz de León nodded. "His plans for a voyage to Spain

are only an old man's dreams of a future that no longer exists."

"Gracias a Dios, that's all the old ladrón (thief) has left now. So, where does that leave us? With the exception of the commandant, we haven't much to show for all our efforts."

"Not much at all. The governor will not like my report."

"That can't be helped!" Martínez spoke sharply.

"I don't suppose Delaney's murder can be compared to the killing of Gloria. It also was a stabbing." Dorado held his hands out palms up.

"No, Delaney was stabbed over some whore – I don't recall her name. I did the autopsy and no mutilation was involved."

"What about María Rosa Morones? Was she murdered, sir?" asked Dorado.

"I'm still uncertain. It would help if Harmon turned up and was questioned. I don't suppose that's happened."

Ruiz de León shook his head. "We have no idea where he went. Of course, our patrols are still out looking for him."

"It seems we're at a standstill." Dorado immediately regretted saying the obvious.

"That's the way it looks," muttered Martínez, slowly rising from the floor. "Listen to my bones snap and complain."

"You're not the only one who hears that chorus." Ruiz de León also stood. "I hear it every morning when I get out of bed."

"Listen to the old men moaning about their aches and pains." Martínez put his hand on the young man's arm. "Don't we sound pitiful?"

Dorado smiled, but said nothing.

"Speaking of bones, I looked at the leg again and I could see where a dog had gnawed on it. So, it seems Fish was telling the truth about that anyway. Of course, we still don't know whose leg it was – though it looks like a man's leg."

"It might be Harmon's leg since he hasn't been found."

"Maybe. Tell me, Dorado how's your budding romance with Serena Rodríguez? Look at that smile, Ricardo. Nothing to say, Don Juan?"

"Thank you for helping me meet Serena, sir. I'm grateful."

"Listen to him, Ricardo; that's all he'll say. Isn't he the smug one?" Martínez grinned.

"Leave him alone, Carlos. He's a caballero (gentleman) and won't say a word about the girl. Isn't that so, Lieutenant?"

Dorado nodded. "I've heard it said, 'if we boast about women we're braggarts, and if we complain about them, we're fools to be with them.'"

"That sounds like something Uncle Ernesto said. But it's true whoever said it."

"It was, sir," said Dorado as he buttoned up his coat.

"Well, Lieutenant, you can surely tell me about your chess games. Who's winning?"

"We're closely matched," replied Ruiz de León.

"I don't know about that." Dorado shook his head from side to side. "As of now, Don Ricardo has won six games. I've won three and we have two draws."

"That's much better than I've done against him even sober! Well, it's time to go home and put my weary bones to bed."

"I'll go out with you, sir."

Martínez turned, his huge hand holding the door knob. "Ricardo, do get some rest, stay home tomorrow. That cough isn't to be ignored. Do you hear me?"

"I'll rest all day Saturday."

He sat on the seawall watching the water birds. At sunset in the last light, they were busy fishing in the bay. He counted eight different species in his study of the sky. The birds were looking for the last food of the day and their squawks dominated all other sound, except the roar of the waves rolling onto shore. It was five-thirty and night was near. The bay's blues and greens had already turned to gray as darkness descended over the town. He stood to leave, hoping to see one last formation of pelicans. Within seconds, a line of the birds flew out of the north and soared silently over the bay. They glided on air currents without flapping their wings. Their effortless flight never ceased to fascinate him and he would watch them for hours.

As he stood peering into the dusk, the brown pelicans performed his favorite act. One after another in sequence, they dove down into a school of tiny fish. With their feathered wings pulled back and bills pushed forward, the diving pelicans looked like arrows sent from the bow of an archer. Despite the height of their dive and the explosive splash of water as they plunged into the sea, the sharp-eyed birds seldom missed their targets.

Their accuracy never ceased to amaze him. The pelicans would invariably surface with a fish or two in their bills. It was no different that afternoon. The birds fished with their usual finesse and then floated serenely on the swell of the waves like so many ducks on a pond. He left as the last pelican of the formation settled onto the surface of the bay.

"What it must be like to see the whole world from the sky," he said aloud. He sighed and slowly walked on wondering why God had not given man the gift of flight.

Other thoughts occupied his mind as he set out for home. They were the same thoughts he had hoped to escape while watching the pelicans fly about the bay. Uninvited, they arrived, crowding into his mind despite all his efforts to push them away. He knew it was futile to fight against them. His resistance would only result in one of his intolerable headaches.

He was relieved when the thoughts did not dwell upon

the past or remind him of what had happened in the woods. Instead, they appeared more interested in the present. He sighed with relief when he realized the thoughts only wanted to talk about the investigation.

At first, the thoughts told him he had nothing to fear. There was no reason for anyone to suspect him. No one had seen him in the woods or on the road to and from his rendezvous with her. Nothing, in fact, had been found to involve him in any way. He seemed to be free of all suspicion for now.

But his nagging concerns could not be so easily dismissed and he continued to worry. How could he not worry, especially after the past ten days with so many new problems now confronting him? The future seemed to be full of peril as well. It frightened him.

The thoughts now worried with him, wondering what unexpected dangers lurked ahead in the coming weeks. He feared the future would be a time of constant struggles trying to evade their scrutiny. He would need to be alert to all their endeavors. They now might know more about him than he realized. They were clever and should never be taken for granted. Though unlikely, it was possible they already suspected him. The more he thought, the more he worried and, as he neared home, he admitted to himself that there was good reason to worry.

The man felt weary as he reached the street to his house. What had been a picturesque sunset watching the pelicans was ruined. One of his horrible headaches was on the way. The usual nausea and the all too predictable ache behind his right eye signaled its arrival. He knew the coming night would be a time of inescapable sickness and pain. Unable to sleep, he would toss and turn in bed, hoping his suffering would end with the dawn.

As he hurried the last few steps down the street, it occurred to him that all his suffering was because of her –

because of that treacherous little slut. She was the cause of all his misery. He marveled how it could be possible. All the risks he faced, all his wretchedness was because of her. He wondered why the whore would be worth so much concern. It astonished him.

CHAPTER ELEVEN

NOVEMBER 14-23, 1788

A sentry at the drawbridge told Dorado to go to the doctor's office when he arrived at dawn on the cold morning of November 14. His hands deep in his coat pockets, he hurried into the fort, signed in and quickly crossed the parade grounds to the office. Dorado found Martínez bent over a man on the table in the surgery.

He motioned to a stool by the wall. "Sit over there, Lieutenant. We need to talk. I'll be done in a minute or two."

"I see they made a new examining table for you. It looks sturdy."

"Sí, al fin (Yes, finally). It's well made, I'll say that for them. They even sanded it. I no longer have to put a mat over it to examine patients. The top is as smooth as a young girl's breast. How does it feel to you, Peralta?"

"Fine, sir."

Dorado took the stool and sat across the table from Peralta, who lay on his stomach, his breeches down at his knees. Martínez was applying alcohol to a red swelling on the left cheek of the man's buttocks. He swabbed the swelling several times and then leaned over to study it.

"It's infected as I suspected." Martínez squeezed the raised area and a small amount of white liquid leaked out from the center. The man grunted, but did not cry out. "Well, Peralta, you'll be watching where you sit in the future, won't you?"

"Yes, sir."

The patient turned his face to Dorado and smiled. Returning the smile, he realized the man was José Peralta, a soldier who often served as a sentry at the Castillo. Dorado recalled seeing him the night he returned from the woods with Gloria's body.

"Peralta here has a serious pain in the ass." Martínez guffawed.

"Yes, sir. I sat in the wrong place."

"I should say so! He sat on a red scorpion." Martínez smiled at Dorado. "Now, I have to get the stinger out of his ass and it's going to hurt. Are you ready, Peralta?"

The soldier gritted his teeth as Martínez stuck his scalpel into the center of the swelling. Yellow mucus squirted out of the opening and the doctor used his fingers to squeeze out more of the mucus. He continued squeezing even though Peralta writhed beneath him.

"Ayhh! Suficiente (Enough)!" Peralta struck the sides of the table with his hands.

"Hold still, damn it! There it is." The doctor used the nails of his forefinger and thumb to pluck the stinger from the wound. "Look at the size of it – it's at least a half-inch long!" He showed Peralta the stinger on the tip of his forefinger. "You certainly sat on a big one – it's no wonder it was infected."

"Ayhh! That burns!" complained Peralta as Martínez applied alcohol to the wound.

"The pain should be gone in a day or so. If the swelling doesn't go down in that time, come see me. From now on, take your wenches someplace inside. Do you hear me, José?"

"Sí, señor, gracias." Red-faced, Peralta quickly pulled his breeches up and jumped off the table. He put on his coat and, after thanking the doctor again, hurried out the door.

Martínez motioned for Dorado to follow him into his office. "I got a letter today from Esteban. He wants me to come to Havana and look through the murder files myself. But I can't possibly go now. The cough is everywhere; it's a new plague. With so many sick, I must stay and do what I can here. Old Doctor Domínguez in town can't manage more than a few cases a day. Since he's so feeble, I worry he may get sick as well. If that happens, I would be the only physician in the presidio. So you must go to Havana in my place."

"But isn't your friend expecting you?"

"Yes, but that can't be helped. Esteban will welcome you as he would me. Believe me, Dorado, I'd like to go. Some free time to enjoy the fine food and women of Havana would do me good. But with this plague, I just can't leave now."

"When am I to go, sir?" Dorado toyed with the cockade on his hat.

"Tomorrow."

"Tomorrow! So soon?" Dorado made a face.

"Yes. *La Santísima Trinidad* sails tomorrow on the afternoon tide. Be aboard ship by two. Ricardo made all the arrangements. Go see him, he's at home supposedly resting on the orders of his doctor." Martínez shook his head.

"I hope he listens to you."

"If he does, he'll be better in a week or so. He seems to have a mild form of the illness, though he looks terrible. He'll give you the necessary letters for the king's officials in

Havana. The governor signed them this morning."

"Where am I to stay? I could stay with my brother, Miguel; he's stationed in Havana."

"No. I want you to stay with Esteban while you're there. I wrote to him and explained the situation. Here, you can read what I've written." He handed Dorado the folded letter.

"I don't want to intrude on his family, sir."

"You won't be intruding. Esteban has a large house with many rooms. There're always friends and relatives staying there – some from Spain. You'll be welcomed with open arms by his family and Esteban's wife, Beatriz, will treat you like a son."

"All right." Dorado frowned. "But I want to spend some time with my brother, Miguel – at least a couple of days while I'm there."

"Fine. You'll need some diversions from your duties. So, enjoy time with your brother or anyone else you might meet."

"What do you mean by that, sir?"

Martínez smiled. "Do keep in mind, Dorado, you aren't married yet!"

"I'm not getting married and you know it."

"Yes, my young friend, and I also know Serena Rodríguez will still be here when you return. There are many lovely girls in Havana and life is much too short to be celibate at your age. Believe me, your youth is gone before you know it. So, take whatever good fortune brings your way, especially if it's some winsome wench who gives you those big eyes. But avoid the putas – they cost too much and carry the pox."

"I have no intention of spending time with whores." Dorado glared at Martínez.

"Oh, stop being so stuffy." Martínez clapped Dorado on the back. There was a sting to the blow. "Go and try to enjoy Havana in spite of yourself. You're like Ricardo – too damned serious. I think the men from the high country are too serious to enjoy life. It must be the cold air blowing off the Cantabrian Mountains. The cold air apparently freezes their balls."

Dorado laughed despite his annoyance. "Do you have any other critical instructions?"

"No. I know you'll keep us informed of what you learn. Inform Esteban as well. He knows much about many things and will always give you good counsel. You'll like him once you learn to tolerate his complaining. We are much alike."

"That shouldn't be hard. I've learned tolerance from un buen maestro (a good teacher)."

Martínez laughed and again clapped Dorado on the back. The blow was much softer than the first one. "Go on now and get ready for the voyage."

Dorado sat on the aft deck of La Santísima Trinidad watching the crew work the lines. They were busy moving the schooner's mainsail back and forth from port to starboard trying to catch the wind. The sailors had struggled to fill the sails all morning. Blowing in brief gusts, first on one side of the ship and then on the other, the wind was hard to hold for any length of time. Without a constant wind they could not hope to stay on course against the strong current of the Bahama Channel. Already four days out of St. Augustine, La Santísima Trinidad still had not sighted Boca de Ratones (shallow inlet of sharp rocks), the halfway point to Havana.

Dorado felt seasick. He was an admitted man of the land and counted the days aboard ship. Dorado suffered sieges of dizziness and vomiting in heavy seas and would likely faint if he stayed below decks in a storm. He felt worse in a prolonged calm when a ship pitched and rolled or bobbed up and down in the water.

His first sea trip took him from Cádiz to the Canary Islands, where he served a year at Las Palmas. It was a smooth sailing in the autumn of 1785 and the sight of blue whales on the same course made that voyage memorable. But Dorado found life at sea boring with too little to do. Time passed slowly and the sailing seemed endless. When the frigate finally arrived at Las Palmas, Dorado leaped off the boat, glad to be on land again.

His second voyage, eleven months later, was aboard a Portuguese brigantine en route from Lisbon to Havana carrying furniture and Persian rugs. Only a week after Dorado boarded the ship at Las Palmas, it stalled at sea in an Atlantic calm that lasted four days and nights. He became so ill that a priest aboard administered last rites. No sooner had he recovered, than the lumbering vessel sailed into a gale with the strongest winds the crew said they ever had seen.

Awash in mountains of seawater, the brigantine seemed certain to sink. Three times the old ship, listing too far to one side, almost capsized. Each time it happened, everyone aboard assumed the end was near, but the brigantine stayed afloat and survived what the Portuguese captain called a *November Nightmare*. Afterward, the sodden ship labored sluggishly through the heavy seas, but made the remainder of the voyage without incident. Waterlogged and lying perilously low in the water, the brigantine would have sunk in another storm.

Once settled in Havana, Dorado spoke of the sea as his sworn enemy. He stayed away from the water during his entire assignment in Cuba. Dorado refused to go near the ocean even to catch crabs or fish with other officers on their time off. It was not until the young lieutenant was ordered to St. Augustine, almost a year later, that he sailed again.

The longer Dorado watched the exhausted crew move the limp mainsail back and forth without effect, the more he worried. Feeling nauseous, he closed his eyes and put a hand over his mouth. Dorado knew he would vomit any moment. He crawled to the starboard side of the schooner and hung his head out over the sea.

Dorado opened his eyes when he heard a shout from the lookout in the crow's nest. He saw a sailor staring at the canvas mainsheet, now pulled hard around to the starboard side. The schooner had finally found the wind and was under full sail. For the first time that morning, the sailors were smiling, though some of them crossed themselves praying the wind would hold.

Dorado sat back against a water barrel and exhaled his breath. He now could think of other things. He first thought of Serena Rodríguez, who met him in the main plaza and walked with him to the ship. She stood and waited at the dock while the crew cast off and then waved to him as the big schooner set sail across the bay. Dorado could still see her in his mind's eye, a small figure in white waving from afar.

They were spending more time together now, at least three early evenings a week and much of Saturday. One of her cousins usually accompanied Serena when they met at night, but, now and then, they were permitted a few moments alone. His new assignment allowed Dorado more free time and he used it to be with her. Dorado found Serena affectionate, good humored and interesting. She could carry on a decent conversation, unlike so many other Spanish girls, who would say little more than "Sí," "No," or "Whatever you wish, Dorado."

Dorado knew his mother would disapprove of Serena Rodríguez. She was a commoner without land or money and therefore unsuitable for marriage. He could hear his mother saying, "Roberto, she's not for you, surely you know that. There are many lovely girls for you in your *own class.*" He recalled her words when he had shown interest in a shopkeeper's daughter.

Pedro, his very practical older brother, would remind him of his family responsibilities. "Young man, you know very well what you should do," he would say with his usual sad face. Dorado was expected to marry a wealthy noblewoman, whose dowry would bring property or money to the family in Asturias, hopefully near their own small holdings.

Ever since the death of their father, both he and his brother Miguel had been instructed to make good marriages which would improve the meager family fortunes. When the time for marriage came, typically in their late twenties or early thirties, the two brothers were expected to court and wed a *proper girl* from an affluent family. Pedro's marriage had added a piece of pasturing property to the family holdings in Asturias.

Only Miguel would tell him to do what he wanted with Serena Rodríguez. "It's your life," Miguel would say. "Do what you wish. If we do what Pedro tells us to do, we will end up like him — God help us! — married to some unattractive country woman. Of course, with a sizeable dowry of pesetas and property."

Dorado smiled, thinking of the last night they spent together in Havana before he sailed to St. Augustine. It had been a time of talking and drinking too much wine, the kind of evening he always enjoyed with Miguel. When they parted the next morning in the street, both of them were exhausted. As Miguel left, he hugged Dorado and then cuffed his head. "Hit you last," he shouted and ran off down the street. Only a few steps away, Dorado lost sight of his brother in the morning fog that had rolled in from the sea.

The memory made Dorado think of Miguel as a small boy, always in trouble. He could see him now, his eyes shining with glee, as he planned some prank sure to infuriate his mother or Uncle Ernesto. "That boy will be the death of me," his mother would say.

Dorado looked forward to seeing Miguel after eight months in St. Augustine. His visit to Havana would be as much a surprise to his brother as it had been to him. Dorado visualized a stunned look on Miguel's face when he suddenly appeared in front of him.

As he sat in the sun on deck, Dorado let his mind wander from one topic to another. At first, he thought about the letters in his pocket. Dorado kept them with him at all times, fearing he might lose them. Instead of storing the papers in the schooner's strongbox, he put them in a buttoned pocket, where he was always aware of their bulk.

Along with the official letters permitting passage into Havana, Dorado carried the letter to Major Esteban Morales y Barrientos and the brief message the Cuban physician had written to Martínez. The message had stunned them all. As he sat on the deck watching the wake, Dorado repeated the words to himself from memory.

"After a two-hour search of Doctor Vilar's files, I found a case of murder-mutilation of a girl in October, 1770. There is a similar murder recorded for 1777, but I can't seem to locate it. Come to Havana and see the autopsy reports yourself."

Dorado could not stop thinking about the message and what it meant. The possibilities for the investigation now seemed endless and he lay sleepless at nights wondering about them. Dorado hoped to sail back to Florida with the identity of the murderer or, at least, information that would lead to his arrest. In his daydreams, he pictured the governor smiling as he pinned a medal on his chest and promoted him to captain.

Dorado knew his hopes depended on what the files revealed. If the mutilations in the files were similar, he would know the murderer had lived in Havana in 1770 and 1777 and St. Augustine in 1788. He would also know the man was a Spanish subject. His identity might then be discovered by the dates and places of his killings. In Havana, the Building of Records held the passenger lists for all the ships sailing to and from Cuba as well as the service record of every Spanish official and soldier in America. Those records showed assignments, periods of appointment and places of service. No one was excluded and nothing was left out.

Dorado instantly thought of the commandant. He wondered if the colonel had served in Havana in 1770 and 1777. Could it be, as Martínez suspected, that the commandant was the murderer after all? It was something to think about as he looked through the medical records.

Dorado nodded, thinking there were many things to pursue in the Building of Records. All of the colonial records for Cuba, the other Spanish islands in the Caribbean Sea and Florida were stored in the building, an old church situated in the center of the city. Constructed by the Dominicans in the early sixteenth century, the church served as an archive for official letters, papers and reports. It held millions of documents, from the colonization of Caribbean islands to the late eighteenth century.

The bundled documents were placed on shelves set in tiers along the inner walls. The tiers stood seventy-five feet high. In the center, where the main altar and nave had been built, other stacked shelves stood in rows twenty-five feet high. The rows ran the entire length of the building. All the available space was used to house the vast collection of handwritten records.

The rows and tiers of bundled documents reminded Dorado of the Minoan labyrinth he had read about in Greek mythology. Although no Minotaur lurked in the maze of narrow aisles, it was easy to get lost in the archive. It had happened to him on his first visit to the Building of Records. A few weeks before his transfer to St. Augustine, he had been sent there to look for a document and lost his way in the dark building at the end of the afternoon. It took him twenty minutes to find an escape. Afterwards, whenever Dorado entered the archive, he carried an oil lamp and carefully mapped a mental route through the rows.

Despite the difficulty of searching for something in the huge archive, Dorado knew the identity of the murderer could be found somewhere within its walls. It would be tedious work sifting through dusty documents, but Dorado was certain he could find something significant in time. Everything depended upon what the physician's files revealed. If the murders in Havana turned out to be unlike the killing of the governor's niece, his trip to Cuba would be worthless. He would return to Florida with nothing to report and no prospects for a promotion.

Feeling the sun's rays on his shoulders, Dorado took off his woolen jacket and rolled up his shirt sleeves. Despite the steadily blowing wind, it was hot on deck as the schooner sailed south through the Bahama Channel. He stood, stretched and looked out to sea. Seeing nothing except the endless blue sea, Dorado sighed and sat back down.

As he leaned back against the water barrel, Dorado saw a man approaching him out of the corner of his eye. He recognized Father Jon Fullondo, who had already been aboard when Serena accompanied him to the ship. Dorado stood and bowed to the priest.

"Siéntese, Teniente, siéntese. (Sit, Lieutenant, sit.)" The priest reached over and patted Dorado's arm. "May I sit with you?"

"Of course, Father. I suggest you sit against the barrel."

"I don't want to take your place." Carefully arranging his cassock, the priest lowered himself across from the barrel, one hand clasping a black leather bible to his chest.

"Are you sure you will be comfortable there?" Seeing

Fullondo nod, Dorado sat down facing him. He laid his sword on the deck.

"Gracias, Lieutenant." Fullondo smiled at Dorado. "We are fortunate they finally found the wind, I get seasick even in calm seas."

"So do I. In fact, I get seasick in almost any sea."

"I'm not much of a sailor either." The priest smiled showing small irregular teeth.

Father Fullondo was a thin man with a long narrow face ending in a pointed chin. He had a pointed nose as well. His accent and light skin color suggested a Basque ancestry. His fair hair and almost hairless face added to that impression. He looked like a boy who had not yet shaved for the first time.

"I've wanted to talk to you ever since we met our first day out. After all, there're only the two of us aboard, with the exception of the Portuguese crew. I thought of approaching you on several occasions, but hesitated since you looked to be preoccupied."

"I'm glad you did. It's good to talk to someone at sea." Dorado did not reveal what had occupied his mind.

"It is. These voyages seem endless."

"They do. I understand you boarded ship in Pensacola? I heard one of the crew speak of it – I understand a little Portuguese."

"Yes. I've been recalled to Havana." Father Fullondo turned his mouth down. "The bishop disapproves of my sermons."

"Oh." Dorado wondered why his sermons were questioned, but hesitated asking the priest about them.

"You see, Lieutenant, it's all about God's gift of love to mankind. Love – that's what the New Testament is all about." Father Fullondo nodded to emphasize his statement.

Dorado sighed. He knew a sermon was coming and there was no polite way to escape hearing it. He now regretted inviting the priest to sit with him.

"Moses brought only ten commandments down from Mount Sinai." The priest pointed his finger at Dorado. "That's what is wrong with the old bible of the Hebrews. Love isn't in it. No. That's why we were given a new testament – a testament to tell us that God sent his only son, Jesus Christ, to bring the gift of love to mankind. Though you would never know it from what the priests tell the people. Instead of celebrating God's gift, they talk on and on about sin and salvation. I often wonder if they've ever read the word of God themselves. What's more important – they neglect to tell the people who can't read Spanish, never mind Latin, what God did for us. What did he do? He sent Christ to us with his gift of love."

Dorado said nothing. Even if he wanted to comment, it would have been impossible since the priest spoke without a pause. He even asked and answered his own questions.

"What about sin, you say? There's only one cardinal sin we need worry about – the sin of not loving. Never mind what the priests say. Not loving God! Not loving our Lord, Jesus Christ! Not loving others. 'Thou shalt love thy neighbor as thyself.' It's there in the bible as clear as day. So, beware those who do not love God. Those who do not love – they sin! And the wages of sin is death."

Father Fullondo abruptly stopped speaking. He closed his eyes and sighed. When his eyes opened again they were wet with tears. "Perdóneme, por favor, Teniente (Please forgive me, Lieutenant). I didn't come here intending to give you a sermon. But God's truth is inside me and I can't keep it to myself."

"I understand." Dorado was touched by the priest's sincerity and smiled at him.

"You can see why I'm being recalled." Father Fullondo pursed his lips. "They don't want me around the parishioners. They think I'll corrupt them."

"What do you think they'll do with you in Havana?"

"I'll be sent to some seminary to learn Church doctrine – again! Then, they'll probably assign me to a one of the church's offices to serve as a clerk or an isolated library where I can only corrupt the books and documents. Eventually, I'll be given a parish again because of the continuing shortage of priests in America. But it'll be at least ten years before they let me out into the world again. Of course, I'll be watched carefully during that long period. By then, I'll be fifty and who knows what I will say to the parishioners when I'm an old man. The Church knows well that time changes us all." His eyes teared again.

Dorado shook his head, feeling sorry for the priest.

"So much for me and my travails – I've talked far too long about myself. What about you, Lieutenant? What are your prospects?"

Dorado told him about his early life as well as his time in the army. He was tempted to tell him about his assignment, but hesitated to speak of it to a stranger.

"Father, would you answer a question for me?"

"I'll try, mi hijo." The priest held his hand out palm up.

"I'm wondering Father, can a woman love too much?"

"You don't mean love God, do you?"

"No, I mean love too much with her body." Dorado blushed.

"Are you speaking of fornication – outside the sacred state of marriage?"

"Not fornication, but permitting bodily passion."

"Speak plainly, mi hijo. Tell me exactly what you mean."

Dorado hesitated, but then explained. "I'm speaking of a woman who would touch and be touched by a man – intimately."

"Ah. I assume the touching takes place outside the sacred state of marriage."

"Yes, Father, and with more than one man – in fact, with

many men, but not for money. The girl was not a puta."
Dorado exhaled audibly.

"Why don't you tell me about the girl? I need to know more precisely what she did so I can properly answer your question."

Dorado told the priest what he knew about Gloria Márquez García y Morera, but made no mention of her murder.

"The girl is committing sin – mortal sin! In no manner can her bodily acts with men be considered any form of love. What she does is sinful! Surely you know that."

"Yes. I'm simply trying to understand why she would do such things."

"From what you tell me, it seems the girl is morally reckless and unrepentant. I would say the girl has not only lost her way to God, she may be possessed as well."

Dorado nodded, recalling Ruiz de León's similar words. Feeling close to the priest, he then related the details of the girl's murder and told him the purpose of his trip to Havana.

"Dios mío, what a world we live in." The priest pressed the bible to his heart.

"Father, please answer another question?" Seeing his nod, Dorado asked him about the girl's mutilation. "Do you think a Catholic could have cut the cross on the girl's corpse? It's hard for me to imagine one of our people doing such a thing. It's so blasphemous!"

"Yes, I'm afraid so." The priest nodded, a sad expression on his face.

"Why not a Protestant? I've always thought one of them was the fiend who mutilated the girl in that manner. Of course, now with the possibility of finding other similar murders in Cuba, I wonder. If similar, the murderer must be a Catholic."

Father Fullondo did not reply immediately. He stroked his chin for a time and looked out to sea. When his eyes returned to Dorado, he nodded.

"I'm afraid it's more likely the blasphemous act of a Catholic rather than a Protestant. I'm sorry to say such a thing, but it's true. The terrible acts of Catholic fanatics are well known in the history of the Church. The murderer is a man who surely knows what the crucifix means to us and knowingly kills in a blasphemous manner. He is a Catholic fanatic, I'm certain."

On the last day of the voyage, Dorado sat on the deck in the late afternoon. The sun had shifted farther to the west and left him in shade, where he felt the bite of the wind. Sunset was not far off and he felt chilly sitting on deck. The days were much shorter and colder now that December was near even in the southern seas.

As he moved to a sunnier spot on deck, Dorado thought of the last time he had talked to Ruiz de León, after learning of his orders to sail to Havana. At noon, the standing water in the presidio was still covered with a thin layer of ice when he walked to his house. Dorado found the sick man huddled only a foot from the flaming wood in the fireplace.

"It's easy to criticize the governor." Ruiz de León made a face. He sat bundled up in a woolen blanket in his favorite chair. One hand was hidden beneath the folds of the blanket, the other held a half-full teacup close to his face.

Dorado, sitting beside him, nodded without speaking.

"He is rarely appreciated for his constant dedication to this remote colony. Instead, the governor is denounced for what he does and denounced for what he doesn't do. Tell me, is it his fault the investigation has lasted so long? What more can he do? I ask you, what more can any of us do?" He coughed and spat into a handkerchief. "Perdóneme (pardon me), Dorado."

"No importa, Don Ricardo. I thought you would want to know what they're saying in town about the governor."

"I understand. Thank you, Lieutenant." Ruiz de León spoke in a hoarse voice. "We need to calm the townspeople. We can't have panic in the streets."

Dorado nodded again. He had been studying Ruiz de León while they talked. The man looked very sick. There were dark shadows around his eyes and his sallow cheeks seemed sunk into his face. Bundled up in the blanket, the small man looked like a child who had fled from his bed because of a bad dream.

"How are you feeling, Don Ricardo?" Dorado sat in a chair across from the captain.

"Oh, I'm fine. I'm sure the worst is over. Tell me Lieutenant, is there anything new to report? Carlos has told me little of the investigation lately."

"That missing Englishman hasn't been found yet, but the patrols are still out looking for him. A couple of sightings place the man near the western woods, so the commandant has sent a squad of men into the lost lands in search of him."

"God help them. I hope they get back from that awful place."

"So do I. I wouldn't want to lead that patrol."

"No, indeed. What about the Morones girl? Has Carlos come to any conclusions about her death? We haven't had a chance to talk at length. He's here and gone in five minutes."

"No, sir. He hasn't said anything new to me about her. The last time we spoke, he said her death might have been the murderer's doing, but he wasn't certain. It seems there were too many tooth punctures on the girl's corpse to tell if she was mutilated in any way. The alligators so crushed her chest that it was impossible to see if a cross was cut into her flesh."

"I see." Ruiz de León sipped his tea. "What about the

leg? Do we know whose it is?"

"No, sir. It's not the dead girl's leg. And no one in town has been reported missing, so we don't know whose leg it might be. If the Englishman hadn't been seen recently, we would suspect he was taken by the alligators, too."

Ruiz de León nodded. He blew his nose into a handkerchief he kept under the blanket.

Dorado was distracted by a burning log falling out of the fireplace. He got up, grasped the log by an end and shoved it back into the flames. He stood by the fireplace as he brushed the soot off his hands.

"Do you have any instructions for me, Don Ricardo? I, of course, will send you reports of what I find in Havana."

"No, Lieutenant, you know well what to do. I'll look forward to receiving your reports from abroad, though I'll be sad to see you leave. I'll miss our times together." He turned his head to the side and coughed; it was a long rasping cough that left him gasping for breath.

"I'll miss them, too. I've enjoyed our chess games and the talks we had together. They have meant much to me." Dorado blushed. "As I've told Serena, when I am here I feel like I'm home with my family. It's a good feeling."

"It is the same for me with you in the house." Ruiz de León looked into the crackling fire. "Your presence has made me happy and I will look forward to your return. Until then, I'll survive with Carlos' careless efforts at chess." He smiled weakly.

Dorado used the iron poker to rearrange the logs in the fireplace. He added four dry pieces from the stack standing beside the sick man's chair. They immediately flamed.

"Do you want me to make any more tea, Don Ricardo?"

"No. Not unless you want some yourself. I'm fine for now." He sighed and leaned back in his chair. His eyes were half closed. "Thank you for adding the firewood."

"Por nada. Do you want me to leave now, Don Ricardo?"

"No, not yet. Sit a few minutes more and tell me what you plan to do in Havana."

Dorado sat as he was told and saw the sick man's weariness. "I'll read the autopsy reports first and inform you immediately of what I find."

"Good. That's probably all you should plan to do." The sick man opened and closed his eyes several times, trying to stay awake. "The reports will provide a good starting point."

"Yes, sir. Everything depends on what's in the autopsy report of 1770."

"Verdad. Havana appears to be the only place left with any information. There's little if anything left to find here in town." Ruiz de León spoke without trying to open his eyes.

"That's what Captain Martínez says. It seems we can no longer suspect Barton and Fish since they were together on the island that morning. We were fortunate to get a reliable report from the man who saw them there at the time."

"They're fortunate as well." Ruiz de León smiled slightly. He opened his eyes briefly to see Dorado smiling with him.

"They are indeed, Don Ricardo."

One of the Barton's servants, a freedman named Abraham, had informed Ruiz de León of the Englishmen's meeting that morning. Abraham was one of eleven freedmen paid by Ruiz de León to observe the foreigners in town. He had rowed Barton to Anastasia Island and, later, told the Spanish captain about their meeting on Fish Island. Dorado now knew the names of all the spies in St. Augustine. Ruiz de León had told no one else, not even Carlos Martínez. The secret they shared made Dorado feel close to the older man.

"Even if Jesse Fish had time to rendezvous with Gloria after his meeting with Barton, it seems unlikely the old man could row so far in his frail physical state. Anyway, according to the Indian boy, Mateo, there was only one boat grounded there on the shore that morning – and that was Gloria's canoe." Dorado made a face. "So, where does that leave us?"

"So, it seems the commandant is the only one left as a possibility." Ruiz de León awoke after nodding off to sleep for a few seconds. "But, you know, I doubt his involvement."

"Even Captain Martínez says he's no longer as suspicious of him. Of course, we can't ignore his romance with the girl and his fears of her compromising his career. He also had the time to murder her, but even that's uncertain. We don't know when he returned to the Castillo that morning since neither of the drawbridge sentries thought to record the time in the register."

Dorado stopped speaking when he saw Ruiz de León was asleep. He lay back against the chair, his head lolling to the side. The sick man was breathing unevenly through his open mouth. Dorado got up quietly, trying not to disturb him, and tiptoed to the door. As he put his hand on the latch, Ruiz de León spoke from behind him.

"Lieutenant! Don't forget the letters of transit signed by the governor. They're over there on the table near the door."

"I thought you were asleep." Dorado turned to face him.

"Not yet. Though I will be soon since it's obvious I can't keep my eyes open." Ruiz de León stood, still wrapped in the blanket, and beckoned to Dorado. "I want to wish you un buen viaje, mi estimado Dorado."

The lieutenant smiled, pleased that his superior had used his given name. He went back to him and gently embraced him. It was an affectionate abrazo that lasted a few seconds. Ruiz de León felt small and frail to Dorado as he held him in his arms.

"Adiós, Don Ricardo." Dorado turned again as he reached the door. "I hope you feel better soon. I'll see you in a few weeks. Take care of yourself and do listen to your doctor!"

"I'll be fine. Adiós, mi amigo."

Dorado turned his thoughts to what lay ahead of him in Havana. There was so much to do. He stood and watched the last of the orange sun fall into the ocean and, when a sharp wind blew across the deck, he went below to pack his clothes. He had been told the schooner would be within hailing distance of the port-city's fortress in another hour. Dorado took a last look to the east and saw the island of Cuba on the horizon. It appeared in the darkening dusk as a long black shape of a sea dragon rising up out of the waves.

Below decks, he gathered up his shaving items, stockings, underwear and spent a few minutes folding his two extra shirts. He packed everything in the leather haversack Uncle Ernesto had given him when he first left home for the army. His packing completed quickly, Dorado lay in his hammock to await the shouts of the crew as the schooner neared the inlet to Havana. He stayed below only a half hour. Even if cold on deck, his impatience to land drove him up the ladder. He paused only to put on his wig which he had not worn since boarding *La Santísima Trinidad*. Carrying his haversack over one shoulder, he climbed up to the deck and went forward to the bow as the ship sailed along the island's coast toward Havana.

Dorado felt a surge of warmth run through him when he saw the stone watchtowers of El Morro, the great fort that guarded the entry channel into Havana. The sight of the fortress named El Castillo de Los Tres Magos del Morro (the Castle of the Three Magi of the Cliff) always made him feel proud to be a Spaniard. Built high up on the headlands overlooking the ocean, it was an engineering marvel that never ceased to amaze him.

He thought of his brother as the schooner sailed toward El Morro. Miguel served at the fort as an artillery officer and might even be there now as the ship approached Havana. He smiled, thinking of seeing his brother. There would be much to talk about and, for once, he had something unusual to tell Miguel. Dorado knew his part in the murder investigation would surprise him and he pictured Miguel's startled look when he heard about it. He would tell him over a meal or on a walk rather than in a noisy tavern where they usually went at night.

Dorado's thoughts then turned to the quest that had brought him to Cuba. Excited by his hopes of what he would find in the medical records, he paced the deck imagining what they would reveal to him. With luck, he would return to St. Augustine in triumph, the name of the murderer on his lips. He ceased pacing and stood picturing his reception by Ruiz de León when he entered his office. Dorado saw him rise from his chair and commend him with a smile as he told him the man's name. Carlos Martínez then appeared and said, "Buen trabajo, Dorado."

Dorado sighed with the realization that it was also possible he might find nothing at all helpful in the medical records. The murders in Havana might not be similar to the murder of Gloria Márquez García. His mission in Cuba might be a failure and he would sail back to St. Augustine with nothing to show for his efforts. That distinct possibility made him worry about how he would then be regarded by Ruiz de León and the ever critical Carlos Martínez. Dorado felt his throat constrict as he thought about the many things that could go wrong.

Father Fullondo joined him at the bow as the first lights of the watchtowers appeared in the distance. The priest patted Dorado on the back. "Are you glad to be in Havana again?"

"In many ways, Father." Dorado looked at the lights in the darkness. "I look forward to seeing my brother; it's been almost nine months since we were together. I also look forward to being in a city again after so long on the Florida frontier."

Father Fullondo smiled. "I understand completely."

"The food alone is worth the voyage here. My mouth already waters thinking about it."

Lantern-lit ships of all sizes were about them a half hour later as a harbor pilot boarded the schooner to guide it into the long channel leading to the city docks. Looming above them, they saw the cannon muzzles and massive walls of the Castillo del Morro and Fortaleza de San Carlos, the fortresses guarding the inlet into Havana. The captain, following the instructions of the harbor pilot, ordered the crew to lower the sails as the ship proceeded through the channel and passed the forts. Sailors on outbound ships waved to them as they glided by.

As the schooner approached the pier, the sounds of the busy commercial port reached them across the water. They heard shouted commands, snorting horses and carts and carriages clattering over cobblestones. The pilot directed the ship's helmsman to steer the schooner into an empty berth and deck hands threw out mooring lines to waiting men on the wharf. Within seconds, *La Santísima Trinidad* was tied up securely and ready to be unloaded.

Father Fullondo walked down the gangplank in front of Dorado and the two men said their farewells beside the ship. It was seven o'clock and completely dark outside when they went their separate ways. A priest met Father Fullondo and accompanied him into the city. Dorado received his entry clearance from a regimental station at the entrance to the port. He heard the church bells chime the hour as he left the station and returned the sentry's salute.

At seven o'clock, Havana still bustled with hordes of people hurrying here and there and vendors peddling their wares in the dark streets. Unlike the frontier town of St. Augustine, which fell silent soon after sunset, Havana was noisy almost all night. There seemed to be no time even after midnight or in the early morning before first light when the city streets emptied completely. People always were about. When Dorado first arrived in Havana from Spain, he wondered if the Cubans ever went to bed. Every street corner in the center of the city seemed to have its cooking fire encircled by men and boys even in the dead of night.

Dorado smelled the frying food as soon he stepped from the gangplank. The smell of it was irresistible after a week of tasteless shipboard fare. His mouth watered and he decided to eat some of the food before walking to the house of the Cuban physician. He saw a stall only ten steps up from the docks and bought a bowl of seafood and rice. The full bowl came with sizzling hot plantains and two pieces of toasted bread. Dorado sat against a wall among seven other men holding the steaming bowls on their knees. The spicy food tasted delicious and he devoured every single grain of rice, sopping up the sauce with the last of his bread. Dorado finished his meal with a slice of pineapple and a cup of lukewarm tea. Satisfied, he stood and walked away feeling full and ready to face the long walk ahead of him.

On his way toward the center of the city, Dorado proceeded through the barrios beside the water where the poor lived in hovels and the littered streets smelled of excrement, urine and rotting food. He hurried through the filthy barrios, kicking at the stray dogs that followed him nipping at his ankles. He passed bread, meat and produce stands, shops selling clothing, fabric, furniture, household goods and carts full of new and old tools for sale. Squalid taverns stood on every block along the way and drunken men staggered about the streets or lay sick or asleep on the ground. Dorado was besieged by begging blind men, cripples and pleading children pulling at his clothes, their soiled hands held out for food or pesetas. Painted prostitutes leaned toward him from candlelit doorways and windows, shouting the bodily pleasures they offered him.

When Dorado reached the Plaza of the Cathedral in the center of Havana, most of the foul odors and noise were behind him. He inhaled deeply for the first time since leaving the dock. Under one of the night lamps in the plaza, he examined the rough map drawn by Carlos Martínez. It showed him which road to take of the several that extended from the plaza and he set out in the darkness confident of the directions.

Dorado reached the mansion of Esteban Morales Muñoz at eight-thirty. The huge house was situated in an old but affluent area, along the tree-lined Alameda de Paula. Dorado knew he had found the Alamada when he saw the numerous beds of flowers that were planted along the road. Martinez had told him he would see the flowers as well as sculptured fountains built on every other block. Dorado no longer needed the map and put it away in his pocket. From a block away, he saw the huge three-story structure described by the doctor. It was clearly visible in the light of the full moon.

Dorado stopped and washed his face and hands in one of the sculptured fountains that had been built at the far end of the house. He laid his hat and wig on the edge of the fountain while he washed. He dried himself with a towel he carried in his haversack. Dorado wanted to look as clean and proper as possible when presenting himself to the physician's family.

He then examined his blue coat, holding it up in the moonlight. He wet his fingers in the fountain and used them to brush the coat. When finished, he carefully arranged his wig on his head, put on his tricorn hat and secured his sword and scabbard at his side. A moment later, groomed to the best of his ability in the dark, Dorado was ready to knock on the door.

CHAPTER TWELVE

NOVEMBER 23-29, 1788

Dorado knocked twice and waited for someone to open the oak door. While waiting, he looked at the front of the house. The moonlight allowed him to see its immense size as well as the wide shuttered windows on all floors. In the morning, Dorado would see that the mansion was white-washed and had a red tiled roof.

A mulatto manservant, lantern in hand, finally opened the door. He looked Dorado over and, after learning what he wanted, invited him inside. Dorado smelled the sweet fragrance of citrus flowers as soon as he entered the vestibule. Somewhere near, he knew there were orange and lemon trees in winter blossom. Standing inside, he heard flamenco music coming from a nearby room. Someone was playing a Spanish guitar and he recognized the piece as *Sitios de Zaragoza* (*Sites of Zaragoza*).

The servant asked Dorado to wait in the vestibule, while

he told Doctor Morales Muñoz of his presence. Moments later, the doctor arrived and greeted the lieutenant. Dorado saluted him and handed him the letter from Carlos Martínez. He scanned it a quickly.

Esteban Morales Muñoz did not look as Dorado had pictured him. Instead of short and slender, the doctor was broad and muscular and looked like one of the wrestlers he had seen at a match in Madrid. There was a width about him like an oak door. Although Esteban smiled easily, his dark face looked foreboding with distinct lines etched on his brow between his eyes.

"So, he's not coming."

"No, sir."

"That's too bad. It seems Carlos has his hands full in Florida. Unfortunately, we have the same sickness here in Havana. It's apparently everywhere in the colonies."

"Yes, sir."

"So, you're here to serve in his place." The physician smiled. "Well, Lieutenant, you have a large space to fill – in more ways than one."

"Sí, señor."

"Come on in, Lieutenant. Nuestra casa es tu casa."

"Gracias, señor."

"Thanks aren't necessary – a friend of Carlos is our friend as well." He took Dorado's arm. "Come, Lieutenant, let's go meet everyone. The children are asleep, but you'll meet the rest of the family. We also have good friends here with us tonight."

The manservant took Dorado's haversack and sword as the doctor ushered him into the living room. The room was elegantly decorated with paintings and tapestries on the walls and plush Persian rugs on the floor. As he entered the doorway, Dorado saw seven people sitting in soft chairs around a low table where bottles of wine and plates of food were within easy reach.

Dorado followed his host as he introduced him to everyone in the room. The doctor's family included his wife, Beatriz, her father and mother, Ignacio and María Teresa Soto Iglesias, her cousin from Spain, María Luisa Meléndez Vilas and Esteban's mother, the widow Sofía Morales Sedonia. A Doctor Diego Garrido Costas and his wife, María Isabel, were also there as dinner guests. They left soon after Dorado's arrival despite protests from everyone. The doctor had been playing the guitar.

It was past midnight and Dorado lay in bed, thinking about the warm welcome he had received from the doctor and his family. He had been settled into a big bedroom on the third floor and, now stretched out on a soft feather mattress, he sighed contentedly. Dorado had enjoyed a full glass of sherry and taken a leisurely bath before climbing the stairs to his room. A servant had prepared his bath, brought him the glass of wine while he bathed and took his underclothes to be washed. He also left him a robe to wear up to his room.

Dorado lay on his back with his hands held behind his head. He recalled the evening and pictured everyone he had met. Beatriz was a tiny woman, less than five feet tall. Smiling and vivacious, she never seemed to stop moving. Her lively little hands appeared perpetually in motion. When not pouring wine in a glass or bustling about serving cheese and dried fruit, she would straighten someone's wayward shirtcollar, rearrange flowers in a vase or adjust an off center painting on the wall. Dorado wondered if she ever stayed still even when asleep.

Her mother seemed an older and heavier version of Beatriz. She too seemed forever to be fixing whatever was out of order. Seeing the two women in motion made him think of two bumblebees buzzing around a patch of flowers. Beatriz' father, a slender austere looking man, sat quietly, his hands entwined in his lap. He watched the antics of his wife and daughter with the complacence of someone who had seen it all before many times. The seated man did not rise to greet him as he entered the room in front of the doctor. Dorado later learned the elderly man suffered from a painful joint disease which had left him an invalid.

The doctor's mother was a melancholy woman, whose mind had been muddled since the death of her husband, fifteen years earlier. The next morning, Beatriz told him the white-haired woman, with the exception of dressing herself, did little else during the day. She spent hours in a chair by one of the front windows staring out into the street. On the evening of his arrival, she acknowledged him with a nod and never looked at him again.

Before sleeping, Dorado's last thoughts lingered on the lovely María Luisa Meléndez Vilas. She was a striking woman, whose black eyes stared boldly into his when they met. In the morning, the doctor told Dorado that María Luisa was a widow, whose older husband had died of a heart attack. With an audible sigh, he said she had been visiting for eighteen months. No one knew when she would return to her home in Zaragoza, Spain.

María Luisa was a slim, shapely woman with long slender fingers, conspicuous because of the gemstone rings she wore on the middle fingers of each hand. Dorado guessed the large blue stones were sapphires. In the candlelight, María Luisa looked beautiful and regal in a red velvet dress that fell loosely in lengthy folds to the floor. She had luxurious black hair, a light Castilian complexion and a saucy smile. Her beauty beguiled Dorado, even when he bowed before her and saw the tiny age lines around her eyes.

As he lay thinking of María Luisa, a tiny breeze brought the fragrance of citrus blooms wafting into his room. The fragrance drew him out of bed and he went to the window. It was a humid night and all the windows in the house were open to admit whatever slight movement of air might flow in from the outside. Dorado looked down into the patio, now in total darkness. There was only enough moonlight to see the taller trees and the outline of the building.

The huge stone house was constructed in the shape of a square, with its front section, three stories high, facing the outside street. Ten-foot high stone walls extended from both ends of the front section and went around the four acres owned by the Morales Muñoz family. The other three sides of the house were one floor lower and, together with the front side, formed a spacious patio with a fountain in the center. The patio was surrounded by a covered porch open to all the first floor rooms of the house.

In the daylight, Dorado would see that the fountain, apparently spring-fed, bubbled up into a pond full of colorful fish. The pond was encircled by beds of orange calendulas, yellow marigolds, and leafy red flowers Dorado could not identify. A dozen lemon and orange trees covered with fragrant white blossoms stood interspersed among the flower beds. Pineapple plants, in full blossom with lavender flowers, grew in all four corners of the patio along with pink and white dogbane.

Other buildings stood behind the huge house, as Dorado would see in the morning from his window. In addition to servants' quarters, there were stables, a pasture for the horses and cattle, enclosures for chickens and pigs, a blacksmith's stall and a coach house on the property. There was also a large vegetable garden situated near the pasture and a wild area full of trees left uncultivated along the rear walls.

As Dorado looked out into the darkness, he noticed a light on the opposite side of the building. It came from a window on the floor below. The light flickered from side to side as someone in the room moved about with a candle in hand.

The light suddenly stopped moving and Dorado saw a woman standing in front of the open window. Within the yellow circle made by candlelight, he saw the woman was naked, her bare breasts clearly visible to him. Dorado blinked his eyes to see better, but the candle was put out and he saw nothing more. He waited awhile, hoping the woman would reappear, but the room remained in darkness. The next day, Dorado learned the suite of rooms across the patio was occupied by the lovely María Luisa Meléndez Vilas.

Early in the morning, Dorado awoke with slender arms wrapped around his neck. A warm body was lying on top of him and brown eyes were peering into his face. The giggling and tickling started as soon as he opened his eyes. Little Angel, five years old, held a long thin feather poised to tickle his nose. His older brother, Julio, stood beside the bed giggling and giving instructions. Fully awake, Dorado seized both boys and rolled them up in the bedcovers. He tickled them, until exhausted from laughing, they finally surrendered and ran out of the room. Later at breakfast, Julio regaled his father with a detailed description of the bedroom battle. In Julio's account, the struggle ended with his bold escape from under the covers. He smiled sheepishly when his father asked him if he was sure it had ended that way.

After a tour of his house and grounds, the doctor invited Dorado to share a coach ride with him to his quarters in the Plaza of the Cathedral. Kissing his sons goodbye, they left the house moments later. The coach trip was brief and they arrived at the plaza at seven o'clock.

The offices of the presidio physician were located in a long abandoned Augustinian church and monastery. Finished in the first years of the seventeenth century, the massive stone structure had been designed with the church in front and the monastery in the rear. The old structure was built in the second century of Spanish occupation and its architectural style included little ornamentation. Viewed from the street, the building had a simple façade with four partially enclosed columns and statues of the Madonna and St. Augustine. The statues were sculptured into niches on either side of the church door. With the exception of a number of small upper windows cut into the stonework, nothing else appeared on the exterior walls.

The Havana medical facilities included four surgeries, each with two treatment tables, five doctors' offices and a hospital. Medical treatment was performed in the church portion of the building and patients requiring additional care were carried back to the monastery which served as a hospital. The surgeries, partitioned by pine planking, had been set up in what had been the main seating area of the church. Unlike the small, cramped surgery in St. Augustine, the surgeries were spacious enough for families and friends to stand about comforting patients enduring a variety of painful treatments including surgery. The monastery hospital housed as many as a hundred sick and surgical patients sent there to recover or die in bed. Nursing care was available to those fortunate patients whose families lived in Havana.

Eight experienced doctors worked under the direction of the Doctor Morales Muñoz and they bustled about the surgeries treating the living and examining the dead. They worked from dawn until dusk with only a few moments stolen for meals. When there were unexpected surgeries or emergencies, they even missed their midday lunch. At the busiest times, Doctor Morales Muñoz also treated patients.

It was a noisy place with people coming and going throughout the day. The doctor told Dorado that more than

500 patients received treatment there each week. With so many people waiting to be examined or witnessing treatment, there was a constant murmur of voices. They hushed only when a loud scream of pain emerged from one of the surgeries. The talking then resumed until the next outcry startled them into silence. At times, amid all the commotion that echoed throughout the building, the doctors often shouted to be heard by their patients.

The physicians usually performed their autopsies early in the morning before patients were permitted into the waiting room. But, now and then, the unexplained death of a Spanish nobleman or a prominent Cuban required an immediate autopsy and it would be performed in the same surgery where a sick patient was receiving treatment on the other table. With a wry smile, the doctor told Dorado the sight of a dead man lying beside an ill patient often helped him tolerate the excruciating pain of surgery, even when amputation was required.

The foul-smelling surgeries upset Dorado's stomach. He could not escape the gagging odor of decomposing corpses, gangrenous flesh, bloody rags and bodily excretions, even with his nostrils pinched shut. When his host was called away by another doctor, Dorado hurriedly left the surgeries. Fearing he would vomit if he stayed there any longer, he went to the rear of the church where the physicians had their offices. The smell of the surgeries was bearable at that distance. One of the doctors later told him that the stench defied all attempts to remove it from the building. It remained despite twice daily cleaning with buckets of lye and water.

All the offices were in use by the time Dorado arrived. The building was full of ailing people and a line of thirty soldiers sat or stood waiting for examinations. Some were bleeding, others had bandages wrapped around arms or legs and several lay on the floor too sick to stand up. One man had spit up blood on his shirt and another lay moaning on the stone floor, his head cradled in his hands. A third man with a swollen left arm sat against the wall sobbing.

Dorado waited two hours to enter the office where he had been told the medical records were stored. He paced the outside hall as patients went in and out of the room. Finally, when a doctor opened the office door and called out for an orderly, he hurried over to him.

"What do you want?" The physician, a stout bald man, stood in the doorway with hands on his hips.

"I'm Lieutenant Dorado Delgado. Major Morales Muñoz has given me permission to look in the files." Dorado looked over the man's head to the closed closet, which he knew held the records he needed to see.

"I see. I'm Doctor Alejandro Ramos Escobedo. You'll have to hurry, Lieutenant. I have patients to see. So be quick about it."

"Yes, sir. I was hoping to find a file here and read it."

"You can't read it here. We need this room, as I told you."

"If I can't read it here, where can I go, sir?" asked Dorado, seeing the portly physician as an overfilled wine barrel.

"How would I know? Ask Esteban." He dismissed Dorado with a frown and the flip of his wrist. "Get the file and go see him. Hurry up, I've got work to do." The doctor clucked his tongue loudly and sat down at the one table in the room.

Dorado went directly to the closet and opened the door. He gasped at the sight of seven overflowing shelves of bundled papers facing him. He had no idea where to begin looking for the autopsy file. And, then, Dorado saw the faded, almost illegible labels on the edges of the shelves. Since the upper shelves held patient case files, he kneeled down on the hard floor to read the lower labels. On the bottom shelf, he found *Murders and Unexplained Deaths*.

The files, tied by year into thick packets, had been placed on the shelf in chronological order beginning in 1700 and ending in 1787. Tagged with a protruding red ribbon by Esteban, the packet for the year 1770 was easy to spot. Dorado took it from the shelf, well aware of the doctor impatiently drumming his fingers on the table behind him. Ramos sat with his back to Dorado, but watched him out of the corner of his eye. As Dorado stood with the packet in his hand, the physician turned his eyes down to a patient's file on the table.

"Now, I can return to my patients," he muttered without looking at the officer.

"Thank you, sir." Dorado spoke to the man's back and thought, "What a pompous ass," as he left the office.

Minutes later, apologizing for the cramped space, Esteban led Dorado to a stuffy room near his office. It was cluttered with broken furniture, piles of old clothing, rusted instruments and old medical volumes. A layer of dust covered everything he touched. Dorado cleared one corner of the storage room and shoved a battered desk into the space. He wiped the top of the desk with a blood-splattered shirt he found in one of the clothing piles. Dorado made sure he brushed the dust away from the clean uniform he now wore; when he awoke that morning, he found all his clothing had been washed and his uniform thoroughly brushed.

Since there were no unbroken chairs in the room, Dorado climbed onto the desk and sat with his back against the wall. A candle given him by Esteban offered sufficient light to read. He now was ready to see the autopsy report that had been on his mind for so long. He quickly untied the thick packet that held the files for 1770 and leafed through them until he found the file of Carlota Ramírez Cruz. It was organized by month and placed among six other murders in October. The file contained twenty-five sheets of paper and Dorado cautiously separated them from other files. He wanted to make sure he saw everything of importance in the report.

Dorado laid the file in his lap as he began to read. Once he began, the ceaseless noise in the waiting room faded away. Dorado read with rapt concentration, aware of only the report in his lap. For a time, he even forgot about the stench from the surgeries.

Turning over the cover page, Dorado immediately saw the brief note written and signed by the crown's investigating officer, Captain José Caminero de Castilla. The captain wrote his note in large bold letters and his similar signature with a complicated flourish extended almost the entire width of the page. It was dated December 22, 1777.

"Ah, there it is," Dorado said aloud.

"The enclosed unsolved case (#52 in the year 1770) of the killing of Carlota Ramírez Cruz (October 14, 1770) shows a number of the same characteristics as the killing of María Palés Molina (November 28, 1777), presently under investigation (Case # 68 in the year 1777). The method of mutilation appears to be similar for both murders. Both victims were murdered in the same district of the city. See my report of December 24, 1777."

Dorado quickly perused through the many routine documents employed in the imperial system. They included receipts of the report with the signatures of secretaries and clerks, all with official seals. Dorado sighed seeing the paperwork. He recalled Martínez' criticism of the paperwork and protocol of Spain's expanding bureaucracy. "It's mierda admininistrativa (administrative shit) that's slowly, but surely destroying the Spanish Empire in America."

After flipping through five pages of receipts, he found a report relating the discovery of the corpse of Carlota Ramírez Cruz. He skimmed the three page statement anxious to read the physician's autopsy report. The details of the discovery and disposition of the body would be significant only if the method of her murder was the same or similar to the murder of Gloria Márquez García y Morera.

A number of accounts of people who lived near the site of the murder followed. There were then statements from family members, friends and neighbors as well as a couple of street gossips. The final one was written by the victim's fiancée, Lieutenant Eduardo Velarde Oviedo. It was a sad memorial from a man lamenting the loss of his loved one.

Dorado next read the report penned by the crown's officer assigned to investigate the murder. Written three weeks after the discovery of the corpse, it was a concise description of what was known about the murder of Carlota Ramírez Cruz. The crown's officer, Lieutenant Mario Salinas de Mendoza, summed up the investigation in a paragraph.

"The girl was murdered and mutilated by an unknown assailant for unknown reasons. The murderer is probably a madman, who never will be found. A random killing of this kind is much too ordinary in Havana to waste the crown's time and pesetas on a lengthy investigation. It is therefore my recommendation that the Case # 52, The Murder of Carlota Ramíerz Cruz, be closed unless additional information is found within the next thirty days."

"The lazy dog!" Dorado struck the table with his hand. He knew the man had expended little effort to write the report and suspected him of an equally limited investigation. As Uncle Ernesto had said, "What a man does in one situation, he'll surely do again in another."

It was obvious the officer intended to avoid further work on the murder investigation. His conclusion that a continuing investigation would waste the crown's money assured the end of any official attempts to find the girl's murderer. The ever-thrifty royal officials in Havana would need no better excuse to close the case.

Dorado frowned, turning over the report in disgust. His mood instantly changed when he found himself looking at the autopsy report, six pages in all. The report was written and signed by Doctor Luis Aguilera Gayón, the Presidio Physician of Havana. The doctor wrote legibly, though his lettering was tiny and his sentences were crowded together on every page. He wrote as if trying to fill every bit of space on the paper. Dorado wondered if the crown's officials had given the Presidio Physician one of their capricious orders to conserve paper.

His stomach tightened as he read the first page. In minutes, he would know whether or not his voyage to Havana was worthwhile. He read each sentence with growing excitement, scrutinizing every word to make certain he missed nothing. Then, he reread it. On his second reading, Dorado paused occasionally to write notes on a piece of torn paper he picked up from the littered floor. By noon, he had finished looking at the file and retied it with the ribbon.

A few minutes later, Dorado went to lunch with his host. The doctor opened the door as he was tying up the packet of files. "Do you have time for lunch, Lieutenant? If so, we must go now before the taverns fill up for the midday meal."

Dorado nodded, placed the file under his arm and followed the doctor out to the street. In the plaza, the physician led him to a small tavern behind the cathedral. Still early with only three other tables occupied, they ordered immediately to save enough time for talking. Dorado followed the Cuban's recommendation and enjoyed roasted chicken and rice with crisp bread. He told the doctor about his findings in the murder file and they talked about the investigation in St. Augustine. After lunch, the doctor returned to his office and Dorado took a longboat to El Morro. He hoped his brother, Miguel, might be inside the fort that afternoon.

After dinner that night, Dorado wrote to Serena Rodríguez and Ruiz de León. He spent three hours writing the letters and finished at midnight. Dorado had been told a ship was sailing for Florida the next day and he wanted the letters sent out in the morning mail.

His letter to Serena flowed easily. Dorado began by telling her what had happened to him since sailing to Cuba. He told her how warmly the Morales Muñoz family had welcomed him into their home and described their luxurious house and the scenic property surrounding it. His description of the house included his third floor bedroom overlooking the patio.

"My bedroom is as big as Don Ricardo's entire house," he wrote, "and it has a splendid featherbed. The house has twenty rooms, several bathing closets and an enclosed patio with a fountain, beautiful flowers and orange and lemon trees. All the downstairs rooms have marble floor tiles brought from Mexico and there are colorful tapestries and paintings on all the walls. In the main living room, there is a painting of San Francisco by José de Ribera. I don't know much about painters, but I have heard the name of José de Ribera."

Dorado described everyone in the house with the exception of María Luisa Meléndez Vilas. He never mentioned her name in any of his correspondence to Serena Rodríguez. It was as if she did not exist.

Several paragraphs were devoted to the adventures of Angel and Julio. Dorado knew how much Serena loved children and he told her of his time playing with them. "Almost every morning, they awaken me and we wrestle in bed," he wrote.

In the last paragraph, Dorado told Serena he missed her very much and looked forward to seeing her soon. Dorado hesitated to write of his feelings for her, fearful she might expect a marriage proposal on his return to Florida. Instead, he said she was always in his thoughts and frequently in his dreams at night. As an afterthought, Dorado added that his heart felt heavy without her. He closed his letter with, "Te quiero."

In a postscript, Dorado said he had not seen his brother. He told Serena that Miguel's regiment had gone on maneuvers in the mountains and the time of its return was not known. Dorado told her he feared finishing his mission before Miguel returned to Havana.

Dorado wrote two letters to Ruiz de León, one a private note, the other a detailed report of his time in Havana. Dorado wrote slowly and carefully. When he found the slightest error, unclear lettering or an ink spot, he immediately discarded that sheet. He read each completed page three times to insure his grammar was correct and there were no misspellings. By the time Dorado finished writing, ten sheets of paper were balled up on the floor. Since Ruiz de León would read both the letters and the governor would probably read the report, he wanted them to be as perfect as possible.

Dorado began his writing after looking in vain for candlelight in the bedroom across the patio. Several other times as he paused to compose a sentence, he would walk to the window to see if light appeared in the suite opposite him. But there was no light to be seen that night and no naked woman standing near the open window.

In his first letter, Dorado wrote a brief account of his arrival in Havana. He considered describing the elegant house, but decided not to say anything the staid captain might regard as trivial. It was better to be brief and concentrate on what was important to the investigation.

Captain Ricardo Ruiz de Leon,

I hope this letter finds you feeling better and up and about. By now, you must be back in your office making up for lost time. Hopefully, the illness has finally left the presidio.

The sea voyage to Havana was smooth and uneventful, Gracias a Dios. Major Esteban Morales Muñoz y Barrientos welcomed me into his home as Captain Martínez said he would. The entire family has made me feel at home and I am now comfortably situated in a bedroom on the third floor. It overlooks a patio with flowering orange and lemon trees. The house is in a quiet district away from the center of the city.

Havana seems more crowded than ever. After my time in St. Augustine, I find this city filthy and noisy. It is much worse than I remembered. I'll be glad to return to Florida.

Doctor Morales Muñoz y Barrientos has been very helpful and he has given me the use of his office where the medical files are stored. He marked the file of Case # 52, The Murder of Carlota Ramírez Cruz (October 14, 1770) with a red ribbon which made it easy to find. We have already discussed the murder of the governor's niece and he has given me good counsel.

I have not yet played chess with my host, but I look forward to it. I miss our games as well as our evenings of conversation. It is my hope that I will return soon to St. Augustine and resume our pleasurable evenings together.

Adiós, Mi Capitán.

Reciba mi más atento salud,
Lieutenant Roberto Dorado Delgado y Estrada

Dorado sat awhile, thinking about the official report he would write to Ruiz de León. Much of it was already composed in his mind. He got up from his chair, went to the window and, for the fourth time, looked at the room across the patio. Seeing no candlelight, he sighed and returned to the desk.

Captain Ricardo Ruiz de León
Fourth Infantry Regiment of Havana
Presidio of St. Augustine

Capitan Ruiz de León, Señor,

I am writing to report my activities since leaving La Florida on November 15, 1788. The voyage on La Santísima Trinidad lasted seven days and I arrived in Havana on the night of November 23. I then proceeded to the house of Major Esteban Morales Muñoz y Barrientos, Presidio Physician of Havana, where I received quarters for the duration of my assignment in Cuba. As instructed, I will report to Major Morales Muñoz y Barrientos.

This morning, November 24, 1788, I accompanied Major Morales Muñoz y Barrientos to his office to examine the murder records for the city of Havana in the year 1770. In those records, I found Case # 52: The Murder of Carlota Ramírez Cruz dated October 14, 1770. The murder file includes twenty-five written pages and contains the following inclusions:

1. Statement made by Captain José Caminero de Castilla, the Crown's investigating officer for the murder of María Palés Molina (November 28, 1777).

2. Letters of dispatch and receipt for Case # 52: The Murder of Carlota Ramírez Cruz.

3. Report of discovery and transfer of the victim's corpse to the presidio physician.

4. Depositions from the family, friends, neighbors and the vegetable vendor, Jaime Figueres, who found the body of Carlota Ramírez Cruz.

5. Report made by Lieutenant Mario Salinas de Mendoza, the crown's investigating officer for the murder of Carlota Ramírez Cruz (November 5, 1770).

6. Autopsy report prepared by Doctor Luis Aguilera Gayón, Presidio Physician of Havana (October 20, 1770).

The following is a summary of the known events of the murder for your consideration: Carlota Ramírez Cruz was killed on the evening of October 14, 1770, in a pasture near the market on La Calle Santa Clara. Carlota was seventeen when she died, born September 13, 1753, in Havana. She was betrothed to Lieutenant Eduardo Velarde Oviedo in December. The girl was the third child of a family of five children with two older sisters and two younger brothers. Her father, Alejandro Ramírez Cruz, served an accounts clerk in the governor's office. Statements made by her friends and neighbors affirm that the family was well-respected in the barrio. Carlota was an obedient, proper and pious girl, who accompanied her mother to Mass every day. She was never known to say an offensive word to anyone in the neighborhood.

On the night of October 14, 1770, Carlota left home after dinner without the knowledge of anyone in the family. No one knew why she left the house or where she was going. When she was missed sometime later, it was thought she had gone across the street to visit her friend, Ana María Sánchez Portes. No one was alarmed until her fiancée, Lieutenant Velarde Oviedo, arrived to see her at eight o'clock and she was not to be found. Ana María admitted Carlota had visited her, but said she left without mentioning her destination. Once the family realized she was missing, everyone in the neighborhood searched for her. Carlota was not found that night.

The next morning, at six-thirty, the vegetable vendor, Jaime Figueres, found her body while pushing his cart past the cattle pasture. He saw her legs sticking out from underbrush near the path he used every day. It was a route Figueres took on the way to and from the site where he sold his vegetables on La Calle Santa Clara.

The body of the girl lay in thick underbrush. It had been dragged there from eleven feet away, where the killing took place. Lines in the dirt indicated the girl had been dragged to the underbrush. The site of the murder was a secluded spot in a thicket of trees.

The corpse of Carlota Ramírez Cruz was found completely undressed and none of her clothing was ever found.

It was assumed the murderer stripped her body after her murder and carried away everything she wore. No reason for the removal of her clothing was suggested.

Doctor Luis Aguilera Gayón reported that Carlota Ramírez Cruz was stabbed to death and then mutilated. The doctor found four knife wounds on her cadaver: one in the throat, one in each breast and one between her legs. He concluded that the girl died from the knife wound in her throat. The doctor did not mention any significant loss of blood.

Doctor Aguilera Gayón found bruises on the sides of Carlota's neck and concluded the murderer had seized the girl by the neck, pushed her to the ground and, then, stabbed her with a knife. The bruises on her neck as well as her bloated face he attributed to the murderer's hands holding her by the neck. He determined the murderer mutilated her corpse when it lay on the ground. Doctor Aguilera Gayón thought the mutilation was the work of a madman.

The crown's investigating officer, Lieutenant Mario Salinas de Mendoza, summarized the findings of the presidio physician. He said Carlota Ramírez Cruz was murdered by an unknown assailant, probably a madman, for unknown reasons. He recommended ending the investigation unless additional information was found within three weeks' time. His report was written on November 5, 1770, and the investigation was terminated as he recommended.

In 1777, Captain José Caminero de Castilla, the crown's investigating officer for the murder of María Palés Molina (November 28, 1777), found the file for Carlota Ramírez Cruz (Case #52 of the year 1770). Captain Caminero de Castilla compared the autopsy reports for the murders and found similar characteristics in them. He wrote, "The method of mutilation appears to be similar for both murders." His statement is included in the file of Case # 52 for the year 1770 and refers readers to examine Case # 68 for the year 1777.

Captain Caminero de Castilla's report of the murder of María Palés Molina was written on December 24, 1777, and should be found in the files as Case # 68 for that year. Tomorrow, I will read Captain Caminero de Castilla's report and inform you of my findings.

From the information acquired in Case File # 52, it appears that the murders of Carlota Ramírez Cruz and Gloria Márquez García y Morera are much alike. A list of the similarities is presented below:

1. Both victims were seventeen-year-old girls.
2. Both were murdered in remote locations.
3. Both were stripped of their clothing and left naked.
4. Both were murdered in one place and then dragged to a nearby location.
5. Both were murdered first and then mutilated
6. Both bodies were placed on their backs.
7. Both were stabbed in the throat, breasts and female area.
8. Both bodies show finger and thumb bruises on their necks.
9. Both bodies had bloated faces.

The most significant difference between the two murders is the doctors' determination of the cause of death. Doctor Aguilera Gayón reported that Carlota Ramírez Cruz was stabbed to death, while Doctor Carlos Martínez concluded that Gloria Marquez García was strangled to death. Doctor Morales Muñoz y Barrientos, who knows the results of both autopsies, believes Carlota Ramírez Cruz was strangled, not stabbed, to death. The finger and thumb marks on the victim's neck, the bloated face and the absence of any significant amount of blood on the body or at the site of the murder indicate death by strangulation. He thinks Doctor Aguilera Gayón, not knowing the significance of lividity at that time, mistakenly diagnosed the cause of death.

Doctor Morales Muñoz y Barrientos believes both victims

were strangled and mutilated in exactly the same way – they were marked by the sign of the cross. He said there was only one difference between them; the points of the cross on the corpse of Carlota Ramírez Cruz were not connected by lines cut on the corpse of Gloria Márquez García y Morera. He thinks the victims were mutilated in the same sequence. They were stabbed first in the throat, then between the legs and lastly in the left and right breasts.

Doctor Morales Muñoz y Barrientos thinks the murderer has killed a number of times, all in a similar manner. He expects, when the report of murder of María Rosa Molina in 1777 is seen, it will show the same characteristics as the other murders. He trusts the assessment of Captain José Caminero de Castilla, who saw similarities in the two murders of 1770 and 1777.

The captain is still alive, although now well over seventy years of age. Doctor Morales Muñoz de Barrientos knows him from previous investigations and says his mind is as active as ever. The captain lives on a finca, south of Havana, near Santiago de las Vegas. I intend to go to his home and interview him in the next few days.

This concludes my first official report from Havana, Cuba. November 24, 1788.

Respectfully submitted,
Roberto Dorado Delgado y Estrada, Lieutenant
Third Infantry Regiment of Havana

Four days later, Dorado was in an ill humor. For one reason or another, nothing he tried had succeeded. He failed to find the murder file of 1777, though he spent three days searching for it. He was then refused permission to look for a copy of the file in the Building of Records. In addition, Dorado had been unable to contact Captain José Caminero de Castilla.

He had no better luck trying to see his brother. Miguel remained away on a maneuver and no one at El Morro knew when he would return. Dorado wondered if he would ever see him while in Cuba. He sat glumly in his bedroom before dinner on Saturday night, brooding over his bad luck. He was so close and yet so far from the information he had hoped to find.

Dorado had spent an entire day in Esteban's office looking through the murder cases. Doctor Ramos was busy elsewhere doing surgery. On his way to lunch, Dorado passed him in the hall and the haughty doctor ignored his polite greeting of "Buenas tardes, Doctor Ramos."

Dorado initially looked through every murder file for the year 1777. The file he sought was not among the murder cases for the year, nor was it misfiled among the death reports for accidents, illness or starvation. After lunch, Dorado opened every tied packet to see if the file might have been mistakenly bundled with one of the other 107 murder reports. But Case #68, which should have been found between Case #67, the machete murder of a drunken sailor on November 10, and Case #69, a throat stabbing in a lovers' quarrel on November 30, was gone. A second day looking through the files for 1776 and 1778 was no more successful. Again, he had access to the office and again he found nothing. By that evening, Dorado knew he would not find the missing file. For some unknown reason, it had been removed from the file closet.

At the time, Dorado was not worried because he knew a copy of the file existed in the Building of Records. Though difficult to find in the overflowing aisles of bundled documents, he expected it would take no more than two days to locate a copy in the records for 1777. He decided to start his search the next day when the archive opened.

In the morning, following a coach ride to the plaza with his host, Dorado walked to the nearby Building of Records, located on Merced Street beside the Municipal Palace. There, he met Rubén Ballesteros Bazón, director of the archive, in his cramped little office situated only a few steps from the entrance. The portly director wore thick spectacles and, while they talked, looked at Dorado with glass-enlarged eyes. He stood up when his visitor was ushered into his office by the old crippled man who served as a receptionist. The newspaper *Papel Periódico de la Havana* lay open on his desk where he had been reading it. The director sat immediately after Dorado introduced himself. He leaned back in his squeaky chair, with his fingers crossed over his stomach. He did not invite Dorado to sit down in the chair that stood to the side of his desk.

His face was round with prominent cheeks. Dorado later told Esteban that Ballesteros looked like a squirrel with acorns stored in the sides of his mouth. The man's mouth, captured between his plump cheeks, appeared permanently pursed. When the man spoke, it looked as if the words bubbled out from his lips.

"You will need an official authorization, Lieutenant, to enter the Building of Records. We do not permit anyone off the street to come in here and look around, you know. This is an archive for serious study." He sniffed and pushed his nose into the air.

"I'm not anyone off the street, señor." Dorado raised his voice. "I've been sent to Cuba by the governor of Florida on an important mission! It involves serious study in the Building of Records." He placed Zéspedes' letter of introduction on the desk in front of Ballesteros.

His chair squeaked as Ballesteros leaned forward and peered over his thick glasses. He did not pick up the letter to be polite, but kept his fingers crossed over his stomach. "That letter will not allow you to enter the Building of Records. No, no, absolutely not! Here in Havana, Lieutenant, you will need an entry authorization from our governor – Gobernador José Manuel de Expeleta. He's the only one who has the authority to grant authorizations."

"I've been sent to the Building of Records by the presidio physician, Major Morales Muñoz y Barrientos," lied Dorado. "He sent me here to find a critical file in an investigation – a murder investigation!"

Ballesteros shook his head from side to side. "The presidio physician cannot grant you an entry authorization to the Building of Records. No! No, indeed! That's a prerogative of the governor of Cuba only." His pursed lips emphasized the p's of presidio and prerogative.

Red-faced with anger, Dorado turned and left the Building of Records. He thought of telling Esteban his predicament, but decided instead to go to the governor's office and request an entry authorization. Dorado was sure an aide in the office would assist him once he showed him his official letters and explained his need to enter the Building of Records.

The governor's offices were located on the first floor of the Municipal Palace. A sentry led him to the reception room. As soon as the door closed, Dorado saw a familiar face in the office. It took him a second to recognize Lieutenant López Sierra, who sat at a desk across the room. López Sierra stared at him and then, recognizing Dorado, smiled at him.

"Well, well. If it isn't Lieutenant Dorado Delgado from the Florida frontier. What are you doing here in Havana?" he asked, standing and nodding a perfunctory greeting.

"I'm still involved in the murder investigation." Dorado nodded in return. "I need to see the governor about it."

"You do? What about, Lieutenant?"

"It's an ... official matter."

"I see. But it concerns the investigation?" López Sierra walked toward Dorado.

"Yes. When can I see him?"

"Ah." López Sierra nodded knowingly. "You want to see the governor on an official matter. I wonder if it has to do with an authorization to enter the Building of Records?"

"Yes, yes." Dorado sighed loudly.

"Well, Lieutenant, why didn't you say so immediately? I'm sure I can assist you." He nodded his head agreeably. "Do sit down and we'll discuss it." López Sierra motioned him to a chair in front of his desk.

"I would be very grateful for your help." Dorado remained standing.

"I'm sure you would." López Sierra's eyes glistened. "Of course, I'll help you. You can count on me. I'll see to it that you get an authorization from the governor. It shouldn't take more than, ah, three or four weeks." He smiled maliciously.

"Three or four weeks!" Dorado grimaced, blaming himself for being so gullible to believe López Sierra would help him. "I can't wait that long."

"That's too bad. These things take time, you know, Lieutenant." López Sierra smiled again. "Rome wasn't built in a day, as they say."

"I want to talk to the governor, Lieutenant." Dorado glared at López Sierra. "I have a letter from Governor Zéspedes, requesting his assistance." He took the letter out of his pocket.

"Of course you do." López Sierra scanned the letter quickly and dropped it on a nearby table. "It won't be easy to see the governor."

"I must see him." Dorado gritted his teeth.

"Must see him, Lieutenant?"

"I need to see him. I need his authorization to enter the Building of Records."

"Yes, Lieutenant Dorado Delgado, you do need the governor's authorization since you won't accept my help. If you would only be a bit more patient, I would assist you."

"I can't wait three weeks. I need to see the governor, now!"

"He's much too busy to see you now, Lieutenant. But if you return in a week or so, he might see you then. You must be patient. As you surely know, Lieutenant, patience is one of the heavenly virtues. St. Paul said it was a fruit of the soul." López Sierra spoke slowly and softly in the same patronizing way Dorado had spoken to him in St. Augustine.

"I need to see him, now." Dorado raised his voice. "It will only take a few minutes."

"I understand your needs, Lieutenant Dorado Delgado, but it's not possible to see him now. And raising your voice won't help you to see him any sooner." López Sierra smiled.

Dorado felt the heat in his cheeks and knew his face was flushed in anger. He wanted to knock López Sierra to the floor. But he lowered his voice and spoke calmly. "I need only a minute or so of the governor's time to request a routine authorization. It's a simple request, so why can't I see him when he has the time? I'll wait here as long as necessary."

"No, no. This office is not a waiting room for uninvited visitors." López Sierra's face reddened and he raised his voice. "This is the administrative office of the governor of Havana, young man, the most important port in all of America! Not some insignificant little outpost on the remote Florida frontier. The governor is busy with important matters concerning the king's possessions in the entire Caribbean. That's why you can't see him now. Do you understand?"

"Oh, yes, Lieutenant, I understand everything!" Dorado scowled at López Sierra, but said nothing more. A further display of anger might keep him from ever seeing the governor and getting the entry authorization for the Building of Records. He looked around and saw the other soldiers in the office staring at him. A couple of the sergeants had smiles on their faces.

"I'm glad you understand." López Sierra now spoke in a soft pleasant voice. He also was aware of the attention focused on them. "Come back in a week, Lieutenant, and I'll see what I can do for you." He smiled. "I'm sure the Building of Records will still be standing."

Dorado knew it was futile to argue any longer. He picked up the governor's letter from the table and left the office. As Dorado walked away, he decided to ask Esteban for help.

"What damned nonsense!" exclaimed Esteban that evening when Dorado told him what had happened to him that day. "I've never heard of such an authorization to enter the Building of Records and I've gone there countless numbers of times. So have all the other physicians on my staff. I'll go see the governor in the morning and find out about it. If an authorization is indeed needed, I'll get one for you. Meanwhile, let's contact Caminero de Castilla. We can set up an interview with him for next week. I'll send a man down to Santiago de las Vegas to make the necessary arrangements."

Now, days later, Dorado still had not been granted authorization to enter the Building of Records. The governor was home sick with a harsh cough and high fever. He fell ill on the same afternoon Dorado had gone to his office and it was rumored the governor had gotten the plague that was spreading through Havana.

Dorado had no better luck trying to contact Captain Caminero de Castilla. Esteban sent his stableman, Simón Andrade, to Santiago de las Vegas to schedule a meeting with him, but the captain was not home when he arrived. The captain's wife told Andrade her husband had gone hunting in the mountains. She had no notion when he would return.

Despondent over his lack of progress, Dorado went to bed early Saturday night. After dinner, he talked to Esteban for an hour and, then, excused himself to go to his room. He was in bed by nine o'clock and asleep a few minutes later.

María Luisa made up her mind during dinner. It was

a plan she had considered since Dorado's arrival at her cousin's home. María Luisa had immediately liked Dorado's greenish-blue eyes that looked directly into hers, his strong face and chin and what she could see of his hard young body beneath his uniform. She also liked his courteous manners and the way he treated everyone with respect, even the servants. Unlike so many arrogant Spanish caballeros who typically ignored those people who served them, Dorado thanked them every time they brought him something, even if only a cup of tea. María Luisa knew from their conversations that he was unsophisticated and generally ignorant of art, literature and music, but she found his eagerness to learn quite charming. She even enjoyed his rustic Spanish and concealed her amusement when he mispronounced words that were new to him.

Seeing Dorado looking so forlorn Saturday night, María Luisa decided to take the risk that had been on her mind for days. The very thought of it made her feel warm all over and she wished she could fan herself at the dinner table. Seeing him sit so quietly, his fingers stroking his chin, she felt her face flush as if she suffered a sudden fever. The warmth remained with her all during dinner and for the rest of the evening as she talked with Beatriz. Busy as usual, writing letters to family friends, Beatriz did not initially notice the color in her cousin's cheeks. When she did see and inquire about it, María Luisa said she was a little overheated from the hot tea she had sipped too quickly. The warmth diminished after awhile, but then she felt her heart flutter when the Dorado stood, bowed politely and said good night to everyone.

Afterwards, María Luisa sat in the living room talking to Beatriz while she sewed the sleeves on a new shirt for little Angel. Time passed slowly as she anxiously awaited the time when everyone would go upstairs to bed. Finally, at ten o'clock, Esteban took the dogs out for their final walk and

Beatriz put her sewing away. Fifteen minutes later, they all mounted the stairs to their bedrooms.

María Luisa waited in her room until she thought everyone was asleep and the two dogs had settled down for the night. They patrolled the halls for awhile after the family went to bed. When the house was quiet, María Luisa slipped out of her room, paused a moment to listen for any sound of activity. Hearing none, climbed stealthily up the stairway to the third floor.

María Luisa opened the door to Dorado's bedroom without a sound, her hand shaking as she stepped cautiously inside. For a few seconds, she stood still by the door, adjusting her eyes to the darkness. A thin shaft of moonlight coming in through a window allowed her to see the outline of the bed where Dorado was sleeping. He lay on his right side, his head on a pillow, his body a mound beneath the bedcover.

María Luisa paused a few seconds more, sighed quietly and tiptoed toward the sleeping man. Beside the bed, she slipped off her silk robe and dropped it to the floor. Carefully lifting the light cover, she crawled into bed behind him. Dorado did not awaken. Trembling, María Luisa slid slowly across the bed sheet until her body barely touched him. Her nipples brushed his back, her thighs lightly touched his buttocks. Gently but firmly, María Luisa pressed her breasts against his back and waited for him to awaken.

"Do you want me here?" she asked when Dorado had turned and faced her, his mouth close to hers.

"Oh, yes." Dorado kissed her hard and wrapped his arms around her.

Pulling her lips away from his, María Luisa moved her head slowly down to his chest and rubbed her cheek against his soft hair. "Are you certain? Let me hear you say it."

"Yes, I want you here with me."

"Oh, I'm so glad you do." María Luisa rolled on top of Dorado and teased him with little bites on his chest and neck.

She then lifted her head to kiss his lips again. Her tongue probed his mouth as he hugged her, his strong hands pressing her body to him.

Still kissing him hard, María Luisa rubbed her body rhythmically against him. Dorado groaned and let his hands fall uselessly to his sides. As he lay unmoving upon his back, María Luisa moved her mouth from his and kissed his chin, neck and chest. Holding his hands down on the bed, she very slowly slid her face down his chest to his stomach, kissing and licking his body. He gasped with surprise when she licked his navel and then shuddered as her tongue moved over his erection and engulfed him. Moments later, Dorado pulled her head up to face him and kissed her eyes and ears and then her lips again. They kissed deeply, their bodies pressed together, their arms around each other. Dorado then gently turned María Luisa over on her back and entered her. Her legs held tightly around him, they were entwined for the first of many times that night.

Afterwards in the darkness, they remained cuddled closely for hours. As María Luisa had come to Dorado in bed, she cradled him from behind with her breasts pressed against his back. At first light, she left as he lay sleeping on his side. Before leaving the bedroom, María Luisa straightened the sheet over him, stroked his covered back and kissed him lightly on the cheek. She stood beside the bed a few seconds more looking at him and then stole out of the room as soundlessly as she had entered.

CHAPTER THIRTEEN

December 1-20, 1788

Dorado left early Tuesday morning for Santiago de las Vegas. The lamplighters were extinguishing the streetlights as he rode out of the city. He had planned to leave Monday, but heavy rain kept him inside all day. Dorado decided to take the trip himself and wait as long as necessary to interview Captain Caminero de Castilla. At Esteban's insistence, he rode his host's favorite horse, a strong chestnut-brown stallion bred from Spanish Andalusian stock.

To his surprise, Dorado found the dirt road south firm with few potholes and puddles in the way. With the rain clouds gone and the sun rising in the east, it looked to be a clear day for his journey. The narrow road remained hard and uncluttered as he rode through long stretches of open pasture land bordered by intermittent tobacco fields. "Agriculture is coming," Esteban had told him, "and the old hacendados (ranchers) who raise cattle can't do anything to stop it. We're seeing tobacco everywhere now and sugar-cane will surely follow."

For much of his ride south, Dorado thought about María Luisa and their night together. He thought of little else as he rode easily on the hard road. He saw her in countless fantasies that flashed through his mind and reminded him of the reckless passion they had shared. With María Luisa, Dorado had discovered bodily pleasures he had never known before and hoped to have again and again in the future.

Dorado missed her in the morning when he came downstairs for breakfast. Beatriz told him María Luisa had gone to morning Mass and, afterwards, would be taken by coach to visit a cousin who lived in Santa Cruz, a city east of Havana. Learning she would be away a week, he turned away to hide his disappointment. Dorado could not stop thinking about his night with her and he almost dropped the reins when the stallion stumbled over a large rock in the road.

Afterwards, Dorado concentrated on the pitted and stone surface he now saw ahead of him. The stony rubble remained on the road for the next several miles and he rode cautiously until it diminished near his destination. He arrived in Santiago de las Vegas at midmorning.

A few minutes later, following the directions of a campesino, Dorado reached the ranch of José Caminero de Castilla. He dismounted at the gate and led his tired horse up the path to the house. Cattle grazed in green pastures on both sides of the path.

The captain's ranch appeared as the stableman had described it. Everything seemed to be in perfect order. The house had been whitewashed recently and the roof tiles had either been cleaned or new ones had been laid down in the autumn. Not one house plank looked warped and none of the wooden fence slats appeared loose or weather-beaten. There was not even one protruding stone in the long path leading from the iron gate to the front door of the house. The well-tended state of the ranch amazed Dorado, whose family home in Asturias always seemed in need of paint and repair and whose lands were always cluttered with piles of stones, rotting timbers and broken plows and wagons.

A large white dog sat in front of the house and watched Dorado as he led his horse up the path. He stood and growled when they neared the house. Studying the fierce looking dog, Dorado stopped and stood beside his horse. He stood completely still and waited until a man came out the front door of the house.

"Captain Caminero de Castilla?"

"Yes. Are you the one who's been looking for me?"

Caminero de Castilla was a slight, short man with a paunch. He had a head full of gray hair, a long straight nose and a wrinkled forehead. His bright brown eyes looked Dorado over as the lieutenant stood on the path.

"Sí, señor. I'm Lieutenant Roberto Dorado Delgado. Major Esteban Morales Muñoz y Barrientos sent a man here earlier to request a meeting with me."

"I see. You can come over here, Lieutenant. César won't bother you."

As Dorado approached, the dog trotted over to his master and sat down beside his legs. César continued to growl, showing the stranger his teeth. The dog never took his eyes from Dorado as he walked slowly toward them.

The captain leaned over and scratched the dog's ears. "It's all right, César, good boy." He straightened and again looked Dorado over.

"I was hunting. If that's what you'd call it. We got damned little to show for ten days in the woods. Only a few bony birds. I got more gnat bites than anything else." Caminero de Castilla spoke in short brisk sentences, the words seeming to burst out of his mouth like hail in a storm. "Sixteen birds in seven days! It took three men to do it. Some hunters, eh?"

"Yes, sir. Please pardon me for coming unannounced to see you."

"No importa." The captain waved off the apology with the sweep of his hand. "I don't bother with formality, Lieutenant. That's for the pompous Peninsulares. (The Spaniards born in Spain who governed all the colonial born Spaniards in America)."

"Yes, sir. I hope you have time to talk to me, sir."

"I've got too much time. It's been that way since I left the crown's service. All I do these days is take care of this little place. Only forty acres – a bit more than a caballería." He pointed to the pastures beyond the house. "You can see all my land in the blink of an eye. My campesinos do most everything here, anyway. So, I've got more time than good sense." He chuckled at his own joke.

"Yes, sir." Dorado stood holding the reins of his horse.

Caminero de Castilla nodded. "Well, Lieutenant, what do you want to talk about?"

"Sir, it concerns the murder of María Palés Molina in 1777."

"Ah! So, that's it. Let's go inside. Cecilia is making breakfast. I went to town early and missed it." He led Dorado into the house. "We have much to talk about, Lieutenant."

After Caminero de Castilla introduced Dorado to his wife, he went outside to arrange pasturing for the lieutenant's horse. Returning a few minutes later, he sat with his guest at the kitchen table. They drank hot tea as Cecilia made breakfast.

"We were about to eat when you rode here. Not that I need it, as you certainly can see. The melon that sticks out from my stomach arrived after my retirement. It came without my permission. All my life, I ate what I wanted when I wanted without adding a pound. Now, no matter what I eat or don't eat, the damned thing sits there defying me to remove it. I don't even eat that much, do I, Cecilia?" He looked at his wife who only turned to him and smiled.

They ate fried pork strips, brown-sugared blackberries and baked bread with honey for breakfast. After wiping his plate clean with the last piece of bread, the captain took four more pork strips and a second helping of blackberries from the serving dish on the table. He smiled and winked at Dorado. "I need something to eat with my tea."

During their breakfast, the captain complained about the agrarian changes taking place in Cuba. Cecilia, many years younger than her husband, sat with them at the small table. She listened as he condemned Spain's policies in the old colony, but said nothing. For most of the time, she stared down at her hands which lay folded in front of her on the table.

"Too many incompetent officials are sent here from Spain." He raised his voice. "Not one of them knows any-thing about this colony. When will the stupid fools in Ma-drid realize they need us Criollos (creoles) who are born and live here to administer this island? That's who should be in charge here, but, of course, they wouldn't think of doing that. No, oh no! They worry that we might limit the vast wealth they take home from Havana. So, instead, they send us those pathetic Peninsulars; those tontos (fools) know no more than the king's officials who send them here. That's why there are so many problems in the empire. It's the same all over America."

Dorado listened politely. He did not dispute the cap-tain's complaints. In his opinion, the Peninsulars brought Spanish experience to America. Without Spain's help, he believed the Spanish colonies would be no better than the rabble-ruled British provinces.

"Look what's happening here." The old man pointed

toward one of the two windows in the kitchen. The cattle country is slowly, but surely coming under tobacco production. And the stupid Peninsulars let it happen. They don't care. In time, they'll go home to Spain with their pockets full of our pesetas! Damn them!" He slapped the top of the table.

"Isn't it time to show the lieutenant the finca, Pepe?" Cecilia patted her husband's spotted hand and smiled shyly at Dorado.

The captain nodded and got up. "We'll talk afterwards."

After taking turns in the outhouse, Caminero de Castilla led the lieutenant on a tour of the finca. Dorado praised the many improvements the captain had made to his ranch, including the spring-fed fishing pond, new hog pen and flowering citrus grove. César accompanied them, trotting between his master and Dorado. Afterwards, they sat in the patio behind the house, out of the sun under the limb of a red flowering Poinciana (flame tree). They drank cool lemonade brought to them by an old black woman, the wife of one of the campesinos.

"So, the fiend's in St. Augustine." The elderly man sighed when Dorado finished his account of the murder. "I feared he might still be in Cuba somewhere. I hoped he had died."

"Then, you think the same man murdered the governor's niece?"

"There's no doubt about it. The fiend always leaves his mark wherever he goes. He's like some animal peeing near his prey."

"What mark is that?" Dorado had mentioned Gloria's mutilation, but not the cut of the cross on her corpse.

"His mark is a cross. He cuts it on his victims like this." The captain made the sign of the cross, pausing at each position to plunge an imaginary knife downward. "I assume that's how the Governor's niece was mutilated."

Dorado winced as a shiver slid down his spine. "Yes,

that's what he did to her." Watching the elderly man make the cross reminded him of Martínez demonstrating the same sequence of stabbing. With the big man in mind, he almost missed the captain's next words.

"There was another, earlier, murder by the same man. He left his mark then, too."

"Another murder? Like the three others?" Dorado saw Caminero de Castilla nod his head. "When, for God's sake?"

"In 1763." He continued to nod. "I heard about it from an old soldier, now long dead."

"Is the information in the Building of Records?" Dorado pointed north.

"Yes, but it didn't happen in Havana." The captain sipped his lemonade. "It happened in St. Augustine."

"In St. Augustine!" Dorado's mouth dropped open. "In 1763?"

"Yes. It happened there as all the people were leaving the colony after the war. When they moved to Havana."

"Are you certain of it?" In his excitement, Dorado hit the glass of lemonade with his hand and almost knocked it over.

"Yes, absolutely. That old soldier told me about it. It was because of what he said that I discovered the murder of 1770. I wouldn't have learned of it otherwise."

"What did he tell you, sir?" Inpatient to hear about the murder, Dorado had to squelch his intention to hurry the elderly man as he tried to recall the soldier's account.

"Let me think." The captain scratched his ear. "Ah, yes, I remember. He was one of the soldiers who found the girl's corpse. She was missing several days so her body had been mauled by animals. I recall a hand and a foot were gnawed away. Still, the knife wounds were there to be seen. The fiend left his mark even then."

"Sir, where did they find the girl's body?"

"Somewhere outside the city." He scratched his ear again. "I'm not sure exactly where it was. Maybe, in a pine woods?" He frowned trying to remember.

"In a pine woods! Dios mío! The governor's niece was found in the woods, too. I now wonder if they were murdered in the same place."

"I told you the fiend leaves his mark – apparently, more than one. In St. Augustine, he kills them in the woods; in Havana, he kills them in a pasture. Did you know that, Lieutenant?"

"Yes, sir. I read the autopsy report on Carlota Ramírez Cruz."

"What about my report on María Palés Molina in 1777?"

"I haven't read it as yet. It's not in the presidio physician's files and I haven't been able to enter the Building of Records to look for a copy." Dorado told him about his troubles trying to get the governor's authorization.

"You see, that's what I was talking about – incompetent Peninsulars like Ballesteros Bazón. I know that officious fool! He has a head as hard as a paving stone. The whole lot of peninsular tontos should be packed aboard a ship like olives in a barrel and sent back to Spain, once and for all. Damn them! Why must we be plagued with them?" The elderly man's eyes blazed and spittle sprayed from his lips.

Dorado waited to speak until the old man had calmed himself with a drink of lemonade.

"I don't suppose you have a copy of that report, sir?"

"No, I left everything in Havana. I was tired of it all – the endless paper work, the lazy incompetent Peninsulars, the lack of appreciation, the insulting salary they paid me – all of it!"

Caminero de Castilla abruptly stopped speaking and smiled broadly, showing gaps in his upper and lower teeth. Dorado studied the elderly man, wondering what suddenly had amused him. It was the first time he had seen him smile.

"I'll tell you something, Lieutenant." He paused to stare at Dorado before continuing. "Ordinarily, I wouldn't admit this to anyone." He snorted. "Especially some Spaniard with an annoying Castillian accent. Of course, I know you're one of those damned Peninsulars. I knew it when the first polite words came out of your mouth. I may be old, but I'm not stupid."

Dorado smiled. "I think you will find, sir, that I'm neither incompetent nor lazy."

"I know that. Esteban wouldn't have sent you to me if you were either. And, if I had any doubts, I wouldn't have wasted my time talking to you. I would have sent you packing."

"Sí, señor."

"But I know men and can always tell those who are worth their salt. That's why I'm talking to you and that's why I'll tell you what's on my mind. You know, I've always hoped someone would come by and ask me for help. You see, I'm bored here in this quiet campo (countryside). Cecilia thinks I'm content as a clam, but I'm bored." He turned and looked around to see if she might be anywhere nearby.

Dorado nodded.

"The truth is I miss my work in Havana. The uncertain investigations, the satisfaction of capturing a clever killer – most of all, the search itself. I even miss the many failures over the years. I miss it all. Even with the incessant stupidity of the Peninsulars sent from Madrid. Well, never mind all that. I'm glad you're here and need my help. Even as young as you are, you should understand."

"Yes, sir. I do understand. My uncle, Uncle Ernesto, left the king's service to take care of my family. It happened when my father died. He said many of the same things to my brothers and me."

"Then, you understand. Let's continue. I hope what I know will help. That fiend needs to be stopped once and for all."

"I hope so too, sir. Maybe, now, it will be possible." Dorado smiled warmly. "With your permission, sir, I would like to return to the old soldier's account."

"I do ramble on and on, don't I?" He sighed. "I know it's a sign of age and yet one of the few privileges left an old man."

"You're not that old, sir, and your mind is good."

"Don't flatter me, Lieutenant, even though I do like to hear it." He chuckled loudly and Dorado laughed with him.

"You should hear what Doctor Morales Muñoz y Barrientos says about you."

"Oh, what does Esteban say?" The old man's eyes sparkled.

"He said, 'Caminero de Castilla is still alive and, of course, complaining about everyone and everything. He says what's on his mind; he's in his seventies, but still makes good sense.'"

The captain smiled broadly. "Well, you can tell him he's absolutely right. Incidentally, I'm seventy-five and I intend to live to a hundred. And I'll keep complaining to the very end of my life – you can be sure of that! Those who keep quiet are the ones who die young."

"I'll tell him, I promise, sir. Please tell me about the murder of 1763."

He nodded. "When I was investigating the murder of María Palés Molina, in 1777, the news of the girl's mutilation was all over Havana. You know how hard it is to keep a secret in a Spanish city. The grisly details were well known and discussed in every damned tavern."

"It's the same in St. Augustine, sir. Though for now only a few of us know about the cross cut on the girl's corpse."

"Bueno, let's hope it stays that way. The old soldier – I can't think of the man's name to save my life – came to see me. He was a shy fellow and apologized about coming to speak to me. But it was his memory of the girl's corpse –

I don't remember her name either, made him come. The look of her mutilated body was locked in his memory and, from what he had heard about the murder of the Molina girl, he thought there might be some similarities. Among other similarities, the girls were both seventeeen."

"Seventeen! So was Carlota Ramírez Cruz and Gloria Márquez Garcia, the governor's niece." Dorado stared at the captain and saw him nod his head knowingly.

"I'm not surprised. Anyway, the soldier knew the girl by sight in St. Augustine. So, he instantly recognized her when he saw her lying dead on the ground. Her face apparently was untouched, though her body had been mauled. The corpse was found in some woods north of the presidio. I do remember that, now."

"That's where the governor's niece was found as well."

"He said the sight of her maimed corpse made them all vomit. At first, it was thought she had been killed by English Protestants from Savannah, but then the method of mutilation made them realize that someone Catholic in town must have been the murderer."

"Who determined that, sir?"

"I don't know – I don't think the soldier knew."

"What else did the old soldier tell you?"

"He knew little else except the murderer was never arrested. There was not much chance for a thorough investigation then. The king's officials were too busy shipping our people off to Havana. Some were sent to Vera Cruz as well."

"Do you know what happened to the soldier, sir? Where he was sent afterwards?"

"He left St. Augustine with the army and came to Havana. They eventually gave him a small pension and he spent the rest of his life in Havana. He had a tobacco stall in the main plaza. The man was well along in his sixties when I met him and he died a year or so later."

"But he remembered seeing the stab wounds? All of them?"

"Yes, he did! He couldn't forget them. And that's why I looked through all the other files in the office of the presidio physician. Fifteen years of them."

"Fifteen years of files! You looked through all of them?" Dorado stared at the captain and shook his head in amazement.

"Every file from 1763 to 1778! From the time of the first murder to the year following the murder of María Palés Molina. It took me three months! I went through the files every day after the office closed and I returned on Saturday afternoon as well. I would have worked on Sunday, too, but Cecilia wouldn't allow it. I had to do it! It was essential once I knew there was a similar murder in 1763. I did it because I believed the old soldier and my belief in him was well worth it. One month after I began reading the files – it was on a Monday afternoon, I will never forget it – I found the murder case of 1770. I found it on October 16, 1780; the day is still embedded in my memory. A storm struck Havana that morning and it rained all day."

"What an effort! I admire you for what you did. I looked through only three years of files and it exhausted me."

"That's not all. I never forgot the killing of that little girl – María Palés Molina. It was stuck in my mind and wouldn't leave me in peace. So, three months before I left office, I went back and looked through all the files from 1778 to 1785. Every damned one of them! I had to know if there were any more of the fiend's murders before I left the king's service. It took me six, no, it was seven weeks."

"Did you find anything else sir?"

"No. There were no more murders with his mark. I thought the fiend might be dead, but, no, he lives and now is in St. Augustine. He probably sailed to Florida after the colony was returned to the king in 1783."

"That makes sense." Dorado nodded his head up and down.

"Something else occurs to me, now." He patted César's head.

"What's that, sir?"

"We know much more about the fiend now than ever before. We know he was living in St. Augustine in 1763 and went to Havana during the foreign occupation. He then returned to Florida sometime after 1783. That means the murderer must be an old Floridian or someone in the king's service. He could be a royal official, a soldier or even a priest."

"A priest?"

"Yes, of course. Don't think they're all innocents. They're men like you and I, and sin, like the rest of us – even if they wear a cowl or cassock. Only God above knows what goes on behind the closed doors of churches and monasteries." The elderly man raised his eyes as if to heaven. "Surely, you've heard what the monks do among themselves in the monasteries?"

"Their intimacy is one thing, sir, but murder is another."

"True. But, believe me, they're murderers, too. I recall a priest and two monks who were found to be murderers while I was in the crown's service. The monks killed one of their brothers for some trivial reason I don't recall. But I do remember the priest's murder. He poisoned an older priest to get his parish."

Dorado raised his eyebrows. "Dios mío! How did you discover he was the murderer?"

"He told us on his death bed while receiving his last rites. The old priest was known to take a drink or two of the communion wine every evening and the younger priest poisoned the wine after supper one day. No one suspected murder and, as expected, the younger priest was given the parish by the bishop. Then, a few days later, the damned fool forgot he had poisoned the wine and took a drink of it before morning Mass. He was a Peninsular, of course."

Dorado shook his head. "The priest got what he deserved. Sir, you were describing the murderer. What else do we know about him?"

"He's a Catholic. The cut of the cross tells us that."

Dorado nodded. "I didn't want to believe that at first, but I met a priest aboard ship and he said the murderer was probably a Catholic fanatic. He said there have been all too many in the history of the Church."

"All the more reason to think the murderer might be a monk or priest."

"It would have to be one who was in St. Augustine in 1763 as well as 1788. Of course, that also would be true for an official, soldier or old Floridian."

"Yes, which means the fiend must be in his fifties, at least. He couldn't be any younger to have killed the four girls over so long a span of time. There are twenty-five years between the first murder, in 1763, and the last one – this year." He sat back and smiled. "Maybe I still have my mind, at that."

"I'm certain of it, señor. We may know one more of his killings." Dorado told him about the disappearance of Patricia Hernández Parral.

"I doubt she was one of his victims. Would he murder a girl without leaving his mark to be seen on her body? With what we know about him, is that likely?"

"That's a good question. Yet, something tells me the girl was one of his victims. I ..."

Dorado was interrupted by Cecilia's arrival with a pitcher of juice. She blushed when he smiled and thanked her.

"It's made from lemons and fresh mint and only a little rum," she told him. "We call it a 'Mojito Criollo.' It's Pepe's favorite drink." She filled the glasses and walked quickly away.

"Sir, didn't you say the case file for the murder of 1763

is in the Building of Records?" Dorado licked his lips after his first sip of the Mojito Criollo. "Delicioso."

"It is delicious. Yes, it's there, Lieutenant. But, when I was investigating the murder of María Palés Molina, the file couldn't be found." The captain frowned. "In fact, all the Florida files from the early sixties were lost – for five years! Can you imagine that?"

"Lost for five years! Where were they, sir?"

"They were in the Building of Records all that time. Some damned fool put them in the wrong section. It wasn't until years later, in 1782, that they turned up. In that labyrinth, it's a wonder they were ever found. To make matters worse, I didn't learn the files had been found for more than fifteen months. Fifteen months! Even though I left explicit instructions for them to notify me immediately when they were found. First the fools lose the files for five years and then they neglect to notify me. I tell you, the empire is doomed by such incompetence!"

"What happened then?"

"I was finally notified the files were found in August of 1784. It was on a Wednesday, August 14. I heard about it in the morning and read the murder file that afternoon." Caminero Castilla frowned. "No authorization was needed then to enter the Building of Records. Would you like some more Mojito Criollo?"

"Yes, thank you, sir." Dorado had been idly turning the empty glass in his fingers. He found himself becoming impatient with the elderly man's seemingly endless stories. "I assume the file included what you expected."

"It substantiated everything that old soldier told me years earlier. I knew my faith in him was not misplaced."

"Similar wounds were on the corpse?" Dorado asked the expected question.

He nodded. "All four knife wounds were noted in the autopsy. They were like those of the other murders. It was a very brief report. No more than a few pages as I recall. Probably because everyone was busy packing up to leave the colony."

"I must see it when I get into the Building of Records."

"Yes, Lieutenant! Read it very carefully. It may include valuable information that I no longer recall. Among other things, it should show the name of the investigating officer, who might still be alive and available for an interview. He might even live in Havana somewhere." Caminero de Castilla picked up the pitcher and filled both glasses.

"That's true. With the help of the presidio physician I should get authorization in a day or so. As soon as the governor gets better and returns."

"What the governor needs is some fresh country air. It's living in that dirty city and all that paperwork that makes men ill. I haven't been sick a day since I left Havana."

"Sir, please tell me about the murder of María Palés Molina."

"I'll tell you everything I remember. After all, who knows if or when you'll be allowed to enter the Building of Records to read my report."

"Yes, sir. That was my thinking, too." Dorado sipped his drink.

"I recall that murder as if it were yesterday." Seeing Cecilia approaching them with a tray of food, Caminero de Castilla said, "Let's have lunch and then I'll tell you all about it."

Cecilia served them roast pork, fried plantains and yellow rice. She sat and ate with them in the cool patio. Cecilia ate without speaking until Dorado asked about their children. Then, she seemed to awaken as if from a long sleep and talked throughout lunch about her four sons and their families. Her husband smiled with undisguised pride as she spoke of their many accomplishments and the eight beautiful grandchildren they had brought into the world.

After lunch and an hour siesta inside the house, they returned to the patio. The sun was now overhead and they moved their chairs into the shade of a leafy tree limb. César lay at his master's feet.

"A daily siesta always refreshes me. I need no more than an hour. The old don't sleep as well as the young, so I nap after lunch. I've heard it's so the old can have more time to live before they die." He snickered. "I'm sure that's the thinking of some old fart."

Dorado laughed with him.

"Well, let's continue. I want to tell you everything I know."

It was three in the afternoon, when Caminero Castilla finished his detailed account of the murder. He wiped his mouth on his shirt sleeve. "I haven't talked this much in a long time, but it was good to get it all off my mind."

"Thank you, sir. You've given me everything I need. Even if I don't get to read your report, I know the murders were committed by the same man. As you say, there's no doubt about it. There are so many similarities."

"He left his mark on all of the victims, didn't he? It's as if the fiend was following the instructions in an officer's manual. He went about the four murders, step by step, in the same manner: first, the strangulations, then, the stabbings, the cross cut on the corpses, the removal of clothing – all the same. That fiend knows exactly what he's doing."

"That's what Doctor Martínez said when he did the autopsy."

"I've seen many murders in thirty years of service, but none so well planned. Most of them come from anger over something the victims did or didn't do. But, not the murders of these girls! The man may have killed them in a rage, but he mutilated them out of his mind."

"Sir, do you think there might be someone still alive in Havana who would know about the murders? Should I look for any of the family, friends or neighbors of the murdered girls?"

"Don't waste your time." The elderly man shook his head. "Most must be long dead or moved elsewhere by now. It's been more than a decade ago and, even if you found them, what would they remember now? What would they tell you that they didn't tell me?" Red-faced, he raised his voice. "I talked to all of them, believe me! I missed no one and nothing got by me. It's all there in my case report – fifty pages long! Read it!"

"I'm certain it's complete, sir."

"It certainly is complete! Everything is included, believe me. But, young man, if you think you can do better, do it!" The captain's face remained flushed.

"No, sir, I'm certain I can't do better." Dorado was surprised by the man's sudden show of temper. "No one would do better. No one else would look through fifteen years of files."

"You can be sure of that. I left no stone unturned. None!"

"What you say, sir, makes good sense. It would be a waste of time to talk to anyone about the past. I'm sure your report will give me everything I need to know."

"Everything you need is there. It's thorough! Not like the work of the lazy lout who they sent to investigate the murder of 1770. What was the man's name? Ah, yes, Salinas de Mendoza. The fiend might have been stopped then, if he had done his job properly. But the man did nothing! So, the murderer has lived to kill again and again."

"What ever happened to him? Do you know, sir?" inquired Dorado, anxious to change the subject and the mood of the elderly man.

"He was promoted for his work in Havana. Can you believe it? He was later sent to Santo Domingo. The last I heard of him, he was a major in San Juan."

"A major?" Dorado sat up in his seat.

"He's probably a colonel by now and surely as lazy and incompetent as ever. Salinas de Mendoza must know some-one in the king's court."

"Promoted two ranks in ten years! That's hard to believe, even with influence at court."

"Why? He's a Peninsular from a rich family in Córdoba. It happens all the time. The Peninsulars are always promot-ed in the king's service. But it's never easy for us, not for those Spaniards born in the colonies." He gritted his teeth. "No, after a lifetime in the army – thirty years! – I was pro-moted only once! They made me captain five years before I left the service."

Dorado said nothing. He knew many Spanish officers from Spain who found no better fortune in the king's service. But, in his host's home, it would have been im-polite to argue.

"One day, the damn fools in Spain will regret what they have done here in America. You'll see, Lieutenant, after I'm dead and buried, this empire will fall because of Ma-drid's stupid policies and the incompetent officials they send to the colonies. It's already showing deterioration and weakness. Everyone sees it – except the opportunistic Peninsulars."

"Pardon me, sir. I must go to the outhouse."

"So must I." The captain stood. "Afterwards, let's try our luck in the fish pond. I saw a couple of large bass last week."

At the urging of the captain, Dorado stayed for the night. He had hoped to leave in the afternoon, but remained as the old investigator requested. Dorado felt obliged to stay after all the help the man had given him. They ate a meal of black bean soup and bread and then went outside to the patio to watch the sunset. A lingering line of clouds in the west colored the sky in subtle shades of pink and purple. The men sat and sipped an aged brandy the captain served on special occasions. They stayed outside to see the moon rise and stars appear, but when the darkness brought the biting gnats and mosquitoes, they went inside and talked until bedtime.

Dorado left early the next morning, following abrazos (hugs) and his sworn promise to write Caminero de Castilla about the results of the investigation. His hosts walked with him down the path to the gate and watched him mount his horse. César stood there with them as always their vigilant guard dog. A few moments later, Dorado was riding north to Havana.

Nothing had changed during his trip to Santiago de las Vegas. The governor was still sick at home. Without even asking Esteban, he knew there was no entry authorization for the Building of Records. Dorado also learned that Miguel was still away on regimental maneuvers in the field. The sergeant in the commandant's office told him the regiment was on the march east of Havana. "It's to assure our readiness in the event of an enemy attack, even though we're not at war. It's an order from the governor's office," grumbled the bald sergeant.

Nothing changed during the week and Dorado waited with growing impatience. The governor remained sick at home and his brother's regiment was still in the field. He took daily trips to El Morro, only to return each time dispirited.

While waiting with little to do, Dorado spent much of his time talking to Beatriz' father about the murders. They met in the morning, before Dorado rode into town and, at night, after everyone else went to sleep. Talking with the sedentary man helped him pass the time. Still, he found himself with many unoccupied hours, especially in the afternoons.

At those times, he would think of Serena Rodríguez. Dorado recalled his conversations with her, his long walks in the plaza and their endless kisses in the house of Esperanza Chavez. Thinking about Serena made him feel warm all over. Dorado first noticed it aboard ship when the feeling came over him one cold day on deck. The feeling reminded him of the spreading warmth of the sun as it suddenly emerged from the shadow of a dark cloud. With her warmth about him like a cloak, he would recall Serena's gentle hand upon his cheek and the way she turned and tilted her head to look at him out of the sides of her eyes.

During the day, Dorado often thought about her as he went about his everyday errands in town. It would happen unexpectedly, when he saw something unusual or wanted to tell her an amusing story. A bed of beautiful red roses he saw on the Calle Obispo or the family's lazy house dog, who always looked to be laughing, were sights he wished to point out to her.

His frequent thoughts of Serena made him feel guilty about his unforgettable night with María Luisa. But, despite his guilt, Dorado knew he would welcome the Spanish woman in his bed again and, at night in the darkness, he would lie on his back and recall their time together. His mind would flood with vivid memories of María Luisa kissing, licking and rhythmically moving against him. He would hear her whispered words of urging and see her poised above him, her brown-nippled breasts over his face. In the end, Dorado would use his hand and then sleep until morning when the boys would sneak into his room and tickle him awake.

At the end of the week, on Saturday, Esteban told him the governor was feeling better. He had risen from bed and, although still weak, he seemed to be recovering. His fever was finally gone and visitors to his house said he was eating normally. His aides expected him to return to his office one day the following week.

There was also a report that Miguel's regiment was finally heading back to Havana. On Monday morning, a messenger from the field informed the commandant that the regiment was no more than a ten-day march from the city. Dorado's spirits lifted as he looked forward to the coming weeks in the company of his brother. After the long wait, he hoped they would be able to spend Christmas together.

His mood changed again with the arrival of two letters from St. Augustine. They were delivered to the presidio physician's office on Thursday afternoon and Esteban brought them home that night. One was a short letter from Serena Rodríguez, the other, a hurriedly scrawled message from Carlos Martínez.

Dorado read Serena's letter first and was surprised it was so brief, no more than forty widely spaced lines and barely two pages long. He had written her four letters and every one of them had been lengthy and informative. It annoyed him that she wrote so little in return.

He did not know Serena had written him three lengthy letters as well, but only one was en route to Havana. She burned the first two in her cousin's fireplace. After half a day spent on the letters and writing many lines of her love for him, Serena angrily threw them in the fire. She thought the letters yielded too much of herself to him and feared he did not love her.

The first letter she received from Dorado, after two weeks, only worsened her fears. It said too little about his feelings for her. She read his letter several times and concluded the "Te Quiero" at the end was an afterthought. The lack of feelings she found in his letter convinced her that Dorado would eventually spurn her for a wealthy noblewoman in Havana. With such convictions in mind, she vowed not to give any more of herself to him, even in letters.

Her fears were exacerbated by his absence and her knowledge of the many unmarried noblewomen in Havana. She worried Dorado would meet one of them in the grand mansion of Esteban Morales Muñoz. In her imagination, she envisioned nightly fiestas in the house, where richly dressed women came to meet the handsome young officer from Spain. Serena could see them smiling seductively, while Dorado willingly kissed their outstretched hands.

Whatever her doubts about him, the mood that enveloped her in the house of Esperanza Chávez made them worse. Almost everyday, something was said by one of her cousins about the perfidy of men and the misery they brought women. They were too selfish to be trusted.

"What selfish beasts they are," Esperanza Chávez often would say with a snort. "All they want is your body in bed. When they're finished, it's food and service they want."

"That's what they want," María Valdez would add on one of her afternoon visits to her sister's house. "They think every woman is there for their pleasure. Then, they come and go as they please, without a word of explanation. You're to be overjoyed whenever they appear, whether day or night. And, if you should dare say something about it, then you pay for it."

Disturbed by her doubts of Dorado's love, the letter Serena wrote to him was brusquely factual. She wrote a warmer second letter after receiving two others from him which spoke of his love and need for her. Dorado's third letter telling Serena how lonely he was without her changed her mood for days and she went around with a smile on her lips.

In the letter Dorado did receive from Serena, she said the

plague was still in the city. She told him the elderly woman who lived next to Esperanza Chávez had died of it. Señora Sánchez, the widow whose rooms he rented, also had been very sick, but now seemed better. "No children have died yet, Gracias a Dios!" she wrote, "though all too many of the little ones have high fevers and suffer from a wracking cough." Serena said she and her cousins so far had escaped the sickness.

At the end of her letter, she told him about Ruiz de León's condition. "He has been sick for more than a month now and everyone is worried about him. They say he is quite frail. The doctor says he was recovering until very recently, when he had a serious setback."

Dorado was surprised to read the bad news about Ruiz de León. He had hoped to hear of his recovery in the doctor's note. The young man paused in thought before reading the rest of her letter. In the last paragraph, Serena told him María Valdez had left Martínez. She said it followed a loud quarrel one late night that awoke the neighbors. Dorado was startled by the words Serena used to tell him about it.

"The brute almost killed her. He choked her in a drunken rage. It was over something María said about his incessant drinking. María has his finger marks on her neck to this day."

Dorado felt his stomach tighten as he reread Serena's words. Frowning, he placed her letter on his bed and opened the one from Martínez. The doctor did not mention María Valdez in the two scrawled pages he penned to Dorado. His letter only concerned the sickness of Ruiz de León and the murder investigation.

Lieutenant,

I'm replying to your report because Ricardo is too ill to do it. I am very worried about him, but not without hope. He was getting better for a time, but then took a turn for the worse. He has high fever and his breathing is labored. He has lost much weight and is too weak to get out of bed. I must tell you I fear for his life.

Sad to say, his promotion papers arrived from Havana the very same day his fever rose and the sickness took hold of him. What a cruel irony! It's been more than nine months since they were submitted to Havana. We can only hope he lives to wear his Major's insignia.

He talks of you often. I think it might help him now if you return, but you must make that decision. I am enclosing a letter of transit signed by the governor if you should decide to return to St. Augustine.

Your report was thorough. There are clearly many similarities between the murders of 1770 and 1788. Your list of them is impressive. I will be anxious to hear what the file of 1777 reveals. I concur with Esteban's conclusions about the murderer. I also think he has murdered before, maybe many times. If the murder of 1777 shows the same characteristics as those of 1770 and 1788, we will know the man has killed at least three times.

It now appears the Morones girl was not murdered. Her sister, Sara, told us that María Rosa went to the island with that Englishman, Matthew Harmon. It was the day of the strong winds and their canoe must have overturned amid those alligators. A shipmate of the young Englishman said the pipe you found was Harmon's, so we must assume the alligators got him, too. The reports of him being seen after the girl was mutilated were found to be no more than rumor. I think it was Harmon's leg that Fish's dogs dragged to his house.

Zéspedes is in a foul humor. Without Ricardo in the office, he seems lost and Suárez says he is irritable and quick to anger. Whenever the governor sees me, he complains about the time spent on what he calls, "the continuing unsolved murder investigation." I try to avoid him and stay *away from Government House.*

The plague is finally showing signs of ending. Fifteen already have died from it and a few older people are in serious trouble. That old bastard, Jesse Fish, is sick, too, gracias a Dios. I hear the plague has spread to Santo Domingo and Havana and both governors are ill with it. I better not get it, but I'm not really worried. As long as I scrape the bowl as always, drink a half bottle of medicinal wine at night and keep my member moving, I should be fine.

Carlos Martínez

Dorado remained nine more days in Havana. Unable to find a ship sailing to Florida, he arranged passage aboard a Portuguese schooner, the *Santa Catarina*, headed for Savannah. With a payment of fifty pesetas, Dorado persuaded the ship's captain to stop at St. Augustine, only long enough to drop him off at the city pier. He left Cuba on December 20. A message, notifying Carlos Martínez of his return voyage, was sent on a Spanish warship a week earlier.

Dorado still hoped to see his brother before leaving Havana. He also hoped to read the murder file of 1777, if permitted to enter the Building of Records in time. Neither of his hopes was realized. Governor Ezpeleta suffered a relapse and remained home in bed and Miguel did not reach Havana until Dorado was already out at sea.

While waiting, Dorado played with the children, took daily walks in and about Havana and spent his evenings talking to Beatriz' father and Esteban when he came home at night. He also wrote his final report. The twenty-two page paper described everything he had discovered in Havana. On the last page, Dorado summarized what was known about the murderer and the apparent step by step pattern he followed in the four murders. An additional page later penned aboard ship included his host's observations about the murderer. The physician spoke to him at length on the evening before he sailed.

They sat in the library which was filled with leather-bound books. The books stood side by side on four shelves that extended around the room on all the walls. With the exception of the shelves beside the door to the hallway, which held rolled maps and stacked documents, the others held an assortment of books written by well-known authors. The library contained an extensive collection of historical chronicles and theological works, including Thomas Aquinas' *Summa Theologica* and Ignatius Loyola's *Exercitia Spiritualia*. In addition, there were a number of mathematics and philosophy volumes written in the seventeenth century. Greek and Roman classics were also included in the library as well as the writings of the famous Spanish authors of the past. Collections of Pedro Calderón de la Barca, Cervantes, Lope de Vega and Luis de Góngora stood on shelves beside the one window in the room.

The library included few works of the eighteenth century, with the exception of medical texts. Dorado made that discovery on an idle day when he went there in search of something to read. It was as if nothing of worth had been written in the Age of the Enlightenment. Esteban told him most of the books in the library had belonged to his father, who had hated everything written in the eighteenth century.

"My father detested the changes he saw during his lifetime," Esteban told Dorado. "He was a very religious man who viewed this century as the time of man's fall from God's grace. He said the eighteenth century was 'empty of the soul of man and, as a consequence, would be empty of the love of God.'"

They sat in the library's pillowed chairs and talked late into the night. Beatriz' father, Ignacio Soto Ignesias, was with them. Servants carried the infirm man upstairs to the library, where he sat smoking his pipe. When asked to join them, he had smiled, pleased to be invited. They sipped cognac from crystal glasses. The bottle was placed on a table, within easy reach of the crippled man.

"The murderer is not a madman!" said Esteban, after listening to Dorado's comparison of the four murders. "Definitely not!"

"Not a madman?" Ignacio Soto Ignesias stared in disbelief at Esteban.

"Yes! The murderer knows exactly what he's doing and follows a plan. He leaves his mark, as Caminero de Castilla called it, on all his victims. He shrewdly arranges secret trysts with them in remote places. He takes off their clothing and leaves them naked. He slips away after the mutilations without ever being seen. All those acts are very well planned and suggest the use of a fine functioning mind. No, he is not a madman." Esteban shook his head.

"You're saying he's sane because of his use of reason in everything he does?" Dorado studied the doctor who reminded him, at that moment, of Carlos Martínez.

"Yes. The repetition of the method of murder and mutilation on all the victims shows us that. He's methodical. Cleverly methodical."

"So, all the girls were killed according to his diabolical design." Soto Iglesias looked up from packing his pipe with tobacco.

"It looks that way to me." Esteban nodded. "He makes sure they meet in places where there is little if any chance of being seen – a secluded spot where he carries out his killings. The girls come to him willingly. Though they don't know it, they are doomed when they come."

"How does he convince them to meet him alone, telling no one where they are going?" Dorado shook his head. "It amazes me they willing to go to such remote places to meet him."

"He must have a way with women." Beatriz' father pointed his pipe at Dorado. "Of course, we must wonder why such young girls would want to meet him – a much older man. We know he's years older than the girls who meet him. I don't understand it. He must be the Pied Piper of young girls."

"Perhaps." The doctor frowned, his bushy eyebrows almost meeting. "Whatever way he entices them to meet him, they unfortunately go – like lambs to the slaughter."

Dorado leaned forward in his chair. "What you say about his mind makes sense, señor, but what about his awful acts of mutilation? What are those acts, but the work of a madman? Who else would commit such murders and mutilations? Who else would kill innocent girls?"

"That's the critical question, isn't it?" Esteban nodded. "If not a madman, why would he commit such cruel killings?"

"Perhaps, the man's madness comes and goes." Soto Iglesias lit his pipe with the table candle. "It might be only temporary like the madness that overwhelms all too many men when they drink too much. It could also be quite occasional like the madness that comes from fury. We know what rage can make men do."

"Yes, but I don't think an enraged man could carry out such methodical mutilations." Esteban looked at Dorado. "I agree with what Caminero de Castilla said about the murderer. I believe his words were, 'the man may have killed her in a rage, but he mutilated her out of his mind.' There is simply too much mind evident in the murders to be the acts of a madman. It seems there's even a schedule to his killings."

"What do you mean, sir?" Dorado studied the doctor.

"Except for the murder of the governor's niece, in 1788, the other three girls were killed in a sequence separated by seven years – in 1763, 1770 and 1777. Isn't that right?"

Dorado nodded. "It is and I know of another possible murder in 1784, that fits such a schedule." He told them about the strange disappearance of Patricia Hernández Parral. "She could well be his fourth victim, unless there are others not yet known to us."

"Without her corpse to examine, we can't be sure she was murdered."

"That's certainly true." Dorado frowned, looking at Esteban. "Well, then, what can we then say about the murderer if he's not mad?"

"The French call such murderers, *piquers*. The term comes from the word pique which means to prick or strike with a pointed instrument. I found a volume entitled *Legal Medicine and Public Health* here in the library that discussed the subject in some detail."

"There are other murderers like him?" Dorado raised an eyebrow.

"Yes. I was surprised to read about a number of cases of what the French physicians call piquerism. In 1767, Doctor Chaussier, a physician at the prison in Dijon, described their cruel acts in detail. None mentioned a cross cut on victims, but there were other similarities."

"What similarities?" asked Soto Iglesias.

"One similarity we discussed only a few minutes ago. According to Doctor Chaussier, the piquer typically kills his victims in secluded places where interference is unlikely."

"That certainly fits this murderer, sir." Dorado finished the last of his brandy.

"It fits him perfectly! There're other similarities. A piquer kills and mutilates without compassion. It starts with the killing itself and continues with his cutting and slashing, even after death. One other important similarity –

women are invariably their victims."

"Only girls?" Soto Iglesias stared at his son-in-law.

"No. Piquers have been known to murder old women as well."

"Are there other similarities, sir?" asked Dorado.

"Yes. The piquers methodically mutilate the corpses of their victims. There's a pattern to their cruelty and their mutilations can be much worse than those in this investigation."

"Much worse?" Dorado frowned in disbelief.

"Yes, they slash their victims, sometimes hundreds of times. They commonly slice off the nipples and repeatedly stab the breasts, stomach and female opening. The piquers amputate feet, fingers and hands. They cut out eyes and cut off ears. There have even been attempts to disembowel and decapitate victims. They sometimes take bites of flesh from the bodies."

"Madre de Dios!" Dorado gasped in horror.

"At least their victims were already dead and spared the terrible pain of such cruelty." Soto Iglesias sighed.

"Not always." Esteban shook his head slowly. "According to Chaussier, some piquers mutilate their victims while they are still alive. The fiends torture them slowly to see the agony they endure before dying. They should be struck down like snakes on the ground."

"I should say so. Such monsters should not be allowed to live in this world."

"One more similarity should be mentioned. Piquers typically avoid bodily contact with their victims. That's why the governor's niece was found to be a virgin. Doctor Chaussier said it's a characteristic of their mutilations."

Dorado nodded. "María Palés Molina was also a virgin. Captain Caminero de Castilla remembered it was in his report. I don't know about Carlota Ramírez Cruz; it's not included in the autopsy report of 1770. Nor do we know about the girl in 1763."

"I doubt if we'll ever know," said Esteban. "Female corpses were not examined for such findings in the past. The practice only began at the end of the seventies."

"Well, at least now we know the murderer is a piquer." Soto Iglesias stifled a yawn.

"Yes, and he must be found soon and executed forthwith." Esteban stood. "Unless we have missed something, it's time to go to bed."

Dorado left Sunday morning after eating breakfast with Esteban. The doctor's driver waited in his coach outside the house. While drinking tea, they discussed copying the critical files in the Building of Records. Once the governor signed the entry authorization, one of the clerks from Esteban's office would be sent to copy the documents. It was decided the brief file of 1763 would be copied first and sent to Florida. The longer report, written by Caminero de Castilla, would follow afterward. They both stood once the arrangements had been made.

"I'll keep you fully informed of the investigation, señor." Dorado bowed formally to Esteban, who also bowed politely. Dorado thought of hugging him, but then hesitated. He saw the physician as a reserved man, who kept his distance from most people. Esteban was affectionate to his wife and children, but not demonstrative to anyone else.

"Good. Tell Carlos I'll look forward to scraping the bowl with him, whenever he can come to Havana."

"I'll tell him, sir." Dorado smiled. "Thank you for your hospitality, Don Esteban. Adiós. I hope we meet again soon."

"I'm sure we shall. Buen viaje, Dorado. We enjoyed

having you here." To Dorado's surprise, Esteban patted his shoulder and squeezed his arm. He turned back at the doorway and smiled at him. "I regret we spent so little time together, Dorado. We must do better the next time you're here. We should at least play a few games of chess."

When Esteban had gone, Dorado went upstairs to finish his packing. Coming down the stairway, he saw Beatriz and the two boys waiting for him in the doorway. Little Angel held his hand as he walked outside to the waiting carriage. There were hugs and kisses and cross-my-heart promises of return visits as he said his farewells to the family. They all had tears in their eyes as they stood huddled together.

María Luisa arrived as Dorado was about to leave for the city docks. He was shoving his haversack into the carriage, when her coach came clattering along the road and stopped in front of the door. Following Beatriz and the boys, Dorado went over to her as a manservant helped her out of the coach. To his surprise, María Luisa seemed indifferent in him. As he bowed and kissed her hand, she barely looked at him. Her eyes were empty of any feeling he could see as she turned to embrace and kiss Beatriz. Before Dorado could say a word to her, María Luisa was gone, striding toward the house with the children pulling at her skirts.

Dorado thought about María Luisa for much of the voyage to St. Augustine. He could not explain what had happened to her passionate feelings for him. Over and over, he pictured her cold eyes as they passed over him without the slightest interest or warmth. At first, Dorado thought her apathy was an act to hide her passion for him, but later he knew it was the way she felt about him.

It bewildered him that María Luisa could come so amorously to his bed one night and then, only three weeks later, ignore him as easily as a spoiled house dog would dismiss a dried-up bone. In his mind, Dorado asked end-less questions about her, all without satisfactory answers. The irresistible Spanish woman would remain mysterious to him ever after. Even years later when some sudden memory of the past would bring María Luisa to his mind, Dorado would wonder about her.

CHAPTER FOURTEEN

DECEMBER 27-31, 1788

Dorado sat at the bedside of Ruiz de León drinking tea. Already worried about the ailing man's uneven breathing, he frowned seeing him shiver in his sleep. He covered him with another blanket as Señora Salgado entered the room with a pot of tea.

Dorado had sailed into St. Augustine two days after Christmas. The *Santa Catarina* arrived in the sea outside town a little after noon, but the captain waited four hours to enter the inlet at high tide. No experienced captain would risk taking his ship through the treacherous shoals at any other time. More than 200 vessels had been grounded and broken to pieces on the sand and oyster bars that guarded the shallow entrance into the bay of St. Augustine.

Dorado was seasick as the ship sailed in slow and seemingly endless circles outside the bay. Without any wind in the sails, the schooner pitched and rolled, making him miserably ill.

Even though he remained above decks in the fresh air, he vomited four times in the first hour. It seemed to him that his head hung over the side all afternoon.

At twilight, the tide was full and the vessel cautiously ventured into the inlet and sailed slowly past the hazardous sand bars. Once in the deepwater of the bay, the ship moved swiftly on the incoming tide. The short trip to the presidio pier was routine, but the sun had set by the time Dorado walked down the gangplank. He still felt sick to his stomach.

Serena stood on the pier awaiting him. The *Santa Catarina* had been seen earlier from the lighthouse and everyone knew of its arrival. She waved to Dorado when he was visible on deck. A few feet from the seawall, he threw his leather bag to a boy on the pier. Stepping ashore, he went to Serena and took her hand. He did not embrace her in view of the sailors on the deck of the ship. Dorado knew they would hoot and shout obscene words if he showed Serena any affection. He waved to the crew as they pushed off and the schooner set out to sea.

Dorado walked with Serena to the house of Esperanza Chavez. They held hands and looked at each other the entire way. Even though their pace was slow and they talked as they walked, they reached the house in only a few minutes. Seeing no one about the street, Dorado kissed Serena outside the house. They stood holding each other tightly until he sighed, kissed her again and turned to go. With a last smile over his shoulder, Dorado left her at the doorstep. Serena followed him with her eyes as long as he was in sight.

All the street lanterns were lighted by the time Dorado arrived at the house of Ruiz de León. He found him sitting in his favorite chair facing the fireplace. Despite his weakness, the sick man forced himself out of bed when he heard the *Santa Catarina* had been sighted sailing into the bay. He did not want Dorado to see him lying in bed.

"It's so good to see you, Lieutenant." Ruiz de León spoke in a hoarse voice. "You're a welcome sight for these old eyes."

"It's good to see you, too, Don Ricardo." Dorado went across the room and embraced the older man. He pulled up a chair to be near him.

"I'm glad you're here at last." Ruiz de León cleared his throat, but still spoke in a harsh whisper. He coughed and Dorado heard the congestion in his chest.

The sick man looked thin, almost skeletal. He looked much worse than when Dorado had seen him a month earlier. His coughing now lasted much longer and left him exhausted and obviously in pain. The pain made him frown. The sick man wheezed whenever he took even a short breath and shivered on and off while they talked.

"Did you know I was coming in on the *Santa Catarina*, today?"

"I heard it was due here today or tomorrow. A while ago, the widow woman next door barged in to tell me the ship was in sight. That woman tells me everything going on in town." He made a sour face. "She tells me much more than I want to know. The old woman is utterly consumed with the town gossip."

"Is that Señora Salgado, sir?"

"Yes. The woman means well, but she never leaves me in peace. She's always in here for something or other. If she's not here with a bowl of soup or cup of hot tea, she finds some other excuse to look in on me. I'm certain Carlos has put her up to it."

"Surely, he would never do such a thing." Dorado smiled.

"You know very well he would. I'm sure he's behind her incessant intrusions. The old woman even wants to bathe me. Can you believe it? It's all I can do to keep her from cleaning the house and meddling with my things." Ruiz de León coughed, laboring to get a breath of air. He held his chest with a thin hand.

"Now that I'm here, sir, I'll see to it she doesn't come around as much. Although I'm sure she means well and is only trying to be helpful."

"I suppose so. Now, tell me all you discovered in Havana. I've heard some of it since Carlos read me your report. It was well done, Lieutenant."

Dorado spent the next hour talking about his trip to Havana. His detailed account of the interview with Caminero de Castilla took up most of the time. In the end, he listed the many similarities of the four murders and the new facts known about the murderer. Ruiz de León nodded as Dorado described them one by one.

"With what we now know, his identity should be revealed soon – especially since we know his whereabouts at the time of the four murders. We know he was here in St. Augustine in 1763, in Havana in 1770 and 1777 and here again in 1788. There can't be too many men in town who were in those places at those times."

"I wouldn't think so." Ruiz de León leaned his head against the back of the chair.

"We should be able to find the man's name in some roster for the years he was here in Florida. I recommend we start with the presidio census lists. Do you know if any lists were made for the last years, before the foreign occupation?"

"I think so." Ruiz de León nodded. "But even if not, there's a complete list of every man, woman and child who left Florida in 1763. I remember seeing it somewhere here. Ask Sergeant Suárez, he should know where it's located."

"That means the murderer's name should appear in one of those lists from 1763 as well as in the census of 1786. It shouldn't be hard to find him, now."

"I wouldn't think so." Ruiz de León coughed again. "All that's needed is someone to look through the lists."

"Yes, sir, that should do it. Of course, everything depends on those two reports from Havana. I hope Doctor Morales

Muñoz finds them."

"I expect he'll find them eventually." The sick man started to nod off to sleep.

"Even if he doesn't find them, we still have what I was told by Caminero de Castilla. I am certain his information is accurate. He has all of his mind and still much of his memory."

"From what you've said about him, I'm sure that's true." The sick man's eyes were shut as he spoke.

"You should get some sleep, Don Ricardo," said Dorado, seeing him struggling to keep his eyes open. With his hands tucked down beneath the blankets, he looked like a small child. Only his wrinkled face and mustache made his age apparent.

"You're quite right. I'm certainly not contributing much to this conversation." Ruiz de León smiled weakly. "Before you go, I'm afraid I'll need some help getting back to bed."

Holding tightly to the younger man's arm, he managed to walk slowly to his bedroom. Dorado could feel the heat of his body as he helped him into bed. The sick man fell asleep as soon as his eyes closed. In the dim candlelight, he looked like one of the dead bodies Dorado had seen on the doctor's examining table.

A few minutes later, Señora Salgado arrived with hot tea for the sick man. She was a short round woman with little hair left on her head. Seeing Ruiz de León asleep, she handed the tea to Dorado. She described his condition in whispers and raised her eyes to heaven as if to say his life was in God's hands.

Dorado sat at his bedside until he finished the tea. An hour later, he rose from his chair and quietly tiptoed from the room. Before leaving, he straightened the bedcovers and emptied the chamber pot. When everything was in order, Dorado put out all the candles, looked in once more at the sleeping man and then silently left the house.

"He looks terrible," Dorado told Serena. Following a late meal, they sat talking in the house of Esperanza Chávez. She had eaten dinner with them and then gone across the street to speak to a neighbor. Dorado and Serena remained sitting at the kitchen table.

"He's so tiny — like a small sick child. I fear for his life. What have you heard?"

She stroked Dorado's hand on the table. "They say he's near death. But that's not what your friend, Doctor Martínez, says. He thinks Don Ricardo has a good chance to live. He told María that you being here will surely help him."

"That's what he said in his letter. What else do you know?"

"That's all I know. María told me. She's back with him again." Serena made a face, showing her displeasure with María's decision to return to Martínez.

"When does he visit Don Ricardo?" Dorado saw her grimace, but chose to ignore it.

"Every day," she said grudgingly. "He visits Don Ricardo early in the morning and late in the afternoon. At times, he even goes to see him at night. He's hired Señora Salgado to look in on him during the day. No one else is allowed inside the house."

"How long has Don Ricardo been so sick?"

"Two weeks or more. A sentry has been posted at his door on the governor's orders. He is there to report any emergency to Doctor Martínez."

"Who is with him at night?"

"Sergeant Suárez visits him after supper and stays there until Don Ricardo falls asleep."

"He wasn't there tonight."

"No. When the *Santa Catarina* was sighted this afternoon, he knew you would be with him tonight. He told Señora Salgado to tell you he will available anytime you need him."

"Who's with him later in the night?"

"The young brothers from the monastery. They take turns spending the night with him. Father Hassett has spent time with him, too. Even the bishop has been to visit him."

"Good." Dorado nodded, feeling relieved. "He certainly needs to be closely watched. I'll be with him every day from now on."

"That will be good for him." She smiled at him and noticed how tired he looked.

"Has the governor come to see him?"

"Oh, yes. He comes every day before lunch. The governor has had several Masses said for him. Father Hassett mentioned him by name at Christmas Mass and Don Ricardo is always among those mentioned in prayer at the cabildo (municipal council) meetings. Even those townspeople who know him little have lit candles in the church for him."

"Good!" Dorado sighed. "What a sad Christmas it has been."

"Yes, it's been a sad time for so many. Twenty people have already died in town and some, like Don Ricardo, are still struggling to survive. Gracias a Dios, the children have been mercifully spared so far. So have I. None of us has been sick." Serena crossed herself.

"Good, I'm glad to know you have been well. I didn't know so many people had died here. Dios mío! It's the same in Havana, with hundreds sick and who knows how many dead."

"So I've heard. We're all worried about Mama Claudia. She hasn't written since the middle of November."

"That long ago? I hope you hear from her soon. It's been a terrible time for everyone."

Serena nodded.

"I'd hoped to spend Christmas with Miguel, but I missed him by only a couple of days. His regiment was returning from the field as I left. Can you imagine it? All that time there in Havana and I never spent a moment with him." Dorado shook his head.

"How sad!" Serena squeezed his hand.

"I don't know when I'll see him again. With Don Ricardo so sick and the investigation continuing on and on, it may be weeks, if not months before I return to Havana." He sighed.

"What did you do while in Havana?" asked Serena, worried he might have met another woman in the house of his Cuban host.

"I spent my time reading files and writing reports. I also made God knows how many trips out to Morro Castle hoping to see Miguel. I took the long boat to the fort so many times, I met all the men who row there during the day."

"Did you spend any time with old friends?"

"No. Except to say a word or two to a couple of officers I know at the fort. I spent all of my time with the Morales Muñoz family."

"What happened in their home? Were there any fiestas while you were there?"

"Not while I was there. Esteban works until dark almost every day. Most nights, he eats when he comes home and then goes to bed. We never played even one game of chess."

"So, you saw very little of Havana in all that time."

"Very little. From what I saw, the city looks much the same. It's as busy as ever, full of unwashed people and smells terrible. During the day, it's impossible to walk in the streets without bumping into someone who needs a bath or babbles in a foreign language. The city seems even dirtier than my memory of it."

"That's the way it was when I was home. Havana has changed so much since I was a little girl. As you say, there are too many foreigners now in the city. You can't go anywhere without them staring at you."

"That's true. And there're too many street urchins begging

for food or pesetas. They follow your every step if you dare walk in the Central Plaza. That's where I found the green velvet." He motioned to the roll of fabric he had brought Serena from Havana.

"Thank you again for the material; it will make a beautiful dress. I also love the brush and combs for my hair. What lovely Christmas gifts."

"Por nada. Well, it's late, I must be going home." Wearily, he stood up from the table. "I don't want to awaken the Señora when I climb the stairs to my rooms."

"I wish you didn't have to go." She hugged him to her.

"I wish it, too. I would like to stay with you all night."

"I would like that, too." Serena blushed.

Now that she was with him, all her earlier fears seemed foolish. Once again, she felt the urge to yield herself completely to him. Serena imagined herself in bed with him holding his head on her breast, his heart beating against her. She sighed as Dorado took her hand and walked toward the door.

They embraced at the door, holding each other without moving. Dorado lowered his head and rested his face on her cheek, his jaw on her shoulder. Holding her, he felt at home in her arms. When he knew it was time to go, Dorado kissed her deeply, hugged her to him for a moment more and went out into the night.

Early the next morning, Dorado met the doctor at the house of Ruiz de León. He was bent over listening to the sick man's heart when Dorado entered the bedroom. Martínez looked up with his eyes and reached over the bed to shake his hand.

"It's good to see you, Lieutenant." Martínez gave him a broad smile.

"It's good to see you, too, señor." Dorado sat in the chair beside the bed and touched the sick man's thin hand. "How are you feeling this morning, Don Ricardo?"

"I'm doing better." He looked at Martínez, who nodded in agreement.

The doctor helped Ruiz de León sit up with his head resting against the oak headboard. He then shaved the sick man with his razor and the warm water he had heated earlier in the pot over the fireplace. As Martínez finished shaving him, he nicked his friend's left ear and a drop of blood fell on the towel in his lap. Ruiz de León scowled, but made no complaint.

"You can spare that speck of blood, Ricardo." Martínez chuckled. "Think of how much you would have lost earlier in the century when doctors bled their patients."

Dorado arranged the bedroom while Ruiz de León sat up for his shave. He made fresh tea, filled the oil lamps, straightened the covers and emptied the chamber pot. The sick man thanked him with his eyes. Dorado did all the things he had done every day, as a boy, for his bedridden father. The routine was so familiar to him and it occurred to him that in many ways, besides his illness, Ruiz de León reminded him of his father.

They left when Señora Salgado arrived with his breakfast. The sentry was sitting beside the door when the two men came out of the house. Martínez motioned for him to stay seated.

"Gómez, make sure you look in on the captain now and then. Do you understand? I don't want him alone for any length of time. Go in when the church bells ring the hour."

"Sí, mi Capitán."

The officers strolled toward the plaza. It was a pleasant morning warmed by a tropical breeze from the south. They stopped at a tavern for tea and sat at a table near a window.

"How is he today?" Dorado sipped his cassina tea.

"Much the same, he seems to be holding his own. At least, he's not any worse. He still can breathe, but with difficulty.

He's certainly well enough to glare at me for nicking his ear.
You know, he made me promise to shave him every morning
no matter how sick he might be. Appearance and propriety
are so damned important to him. The man wants to look as
if he's still working in his office. It's a wonder he doesn't wear
his uniform and wig to bed."

Dorado nodded, but did not smile. "Is this the worst he
has been?"

"Yes, though there's one good sign I see now. He's begun
spitting up the congestion in his chest. Still, he's very sick and
I don't know what his chances are. I hope your presence will
help him. He needs every bit of help he can get."

"I'll be there with him every day from now on. What else
should I do, sir?"

"You might read to him since his mind needs to stay alert;
I suggest *Don Quixote*. You know how he loves Cervantes.
Talking to him about the investigation will also interest him."

"I'll start reading *Don Quixote* to him this afternoon."

"Good. Read on and off to him, whenever he's in the
mood."

"Is there anything else I can do?"

"Yes. Make sure he eats what Señora Salgado prepares for
him. He needs to eat to stay alive, even though he doesn't
have much of an appetite. Of course, that's nothing new, the
man always has eaten like a sparrow."

"I'll make sure he eats, even if I have to feed him myself."

"Good. He may need that in time. He's a very sick man.
You know, Dorado, I thought he might die while you were
away."

"Didn't you say this is the worst he's been?"

"It is, but he's been sick for so long – I worried he might
die at any time."

"Can he continue this way for long?"

"I doubt it. This sickness has seriously weakened him and
he's having difficulty making water. That's an old problem

for him, but it's much worse now that he's so sick and weak."

"Does that come with the plague?"

"No, but it's made much worse by his sickness. Most men will have the problem sooner or later, if they live long enough."

"The more I hear about old age, the less I think it's worth living a long time."

"I won't argue with you, though that's easy to say when you're so young. Speaking of old age, I hear Jesse Fish is also very sick? Some say he's near death – God willing!"

"Have you seen him, sir?"

"Not recently. I've heard he doesn't trust me as a doctor." Martínez chuckled. "Of course, I can't blame him, can you?"

Dorado smiled. "Not after you told him to enjoy his pain as a sign of still being alive."

"Verdad. Anyway, what do I care about that English bastard. He's stolen everything he owns from our people. He lives like a fat tick off Spanish blood." He pounded the table with the flat of his hand. "Damn him! He can die and go to hell for all I care."

Dorado saw the other men in the tavern stare at them.

"I'll tell you something else." Martínez spoke softly. "Fish was in Havana in 1770 and 1777. What do you think of that? He was there, he says, to settle his debts with our people."

"You talked to him?" Dorado shifted the sword at his side.

"I rowed over to talk to him after reading your report from Havana. That was a good piece of work, Dorado." Martínez reached across the table and patted him on the arm.

"Thank you, sir." Dorado looked down at the table.

"Fish wasn't sick when I talked to him. I visited El Vergel and asked him if Gloria said anything to him on the day she went to the island. Fish claimed he spent all the time of their visit talking to Doña Concepción. She confirmed what he said when I later asked her."

"Did you ask him what he did after Barton left the morning of the murder? As I recall, Barton left the island at nine o'clock, which would have given Fish enough time afterwards to row over and meet Gloria in the north woods."

"No, I didn't ask him that question. Unless the old bastard is stronger than he appears, I can't believe he would be able to row all that way and back."

Dorado nodded. "What else did he say, sir?"

"Fish said the things old men say. He talked about the 'good days of the past' and how the world has changed for the worst. Fish said Gloria's disappearance wouldn't have happened years ago, unless she was taken by Indians. At that time, he said, no one would have dared go anywhere near the governor's niece, never mind murder her. He said such a tragedy is what we should expect with freed slaves and Indians wandering everywhere about town."

"How did you get him to tell you about his trips to Havana?"

"It was easier than I anticipated. After reading your report, I wanted to learn if he had been in Havana at the time of the murders. We know he was here in St. Augustine in 1763. So, I asked him what he thought about the English occupation of Florida." Martínez made a face. "I then had to hear about all the troubles he suffered because of British rule. The old bastard talks like he's a Spaniard. You would think he was one of us."

"That may be why the governor lets him hold so much property here in St. Augustine." Dorado stirred sugar into his tea.

"Perhaps. I then asked if he thought landowners were treated better in other colonies. When he snorted in disgust, I was sure he would tell me what I wanted to know."

"What did he say?" Dorado looked up after sipping his tea.

"He said the same incompetence exists everywhere. It doesn't matter where the colony is located or who rules it.

He complained that the needs of landowners are neglected in all the colonies. Then, he said what I wanted to hear. I recall every word. 'It's the same in Havana. I was there in 1770 and 1777. They do nothing for those who make the land productive.'"

"He actually mentioned those two years, sir? Santa María!"

Martínez smiled. "That's exactly what he said and so I immediately asked him why he went to Cuba in those years. He claimed he went there to settle his financial obligations with the Floridians living in Havana. Fish said he paid them for the properties he sold or still held in St. Augustine. If true, it's a reasonable explanation for him sailing to Havana."

"Did you ask him if he was there in the same months the two girls were murdered?"

"Yes, Lieutenant!" Martínez glared at Dorado. "I may be getting older, but my mind and member still work!"

"Yes, sir. No insult was intended."

"I know that, Lieutenant." He clucked his tongue. "Don't be so damned serious. You and Ricardo – two birds of a feather." The big man got up to get their cups refilled.

"Thank you, sir," said Dorado when Martínez returned with their tea. Though anxious to hear his question answered, he said nothing else.

Martínez smiled. "I won't keep you waiting any longer. Fish was indeed in Havana at the same time María Palés Molina was murdered – in November of 1777! He remembered the hurricane at the end of the month that delayed his return home. But I don't know about the girl in 1770 – Carlota Ramírez Cruz. By the time I found out about his first trip to Havana, it was getting late and I didn't want to row back across the bay in the dark. Besides, I was tired of the man's stink. I'd been cooped up with him too long and I was ready to leave."

"I can understand that. I still remember his stench."

"We'll have no trouble finding that information, anyway.

I'm sure the shipping dates of his voyages to Havana were recorded and should be in the Building of Records. Esteban will help us find whatever we need."

"I hope so." Dorado told Martínez about his inability to enter the Building of Records. "Those bastards deliberately prevented me from carrying out my assignment. I could have left Havana with the murderer's name in mind. If the fiend murders again, it's on their heads."

"I can understand why López Sierra wouldn't help you; he was obviously punishing you for the interview you made him endure here. But I don't understand why Ballesteros Bazón refused your request to enter the Building of Records." Puzzled, Martínez frowned. "Did you know him earlier when you were stationed in Havana?"

Dorado shook his head from side to side.

"What he did was so unnecessary. I can't believe it's that hard to enter the Building of Records. It's as if the man had something against you." Martínez shrugged his shoulders. "Of course, he could be one of those officious fools we see all too often these days in the colonies. They make everyone miserable with all their regulations. Well, you can be certain Ballesteros Bazón won't prevent Esteban from entering the Building of Records."

"Major Morales Muñoz said he would send us whatever we need."

"I'm sure Esteban will do what he said."

"So, we can ask him to find out exactly when Fish was in Havana. Is it possible that Jesse Fish is the one after all?"

"Yes, it's possible, even as old and feeble as he is. It's also possible Jesse Fish might die without telling us anything about it. We can't talk to him, now. He's much too sick."

"That's too bad." Dorado shook his head. "If he's the fiend, I'd like to see him hanged in the plaza for everyone to see."

"You sound just like the governor. That's what he plans to

do with the murderer when he's arrested." Martínez frowned. "But, unfortunately, we still don't know his identity. And, sad to say, I doubt the old bastard is the murderer. Don't forget Ricardo's spy told us Fish was still on the island at midmorning when the girl was killed. It's possible she was killed later that day, but that's not what the autopsy showed me."

"What about the commandant, sir? Do you still suspect him?"

"I don't know what to think about him." Martínez frowned. "He was in Cuba before coming to this presidio, but who knows when and where? Then, there's the murder in 1763. I don't recall seeing him in St. Augustine, while I was here. Surely, I would have seen or heard of him if he was here. Damn! There's no one we know who seems much like the murderer."

"I'm certain his identity will be found in the Building of Records. Some list or report will point him out to us."

"Even if you're right, it will take time. Too much time for the governor. His response now to anything I tell him is, 'I've heard that before' or 'You said that before, but the unending investigation goes on and on.'" Martínez sighed loudly.

"Doesn't he understand we need the reports from Havana?"

"He understands, but doesn't like it. Zéspedes is often in a foul humor, now. Without Ricardo in Government House, he has much more paperwork to do. He finds it demeaning and keeps saying, 'Is this the mierda (shit) I should be doing as the Governor of Florida?'"

"It must be hard to talk to him."

"You'll soon see for yourself. Let's be on our way. I must see some patients still sick with the plague." He stood and stretched, the palms of his hands touching the ceiling.

"I'll walk with you to the plaza. We can meet later at Don Ricardo's house. I'll bring my final report then."

"Fine. I'll read it tonight."

On their way to the plaza, Dorado asked Martínez about his fight with María Valdez. "Serena said you choked her in a fury and left finger marks on her neck. She said you almost choked María to death."

"So, do you think I'm the murderer?" Martínez stopped to look at Dorado. He thrust his big hands out as if to choke him.

"No, sir, I wasn't suggesting that at all."

"Well, my young friend, if I were the murderer, I would have strangled María until she was dead. Then, I would have cut a cross on her. But that didn't happen, did it? No! Why? Because María Valdez is much too old to be my victim."

"What do you mean?" Dorado stood facing Martínez.

"She's thirty, an old woman for the murderer. Don't forget, he only kills girls. All of them under twenty – seventeen actually!"

"That's true. I didn't mean to suggest ..."

"No importa." Martínez flipped his wrist as if casting Dorado's apology away. "I'll tell you what happened and, perhaps, it'll put your mind to rest. It all began because I didn't spend enough time with her. It was at the peak of the plague. After so many days and nights treating the sick, I was just too weary to spend much time with María and, when I was with her, I often fell asleep. I was utterly exhausted. Do you understand?"

"Sí, señor."

"The evening of the fight, María, as usual, complained about the little time I spent with her. She said I only went to see her when I wanted her in bed. I said that wasn't true, but she kept repeating the accusation. So, exasperated, I finally said bed was as good a reason as any other to be with her. Of course, that made her angry. So, I tried to soothe her, but she slapped my face and her finger poked me in the eye. In a fury, I took her by the throat and shook her. It only lasted a few seconds, but she accused me of trying to kill her."

"So, that's all there was to it?"

"Well, it actually started earlier that day. After eating lunch and drinking a couple of bottles of wine with her, she said I was a hopeless borracho (drunk). She told me Esperanza said the same thing. So, I said she was much like her sister – a 'sullen bitch.' With that, she stormed out of the house and didn't return until six in the evening. The fight resumed within minutes of her arrival with the details I've already described. Now, everything is better. After a few days, María came back and apologized. Can you believe it? Any more questions?"

"No, señor."

They separated at the south end of the plaza. Martínez went to his office in the Castillo, while Dorado walked home. In his mind were Martínez' last words. "Tomorrow, we meet the governor. Dios nos ayude (God help us)! He wants to discuss the investigation."

They met the governor at noon. He looked severe sitting behind his desk facing them. It was a serious meeting without the customary glass of Rioja wine or even a comment about the pleasant weather outside.

"How did Ricardo look this morning?" Zéspedes stared at Martínez. The forefinger of his right hand tapped on the arm of his chair. His face was set as if in stone and there was no sign of the good humor Dorado had seen in the garden behind Government House.

"A little better. He's wheezing much less today and continues to spit up the phlegm in his chest. He stayed awake longer yesterday and ate everything Señora Salgado put before him. Isn't that so, Lieutenant?"

"Yes, sir. He ate a plate of rice and squash and had a cup of tea while I was with him." Dorado saw the governor scrutinizing him.

"When were you with him, Lieutenant?"

"Most of the day yesterday, sir, and I was with him early this morning. I'll read to him this afternoon, if he's awake. I'll also go see him again tonight, before he falls asleep."

"Good! Ricardo needs all the attention we can give him. He worries me." Zéspedes sighed. "Last Friday, when I went to see him, he talked to me about writing a will."

"I don't like such thinking. Not at all!" Martínez grimaced. "It's not a good sign – no, not a good sign at all."

"No, it's not. That's what worries me, Carlos." Frowning, Zéspedes looked back and forth between the two officers. "Now, tell me about the investigation."

"We're getting very near the end, sir. With the autopsy reports on the way from Havana, we should soon know the murderer's identity. It's only a matter of time, now."

"I've heard that before. Still no one is arrested. It's now three months since the murder of Gloria. Is there no end to this damned investigation?"

"It will take only a little more time, Don Vicente. We know much about the murderer. It's all summarized in the lieutenant's excellent report. I read it last night, all twenty pages. Do you want to read it, Don Vicente?" He held the report out to him.

"No, I haven't the time. Without Ricardo here in Government House, I'm too damned busy to do anything but office work. It's a wonder I have time to eat my meals." He scowled. "Tell me what you now know about the murderer."

"We believe he has killed four girls and maybe even a fifth. It's possible that missing girl, in 1784, was one of his victims."

"Is that so?" The governor crossed his arms over his chest, the frown still on his face.

"Yes, sir. We also know more about him from the manner of his murders. There's a distinct pattern to them. We'll know much more when we see the reports from Havana."

"You said that before, but the murderer is still at large."

"Yes, Don Vicente. But now we know his methods. Once we see those reports, we should be able to identify him."

"What will you learn that you don't know now?" The governor coughed into his hand.

"We will know where and when he was in Havana and St. Augustine. His identity will be revealed by the places and times of his prior murders. With that knowledge, any number of records will give us his name. It's only a matter of time now."

"You said that before. In fact, you've said it so often the words are meaningless."

"Yes, but now we know which records will identify him. The murderer will not escape us. I'm certain of it!" Martínez looked directly at the frowning man in front of him.

"You better be! This investigation needs to be ended! We need to end it so everyone knows it's safe in St. Augustine. The diablo must be arrested and executed for all to see. Spain must be seen as powerful and resolute no matter who the murderer may be. We need respect! With so many foreigners in Florida, we need respect more than anything else. That's why the murderer must be found!" Zéspedes slapped his hand on the arm of his chair.

Martínez nodded, but said nothing.

"What is it you know about the murderer?" The governor moved his narrowed eyes to Dorado. "Wait! Before I forget it, Lieutenant, you are to look through Ricardo's file closet for the census lists. He thinks they might be there. Tell Suárez to help you. Do whatever it takes to end this damned investigation. Now, Lieutenant, tell me what you know."

"Yes, sir. We know the man must be older than forty since the murders are spread out over twenty-five years. We know he was here in St. Augustine, in 1763, went with our people to Cuba during the foreign occupation and then returned to Florida sometime after 1783 when we regained the colony. He is likely an old resident of this presidio. It's also possible he's a foreigner, who stayed in Florida during the foreign occupation."

"A foreigner?" With a forefinger and thumb, Zéspedes rubbed the bridge of his nose.

"Yes, sir. Someone like Jesse Fish."

"Jesse Fish! No! I don't believe it – not for a moment."

"We think it's a distinct possibility, Don Vicente." Martínez told Zéspedes what was known about the Englishman's two visits to Havana, when the other murders were committed. "Fish also had the opportunity to meet Gloria in the woods the morning of her death."

"I still don't believe it." Zéspedes shook his head.

"There's no one else whose movements fit the schedule of the killings so well. We'll know with certainty when we see the records from Cuba."

"I hear the old man is near death, now." Zéspedes sighed and the two officers smelled the odor of garlic. "Even with the documents, you'll have to convince me; I can't believe that feeble old man could kill a chicken with his hands never mind a young girl. Whatever happens, you better know soon if he's the one. We will look ridiculous if we named a dead man as the murderer. Who, in God's name, would believe us?" He clucked his tongue in exasperation.

"We'll know soon, Don Vicente." Martínez nodded confidently. "The murderer might not be Fish. He might be in the king's service – maybe a soldier or even an officer."

"Santa María! That would be much worse!" Zéspedes scowled at Martínez. "That's all I need – a Spanish officer named as the murderer. Dios ayúdame! (God help me)! When will this nightmare ever end?"

"Soon, Don Vicente, soon."

"Oh, and who will be the murderer? The Archbishop of Havana?"

"Sir, Governor Zéspedes," Dorado spoke softly.

"I don't want to hear anymore. I've heard more than enough!" Zéspedes stood up and glared at them. "I want results, not words. Now, get on with it!"

Dorado sat talking to Ruiz de León in the living room of his house. The ailing man's soft chair had been situated so he could look out the window. Whitecaps blanketed the bay as a cold wind blew into the town from the west. They had to raise their voices to hear each other above the noise of the waves crashing over the seawall. It was the last day of December.

Ruiz de León felt better. His fever had broken and he seemed much stronger. It now was possible for him to get out of bed for five or six hours each day and sleep all night, without anyone watching over him. Everyone knew he felt better when he insisted on dressing himself for dinner and had Señora Salgado serve his meals at the table. Three days earlier, he sent the sentry, who stood at his front door, back to duty. The same day he told Martínez to inform the governor that he wanted Suárez to bring him paperwork from his office.

"When did you say the report of 1763 is due here?" Ruiz de León still spoke in a hoarse voice. He was sipping the hot tea he had made for himself.

"This week. Major Morales Muñoz promised me he would have it copied immediately and sent out on the first ship sailing to St. Augustine. A Dutch schooner was scheduled to sail here a few days after I left Havana. I hope the report is aboard the ship. Of course, everything depends on the major getting a permit to enter the Building of Records."

"What an inexplicable situation – the trouble with that man, Ballesteros Bazón. I can't imagine why he wouldn't let you enter the Building of Records, entry authorization or not. It was so unnecessary."

"I now know why he refused me entry, Don Ricardo."

"Sí. Por qué (why)?"

"I learned about it last night from Serena Rodríguez."

"From Serena Rodríguez?" Ruiz de León looked puzzled.

"Yes, sir. I think Ballesteros Bazón refused to let me enter the Building of Records because of – jealousy!"

"Celosía? No, puedo ser (Jealousy – surely not)!"

"Sí, señor. Ballesteros Bazón courted Serena Rodríguez for months before she came to St. Augustine. He wouldn't accept her refusal of his offer of marriage and went on courting her despite her protests. So, she decided to escape his attentions here with her cousins."

"I see. Are you saying Ballesteros Bazón knew about your romance with the Rodríguez girl? And, because of jealousy, he wouldn't let you enter the Building of Records? Is that it?"

"Yes, sir. That's what I think happened."

"How would he know about you and the girl? Has he recently been in St. Augustine?"

"No, sir, not to my knowledge. But Lieutenant López Sierra could have informed him about it when he returned to Havana from Florida."

"Yes, of course. That could have happened."

"They could be friends or, at least, acquainted with each other. Ballesteros Bazón could have inquired about Serena when he saw López Sierra after his return to Havana."

"That would explain it. If so, he should be reported to the governor of Cuba!" Ruiz de León raised his voice. "You were on an official mission in the king's service and he refused to allow you to enter the Building of Records. Because of jealousy? Disgraceful!"

"Yes, sir. But what we suspect is only an assumption."

"I suppose so, but it seems likely. What a petty man. It's no wonder Serena Rodríguez refused to marry him. What did she say about him?"

"She said he looked like a 'sad little squirrel.'"

"Women do have a way of saying things, don't they?" Ruiz de León smiled slightly.

"Yes, but he does look like a squirrel – one with acorns stored in his cheeks." They both laughed. It was the first time Dorado had seen the sick man laugh since his return.

"How did she happen to tell you about him?"

"I knew there was a man pursuing her. Serena told me about him earlier, but she didn't tell me his name. Then, when I told her about my difficulty trying to get into the Building of Records, she told me about him. Serena's certain jealousy was the reason for it."

"I don't doubt it – it's the only plausible explanation." Ruiz de León looked away into the river. "Ah, yes, what men seem to become because of women."

"Speaking of women, señor, what do you think about what happened between Doctor Martínez and María Valdez?"

"What do you mean?"

"Their awful fight. María Valdez told Serena that he almost strangled her to death."

"Oh, that." He sighed wearily. "It was only another of his ceaseless quarrels with that coarse woman. When Carlos told me about it, I told him they deserve each other. He deserves the misery she gives him and she deserves to be strangled. He didn't like my reply, but knew it was true. As my mother, God rest her soul, used to say, 'Skunks smell sweet to each other.'"

A knock on the door startled them. Dorado opened the door and saw Adolfo Fierro, a sentry stationed at the city dock. Fierro was breathing hard after running from his post.

"Sir, Captain Martínez sent me here with this." He handed Dorado a mail packet. "It arrived aboard the *Nuestra Señora de Concepción*. The ship came in on the afternoon tide."

"The packet hasn't been opened. Didn't the captain look at it?" Dorado saw Martínez' name on the packet. He knew it had been written by Major Morales Muñoz y Barrientos.

"No, sir. Captain Martínez told me to tell you 'to read it with Don Ricardo.'"

"Did he say anything else?" Dorado looked the young man over.

"No, sir – except to run over here as fast as possible."

"I see. Thank you, Fierro. You can return to your post."

"Yes, sir." Fierro saluted and walked away.

"It's the report of 1763," announced Dorado as he closed the door and turned toward Ruiz de León. He held it out to the seated man.

"Read it to me, Lieutenant. My eyes are tired."

Dorado lay awake much of that night unable to sleep. There were too many thoughts on his mind. Even with his head under the pillow and his eyes tightly shut, Dorado could not sleep. Sometime after the church bell rang the one o'clock hour, he gave up the struggle and groped for his tinder box to light the candle on the bedside table.

Dorado decided to read the report again as well as Esteban's accompanying letter. It would be his third reading and the second that evening. He had read the report following his last visit to see Ruiz de León. Every night, at nine o'clock, Dorado made sure the sick man was comfortably settled before going home to bed.

Now, in the cold December night, he sat bundled in the blankets reading the report of 1763. Only the hand holding the papers was outside the covers. Trying to get additional light, Dorado tilted his head toward the candle standing on a bedside table. Some unseen draft made it flicker unpredictably and he leaned his head closer to the table.

The report was exactly as Caminero de Castilla described it, apparently written in haste and barely three pages in length. Dorado found it limited in detail, though the necessary facts seemed to be included. The report had been written by Lieutenant Luciano Navarro de Paula, who attended the autopsy and took notes for the doctor. He wrote the report while the autopsy was in progress and misspelled the medical terms he used. The physician's signature, penned under the lieutenant's name, appeared as a smudged scrawl at the end of the statement.

In the margin, opposite the illegible signature, a short note was written by the man who copied the report. He wrote saying a liquid – probably wine – had been spilled on the original in the past and he had traced the scrawl to make the copy as accurate as possible. A capital "C" or "L" was the only initial clearly discernible from his signature or rank in the army.

The day and month of the autopsy report also were badly smudged and impossible to read, but the year, mil setecientos sesenta y tres (1763), was clearly legible. Dorado assumed the autopsy had been done on one of the last days of September since the girl had been killed on the twenty-seventh of the month. That date appeared on the top of the report.

The girl's name was Elena María Escobar, the only daughter of the king's accountant in St. Augustine, Juan Bautista Escobar Santana. Her father told Lieutenant Navarro that Elena María had celebrated her seventeenth birthday only two weeks before her death. The girl was reported to be pretty, but dull-witted.

A squad of soldiers found her body in the pinewoods north of town near the river. The girl's body had been mauled by animals and the fingers of her right hand and most of the right foot were gnawed away. Her face, covered by her bodice, was untouched.

The report also cited the four knife wounds in the throat, the breasts and between the legs and stated that they appeared to be arranged in a peculiar pattern. Navarro underlined the locations of the wounds and wrote, "Although the loss of blood from any of the wounds could have killed Elena María

Escobar, it seems likely the girl was strangled to death."

Navarro noted the girl's nudity and stated that a lengthy search had been conducted for her clothing. The woods were thoroughly searched, but nothing was ever found, not even her shoes. The searchers concluded the murderer had taken everything away with him.

Nothing of additional importance appeared in the report of 1763. It included none of the description and detail of the later autopsy reports, especially relating to the placement and location of the body. Navarro never even speculated on how the girl reached the place where she was killed. Why she went there was also ignored.

As Caminero de Castilla had said, the autopsy report looked to be written in haste. It ended without mentioning an investigation in progress. The conclusion stated the obvious. "The murder remains unexplained and the murderer is unknown at this time."

Esteban's accompanying letter commented on the murderer and related the governor's reaction to Dorado's inability to enter the Building of Records. He also wrote a paragraph of praise for the lieutenant. Dorado smiled even after his fourth reading of the letter.

Estimado Carlos,

I hope this letter finds you feeling well. Everyone at home is feeling fine. Thank God, the children never got sick during the plague. It's finally over, but many, more than a hundred, died during its worst phase. I hope the king's subjects fared better in St. Augustine.

Dorado did good work here. He's a very intelligent and a diligent young officer – the kind we see too infrequently in the crown's service these days. The family enjoyed having him in our home. Beatriz and the boys fell in love with him and were sad he had to leave. Though I was too busy to spend much time with him, we did discuss the murders on several occasions.

In my opinion, the accompanying autopsy report describes a murder by the same man who struck down Governor Zéspedes' niece. From what Dorado told me of the murders of 1770, 1777 and 1788, it seems he has killed four girls – at least! A fifth victim might include the missing girl in 1784. Since she disappeared in that year, her slaying would fit his apparent schedule of murder every seven years, of course, with the obvious exception of the governor's niece. Whatever his pattern of murder may be, he must be arrested as soon as possible. I dread to think of what this fiend might yet do in St. Augustine or elsewhere if he eludes capture.

Caminero de Castilla's report is now being copied. It will take a week to finish since it is fifty pages long and I can't spare my clerk, Velasco Calderón de Ricla, to copy it every day. He copied the report of 1763. Unlike Dorado, he entered the Building of Records without an authorization signed by the governor. Such a document is required by presidio regulations, but it is rarely necessary. Almost no one bothers to request it and Ballesteros Bazón seldom asks for it. The governor told me he hasn't signed more than six in all his years of service in Cuba. He was furious to hear that Dorado was refused entry into the Building of Records, especially since he showed Ballesteros Bazón the official letter from Governor Zéspedes. The governor intends to look into the unfortunate incident and take punitive action against the director if he is found wanting. And you can be assured, he will do it.

I also informed the governor about López Sierra's unwillingness to assist Dorado while on assignment in Havana. He was even more enraged to hear of such obstructive behavior in his office. You can be certain López Sierra will be severely reprimanded, if not penalized for his actions. As you know, that is not the way we treat our guests in Havana.

Well, Carlos, I must return to my patients. Do come visit us when the investigation is over. We will share a bottle of

Rioja and, of course, scrape the bowl together.

Con todo mi afecto (With all my affection),
Esteban

Dorado fell asleep soon after reading Esteban's letter. As he pulled the blankets about his neck, his thoughts turned to what needed to be done in the coming days. Initially, he would look through the census records of 1763 and 1784 to find out which of the former residents of St. Augustine still lived in the presidio. Using interviews, he then would learn who had visited or resided in Havana in 1770 and 1777. The list should be short and, from the final few names, he would discover the identity of the murderer. He sighed in anticipation of what lay ahead.

"It's only a matter of time, now," Dorado thought as he rolled over on his right side to blow out the bedside candle. He shut his eyes and enjoyed a brief fantasy before falling asleep. Dorado saw himself, sword in hand, pushing the shackled murderer forward to kneel before the governor. Governor Zéspedes nodded his appreciation and glared at the man.

The man sat by the window looking out into the darkness. It was too cold to venture out that winter night. He shivered feeling a sudden draft on his ankles. Even with a wool blanket wrapped about his shoulders, he felt the penetrating cold. It was definitely not a time to be out of bed, he thought, rising from his chair. He could not see anything in the dark anyway. The frigid night held only the cutting wind that no matter the woolen clothing would numb the flesh of anyone foolish enough to go into the streets.

"Such stupid girls!" He spoke to himself when once

again settled in the warmth of his bed under the covers. "They thought they could use me, play me for the fool. Putas (Whores)! Putas estúpidas (Stupid whores)! They finally paid the piper."

CHAPTER FIFTEEN

JANUARY 21-26, 1789

"You get the house and everything in it, Lieutenant. That's what he wanted."

"I don't know what to say, sir," Dorado whispered. His throat tightened and he felt tears forming in his eyes. "I never expected such a thing."

"I know you didn't. No one thought he would die. He seemed to be doing so much better. I still can't believe it." Zéspedes held a handkerchief which he used to wipe his eyes.

"I can't believe it either, sir." Dorado sighed. "One day, he was getting better, the next day he was gone. Doctor Martínez said his sudden death surprised him, too."

"It surprised us all." The governor exhaled a long breath, as usual tainted with garlic.

They were sitting in Zéspedes' office, a day after the funeral of Ruiz de León. He had died in his sleep a week earlier. Señora Salgado found him lying dead in bed, when she went into his house to bring him the baked bread she made that morning. She reluctantly entered his bedroom when he did not reply to her shouted greetings. Ruiz de León died without making a last confession, though Father Hassett had visited him the afternoon before his death.

"I don't want his house, sir. I have no right to it. Shouldn't it go to his family? What about his sister, Rosa María, in Spain?"

"According to his will, you get the house, not his sister! He wrote it a week ago." The governor held the will at arm's length to read it. "See, the date on the bottom of the sheet. It's there as plain as day. January 10, 1789. Do you want to read it, Lieutenant?"

"No, sir. I'm sure it says that."

"Then, that settles it."

"Yes, sir." Dorado looked down at his hands.

"It's what he wanted. You were like a son to him. He told me that himself the last time we talked at length. It was while you were away."

"I would gladly have been his son. He was a wonderful man." Again the tears welled up in his eyes. "But what about his sister, Rosa María, sir? She helped raise him. Shouldn't she get his house and all his possessions?"

"She would never live in the house, as you well know. Ricardo wanted someone who loved the house to own it – like you. If Rosa María got it, she would sell it immediately and the few hundred pesetas it's worth wouldn't change her circumstances one iota; she's an old woman with few wants. No, it's yours and you're to move in as soon as possible."

"Sí, señor." Dorado made a face.

"Don't 'sí señor' me. That's what he wanted, Lieutenant, and you know it!"

"Yes, sir, that's true." Dorado nodded.

"His sister will get his pension and whatever salary he had coming to him. Believe me, that will be plenty for her.

I'll also make sure she gets the money due him for his promotion. What a damned irony! A surprise celebration for his promotion was planned for Friday here in Government House. The commandant and I have been planning it for over a month. We were only waiting for him to get out of bed." Zéspedes shook his head sadly.

Dorado nodded.

"Now, Lieutenant, I want to discuss the investigation." Zéspedes inhaled loudly and leaned back in his chair. His head rested against the leather back, where his family's coat of arms were engraved. "Do you want a glass of wine, while we talk?"

"No, sir, thank you." Dorado looked over the governor's shoulder at the falling rain he saw outside the window. It was a cold, dreary day with intermittent showers and he had run through a heavy downpour to reach Government House. Dorado sat across from the governor, his uniform wet from the rain..

"What progress can you report, Lieutenant? I know you've been distracted by Ricardo's death." Zéspedes stared into Dorado's eyes. "Incidentally, he told me you would be the one to end it. He had much confidence in you, young man." The governor pointed his forefinger at Dorado. "I hope it's deserved. Well, we' shall see, won't we?"

"Sí, señor."

"What's yet to be done before it's over? Where are we now?"

"It's almost finished now."

"I've heard that before – all too often." Governor Zéspedes made a face.

"Yes, sir. I know you have, sir, but we are very close now. We're waiting for two reports from Havana that should end it all."

"And what are those two reports?"

"One is the investigator's report of 1777, the other is the

evacuation list of 1763."

"Hasn't that damned report arrived yet? I thought it was on its way weeks ago. What's happened to it?" Zéspedes frowned.

"I don't know, sir. It should be here by now."

"Did they send it from Madrid instead of Havana?" The governor glared at Dorado.

"No, sir. I think the delay is due to the time needed to copy it. It's fifty pages long."

"That's no excuse. It could be done in a day. What's the other report you mentioned?"

"The evacuation list for 1763."

"Oh, yes. And why is that so important? I know you told me before, but tell me again. I have so much on my mind these days, I can't remember every damned detail."

"Yes, sir. The list includes the names of everyone who lived here in 1763 and left when the colony was transferred to the English. Once we have the list, we will compare it to a copy of the census list of 1786. We expect to find the murderer's name on both lists, which will be the way we identify him."

"Is that so?" Zéspedes stared at Dorado, a frown still on his face. "Suppose you find many of the same names on the two lists? Many of the Floridians who left St. Augustine in 1763 have returned here after the foreign occupation."

"After all those years, we expect only a few of the names to appear on both lists. We doubt there will be even ten names and some of them will be women."

"That remains to be seen. But, even if you are correct in your estimate of the number of men, how will you then find the murderer among them?"

"By interviews, sir. Once we know the men whose names appear on the two lists, we will interview every one of them. Captain Martínez is certain the murderer will reveal himself to us no matter how hard he tries to avoid it."

"Is that so?" Zéspedes made a face. "What conceit! Well, let's hope he's right. This investigation needs to be finished with the murderer in custody. As soon as possible!"

"Yes, sir."

"When was the evacuation list requested?"

"A month ago. An official letter of request, with your seal and signature, was mailed to the governor of Cuba. We gave the letter to the captain of the *Candelaria* to deliver personally as a special assignment."

"I remember the letter, Lieutenant." Zéspedes scowled at Dorado. "I haven't lost my memory! So, from what you've said, Lieutenant, it all should be over in two weeks time – three weeks at the most. In three weeks time, we should have the man in custody. Is that correct?"

"Yes, sir, if ..."

"I don't want any if's, Lieutenant. I want it finished in three weeks. That's my limit! Do you hear me?"

"Yes, sir. But ..."

"No but's! You have three weeks to find the murderer. No more. If you haven't found him by then, I will!"

"Sir?"

"You heard me." The governor pointed a trembling finger at Dorado. "If you don't find the damned murderer – I'll find him. Believe me."

Dorado stood on the balcony searching for the first light on the horizon. The sky was still dark except for a thin, white line where the sun would soon appear. He had been awake for most of the night, thinking of Ruiz de León. Unable to sleep, Dorado dressed before dawn and climbed up the stairway to the balcony to await the sunrise.

It had taken him a week to work up the courage to enter the house given to him. When he did go inside, it was only to sleep on the floor beside the fireplace. He slept only two nights there and no more than four hours each time. He was unable to sleep the night through. When Dorado did sleep, he usually dreamed of the dead man; he would see him across the chess board at the kitchen table or sitting bundled up in blankets in his pillowed chair beside the fireplace. The dreams would awaken him late at night and he would sleep only fitfully afterward. Every sound, even the creak of a windblown shutter or the rasp of a branch on the roof, would startle him and he would lie on his back with his eyes wide open for hours.

Dorado felt like an intruder in the house. It seemed impossible for him to think of it as his house, especially with the captain's things everywhere he looked. Everything remained as it had been when Ruiz de León was alive. He had touched nothing. Dorado had not even considered sleeping in his bed, fearing he would see the sick man as he had looked in the last days of his life.

The bed was as Señora Salgado left it after his death, without sheets or blankets. Only a lone pillow lay there. Now and then, Dorado looked into the bedroom, but never dared enter it. Rather than sleep in the captain's bed, he lay wrapped up in blankets on the floor in front of the fireplace. The smell of burnt wood still lingered in the air even though Señora Salgado had removed the charred remains of the last fire. She had worried something might ignite them.

Though cold on the hardwood floor, Dorado never started a fire. It reminded him too much of his many talks with the sick man in the room, warmed by a crackling fire he made for him. Nor would he sit in Ruiz de León's favorite chair. Dorado sat in the other chair where he always faced him, while talking or playing chess. The only change he made in the living room was to move the captain's chair from where he found it, near the window, to where it usually stood beside the fireplace. He pictured Ruiz de León sitting there as he carried the chair.

On the balcony, Dorado wiped the dew from one of the weathered chairs and sat down. He wrapped the blanket brought up from below around his shoulders. Dorado looked out to sea and awaited the arrival of dawn. He knew it would soon appear when he saw a narrow streak of light on the horizon between the sky and sea.

It was a cold morning, but not unusually cold for late January. A westerly had kept St. Augustine comfortably mild for most of the month. The mornings were cold, but, to the delight of the townspeople, most days were balmy. There had been only two hard frosts and the month of January was almost over. The weather reminded him of late autumn in Asturias.

He was thinking about the investigation, when the sun finally appeared, lighting up the sky. It had been on his mind ever since he awoke hours earlier. A week had passed since his meeting with the governor and Dorado knew they were no closer to the arrest of the murderer. He worried that the man would never be found.

Dorado could still see Zéspedes shaking his finger at him as he said, "If you don't find the damned murderer – I'll find him."

Unsure what the governor's words meant, Dorado thought about them the rest of that day and night. He kept repeating them to himself, trying to make sense of them. They were still on his mind the next afternoon when he went to see Carlos Martínez.

He found the physician sitting at the examining table, where the corpse of a tall bearded man lay unclothed. Martínez was bent over the body, writing up his report. He had placed his writing slab and paper on the man's chest to write the report.

"What do you think he meant by that remark to me?" Dorado repeated the last words the governor had said to him.

Feeling colder in the surgery than outside on the street, Dorado kept his hands buried in his pockets. Apparently unaffected by the cold room, Martínez sat with his sleeves rolled up. One huge hand held a quill, the other lay flat on the bared chest of the dead man. While they talked, Dorado noted that Martínez never once rubbed his hands together for warmth.

Before Dorado's arrival, Martínez had completed the autopsy and written most of the report. The dead man was a mestizo (a man of mixed Indian and Spanish ancestry), who had been shot twice in the chest. Dorado had heard the man, named José Jiménez, had been killed by musket fire while resisting arrest. It was said he had murdered an English planter and then fled into the lost lands. A squad of soldiers, led by an Indian guide, pursued the fugitive in the woods and shot him when he rushed them with a machete. One of the soldiers, Juan Solís, was struck and killed by the mestizo's machete.

"You know what he meant as well as I do, Lieutenant." Martínez lifted his quill from the report and looked up at Dorado.

"I can't believe he would do such a thing."

"Don't be naive, Lieutenant. The governor will do what he sees as necessary. You can be sure of it. He's a practical man, not a philosopher."

"But ..."

"He won't hesitate. If we don't find the man in three weeks, he'll name someone else as the murderer. He'll do it to show the foreigners the strength of Spanish rule."

"Whom could he possibly name?" Dorado moved a chair from the doctor's office into the surgery and sat in it.

"That's a good question. Quién sabe?" Martínez shrugged. "I don't know what the man is thinking. He tells me nothing. With Ricardo gone ..." Martínez sighed. "I thought he might talk to me more often, but he seems even more distant. Damned stoic Castellano!"

"I can't imagine him naming someone who's innocent, can you?"

"No, he wouldn't do that. The man would have to be already dead. Like this mestizo here who has a villainous reputation."

"Maybe, he hasn't anyone in mind for the moment."

"Maybe not." Martínez shrugged. "But knowing Zéspedes, I doubt he would make an idle threat. He must have someone in mind – maybe Jiménez." He pointed to the dead man.

"The mestizo couldn't be Gloria's murderer!" Dorado raised his voice. "I doubt he ever met or talked to the governor's niece."

"That wouldn't matter to Zéspedes. Keep in mind, only two men know about the other murders – you and I! That means anyone could be accused of the killing – living or dead!"

"I suppose so, but I can't believe he would do such a thing."

"Believe it! He would and it wouldn't cost him a moment's sleep. By the way, do you know what happened to Jiménez here?"

"I heard he murdered an Englishman with an axe handle, a man named Clemens. It's said that stolen cattle were involved."

"It was in part. It's a sad story and it comes from Pedro Andrade Parra, who manages his family's lands after the death of his father. He came to see me yesterday and told me about it. Pedro has a pilonidal cyst on the base of his spine that needs to be drained now and then."

Dorado nodded. As usual, he had to wait for Martínez to get to the point of his story.

"Jiménez owned a piece of land near the Englishman's cattle ranch. It was given to him by Pedro's father, Juan Andrade Parra, for his many years of service. The Andrade family has farmlands south of Moultrie Creek and Pedro's father hired Jiménez to work for him. He was a young lad then about ten years old. It was before our people left Florida in 1763 and Jiménez accompanied the Andrade family to Havana. Following the war, they returned together to St. Augustine, a month or so after Don Vicente and Ricardo arrived here."

Martínez sighed. "I still can't believe he's dead. I use his name as if he were still alive. I keep expecting to see him come limping in here with his chess board under his arm. We use my pieces here, but he prefers his own board which was made in Spain. See! I did it again. I talk of him as if he were alive." The big man paused and blinked his wet eyes.

"I do it, too. You know, I still can't go into his house. I'm afraid I'll see him in every room. The governor told me to move in, but I'm not sure if and when I'll do it."

"I understand. You know, Dorado, I don't envy your ownership of his house. Gracias a Dios, he didn't give it to me."

"What were you saying about Jiménez?" Dorado sighed loudly.

"Yes, it's better to speak about Jiménez." Martínez covered the corpse with the same piece of blood stained canvas Dorado had seen on the body of the governor's niece. "Jiménez inherited his land two years ago, when Juan Andrade died, and he built a house beside Moultrie Creek. Once the house was finished, he did little else with the property despite the rich soil it's known to possess. Jiménez, however, did occupy the house and he lived alone there except for the occasional visits of whores and other unsavory characters."

"I know the place, it's about five miles south of town. I've seen it from the old wooden bridge that crosses the creek."

"Exactly. Well, instead of cultivating his fertile property, Jiménez became a smuggler, transporting untaxed products into the colony. He acquired the products from foreign ships and ferried them up Moultrie Creek to his house in the dark of night. Avoiding the Crown's taxes, he profited by selling illicit goods at lower prices than they could be purchased elsewhere."

"Jiménez must have made a fortune from such an enterprise."

"He did, but that's not all. Jiménez also made money stealing livestock. Not long after he built his house, his neighbors began complaining about the disappearance of their cattle and hogs. The governor responded to their complaints on several occasions and sent men down to Moultrie Creek to search for the missing livestock. A squad of ten soldiers went on one search. But none of the lost cattle and hogs ever turned up, not even their bones. Jiménez' house and property were thoroughly searched each time without success. Ricardo suspected Jiménez had a secret storage site where he kept his illegal goods – perhaps, in the nearby woods."

Dorado nodded. "It wouldn't be hard to hide his cache in those thick woods along Moultrie Creek. I assume he slaughtered the livestock and sold the meat in town."

"Probably. Anyway, the loss of livestock continued and so did the complaints of his neighbors. Of course, his nearest neighbor, Henry Clemens, complained the loudest."

"That's not surprising." Dorado smoothed his mustache with a finger.

"No, it isn't. Then, a week ago, two milk cows and two hogs were taken from Clemens' barn in the middle of the night. Furious, Clemens, along with three other English farmers, rode into town and demanded the governor take action against Jiménez. So, once again, a squad of soldiers was sent to the Moultrie Creek and, to no one's surprise, none of the missing livestock was found. It's said that Jiménez smiled the entire time the soldiers searched his property."

"I heard about it from Lieutenant Robles Rivera who led the squad."

"I see. Well, the next night, Jiménez' house burned to the ground. Jiménez was not at home at the time. He was away, probably selling the pork and beef from the stolen livestock. Jiménez returned the next morning to find the charred remains of his house. You can easily imagine what followed then."

"That's when he killed Clemens." Dorado crossed his legs.

"Yes. In a rage, Jiménez ran all the way to Clemens' house. The Englishman saw him coming through the gate, opened the door and stood there with a loaded musket in his hands. But Jiménez bowled him over before he could raise it to his shoulder and, with an axe handle, the mestizo beat him to death. Clemens' hysterical wife witnessed it all."

Dorado shook his head. "Dios mío, pobrecita (poor woman)!"

"Indeed. Jiménez fled into the lost lands and the governor ordered a detachment of men to find and arrest him. It took about a week to locate him, but the Mestizo was eventually seen sneaking along the shores of Moultrie Creek where he had lived. Incidentally, a secret cellar was found beneath his house with ten charred casks of wine, partially burned English furniture, broken crockery, Chinese porcelain and stacks of cattle hides. There was also a chest of gold and silver coins – many minted in foreign countries."

"So, that's where Jiménez concealed his cache."

Martínez nodded. "A squad of seven soldiers armed with muskets eventually caught up with him near the ruins of his house. Jiménez was shot when he attacked and killed one of the soldiers. It was Juan Solís – I'm sure you remember him."

"Yes, of course, the sentry who helped Gloria leave Government House unnoticed the day of her murder. I heard Solís was transferred to the lost lands patrol as punishment for his dereliction of duty, but didn't know he was the soldier killed by Jiménez."

"Yes. As for Jiménez, he had hidden in the lost lands for almost a week and, by then, must have been mad. I say that because I can't imagine any man of reason charging a squad of armed soldiers with a machete."

"Mad or not, he got what he deserved." Dorado looked down at the corpse on the table. "What a terrible time for Clemens' wife."

"Yes. Poor woman! She had already lost her little son, only six years old, a few weeks ago to the plague. Sometimes, life is unnecessarily cruel to some people."

"And too short for others." Dorado thought of Ruiz de León.

"True. As they say, 'The good die early, the bad die late.'"

"That's what my mother said when she spoke of my father. I can see her in my mind's eye shaking her head as she said it to us. Now, it makes me think of Don Ricardo."

"The same thought has been in my mind, too." Martínez exhaled a long breath. "Well, we must go on and end this investigation. I'm sure Ricardo would want it finally settled."

"He said as much only a few days before he died."

"Well, where are we now in the investigation?" Martínez stared at Dorado. "Was there anything in the mail from Havana? I hear the *Nuestra Señora de Dolores* arrived last night."

"Yes. We got the evacuation list at last!"

"What about the report of 1777?"

"It still hasn't arrived and is long overdue. If the ship went down at sea, we should have heard about it by now."

"You would think so. At least we have the evacuation list."

"You'll be amused to know López Sierra copied it. His note said he was happy to assist us." Dorado grinned.

"What a damn liar!" Martínez guffawed. "I'm sure he hated every minute of it. As you know, the Building of Records is filthy and López Sierra hates to get his hands dirty. I'm sure the governor made him copy the list because of his treatment of you. What have you found in the evacuation list? Surely, by now, you compared it to the census of 1786."

"I've found fifteen names showing up on both lists."

"That many?" Martínez raised his eyebrows.

"But there won't be many interviews. Not with these people."

"Why not?" Martínez cocked his head to the side.

"Three are dead – they were very old and died soon after the census was finished. Two were common soldiers, who were moved to Havana before the murder of the governor's niece. Another is Sergeant Rafael Varela, who was transferred to Apalache several weeks ago."

"Varela? I know him. He seems so young."

"The man is only thirty two, now. He was eight years old in 1763." Dorado frowned. "An unlikely murderer, obviously!"

"So, we can forget about Varela and the two soldiers."

"Then, there's Don Ricardo, whose name appears on both lists."

"Of course, our unfortunate friend, Ricardo. As if he would limp out to the woods to murder the governor's niece. Never mind his devotion to Zéspedes, with his dread of snakes, Ricardo wouldn't have gone near the woods. Not for a pot of gold!"

"Eight names are left. Most of them seem unlikely, too."

"I don't suppose the commandant's name is among them?"

"No. He was in Madrid in 1763, in Havana only from 1772 to 1774 and, then, in Santo Domingo until his appointment in Florida. I found his service record in Don Ricardo's files."

"Well, then, who are the others?" Martínez motioned with his hand as if waving them toward him with a wand.

"Yes, sir. One is blind, old José González. Another is the invalid, Enríquez Zorrilla, who is bedridden. His wife, Isabella, is also on the lists. Then, there are the elderly Sierra sisters as well as Olga Gallego. Finally, there is Jesse Fish and you."

"Ah! Of course, I'm among the eight left." Martínez smiled. "Well, Lieutenant, when do you want to interview me?"

"I'm not going to interview you and you know it."

"Why not, Lieutenant? I've been everywhere the killings have been committed and at the same times they occurred. And, don't forget, I almost choked María Valdez to death. She had finger and thumb marks on her throat like Gloria Márquez García y Morera."

Dorado smiled, seeing Martínez stretch his hands toward him as if to be manacled.

"It's time to confess," Martínez said in a shrill voice. "I'm sorry, sir, but I couldn't stop myself from killing them. They were much too beautiful to live."

"I'll call the guards in a moment." Dorado laughed. "But, before I do, you villain, you should know your punishment."

"Oh, sir, what will it be?" Martínez bowed his head and pressed his hands together. He looked like a child begging for sweets.

"You will be brought before the governor in a dark dungeon – that is, after he has eaten one of his wife's dinners spiced with garlic."

"Oh, no, not that! Anything but that!"

They both laughed for a few seconds. Martínez continued to snicker as he looked across the table at Dorado. He shook his finger playfully at the young man.

"Well said, Dorado." He grinned. "You're getting much too clever for your own good. So, where does that leave us?"

"Jesse Fish."

"Fish's name keeps coming up, doesn't it? I hear he's seriously ill. They say he spends most of his time in bed. Apparently, all he does is write petitions to the king. He hopes to get Spanish titles to all the lands he holds. What a futile effort."

"Do we dare interview him?"

"I don't know." Martínez shook his head. "We can expect the governor's anger, if we talk to him without his permission."

"What if we named Fish as the murderer – after he was dead?"

"Zéspedes wouldn't like that either. But, dead or alive, the governor would prefer an Englishman to be the murderer rather than some Spaniard. We must take the risk and talk to him as soon as possible."

Dorado rubbed his cold hands together and stamped his feet on the deck as he watched the sun rise up from the sea. Fish had not been interviewed after all. The old Englishman had been too sick to visit. It was said he went in and out of comas and talked incoherently most of the time. His death was expected any day.

Unable to interview Jesse Fish, Dorado did not know what to do. He wished Ruiz de León were there to give him advice. He already had done all that seemed sensible. He had spent God knows how many hours looking through the army service records and land registers in Ruiz de León's office, all to no avail. What Dorado needed was in the Building of Records in Havana, two weeks at the least away by ship's mail.

Without any ideas of what to do next, Dorado was so dejected he did not even enjoy the sunrise in the eastern sky. Dawn was his favorite time of day. But, on that morning, without sleep or hope for success in the murder investigation, Dorado looked with little interest at the rising sun and the blue and green colors it made of the sea.

Dorado shifted the blanket around his shoulders and shoved his hands into his pockets. He heard a neighbor's rooster crowing in the early daylight and suddenly the murderer's name was on his lips. Dorado now knew everything. It was as if the rooster's cry had awakened his mind to the truth. He knew who had killed the governor's niece and all the other young girls. Dorado always had known, though he never admitted it to himself.

The murderer was Carlos Martínez. So many signs pointed to him, so much connected him to the killings. Dorado listed the facts that now flooded his mind. He counted them out on his fingers as the morning light brightened the sky and spread out over Santa Anastasia Island.

Carlos Martínez was the one man, still alive and strong, who had been everywhere the murders had been committed. He had said that himself, though in jest. No one else's life fit the schedule of killings so well with the exception of Jesse Fish, who, even if healthy, did not have the strength to strangle the governor's niece. Carlos Martínez, however, would have no such trouble choking the life out of anyone, even a strong man. With his huge hands, strangling a girl would be like snapping a twig in two. His recent throttling of María Valdez showed his strength as well as his inclination to strangle a woman in anger. Dorado could easily imagine the big man strangling a girl he believed had enticed him and then refused to bed with him.

That was why he murdered them. It was because of his pride. He had been rejected by the girls and could not stand the humiliation. "I hate being humiliated," Martínez had said. "It would surely infuriate me. If Gloria had made a fool of me, I would want to wring her neck as well." He had spoken vehemently at the time and there was anger in his voice.

Martínez was also the only man in the presidio who would have been old enough to kill the girl in 1763 and still strong enough to murder the governor's niece in 1788. There was no one else like him in St. Augustine. All the others, who were still alive and had lived earlier in town, were too feeble to paddle, ride or walk to the north woods, never mind murder anyone.

What made Dorado certain of his guilt was the memory that came into his mind when the rooster crowed. At that moment, he remembered Martínez had been the only physician in St. Augustine when most of the colony was abandoned. Martínez said he had been sent there in 1763, to help the old and sick move to Cuba. He arrived in August and stayed until January, 1764, when the last Floridians left the presidio. The other physicians had already sailed away. Their names, the ships they boarded and the dates of departure were included in the evacuation records Dorado had examined for so many hours. Martínez remained as the only physician in St. Augustine and what suddenly occurred to Dorado when the rooster crowed was that Elena Escobar Santana was murdered at that time. Yet, Martínez never mentioned the young girl's murder or her autopsy, which revealed the four knife wounds on her corpse. Even though the body was badly mauled, Martínez saw the wounds and cited them in his autopsy report. He stated the four wounds "appeared to be arranged in a peculiar pattern." Navarro wrote the phrase, but the words were Martínez'.

Dorado knew with certainty that Martínez had performed the autopsy on the dead girl in 1763. No other physician was in town to do it. He also now knew it was Martínez' smudged name on the autopsy report. The only capital initial, "C" or "L," visible on the report therefore had to be "C" for "Carlos" – Carlos Martínez.

"Martínez did the autopsy and Navarro took notes for him." Dorado spoke aloud with the realization. "Navarro served as his scribe in 1763 and I was his scribe in 1788. For each of the autopsies, he found some fool like me to help him. It was all part of his fiendish plan."

Dorado stood and looked out at the sunlit sea. "What was it he said about the murderer? Ah, yes, Martínez said, 'There's much thinking in the man's mind.' The arrogant murderer had the audacity to boast about how clever he was. Not only did Martínez murder and mutilate the girls, he did autopsies on them as well. What a fiend! What a clever fiend!"

For a second, Dorado found himself admiring the man's

mind, despite what he had done. Then, he was struck by the brutality of the murders. Martínez had killed innocent young girls whose lives had only just begun. As Esteban said in Havana, the girls had gone to him "like lambs to the slaughter." Martínez was an evil man contemptuous of everything and everyone.

"What arrogance!" Dorado said aloud. "He was certain no one would discover what he had done. What scorn he has for us all." Dorado then recalled his last conversation with Ruiz de León, the night before his death. The sick man made much the same criticism of his friend.

"I won't stay long tonight, Don Ricardo. You look tired."

"I am tired tonight. I don't know why. I certainly don't do much these days, yet it seems I am always tired. Everything seems to exhaust me."

"You've been through a long ordeal, Don Ricardo, and it will take time to feel strong again. As they say, 'Time heals everything, even the wounded spirit of a sad man.'"

"I wish it so. I'm anxious to get out of this house. I feel like a cooped-up chicken." Ruiz de León sighed wearily.

"Doctor Martínez says you're doing much better."

"Does he indeed? Carlos doesn't know everything, you know – not nearly as much as he thinks he does." Ruiz de León coughed.

Dorado said nothing. He could see Ruiz de León was in an ill humor. When the sick man felt tired or weak, he complained about everyone, although lately he criticized Martínez more than anyone else.

"Carlos isn't as clever as he thinks, though he's scornful of everyone else's intelligence – particularly our officials and priests. Who does he think he is? Sometimes, he even has the audacity to disparage Our Savior and the works of

His Church."

Dorado nodded.

"He does it endlessly! He ridicules the Church as a place for fools and foolish beliefs."

"I've heard him say that myself."

"He's forever saying it. Have you also heard his comments on the crucifixion?"

"No, sir." Dorado saw the intensity of his eyes as Ruiz de León spoke.

"He scorns the use of the crucifix in our Catholic practice. What is it he says? Oh, yes, I remember it all too well. He says, 'The Church has its gullible people praying to a crucified statue, instead of God himself. The crucifix is everywhere – on the church alters, at the end of people's rosaries and even around their necks. If Christ had been hanged, I assume Catholics now would be praying to a statue with a noose around its neck.'" Ruiz de León shook a finger as if in warning. "One day, Carlos will regret such blasphemy. You can be certain of it!"

"Dios mío! Is that what he said?" Dorado's eyes widened.

"Yes. That's the kind of contempt Carlos has for the Church and you can be sure he'll pay for it, when the time comes."

Ruiz de León leaned back in his chair, spent from expressing himself so forcefully. He put his head on the pillow behind his head and briefly closed his eyes. When he opened them, Dorado was getting up to go.

"I should leave and let you sleep, Don Ricardo."

Ruiz de León nodded in agreement. He took a breath of air and expelled it slowly. It was still painful for him to breathe.

"I'll see you tomorrow." Dorado stood facing Ruiz de León.

"Before you leave, Lieutenant, I want to say that no matter how I criticize Carlos, I am very fond of him. He has been a very good friend. He is intelligent – probably, too intelligent for his own good. What annoys me is his arrogant assumption that he knows more than anyone else. You know what I mean, don't you, Dorado?"

"Yes, I do. At times, he has made me feel small."

"I'm not surprised. You should play chess with him and show him your superiority. It will do him good to see he doesn't know everything. I'd like to play you myself, but, for now, I can't concentrate long enough to give you a decent game."

"I'm sure you will soon."

"We'll see," said Ruiz de León, closing his eyes again. He was sound asleep by the time Dorado had reached the door.

Dorado's throat tightened as he thought about Ruiz de León. He wished he had told his friend how much he meant to him, but unfortunately it was now too late. He sighed and looked at the sunrise, now spreading its bright orange light over the land and sea.

Dorado thought about Martínez' vociferous contempt for the crucifixion. Besides being blasphemous, what he said mocked the significance of the crucifix and made it look ridiculous. "So, that explains the cross he cuts on his victims," Dorado said aloud. "That's it! He shows his contempt for the crucifixion by cutting a cross on their corpses. That's what he does."

Dorado stood, certain he had discovered it all. He knew the murderer and how and why he had killed his victims. He also now knew what to do next. Governor Zéspedes needed to be notified and then Martínez would be arrested. It would be all over in a few hours.

Dorado shut the door to the balcony and started down the

stairway. It was still dark in the house and he lit an oil lamp to look at his pocket watch. He sighed impatiently, seeing the time. It was only seven o'clock.

Zéspedes would not see him until eight-thirty. Although the governor entered his office an hour earlier every morning, he would see no one until he had eaten his breakfast. Sergeant Suárez served him his food, while he signed the necessary documents of the day. With time to spare, Dorado decided to write all his thoughts down on a piece of paper. He could refer to it if necessary as he made his report to the governor.

Holding the lamp in his hand, Dorado looked for the quill and pot of ink. He went over to the table near the window where Ruiz de León kept them, but they were not there. He was about to look around the room when he remembered bringing them to him in his bedroom the night before he died. Ruiz de León requested the pot of ink and quill as Dorado helped him into bed. He also brought him several sheets of paper.

Ruiz de León said he wanted to write a letter before going to sleep. Since his illness, he often wrote letters and reports in bed. He would sit up with his back against the headboard of his bed and use his chessboard as a writing table in his lap. Ruiz de León always inserted a few sheets of paper beneath his writing to make sure his cherry and oak wood chessboard was not spotted from ink or scratched. When not in use, he kept the chessboard covered with a pillow case and leaned it against his bedside chest.

Dorado saw the feathered end of the quill as soon as he entered the bedroom. It lay on top of the bedside chest, where Ruiz de León kept his stockings and underclothes. The pot of ink stood beside it and a piece of ink-stained paper was folded under the pot. Dorado noticed that the upper drawer of the chest was partially open and, looking down into the drawer, he saw the wooden box containing Ruiz de León's chess pieces. The meticulous man kept the box on the right side of the drawer beside rolled stockings, arranged in uniform rows. Folded underwear was stacked on the left side of the drawer along with handkerchiefs.

Dorado took out the box. It was something he had done many times during his visits to the house. Ruiz de León would send him to fetch the chess board and pieces, while he sat in his chair by the fireplace. They had played chess twice a week before Dorado went to Havana, but only once following his return to St. Augustine. He smiled, recalling that the sick man, though tired and weak, still managed to win their game within an hour.

He sat on the edge of the bed and ran his hand over the polished box. It had been made from oak and its rounded top was smooth to the touch. Out of habit, Dorado opened the box and looked at the chess pieces. The box was partitioned into two compartments; one held the light oak pieces, the other the dark cherry pieces. He took the dark queen from the box and turned it in his fingers. Dorado sighed, remembering how Ruiz de León had used the queen in their last game to corner his king. Seeing checkmate only a few moves ahead, he had resigned. Tears filled his eyes as he thought of the man who had meant so much to him.

Dorado reached over to return the queen to the box, but paused as he was about to place it on the other pieces. He saw a piece of white paper in the side containing the dark chessmen. It had been placed beneath the chess pieces and was barely visible. He almost missed seeing the paper since it had been folded into a small square with only one edge showing.

Carefully removing the remaining dark chessmen from the box, Dorado laid them on the mattress alongside the queen. Then, with his thumb and forefinger, he withdrew the folded piece of paper and opened it. It was a note written by Ruiz de León. He apparently had placed it in the box shortly before his death, perhaps the very night he died. The short note, written in Ruiz de León's flowery penmanship, was addressed to him.

Roberto Dorado Delgado y Estrada,
  Look beneath the woven rug that runs between the bed and the wall. In the corner, near the window, there is a safe box hidden beneath the floorboards. Everything in it is yours.
                                          Ricardo Ruiz de León

Dorado went to the window and kneeled on the floor. He rolled up the bedside rug and ran his fingers along the floor looking for loose boards. The floor felt smooth to his touch and all the boards looked to be firmly in place. Then, he saw a crevice beside one of the boards and when his eyes trailed the crevice to the wall, he found a thumb-sized indentation in one of the boards. The indentation was located at the base of the wall beneath the window sill. Dorado put his forefinger in the indentation and lifted the board. It came up easily and three adjacent boards were loosened at the same time. The boards had been sawed into different lengths and fit so tightly in the floor that no one would have known a compartment was built beneath them.

The compartment was two feet long and a foot and a half wide. The old carpenter, who renovated Ruiz de León's house, designed it to fit between two of the joists that supported the bedroom floor. He nailed two boards to the underside of the joists to make a strong bottom for the compartment.

Dorado saw the wooden chest as soon as he lifted the first board up from the floor. Its size was apparent when the other loose boards were moved aside. Dorado immediately noticed that the chest was hinged to open from the top, but the lock, though unfastened, could not be reached from above. The chest had been made to fit snugly into the compartment with only an inch of space to spare on the sides. Since the hasp was below the floor and out of the grasp of even a child's little fingers, the chest had to be brought out of the compartment to be opened. Brass handles on both ends allowed the wooden chest to be hefted out of its hiding place, but it was very heavy as Dorado discovered when he tried to pick it up.

Leaning over, Dorado wrestled with the chest for more than a minute before bringing it up from below. He initially lifted it onto the floor and then heaved it up on the bed. Impatient to see inside, Dorado quickly wrenched the lock off and pushed up the top. A drawstring purse was the first thing he saw. It held seven two-escudo gold coins (each worth about $750 today) and twenty silver coins of varying weight and value. Knowing Ruiz de León's limited funds, Dorado was surprised to see so much money in the purse.

A pile of loose papers lay beneath the bag of coins. Dorado perused them quickly. He saw the deed to the house, Ruiz de León's commission as Lieutenant, his promotion papers for the rank of Captain, an army service award and an old will. Dorado knew his more recent will was held by the governor. The signed certificate of his promotion to the rank of Major lay on top of the pile. Dorado did not read any of the personal papers. He was much more interested in what was beneath the stack of papers.

A thin piece of wood, which served as a cover, separated the upper section of the chest from what was stored below. The cover had a finger hole in the center, which Dorado used to remove it from the chest. In the lower compartment, he saw a white envelope with his name written on it and the other things that made the box so heavy.

Dorado gasped when he initially saw what was in the bottom of the box. He knew then there was no need to wait to see the governor. He would go get Carlos Martínez, at once. The time had finally come to end the investigation.

Martínez was not home that morning. Dorado knocked repeatedly on his door without any reply. He waited at the door for a minute more and then went around the house looking in all the windows. There was no sign of anyone inside the house. Dorado returned to the front door, wondering if Martínez had already left for his office. As Dorado stood there trying to decide what to do, a man shouted to him from across the street.

"He's not home. He's with his woman." The man's bearded face appeared briefly and then was gone, back into the warmth of his house.

Dorado turned away and trotted to the house of María Valdez. He knocked loudly on the door, but again there was no response. Dorado was about to go around the house and look in the windows, when he heard María's muffled voice above him. He looked up and saw her face at a window on the second floor.

"Dorado!" Wrapped in a white blanket, María Valdez opened the window and leaned out to speak to him. "What do you want?" She scowled at him. "For God's sake, what are you doing here at this hour?" She held the blanket tightly about her breasts.

"I'm looking for Captain Martinez." With a hand, Dorado shielded his eyes from the glare of the first light of the morning.

"Que pasó?" Martínez appeared beside María, his hairy chest exposed in the window.

"I must talk to you. It's important!"

"It better be! I'll be down in a moment."

Hands in his pockets, Dorado paced back and forth in front of the house while he waited for Martínez. He heard angry voices and the banging of a door inside. A few moments later, Martínez emerged from the house, pushing his shirt down into his breeches. He put on his coat after slamming the front door. "Damned women," he muttered, looking back at the house.

As Dorado had planned it, they walked to the seawall to talk. It was only a block away and at that time of day no one would be walking along the wall to interrupt their conversation.

Without surf and at low tide, the bay seemed unusually serene in the first light of day. It was a time of stillness that comes with the ebb tide. And, except for the squawks of the seabirds, the day arrived quietly, without even a whisper of wind in the trees.

No one was about that Dorado could see, except for one sentry standing on the seawall near the plaza. Followed by Martínez, he walked a few steps to where recently cut stones were piled up to repair the wall. He chose a place where a large block stood away from the wall and could be used as a seat. Dorado turned to Martínez, offering it to him.

Martínez shook his head and leaned against the wall facing Dorado. "Well, what's this all about? "He propped a big foot on a fallen block in the path.

"This will tell you." Dorado handed him the envelope. "I found it in his safe box."

Martínez gave Dorado a penetrating look before removing the letter from the envelope and unfolding it. His face lost its color after reading the first paragraph. Again, he looked at Dorado, a frown fixed between his eyes. His big hands shook as he read the rest of the letter. When Martínez finished reading, he turned and stared out to sea.

"So, now you know it all." His back to Dorado, he spoke softly in almost a whisper.

"Yes, but I wish I didn't." Dorado stood and stared

hard at Martínez.

Martínez nodded and handed the letter back to him. They stood in silence for several seconds, looking into each other's eyes. Then, Martínez shook his head and said softly, "I'm ready now. Let's go." Without another word, they walked side by side to Government House.

CHAPTER SIXTEEN

JANUARY 27 - FEBRUARY 27, 1789

The governor looked ill. His pale face was immobile and his mouth hung loosely open as if he had suffered a sudden stroke. His hands hung down at his sides, seemingly of no use to him. Zéspedes stared at the two men in front of him without seeing them.

"I can't believe it," he mumbled in a low voice.

"It's a shock to us, too, Don Vicente. Show him the letter, Lieutenant."

"No." The governor waved it away with a limp hand. "I don't want to see it. You read it, Lieutenant."

"Yes, sir." Dorado read the letter quickly. He kept his eyes on it the entire time, never looking up at his listeners.

My Dear Dorado,

This letter is so very hard to write. God knows, I don't want to write it. I have put it off time and time again, but, now, it must be done. I know there is little time left for me, so I must say what has to be said. Que Dios me ayude (God help me)! I am the one, the man you want.

I wanted to tell you much sooner, but I knew it would change everything. So, I've kept silent all this time. I wasn't willing to lose what existed between us. You have meant so much to me, more than even a son! I would never have lasted through this illness without you. But now the end of my life is near. I know it. God has told me it is my time to go.

It is also my time to tell you all. You would have found it out in time, anyway. Sooner or later, one of the innumerable reports in the Building of Records would have pointed to me. It was inevitable. You are too intelligent to be fooled much longer. It's so ironic. You were initially assigned to the investigation because I never thought you would find out about me. I misjudged you at first, but, now, I know you would have found me out after all. I could see the end coming and there was nothing I could do to stop it.

I couldn't stop what had to be done either. They all deserved it – you know that! They were putas, every one of them, always flirting, teasing and tempting. They make fools of men and don't deserve to live! You said so yourself, when you learned what that little whore Gloria was doing here in town. You know how they are – they are all whores at heart.

They thought they were so clever. Oh yes, they thought they could use me to get what they wanted. They only wanted to use me for their own purposes. They expected me to serve them – to do their selfish bidding like an obedient servant. I was to do whatever they wanted, no matter the difficulty. They wanted promotions and special awards and assignments for their fathers and fiancés. They wanted costly clothing, jewels and pesetas. That's what those putas wanted. That little whore Gloria wanted me to help as she schemed to marry the commandant. She expected me to influence the governor to that end. Like all the others, she only thought of herself and

what I could do for her. They didn't want me. None of them!
No, the putas only wanted me for what I could do for them.

They schemed to use me and that's how God delivered
them into my hands. All I had to do was to agree to help
them in their preposterous plots and they did everything
I told them. It was easy to get them to come alone to my secret places. I promised to help them and they, in turn, promised not to tell anyone of our rendezvous. They came to me
full of glee, certain that everything they wanted was free for
the asking. They expected me to help them for only a pat on
the hand, a polite thank you or a smile from a pretty face.
What foolish girls!

They think men are stupid and will do anything they want
for a flutter of an eyelash or a modest smile. The devil has
taught them all too well. They are all the daughters of Eve
and they do the devil's work, deceiving men with their wom-
en's wiles. They think they can tempt and tease us and get
anything they want. I have seen them do it all my life. You
know what I mean, I'm sure. They never think about paying
the piper.

Smiling Gloria came to me because she expected my help
with her marriage scheme. She came out to the woods exactly as I instructed her. She even boasted how well she could
paddle a canoe. It was an amusing game to her. How she
laughed when I told her to wear the monk's habit when she
left Government House.

It was the same with the Hernández Parral girl. She
laughed, too. I don't know what happened to that one. She
was left in the same spot as the others, but somehow disappeared. Only her canoe was found. It was the opposite with
little Elena. She was later found, but not her canoe. I don't
know what happened to it. All the canoes were pushed out
into the current. I had to wade out into the river to do it.

There is not much else to say. What lies below this letter
will tell you what you want to know. I'm sure there is more

you would like to know, but I don't feel like writing anything else now. The details do not matter anyway.

Some will say I am mad, but you know me better, Dorado. You have known me well, even if only for a short time. Many are the moments I have wished we might have known each other longer or in another place or time. However, sad to say, such wishes were not those God willed to be, so I must be satisfied with the time we had together these last few months.

I want you to have my house, Dorado. That is important to me and I have requested the governor to execute my will to that end. The coins in the safe box are also for you.

I am too tired to write any more. As usual these days, everything takes so much out of me, even this letter to you. I now dread the effort of removing the box from beneath the floor. It will take every bit of strength I have left tonight. Gracias a Dios, I won't feel this exhaustion and weakness much longer.

It all will be over soon. I am at peace now. What is done is done. God knows why! I will die knowing I have done His Service and left His Signs for all to see.

May God's Goodness guide you throughout your life,
Ricardo Ruiz de León

Dorado looked up when he finished reading the letter. He saw the governor leaning forward, his head held in his hands. His face looked sickly white.

"What else was in the chest?" The governor looked at Dorado with watery eyes.

"There were five pairs of women's shoes, sir, and four sets of women's underclothing tied with red ribbon."

"I suppose the shoes tell us there were five murders." Zéspedes exhaled loudly.

"Sí, señor."

"Why, then, only four sets of underclothing?"

"I think he forgot one set in the woods – Gloria's underclothing." Martínez spoke in a soft voice. "Following the murder of your niece, her clothing was found in a folded pile near the river. He apparently forgot to pick up the pile after pulling her body under the palmetto."

"I see." The governor sighed loudly again.

"We also think he dragged her corpse there to get it out of sight from the river. Since it was heavy for him, with his bad leg, he dragged it by the bodice and ..."

"I don't need to know any more details, Carlos." Zéspedes spoke sharply. "That's more than enough information."

"Yes, sir."

"I can't believe it." The governor shook his head from side to side. "How could he do it? How could he do this to me?"

There was a long silence as Zéspedes stared into the fireplace. A fire, started earlier by Sergeant Suárez, still burned and warmed the room. Martínez and Dorado exchanged glances as time passed, but neither of them spoke.

"Well, what's to be done?" Zéspedes shook his head. "What do I say to the community? Madre de Dios! What can I say? What can I possibly say?"

"Don Vicente ..." Martínez was stopped by the governor's command.

"Wait!" Zéspedes held out his hand. "Let me see the letter."

"Yes, sir." Dorado handed it over to the governor.

Zéspedes read the letter slowly. He read it without any expression on his face. A tiny twitch of a jaw muscle was the only sign of his mood. When the governor finished reading, he laid the letter on his desk and covered it with the palm of his hand. He looked back and forth at the two men sitting in front of him.

"I know what must be done now." He spoke with certainty. "I'll tell you both, but what I have decided will be final." He pointed a trembling finger at them. "I don't want to hear any suggestions or differences of opinion. None! Do you hear me?"

"Yes, sir." Dorado answered immediately.

"This is not a staff meeting where I ask for recommendations. Is that clear, Carlos?"

"Sí, Don Vicente."

"The community cannot be told the name of the murderer. No, never! It would weaken our standing here and I won't let that happen. With all the foreigners living here, our position in the presidio is already precarious. Who knows what would happen if the community found out the governor's aide was the murderer? They'll never be told such a thing. No!" His eyes narrowed and he spoke slowly, emphasizing each word he uttered. "You will say nothing about it to anyone! Nothing! Not one word to anyone. That's an order."

"Sir. What ..."

"Don't interrupt me, Lieutenant. Don't speak! Listen!"

"Sí, señor."

"You will be transferred from Florida as soon as possible. Both of you. I'll see to it that you are promoted for your service here in St. Augustine. But you will never reveal what you know to anyone, at any time! Is that understood? I want your pledge on it."

"Yes, sir." Dorado replied immediately, while Martínez nodded in agreement.

"I mean what I say. You'll tell no one! I'll make sure you are ruined if you ever dare mention it to anyone." The governor again pointed his finger at them. "I'm sure, Carlos, you know exactly what I mean."

"Yes, I do, Don Vicente."

"Good. Now, that we've settled that situation, the house must next be considered." He looked at Dorado. "I doubt you'll have any need of it when you assume your duties in Havana as Captain of the king's infantry."

"No, sir."

"Good. Then, the house will be sold and all proceeds, after the usual expenses, will be sent to you. I will make sure you get a good price for it."

"Gracias, señor."

"The money in his safe box also belongs to you as his letter says."

"Sir. What about ..."

"Don't mention his sister to me, Lieutenant! As I told you the other day, at her age, she has no need of anything."

"Sí, señor."

"Now, what else is left to do?" The governor tapped his fingers on the arm of his chair. "Oh, yes, Lieutenant, take whatever you want from his house. Everything left will be sold and the proceeds given to the Church."

Dorado nodded.

"Carlos, do you want any of his possessions?" Zéspedes looked over at Martínez and their tearful eyes met briefly.

"No, I don't want anything." The big man shook his head and wiped his eyes with the back of his hand. He sat slumped in his chair.

"I understand," said Zéspedes with a catch in his voice. He turned away, but could not hold back his tears. One fell on the folded letter lying on his desk.

No one spoke while the governor cleared his throat. He blew his nose and, with the end of his handkerchief, wiped his eyes. "Well, that should settle everything." He looked back and forth at the two men. "Nothing else needs to be said then – except, I remind you of your pledge to say nothing about what you know, no matter what you hear about it later. In time, I'll make a statement about the murder. You can be sure, it will end the investigation once and for all."

As Dorado stood to leave, he looked at the letter lying on the desk. Zéspedes saw him eye the letter as he rose from his chair. Now standing, he stared at the young officer.

"You don't need this letter, Lieutenant, do you? No! No one needs it, now."

The governor walked to the fireplace and leaned over to drop the letter on the burning logs. He stood with his left hand on the oak mantel, watching it burn. Zéspedes did not turn to look at the officers as the letter quickly turned to ash in the flames. "You are dismissed," he said, his back to them.

Dorado and Martínez silently watched the southern tip of Anastasia Island disappear from view. They were on deck of the schooner, *La Esperanza* sailing along the Florida coast, south of St. Augustine. The Spanish ship left the pier before sunrise, warily wended its way through the treacherous inlet on the tide and, now, in the dawn's light, sailed toward Cuba. It was the twenty-seventh of February, one month to the day of their meeting with the governor. It was a bitterly cold day with a cutting wind that blew across the deck. The two men huddled in the stern behind the ship's fresh water barrels. They sat bundled in heavy blankets brought up from below. Martínez had wrapped one of his wool blankets around his head and he looked like a hooded monk.

"Well, the governor kept his word." Dorado spoke loudly to be heard above the sound of sea roiling about them.

"Are you referring to our promotions? Or the transfers to Havana?" Martínez mumbled behind the blanket that covered his mouth.

"Neither. I'm referring to his pledge to end the murder investigation 'once and for all.'" Dorado shivered as the blanket slipped off his shoulders and he felt a cold draft on his neck.

"As I said, he's a practical man. He did what he had to do."

"I know, but I wish he had left me out of it. Why did he tell everyone in town I was the man who found the murderer? Dios mío! How could he lie like that?"

"He didn't lie. You did find the murderer, but not the one he named. Keep in mind, he had to explain your promotion as well as mine; he also had to explain our transfers to Havana."

Dorado frowned.

"'He killed two birds with one stone.' Well, that's an interesting choice of words." Martínez snickered. "The governor announced we found the murderer after a four month investigation and said we would be promoted for our effort. It makes sense, doesn't it?"

"Yes, but it's all based on a lie."

"That one lie settles everything. The investigation is over, the murderer's dead and the presidio is safe again. Most important, the governor's honor is restored and Spanish authority in St. Augustine is seen as strong once again. It's all ended – nice and neatly."

"I suppose so." Dorado made a face and sighed.

"Why the sour face? What's so bad about blaming a dead Mestizo for Gloria's murder, a thief, smuggler and a murderer at that? Don't forget, Dorado, Jiménez killed one of the men sent to arrest him. As you know it was Juan Solís – that stupid sentry who helped Gloria leave Government House and ultimately go to her death. Isn't that ironic?"

"It is, but I still don't like the way the investigation ended."

"Like it or not, it's best for all concerned. Tell me, would you have wanted Zéspedes to name Ricardo as the murderer? He and his family would be dishonored, forever. That, my young friend, is what the truth would do."

"I suppose so."

"The governor made a good decision, Dorado. You know, I've often criticized him in the past, but given these circumstances, he ended the investigation as best as it could be done."

"I guess so, but I still don't like it."

"I understand. But that's the way of the world, my friend.

Truth is too often the dutiful servant of men's needs – particularly in politics. The people are seldom told the truth; instead, they are told whatever some lying official decides to tell them. That's a lesson I had to learn when I was young, too. I didn't like it then myself."

"That's not a lesson I want to learn." Dorado held his hair down with one hand in a futile effort to keep it out of his eyes.

"Perhaps not, but there's no escaping it. You know, the way it ended didn't please me either. I didn't want to leave St. Augustine so soon, although it was a convenient way to leave María Valdez. She was making more and more demands and, in time, I'm sure she would have expected me to marry her. Still, I was quite content in that old town and wanted to stay until I reached sixty. Then, I would have gone home for good."

"So, that was your plan."

"Yes, and now, I don't know what I am going to do. I don't look forward to Havana, even with all the available women. There are too many stupid officials in the city."

"The governor couldn't be convinced to let you stay in St. Augustine?"

"No. Zéspedes didn't want me around. Seeing me would remind him of what happened and what I know, so, I had to go. That's why you were sent away as well. He wants no one in town who knows the truth."

"I suppose that's why the transfer papers were sent to Havana so fast." Dorado put his cold hand back beneath the blanket.

"That's what happened. Speaking of what happened, do you know how Ricardo went in and out of the woods without being seen?"

"Yes, I spoke to Suárez two days ago and discovered everything. We were reminiscing about Don Ricardo, so he had no idea I was questioning him. I steered our conversation to our last times spent with him and the explanation eventually came out of his memory."

"A clever approach." Martínez tightened the blanket around his neck.

Dorado smiled. "We were talking about Don Ricardo's kindness and Suárez recalled how helpful he had been to him on so many occasions. He remembered his help on the day of Gloria's disappearance, in particular. Doña Concepción was frantic when Gloria went missing and she sent Suárez in all directions looking for her. It was then in all the commotion, that Don Ricardo offered to take the wagon horse to the blacksmith to get a new shoe."

"That's right. I remember the sergeant told you the horse was sent over from the stables needing a new shoe. It had to be shoed that morning before the rubbish was carted away."

"Yes, Don Ricardo offered to take the horse, while on errands at the north end of town, near the blacksmith's stall. Suárez said it was 'so typically thoughtful of him.'"

"Dios mío! It was so simple. He took the horse for its shoe and, then, rode through the city gates to the woods. But what about the sentries? Why didn't they mention it to anyone?"

"Don Ricardo told the sentries he would be gone only long enough to test the new shoe. So, he went out to the woods and back without any notice. The sentries did report seeing Don Ricardo riding a horse out of town, but Suárez dismissed it as unimportant."

"Of course!" exclaimed Martínez. "Suárez couldn't imagine the governor's aide doing anything, but his duty. It's exactly as I said. Do you remember? A well-known man in such a small place can come and go without ever being noticed. So, Ricardo took the wagon horse to the blacksmith and then left town in plain sight through the main gates. After killing Gloria, he returned without any worry. I can even imagine him making small talk with the sentries as he rode through the gates. Ricardo got away with the murder because he was a prominent official, who would be considered above suspicion by everyone."

"It looks that way." Dorado adjusted the blanket around his ears. "Everything was so well planned and executed. However, there's one part of the plan that puzzles me. How would he have known the wagon horse needed a shoe when it was brought over from the stables? He would have had to know that with certainty for his scheme to succeed."

"He didn't have to know it. Tell me, what horse in town doesn't need a new shoe? With only two blacksmiths in town, most horses go far too long before they are shoed. So, he knew the wagon horse would need at least one new shoe. It was a clever scheme!"

"It surely was." Dorado winced as a gust of cold wind cut across his face. "I'll tell you something else I found out. I have Núñez and his son to thank for it."

"Oh, what did he tell you?"

"Núñez found me at Don Ricardo's house yesterday afternoon. I went there to pick up his chess set and his old copy of *Don Quixote*. That's all I wanted."

"I'm glad you took the chess set. That's what he would have wanted."

"Incidentally, while I was there in the house I looked in the hidden compartment. The safe box was empty. I assume the governor took the shoes and the underclothing."

"I'm sure he destroyed them. Did you get the coins?"

"Yes, the day after we talked to the governor."

"Good. Now, tell me about Núñez."

"He knew I was leaving and came to say adiós. We talked for awhile and he told me he was surprised to hear that José Jiménez was the murderer. Núñez said none of the fishermen he knew had ever seen Jiménez anywhere near the north woods, never mind at the site of the girl's murder. Núñez is not a fool and it was obvious he doubted the mestizo was the murderer."

"I'm sure there are others who doubt the governor's truth."

"Núñez also told me you questioned him the morning after the murder before I talked to him. He said you told him to say nothing about it to anyone. That's how you knew so much about the girl's body, isn't it?"

"Yes, Núñez described it in some detail." Martínez grinned. "You suspected I was the murderer, didn't you? Don't deny it!"

"No – Yes, I did. You seemed to know so much, but never said how you knew it. For example, how did you know I would find Gloria's clothing along the river? I also realized you were everywhere the murders occurred and at the same time. But what stayed in my mind was your oath that you would wring a woman's neck if you found her fooling you."

"I understand." Martínez pulled the blanket up under his chin. "Believe it or not, it was just a hunch that made me tell you to search for Gloria's clothing along the shore. But I would wring a woman's neck if she tried to play me for a fool." He stared into Dorado's eyes.

"I also wondered about your autopsy of Elena Escobar in 1763. I couldn't imagine how you could forget seeing the four knife wounds on the girl's body – which were mentioned in the report Navarro wrote for you."

"Well, strange as it seems, I have no memory of it. None! I certainly remember young Navarro; I can see him in my mind's eye this very moment. But, for the life of me, I can't recall doing the autopsy on that girl. Damn it!"

"Well, it doesn't matter, now."

"It does to me! Even if I'm getting older, I don't want to think I'm losing my memory. My member probably will be next to go."

Dorado smiled.

"Did Núñez say anything else?"

"He gave me this ..." Dorado reached down beneath the

blanket and fumbled around in his jacket pocket. He finally withdrew a small metal object and put it into Martínez' palm.

"Ah, it's a button from an officer's jacket," said Martínez. He could tell the button was brass, though badly tarnished. "One of the domed buttons used in the last decade."

"Núñez' son, Rafael, found it near where Gloria was murdered. They were fishing at the same spot this week and the boy saw it in the sand, near the river. Núñez brought the button to me and listen to what he said. I remember every word."

"'They say you're leaving tomorrow so I wanted to say adiós and give you this button. My boy found it three days ago where we first saw the governor's niece. I'm sure the button means nothing now that the investigation is over, but I brought it to you anyway. Rafael saw it in the sand, the sunlight made it shine.'"

"It's his, I suppose?" Martínez looked over at Dorado.

"From one of his uniform jackets. After Núñez left, I found the jacket with the missing button; it was hanging on a hook in the bedroom. I remember seeing something shine – it was near where I found Gloria's clothing, but I thought it was a seashell. I was in a hurry to leave before the rain and I didn't return to the spot in the following days. I forgot about it."

"So, it was there all the time. If you had found it, we would have known the murderer was an officer and it would have been easy to find him." Martínez paused as a wave splashed over the deck. "I suppose we were not meant to find it until now."

"I guess not. You know, I remember seeing Don Ricardo down on his hands and knees looking all over the ground. It was the day we found the canoe with the monk's habit in it. At the time, I thought he was searching for something I had missed. Now, I know he was looking for the button. I assume it was torn off in the struggle."

"Apparently. The loss of that button may have been the

only mistake he made in the murder." Martínez nodded. "Ricardo was thorough and his plan was almost perfect."

"What about the forgotten pile of underclothing?"

"Gloria's clothing never helped us. It couldn't give us his identity – like the button. We had no idea what it meant, until you found the other underclothing in his safe box."

"That's true. I'll tell you, when I first saw the shoes and underclothing in the box, I felt the hair on the back of my neck stand up. I was like a dog that sees a snake in the grass."

"I can well imagine it, my friend. You saw what you didn't want to see in his safe box. It was a snake in the grass."

"I'll never forget it."

"I'm sure you won't, Dorado. Now, I'll tell you something I won't forget either. It took me a while to figure it out. Ricardo didn't die of the plague. He was sick, but not sick enough to die. Actually, he was improving and, after you arrived, he looked better every day."

"He looked better to me, too. That's why I was so surprised when he died suddenly."

"I think Ricardo died because he lost the will to live. It happened soon after the report of 1763 arrived here. He could see the investigation closing in on him; his letter said as much. Ricardo knew Caminero de Castilla's account of 1777 would eventually follow and he feared it would expose him to us. Knowing the report was fifty pages long, I understand his worry."

"Yet, it told us no more than we already knew from Caminero de Castilla."

"It didn't help, but no one knew it at the time. All of us, including Ricardo, thought the report would give us what was needed to identify the murderer. It was what we all expected and what we told the governor. So, Ricardo naturally feared its arrival. I think his fear of the report and one other thing brought about his death."

"What was that?" Dorado again brushed the hair from his eyes.

"I think Ricardo lost the will to live because of his fondness for you. He didn't want to face you when you discovered he was the murderer. He cared too much for you to allow that to happen. He thought of you as a son – I'm sure of it."

"That's what the governor told me."

"It's true, his last letter said so. He let the illness take him rather than have you see him as the murderer – the diablo we all condemned."

Martínez sighed and the flesh in his cheeks seemed to droop as he exhaled. He looked much older as if a future portrait of the man had been placed like a mask over his face.

"What you say makes sense, though I didn't know such a thing could happen to a man. I wondered why he died so quickly, when he looked so much better."

Martínez nodded. "It happens often, especially for sick people in insufferable pain. All in all, it was probably the best way for him to die."

"I suppose so." Dorado shook his head. "You know, I still don't really understand why he did what he did. Do you?"

"No. Ricardo's letter said the girls teased and tempted him, but that's surely not reason enough to murder them. If Spanish men murdered all the girls who teased or flirted with them, there would be damn few women in Spain or the colonies."

"It's hard to believe all the girls flirted with him. I can imagine Gloria teasing him; that might explain the laughter the Indian boy heard from his canoe when he saw them together on the shore. But what about Carlota Ramírez Cruz? She was to be married in three months. Can you imagine her flirting with him at that time? And, what about Elena Escobar, the dull witted girl in 1763 – what would she know about teasing or tempting?"

Martínez nodded. "No, his reasons make no sense. I've thought about them for days. What surprises me most of all is that none of the girls came from a prominent or titled family, not even Gloria whose father was a Cuban Criollo (creole). So, why would he approach such common girls? You know how important titles and family names were to Ricardo."

"I suppose we'll never know the answers to such questions. At least we know what really happened, which is more than anyone else knows. Do you intend to keep silent about the story the governor has told in St. Augustine?"

Martínez shrugged. "The pledge he demanded of us means little to me, but I have no need to talk about his deception." He sighed. "Or the sad truth about our friend Ricardo. Of course, I'll tell Esteban about it over a bottle of wine. Knowing what he has seen in Havana, it won't surprise him at all. What about you?"

"What's done is done. The governor's story will be believed by the crown's officials in Havana and Madrid, no matter what I might say about it. So, there's no good reason to tell the truth and risk my future in the king's army. I also hesitate to say anything that would dishonor Don Ricardo and his family in Spain. 'Let sleeping dogs lie,' isn't that the old adage?"

"That's sensible thinking. Good for you, Dorado."

"Of course, I'll tell my brother. I also am obliged to tell Caminero de Castilla the truth. Without his help, I doubt we would have known so much about the other murders Above all, he made us aware of the cut of the cross on all the victims, including the governor's niece. He deserves to know about the end of the investigation and the death of the murderer. By the way, do you know what they are now saying in town about it?"

"No." Martínez studied the man beside him.

"They say Don Ricardo's sudden and unexpected death shows the curse is still alive."

"The so-called Curse of St. Augustine?"

"Yes, it's blamed for his death as well as the madness that made Jiménez murder Gloria, the Englishman and Solís."

"What ignorance!" Martínez shook his head. "But, I suppose it's to be expected, after what they've been told. In time, they may yet know what happened. Keep in mind, the rumors haven't even started. It's only been a month since they were told Jiménez was the murderer."

"And, almost five months since Gloria was killed. It's the twenty seventh, isn't it?"

"Yes. The investigation lasted a long time. Much longer than I thought it would."

Dorado nodded. "Much longer than anyone thought. Of course, it was delayed by the discovery of the earlier murders in Cuba. Incidentally, I met Olga Gallego on my way to the pier this morning. She was going to early Mass. When I spoke to her, she didn't recognize me. In fact, she rushed away as if I might hurt her. Her memory must be gone, now."

"I'm not surprised. It will happen to us all if we live long enough. One day, you can recall every woman you ever bedded, the next day, you can't remember your own name."

Dorado chuckled. "Can you imagine what would have happened if Olga Gallego had not remembered the murder of 1770?"

"I can easily imagine it." He stared into Dorado's eyes. "Yes, and it makes me wonder if we would be better or worse off without the old woman's memory?"

"What do you mean?" Dorado looked intently at Martínez.

"Without it we wouldn't know the identity of the murderer or the names of his victims, but, also without it, Ricardo, God forgive him, might still be alive and we wouldn't be on our way to the official-hell of Havana. However, with or without the old woman's memory, the dead mestizo, a murderer himself, still would be blamed for killing the governor's niece."

EPILOGUE

A week later, Dorado and Martínez arrived in Havana. They learned of the king's death as their ship docked. The announcement had been sent to Florida, four days earlier, carried by a courier aboard the same ship that brought the new army physician to St. Augustine.

Once in Havana, Dorado spent a fortnight with his brother, Miguel. He then rode south to Santiago de las Vegas to tell Caminero de Castilla the results of the investigation. Dorado served three years in Havana and then was sent to Puerto Rico, where he became aide to the commandant. A month after his transfer to Cuba, Serena Rodríguez returned to Havana to be with him. They were married three years later, following his mother's death. Dorado served with distinction in Spain's war against Napoleon and, in 1812, he was promoted to colonel.

Carlos Martínez spent only eight months in Havana. He retired from the king's service and sailed to Spain to practice medicine in Cádiz, the city of his birth. Martínez and Dorado met again during the Napoleonic war, when the Spanish army defended Cádiz and forced the French to give up their siege of the city. Later, in a letter to Esteban Morales Muñoz, Martínez said he intended to marry a much younger woman, who would surely make him miserable.

Jesse Fish survived his illness and lived an additional year to the age of sixty-six. He continued to write futile petitions to the king until the day he died. Buried in February, 1790, his grave at El Vergel was dug up and desecrated by robbers looking for his rumored wealth.

Vicente Manuel de Zéspedes y Velasco retired from the Florida governorship in 1790. His health deteriorated following the death of Ruiz de León and he departed St. Augustine a sick and morose man. He lived the last four years of his life in Havana.

Dear Reader,

If you enjoyed this book, please consider posting a short review on Amazon, or wherever your purchased this book. Reviews help all authors a great deal, helping us to continue writing new books for your enjoyment. Thank you for your interest and support!

Robert L. Gold

ABOUT THE AUTHOR
ROBERT L. GOLD

Robert L. Gold is a Professor Emeritus of History, an entertaining speaker and a prolific writer. He has contributed articles and reviews to many magazines and newspapers in the southeast and especially in Florida, where he has lived for more than thirty years. In St. Augustine, he has written the popular newspaper column, *Essays from El Dorado*, a script for sightseeing train guides and *The Story of St. Augustine*, a brief history of the city given to millions of visiting tourists.

Extensive research in English, French and Spanish history and his book, *Borderland Empires in Transition*, have provided the historical basis for his current project, a trilogy of colonial murder mysteries: *Dead to Rights*, set in Savannah, this book, *Cut of the Cross*, set in St. Augustine, and *Dead and Gone*, set in New Orleans – scheduled for publication in late 2016 by Marcinson Press. In addition to the suspenseful mysteries, the trilogy offers readers a penetrating look into the cultural and political life of colonial America in the eighteenth century. Each of the novels therefore reveals the colonists' everyday struggle for survival, their search for meaning in the world and the simplicity and shortness of their lives. The series also offers a graphic view of the lush and virtually undisturbed landscape that once existed in what is now the southeastern United States.

The author has enjoyed a long professional career in Florida. He has served as state historian in St. Augustine, professor of Latin American history at the University of South Florida and executive director of the Historic St. Augustine Preservation Board. Dr. Gold also has been a speaker for the Florida Humanities Council, giving presentations entitled, "Characters and Crooks in Florida History." A bit of a character himself, he continues to offer those talks throughout North Florida.

Robert Gold lives in Jacksonville, Florida with his wife, LaDonna Morris, and, Baxter, his five-year-old Airedale Terrier. A devoted dog servant, he confesses to being led by the nose of the furry-faced beast, walking him at least six miles a week and spoiling him rotten.

Author's Comments

Dr. Robert L. Gold

Cut of the Cross is a murder mystery set in the Spanish city of St. Augustine in the late eighteenth century. The historic city, now more than 400 years old, was less than half its age in 1788 when the story takes place. At the time, Spain had resumed its rule of the colony after twenty years of English occupation and the division of its territory into two separate colonies, East and West Florida. Spain lost Florida in 1763 after the Seven Years' War and then, in 1783, regained the colony following the American Revolutionary War.

Since the story is set in St. Augustine following the return of Spanish authority, the plot involves the first Spanish governor of Spanish East Florida, Vicente Manuel de Zéspedes y Velasco. The governor is a major character in the book, but except for a brief history of his military career, all his activities described in the mystery are fictional. The same is true for the army engineer, Mariano de la Rocque, as well as the Englishman Jesse Fish, who was a prosperous orange grower and property owner in Spanish Florida.

Fish, in fact, lived in St. Augustine for more than a half-century. He arrived in the 1730s, remained in the city through the British Period and survived into the first years of the Second Spanish Period. Born in the second decade of the century, Jesse Fish was in his late sixties when he died in 1790. Since Protestants were not permitted to be interred in the Catholic presidio, he was buried near his house on Santa Anastasia Island. Sometime later, grave robbers desecrated Fish's sepulcher, searching for the money they believed was buried with him.

Although an attempt has been made to describe the late eighteenth-century city and its surroundings accurately, other descriptive details in the novel are fictitious. For example, Government House was not nearly as elaborate as the murder mystery describes it. The governor's well-appointed office on the first floor and his spacious living quarters on the second floor are embellished to suggest a more luxurious lifestyle than governors of that time ever enjoyed. The quality of the food and wine at that time is also exaggerated.

In addition, there were few, if any, Franciscans living in St. Augustine in the 1780s. The Franciscans left the colony in 1763-64 and their monastery was used as an army barracks in the British Period. Contaminated by such abuse, the Catholic Church never employed the building for any religious purpose again.

The office of medical examiner held by Carlos Martínez in St. Augustine did not exist in the eighteenth century. It would be more than a century before trained physicians studied the dead and performed autopsies in Spain or its former colonies in America. The official position of presidio physician occupied by Esteban Morales Muñoz in Havana is likewise invented.

Like St. Augustine, the late eighteenth-century port-city of Havana has been described as accurately as possible. Most of the historic fortifications still exist and the old city itself still retains many features and structures from the past. But the Building of Records and the medical facilities of the presidio physician, both fictitious, are not among them. The three-story mansion of the Morales Muñoz family is also fictional, although the Alameda de Paula on which the house supposedly stood is the oldest boulevard in Havana.

What is not fictional or anachronistic at the time is the xenophobia often expressed by the characters in St. Augustine. First and foremost, Protestants, whatever their origin, were everywhere vilified. Spaniards also commonly condemned the English and French and, in Florida, the Minorcans. Their obsession with limpieza de sangre (pure blood) ultimately affected everyone in Spain as well as the Spanish Empire in America. In Spain, sixteenth-century laws were promulgated requiring Spaniards to demonstrate their ancestry was not tainted by Jewish or Muslim blood. In America, the Spaniards established a caste system that included Africans, Indians, Mulattos and other mixed people and they even regarded Criollos, Spaniards born in the colonies, as inferiors. The Peninsulares, Spaniards born in Spain and claiming limpieza de sangre, held the important positions in the administration of the empire and kept the Criollos in a secondary status. That status, and the many social and economic limitations that accompanied it, infuriated the Criollos and became one of the motivations leading to the Wars of Independence and the end of the Spanish Empire in America.

PREVIEW
BOOK THREE:
DEAD AND GONE

CHAPTER ONE

NEW ORLEANS: AUGUST 15-30, 1799

Even in the night air, the man was soaked in sweat by the time he paddled the pirogue to the stern of *La Bonne Chance* (Good Fortune). It had been easy paddling in the barely moving water, but the mid-August humidity left him tired and winded. He needed no more than twenty strokes to reach the anchored sloop from the shore and he withdrew his paddle from the water a few feet from the stern. The wind on the lake carried the light pirogue the rest of the way.

At the stern, he stood carefully to avoid tipping the tiny boat over. He put one hand on the sloop's hull and eased the pirogue carefully against its side. The two boats touched without a sound. Hoping to board the ship noiselessly, he had padded the sides of the pirogue with a thick layer of cloth. The man maintained his balance by pressing one hand against the hull. With his other hand, he tossed a bowline up and over a cleat on the deck. He pulled the line taut and tied it to the bow of his pirogue. He paused a few seconds to remove his shoes and, with both hands tightly gripping the line, he hoisted himself up to the deck and crawled over the gunwale.

The man stood cautiously and listened for several minutes. It was a quiet moonless night. He heard nothing except the marsh crickets, the occasional croak of a frog and the water lapping softly alongside the sloop. There was no sound from inside the cabin.

He walked stealthily on tiptoes to the cabin door which was wide open to let in whatever wayward breeze might blow over the water. The door led to a four-step stairway that went down below the deck into the cabin. In the darkness, it suddenly loomed up in front of him sooner than expected and he stubbed the toes of his right foot on the base of the doorway. Barely stifling his scream of pain, he gritted his teeth and kneeled on the deck to massage his toes. He remained on one knee until the pain subsided and then rose slowly to stand on his sore foot. He sighed in relief, realizing a scream would have ruined everything.

A few feet back from the doorway now, the man got down on his hands and knees again and crawled forward to lean his head into the stairway. Listening for any sound of movement, he smiled when he heard snoring from inside the cabin. He listened for a few seconds more and then stood to close the door.

The back of the sloop's cabin was built at a forty-five degree angle above a twenty-inch high base and its sliding door was set into the angular portion of the cabin's back wall. Almost hidden in the left side of the wall when open, the door was closed by sliding it sideways across the opening to the right side. Ending there, the door slid into a deep grove that held it tightly in place. A ring in the door's outer edge was used to open and close it. The door itself, built with four one-inch thick and seven-inch wide boards, was forty inches high and twenty-eight inches wide. It was held together by four similar horizontal boards which were nailed across the top, bottom and center of the vertical boards.

He put his right forefinger in the ring and began to pull the door to the right. It squeaked loudly and he instantly stopped. He stood still and again leaned his head down into the stairway. Hearing the continuing and unchanged snoring, he resumed pulling the sliding door a faction of an inch at a time. His forearms ached from the effort. He only stopped when the door squeaked and he would immediately drop to the deck to listen for any sounds other than snoring from the cabin below. It took time, but no one was awakened and he finally slid the door into the right side grove. It fit snugly with only a faint click.

The man paused again to listen and, hearing no sound from inside, he removed the iron crossbar from the chocks beside the door. The crossbar had been installed on *La Bonne Chance* a month earlier to prevent thieves from entering the cabin. Careful not to let the bar hit anything and make noise, he eased it slowly through the iron rings that secured the door to the side posts. There were four rings in all, one on the left side post, two on the door itself and the fourth ring on the right side post. The bar had a rounded knob on one end to keep it from slipping through the rings and a hole in the other end for a padlock, which at night hung on a hook inside the cabin. He took a nail and a rawhide thong from his pocket and laid them on the cabin roof. He then put the nail in the hole and, while holding it in place with one hand, he bound the thong around both ends of the nail with his other hand. The crossbar was now secured as if it was padlocked. The man stepped back from the door and exhaled his breath. The hardest part was over.

Even if they awoke, they were locked inside the cabin and could not escape. They could not get out the locked door or the portholes. The portholes, built into the walls above the bunks, were no more than six inches in diameter and would not allow anything thicker than a man's arm to reach through them. They were incarcerated as if in a prison cell. He smiled, thinking the little cabin might be better termed a coffin and the sloop a sepulcher. They, of course, would not think of such terms; they would be too horrified, knowing there was no escape from the cabin and they would die. He saw them in his mind's eye, their frantic gestures, their futile screams for help – all in vain. No matter what les plus choyés (pampered ones) tried to do, they were doomed.

The man tiptoed silently back to the stern and climbed down to his pirogue. He took off all his clothes except his drawers and, with his knife in hand, dropped quietly into the water. He swam below the anchored ship to open the three plugged holes he had previously drilled into the bottom of the hull next to the keel. One had been bored into the bow, another amidships below the cabin floor and the third in the stern. The man had drilled the holes in the underside planks while the ship had been docked for repairs. He situated them in the seam between two planks that ran the entire length of the sloop. The openings were an inch in diameter and drilled deep enough to pierce both the inner and outer planking.

At the time, he had pushed a foot-long stick into the holes to make sure the hull had been breached. He then had plugged the holes with tapered wooden dowels to prevent leaks when the sloop was returned to the water. When he finished, no one could find the plugs unless guided to them. At sea, they would be well under water and completely out of sight. Knowing he would return to *La Bonne Chance* at night, he marked their location on the edge of the deck in a way no one else would notice. Only he would be able to feel the tiny carved crosses in the wood.

It had taken him almost an entire night to finish the task at that time, but he knew then his effort had been well spent. The wooden dowels could now be removed as easily as a cork from a bottle of wine. He had only to pry them out with a sharp pointed knife. As expected, it took him eight dives below the sloop to find and open the holes. On his last dive, he swam along the keel to all the openings to make certain water was flowing into the hull. He inserted his forefinger in each of the holes and felt the water flowing steadily into the sloop. A few minutes later, he sat in the pirogue drying himself with a towel he had brought from home. It was now only a matter of time to wait for the ship to sink.

Once dressed, the man untied the bowline from the sloop and paddled to a spot near the shore. He was near enough to see the ship's outline in the dark and hopefully far enough away from the clouds of mosquitoes that converged in the swamp land around the lake. But, no sooner had he laid the paddle at his feet than he heard them buzzing behind his head. The man hurriedly paddled into deeper water, slapping futilely at the mosquitoes following him. They relentlessly pursued him no matter how many he swatted or where he paddled in the lake. He finally gave up all attempts to elude them and put the wet towel over his head while waiting for the ship to sink.

For a while, the sloop looked unchanged as it floated serenely on the lake's surface. But, when the man paddled the pirogue closer, he could see the waterline had risen almost a foot on the side he approached. He felt relieved and, on his next examination, the line was six inches higher. An hour later, the rising water looked to be only a foot from the deck. He knew the cabin floor must be flooded, but those inside apparently slept unaware of the rising water around them.

"How can they possibly sleep with the water flooding the cabin?" he wondered aloud.

He had a moment of fright, thinking they somehow had opened the door and escaped. It occurred to him that they could have found an unknown implement in the cabin allowing them to break through the door. But, then, he calmed himself, realizing there were no sights or sounds of the door breaking or anyone moving on the deck. They were trapped inside the cabin and could not break through the barred door no matter what they did. Still, the man wondered why he had heard no shout or sound from *La Bonne Chance*. Seconds later, he heard shouts from the cabin. It was almost as if they had heard his question and answered him.

The shouts were followed by sounds of them pounding on the locked door. He guessed they must be using their fists and feet since the small stairway entrance into the cabin would not allow them to throw their bodies or shoulders against the door. Only one man at a time had room enough to pound on the door and, as the water rose to their knees, they could only use their fists. Their muskets and pistols were of no use since they were stored in open bins below the bunks and would be much too waterlogged to shoot. The butts of the weapons might have been used to batter the door, but that possibility had not occurred to them. Instead, they apparently took turns pounding their fists on the door. It was the only way they knew to escape the flooding cabin.

ALSO FROM MARCINSON PRESS

Dead to Rights *(First in the Colonial City Series)*

Geezer Dad: How I Survived Infertility Clinics,
Fatherhood Jitters, Adoption Wait Limbo,
and Things That Go "Waaa" in the Night

Little Birds Big Adventures

Awakening East: Moving our Adopted
Children Back to China

Dear Creator: An Anthology of Hope & Prayer
in Word, Image, and Song

COMING SOON

Dead and Gone *(Third in the Colonial City Series)*

Willie Walks: Ireland

Pink Baby Alligator

Sam's Sister

Jazzy's Quest: What Matters Most

Available through amazon.com
and by request through most major
and independent bookstores.

MARCINSON PRESS

www.marcinsonpress.com

Made in the USA
Charleston, SC
11 November 2016